THE DEVIL TO PAY

GARY BLACKWOOD

Black Rose Writing | Texas

The author grants the final approval for this literary material.

First printing

This is a work of fiction. Names, characters, businesses, places, events, and
incidents are either the products of the author's imagination or used in a
fictitious manner. Any resemblance to actual persons, living or dead, or
actual events is purely coincidental.

ISBN: 978-1-68433-950-1
PUBLISHED BY BLACK ROSE WRITING
www.blackrosewriting.com

Printed in the United States of America
Suggested Retail Price (SRP) $20.95

The Devil to Pay is printed in Garamond

*As a planet-friendly publisher, Black Rose Writing does its best to
eliminate unnecessary waste to reduce paper usage and energy costs,
while never compromising the reading experience. As a result, the final
word count vs. page count may not meet common expectations.

Credit: Edna St. Vincent Millay, "Conscientious Objector" from Collected
Poems. Copyright 1934, © 1962 by Edna St. Vincent Millay and Norma Millay
Ellis. Reprinted with the permission of The Permissions Company, LLC on
behalf of Holly Peppe, Literary Executor, The Edna St. Vincent Millay
Society. www.millay.org.

PRAISE FOR

THE
DEVIL
TO PAY

"Blackwood fills the canvas with the psychedelic colors of the sixties: anti-war protests, the draft, Agent Orange, the rise of karate culture, and the sexual objectification of women. Yet beneath this lies a mystery that will send chills up the spine of any respectable wordsmith—a secret text discovered in a library, a mysterious code, an ancient story from an exotic locale. *The Devil to Pay* offers you a devil's bargain you cannot refuse."

–Philp Roy, author of the *Submarine Outlaw* series

"If watching grad student Simon Hannay struggle to break the secret code of an adventure-filled 16th century Portuguese codex while also trying to figure out who is going to such extreme lengths to stop him weren't reasons enough to read *The Devil to Pay*, there are also Simon's deepening feelings for his fellow code-breaker and his friends' efforts to deal with the challenges of the Vietnam-era draft... The details about karate and code-breaking are as fascinating to read as they are integral to the story."

–Jean Hegland, author of *Into the Forest*

"[Blackwood is] so good at bringing history to life... this will be a great addition to university reading lists. I learned lots from reading it... A great story with so many elements all thoughtfully woven together."

–Jan L. Coates, author of *A Hare in the Elephant's Trunk*

THE
DEVIL
TO PAY

CHAPTER ONE

Van Dyne University, Ohio; September, 1969

The worn, vellum-bound journal has been sitting in this same spot, on this same shelf, for longer than anyone can remember. It predates even Mrs. Pitman, who has been working at the Briggs Library ever since her undergraduate days and now must be nearing ninety.

No one is quite sure how the book came to be here. Most of the library staff, if they knew about the book at all, have assumed that it was one of the ten thousand or so volumes that Elias Briggs willed to the University at his death and that made up the bulk of the library's collection when it opened its doors in 1889.

This particular volume is obviously far older than either the library or the university. In the 1940s, a history professor at Van Dyne declared that, judging from the antique laid paper and the stab-sewn binding, the codex (as he called it) must date from the seventeenth century or earlier. It's in remarkably good shape, considering. Some of the pages are foxed and dog-eared, and several have pulled loose from the stitching, but none seem to be missing. There's no insect damage, either; someone at some time was diligent enough to freeze or fumigate the book.

If it did indeed belong to Elias Briggs, there's no way of knowing how it ended up in his hands, or whether he had any notion of what its pages contained. Probably not. Except for a brief passage in Portuguese on the recto page, the handwritten text is totally unreadable. Not that there's any problem with the letters themselves; the author penned them in a neat if slightly shaky Chancery script, in carbon ink that, though it has bled a bit into the porous paper, hasn't faded at all. But anyone who attempts to read past that first page—and not many have tried—will discover that the words on the remaining pages seem to belong to no known language.

No doubt it's just as well that so few people are aware of the journal or what it contains.

Some knowledge is dangerous . . . especially in the wrong hands.

•   •   •

When Simon Hannay was five years old, his father made it clear that he should never, ever hit a girl. And, aside from bumping into a few by accident, Simon never has.

Until now. Now, there's really no way he can avoid it. Well, you can hardly teach the art of self-defense to a bunch of coeds without making contact once in a while, can you?

For the past two weeks, he's been wishing that he'd never agreed to take on the class in the first place. He has enough to do already, with his course load and his master's thesis. And if he doesn't keep at least a three-point GPA, he risks losing his fellowship. A sobering thought--a bit scary, actually, since he knows that, if he does drop out of the graduate program, the Army is eagerly waiting to claim him. Of course, if the Selective Service sets up a lottery system as planned, it may be able to grab him anyway.

Though it's possible that the war will end before that happens, the prospect causes him a certain amount of anxiety—almost as much as the prospect of being surrounded by nubile young women in tights and tank tops. When Simon was asked by the athletic director to teach Self-defense for Women, he could theoretically have refused. The thing is, he really needs the money. Whoever claimed that an NDEA fellowship covers "all expenses" clearly never tried to live on one.

Even if money weren't an issue, there's the other thing: He's always had a little trouble saying "no." Well, okay, a *lot* of trouble. That's what happens when you grow up feeling you have to please everyone. In any case, he's stuck with the job now.

At least he's in familiar territory. For over a year, he's been coming to the wrestling room every Wednesday evening for Karate Club, and he actually relishes the musty stench of sweat, the sultry steam heat, the scuffed, creased vinyl mats that give a little under your feet, like hard-packed snow. If he closes his eyes, he can imagine that he's back in his dad's *dojo* in Garden City.

But he doesn't close his eyes. He has no desire to dwell in the past, and no time for it. He needs to get the room—and himself--in shape for his class. From his locker, he retrieves the worn, slightly dingy karate jacket he's been using ever since his junior year of high school. He used to have matching pants, but they were always sliding off his skinny hips and flapping around his skinny ankles, so he's taken to wearing ordinary gray sweat pants.

Simon wrestles the heavy mats into position so there aren't any gaps; he drags the Karate Club's *makiwara* out of the equipment room and stabilizes it with sandbags; he sets up a card table near the entrance to hold the enrollment forms. He optimistically ran off twenty forms, but he really has no idea how many women he's likely to get; since it's not a credit course, they didn't have to sign up in advance. It's not limited to Van Dyne students, either, so there might even be a few townies.

And in fact, the first one to walk through the door is the short, plump bleached blonde who works the register at Lawson's. Simon has engaged in small talk—miniscule talk, really--with her a hundred times while paying for his orange juice and frozen bagels, but if he ever knew her name, he's forgotten it. Apparently she doesn't know his, either. "Well, hi, there!" she says brightly. "I didn't know *you* were the teacher! Instructor? Coach? What should I call you?"

"Oh. Um, well, I hadn't thought about it. If this were a real *dojo*, you'd call me *sensei*, but--"

"Sen-sigh? That sounds so cool. What does it mean?"

"Something along the lines of 'He who has gone before.'"

She startles him by breaking into the *Star Trek* theme. "Da-daaa-da-dadadada! To boldly go where no man has gone before!" She laughs at her own foolishness, and Simon weakly tries to join in. The woman bites her pink-lipsticked lower lip. "Sorry, *sensei*."

Clearly she's as ill at ease as he is, and somehow that makes Simon more confident. "No, no, it's all right. We don't have to be super-serious or anything."

"Oh, good. I'm not a super-serious sort of person. Except about shopping. I like your belt." She points to the tan *obi*, interwoven with black strands, that's cinched around his waist. "I just thought you'd have . . . I mean . . ."

"You thought it'd be black."

"Well . . . yeah. I mean, you hear about how this guy or that guy is a--" She assumes a dramatic tone and makes air quotes with her fingers. "--*black belt* in karate, so . . . "

Simon shrugs. "My dad always said that wasn't important. He learned karate in Okinawa, after the war, and they didn't care much about rank or belt colors, just skill."

"Sorry. I hope I didn't offend you or anything. I don't really know anything about karate, except what you see on TV. You know, the *Green Hornet* and—"

Nodding, Simon says it with her. "--the *Green Hornet* and *Batman*, I know, I know. Well, that's why you're here, right? To learn."

"Right. So. What do we do first?"

Simon checks his father's watch—he still thinks of it that way, even though his father's been dead for . . . what? Six years, now? "Well, I guess first we wait to see if anybody else shows up. In the meantime, you could take off your shoes." For some reason, this sounds slightly salacious to him, and he feels himself blushing.

"Oh, dear." The Lawson's lady glances anxiously at her hot pink Keds. "Did I wear the wrong kind?"

"No, no, they're fine. It's just that we'll be doing it barefoot." Which sounds even more salacious. He's got to get his act together, start behaving more like a *sensei* and less like a blockhead. As the woman slips off her shoes, Simon assumes a slightly stiff *musubi-dachi* stance. "You'll need to sign this enrollment form," he says, in a tone that's maybe a bit too businesslike, but at least not blockhead-like. He glances surreptitiously at the form as she inks in her name: Felicia. Not that he's likely to remember it anyway.

Simon does a little *shin kokyu* deep breathing, and when the next victim arrives, he's feeling more in control. He bows slightly and says, "*Ohayo.*" Only when the coed gives him a bewildered look does he realize how odd that sounds, as if he's reminding her in what state they're located. Well, not really all that odd, when you think about it; he's been here five years, and he still forgets sometimes that he's not in Kansas anymore. When a third girl enters, he tries "*Konnichiwa*" instead, and that seems to go over better. She even returns his bow.

Though it's well after ten, the advertised starting time, Simon waits a few more awkward minutes before concluding that this is as much of a crowd as he's going to get. It's just as well; when it comes to teaching martial arts techniques, the fewer students the better, and he'll get paid the same, regardless.

He takes a couple more abdominal breaths, deep but silent—never let your opponent see your fear--and strides to the middle of the red and blue patchwork of mats. "Welcome. My name is Simon, and I'll be your instructor for the next ten weeks." He takes a calculated pause. "Assuming you last that long." He's gratified when all three women respond with laughter--though there's an edge of nervousness to it, as if they're not quite sure whether he's joking. It's exactly the way *he* responded when Dr. Espinoza used that line on the first day of his class in Spanish Morphosyntax. As it turned out, the professor wasn't joking.

Neither is Simon, not really. He has no intention of going easy on them or dumbing things down. No matter how anxious we may be to please, to be liked, to live up to other people's expectations, each of us has some area of our being that's off limits, that doesn't allow for bending or compromise. For Simon, it's karate.

"Every martial arts studio," he continues, "has its own *dojo kun*—a sort of motto—and even though this isn't exactly a *dojo*, we do have a *dojo kun*--"

He's interrupted by the clang of the Field House's main entrance door, followed by the echoing sound of wooden-soled sandals clomping and women's voices chattering, giggling. A moment later, the door to the wrestling room flies open and the newcomers burst in like Visigoths storming the gates of Lisbon. There are five of them and, though they don't look like barbarians--they're all very attractive, in fact—they might have taken lessons in decorum from Alaric the Goth.

At least they have enough couth to remove their footwear, but not enough to close their mouths; they go right on chattering, at a slightly lower volume. No doubt one of the things they're going on about is him. It's always that way on the first day of classes, when the professor is still an object of intense curiosity and speculation. Simon doesn't let it bother him; the last thing he needs to do is pull a Coach Gilroy tactic, and yell at them to shut their pie holes. There are better ways of getting their attention.

He walks casually to the blackboard, the one Gilroy and the other coaches use for diagramming football and basketball strategies. Forming his fingers into a claw, Simon drags his nails mercilessly across the surface. The whispering turns to groans of dismay; the laughing faces twist into grimaces.

Simon calmly takes up his position in the middle of the mats again. "As I was saying, we do have a *dojo kun* that I'd like you to keep in mind each time you come here—and maybe even when you're *not* here: 'Prepare for conflict, but pursue peace.' I'm not sure how to say that in Japanese, but we will be using a number of Japanese terms and phrases. Don't worry, you won't be tested on them." There's some tentative but appreciative laughter, even a little from the Visigoth army.

"The first one is: *Karate-do wa rei ni hajimari, rei ni owaru koto wo wasuruna.* 'Karate begins and ends with respect.' As I was saying to . . . um . . . Felicia--" Whew. "--there's no need to be grim or formal, but we should be respectful of each other, and of martial arts traditions. We can start by being on time to every class--" He glances, ever so briefly, at the giggly girls. Some of them actually look chastened. Their leader, a slim young woman with a mane of probably genuine blonde hair and a perky nose, doesn't. "--by removing our footwear, and by performing a *rei*, or bow, like this, more or less--" He demonstrates. "--when we enter and leave the room. Okay. Another term we'll be using a lot, obviously, is *kara-te*, which means either 'Chinese hand' or 'empty hand,' depending on who you believe. According to legend--"

A movement at the rear of the room catches Simon's eye, and he mutters a mild curse--not in Japanese but in Portuguese, which he's been reading so much of lately: "*Merda!*" Not very respectful, to be sure, but appropriate. He's got yet another latecomer, though she's nothing like the Visigoths. In fact it takes him a moment to realize that she's female, thanks to her outfit of combat boots, faded bell-bottoms, and a baggy hooded sweatshirt that bears the legend "Property of Van Dyne University Athletic Department."

Such shirts are sported mainly by jocks--and by girls who are dating jocks and like being regarded as their property. This girl doesn't look like either one. She looks as if she got lost and stumbled into the Field House by accident. She pulls back the hood and glances around warily, almost fearfully.

There's something about her face that strikes Simon almost like a punch to the solar plexus. He wouldn't call her beautiful, exactly, not in the usual sense, more like . . . He settles on another Portuguese word: *atraente*, which can mean attractive but also appealing, alluring, captivating. Her short, choppy haircut gives her a gamine-like appearance, sort of like Audrey Hepburn, or Leslie Caron--or how they might look if they had skin the color of toffee.

Simon was just getting into his groove; suddenly he's way out of it. "Um, were you looking for the self-defense class?"

The girl glances his way, but doesn't meet his gaze. "Yes. That is, I . . . I am not certain that . . ."

"Well, you've come to the right place." Simon bows. "Would you care to join us?"

The girl hesitates a moment longer, then wordlessly shakes her head, flips up the sweatshirt hood, and hurries out of the room.

Simon stares dumbly after her until the Visigoths start their whispering and giggling again. "Well," he says. "I didn't know I was *that* scary. Now, where was I?"

Felicia raises a tentative hand. "You were telling us the meaning of *karate*?"

"Right. Tell you what; let's leave that for another time. I'd like to get started on some basic *kata*." But now the genuine blonde has her hand up. "Yes—I'm sorry, I don't know your name."

"It's Wendy. I have a question."

"Of course, Wendy. Sure. You should feel free to ask questions at any time."

"I was just wondering—how come you don't have a black belt?"

CHAPTER TWO

By the time the class is over, Simon is more exhausted than if he'd done two hours' worth of *kumite*--freestyle sparring. He's also famished. Luckily, he just received his NDEA check, so he can afford to treat himself to a chili dog at the Gedunk. Besides, he's earned it. Except for acting slightly weird when the mysterious hooded gamine appeared, he did okay this morning, much better than he expected.

It's easier, somehow, to address a whole group of women than to conduct a conversation with just one. Teaching is a lot like performing *kata*--a sequence of well-rehearsed moves; talking one on one is more like *kumite*, where you don't know what your opponent will do next. Simon is good at reading his martial arts partners, anticipating their moves and responding. But when it comes to verbal sparring, he could use a couple of years of training at a social interaction *dojo*.

Five minutes after he takes a solitary seat with his chili dog and Coke, his friend Mack passes by the window and Simon waves him in. Mack is one of the few people, male or female, with whom he can have a reasonably relaxed, unself-conscious conversation--which is odd, really, considering how different they are.

The big guy is grinning rather sheepishly and limping rather alarmingly. He plunks down—so heavily that the structural integrity of the chair is in danger---across the table from Simon. Trying to sound like the Hippy-dippy Weatherman and failing miserably, he says, "*Qué pasa*, man? *Qué* what you call your *pasa*?"

Qué pasa is about the extent of Mack's Spanish, which is why Simon replies, "*Tuve una muy buena mañana--*"

"Okay, okay, Mister I-Speak-Five-Languages."

"Only four, if you don't count Japanese. I'm not sure you can count Latin, either. Nobody really *speaks* it."

"Yeah, well, I'm lucky to be able to manage one."

"Oh? Which one is that?"

"Har, har."

"Looks like you're barely managing to walk, too. What happened? I thought your knee was pretty well healed up."

Mack responds the way he always does when he's done something he shouldn't have and gets caught out—which is fairly often: He ducks his head and, almost Stan Laurel fashion, massages his buzz-cut scalp with one massive hand. It must be some sort of carry-over from his childhood; Mack seldom talks about his father, but he once let it slip that the old man had a habit of smacking him on the head whenever he screwed up. "Twisted it," he mutters. "Running."

"*Running?* Did the coach say you could do that?"

"Not exactly. What he said was, if I don't get back in shape pretty soon, I probably won't play at all this season. And you *know* what that means."

Simon nods grimly. "You'll lose your scholarship."

"Right. So . . ." He performs another of his signature moves: a shrug of his beefy shoulders that says *Hey, it wasn't my fault.* "So, I started getting in shape."

"By running."

"Yeah."

"Where, exactly?"

"Up the stadium steps," murmurs Mack.

"Pardon me? For a moment there, I thought you said the stadium steps."

"I did. Dumb, I know. I just . . . I don't even care about the scholarship; I just want to *play*, you know?"

"Yeah," says Simon. "I do know." For all their differences, that's one thing they have in common: football holds the same importance for Mack that karate does for Simon. It's the only thing in his life that makes any real sense. The big guy isn't stupid, by any means; if he really applied himself, he could easily maintain a B average. It's just that he doesn't see the point.

Compared to some of the Sliders--as Van Dyne athletes are so curiously called--Mack isn't really all that huge; even if his knee makes a miraculous recovery, it's doubtful he'll ever be drafted by the NFL. And yet he's like an irresistible force out there on the field. Off the field, his strategy has always been to coast along, cramming at the last possible moment just hard enough to pass.

Most of the time. When that strategy fails, he drops back and punts, in his words—changes his major, in ordinary language. So far, to Simon's knowledge, he's dipped his toe into the shallow end of Sociology, Kinesiology, World History, and this semester's special, Psychology. One of these days, Mack swears, he's going to find his "nitch." No matter how mixed the company he's in, he invariably adds, "I mean, every jock has a nitch, right?"

Simon has seldom seen him so bummed. Luckily, he knows a little psychology of his own for dealing with mild, non-clinical depression. "Hey, how about a nice chili dog?"

Mack's grin starts to surface again. "Sure; thanks, man." One big paw reaches for Simon's plate.

"Not *mine*, you moron. I meant I'll treat you."

"Oh. Okay. If you can afford it. I don't want you turning into one of the Living Dead come the end of October. You're already a bag of bones."

Despite Simon's head start, Mack is the first to finish off his chili dog; somehow he also manages to keep up a mostly intelligible conversation. "So, how big is your harem?"

"My *harem*?" Simon rolls his eyes. "Jeez, Mack. Maybe you should consider majoring in Etiquette. If you mean how many women signed up for my self-defense class, the answer is eight. Tune in next week to find out how many of them return." He takes a thoughtful bite of bun. "Actually, I might have nine."

"One of them is pregnant?"

Simon can't help laughing. "No! This one woman came in late, and then she turned around and left. I'm kind of hoping she'll be back."

"Man, there's no pleasing some people. Eight women isn't *enough* for you?" Mack's lung power is in keeping with the rest of his physique; his voice seems to fill up the room. With that kind of projection, maybe he really should major in Theatre. Not that he'd ever make it as an actor; he's probably incapable of playing any character except Mack.

"Could you possibly keep it down a little?" grumbles Simon. "People are *looking!*"

"Let 'em look." Mack turns and waves cheerfully to the Gedunk at large. Several of the students who are chowing down wave back; some just look at him as if he's demented.

Simon lets out a sigh, but can't suppress a smile. As irksome as Mack can be sometimes, you can't help admiring his lack of inhibition. Mack, in turn, admires

10

Simon's devotion to his studies. "It's like you're pumping iron twelve hours a day, only with your brain."

They've settled into a mutually beneficial partnership: Simon helps Mack study for his Research Methods and Statistics tests, and in return gets dragged downtown to the Turtle Tap once a week, where they spend an evening playing pool and pinball, drinking Sloe Gin Sliders and, on a good night, chatting with a couple of coeds until curfew calls the women away.

"So," says Mack, in a more subdued tone, "what's so special about Bachelorette Number Nine?"

"I don't know, exactly. There's just something about her, something kind of . . . *poignant*, I guess you'd say."

"*I* wouldn't say it, since I don't know what it means."

"*Soulful*, would be another word."

"That one I know." He gives a James Brown screech. "*Waow!* Sorry. Maybe I've seen her around campus. What does she look like?" To Simon's surprise, when he describes her appearance and her unconventional attire, Mack IDs her at once. "Gabriela. It's gotta be. You don't see too many chicks wearing combat boots."

"You know her?"

"I know *of* her. Bear used to talk about her a lot."

"*Bear?*"

"Bear O'Hara, our running back."

"What did he say about her?"

"You don't want to hear it, man."

"Yes, I do. I'm going to encourage her to join the class, and I want to know what I'm getting into."

"Okay. If you really want to know, Bear says she's a slut, that she'll put out for just about anybody, but she prefers jocks." He wiggles his gnarly eyebrows, one of which is bisected by a sizable scar. "As do all women, of course."

A lump of disappointment lodges in Simon's chest, like an oversized bite of chili dog. "Oh. Do you . . . do you know anything else about her?"

"Well, I know she's from South America—Argentina, maybe? Or Brazil. One of those big countries. And I think she's a History major; she was in my Ancient Civ class. She wasn't wearing combat boots and sweatshirts at that point, though, and her hair was long."

"Really? Hmm. I wonder what happened."

"Probably fell in with the hippie contingent and started smoking pot--which, as you know, is the first big step on the road to the depths of degradation."

Simon doesn't reply. He's thinking: *South America.* That would explain the hint of an accent he heard. It would also help explain why he was so struck by her. He's had kind of a thing for Latin women ever since the day, in sixth grade, when Peri Jurado walked into his homeroom. Her ankle-length circle skirt made it look more as though she were floating. The colorful skirt drew so many sneers from the Anglo girls that she soon switched to drab plaid wrap-arounds obviously foraged from the thrift store. Sometimes he wonders what became of Peri. Probably, as with Gabriela, he's better off not knowing.

Despite his long-standing reluctance to say no, he manages to fend off Mack's attempts at luring him to the Turtle Tap—"Hey, man, it's Saturday! Nobody studies on Saturday!" Instead he heads back to his one-room apartment, dubbed the Gas Chamber because it sits above the Horvaths' one-car garage and sometimes reeks of exhaust fumes. He really needs to make some inroads into the stacks of research materials that are threatening to take over the place. A person would swear they're multiplying. At any rate, they're getting every bit as much sex as he is, lately.

He might be more motivated if he were really keen on his thesis topic: portrayals of the Devil in medieval and Renaissance literature. The field of Comp Lit is a lot like the California gold fields in 1850 —you have to dig pretty deep to find a vein that hasn't already been mined out. When Dr. Espinoza suggested that the medieval *Cantigas de Santa Maria* were pretty much virgin territory—pun intended--Simon took the hint, since he didn't have a better idea. Now just about any idea seems better.

Over the past four months, he's slogged through all 420 of the poems and translated those that feature the Devil, but the effort has left him feeling listless and lethargic. He needs to take a page from Mack's playbook. He's not about to switch majors, but he can at least change his game plan. Why is it that, after spending time with Mack, he starts thinking in football metaphors?

He decides to have a closer look at the playwright whose work will put the Comparative in Comparative Literature. Simon digs out the first volume of the *Copilaçam de Todalas Obras de Gil Vicente* and tosses it onto the sagging armchair, which sends up a cloud of dust. Before he's ready to tackle Vicente—there he goes again with the football terms--he needs a cup of tea.

It's just as well he had the chili dog, since there's precious little to eat in this place. Not that there's room for much; the refrigerator is the size of a two-drawer file cabinet, and the cupboard is not a whole lot larger. He sticks a kettle of water on the single-burner hot plate and takes down a mostly empty box of mostly stale Ritz crackers. Just as he's about to settle into the armchair—it's impossible to sit there without settling in—the music starts.

Simon lets out a tortured groan. He didn't mind Neil Diamond so much, but now the landlord's daughter has a new favorite—Gary Puckett and the Union Gap. Specifically "This Girl is a Woman Now," which she plays over and over, and which she no doubt imagines was written expressly for her. Though she can't be much more than sixteen, she's doing her best to tack on a few years.

If she'd only keep her damned bedroom window closed. But no, Rhonda Horvath is one of those insouciant beings who want to share their music with the world, regardless of what the world wants. Simon has tried stuffing Kleenex in his ears, but all that does is make his ears hurt. Maybe he should be thankful; though it's warm enough for open windows, she probably won't be carrying her transistor radio into the yard and sunbathing in her bikini, which roughly triples the distraction factor of the radio alone.

The music is having much the same effect as running his fingernails across the blackboard. If he goes on sitting here, he'll start to seethe, and if he seethes long enough he may do something he'll regret—such as packing up and moving out. He can't afford to do that. He'd be lucky to find an apartment of any sort at this time of year, let alone one this cheap.

All he can do is follow his father's advice about dealing with sticky situations: "Take your sails out of their wind." It doesn't usually solve anything in the long run, but in the short run it works remarkably well. He shoves the Vicente text and a notebook into his leather briefcase—another inheritance from his dad—and decamps to the Briggs Library.

Actually, if they'd let him, he'd be content to live at the Briggs. And why not? The Athletic Department—admittedly without official approval—lets a few scholarship students, including Mack, bunk at the Field House. Fair is fair. Simon could move into one of the cozy study rooms on the third floor, maybe bring his hot plate and fridge, put up some curtains. Several of the rooms even have armchairs that don't sag or spew dust. Granted that it wouldn't be a great place to entertain a girl, but neither is the Gas Chamber. In any case, that hasn't exactly been an issue for a while now. Ever since he started on this *miserável* thesis, Santa Maria has been his sole mistress, and a jealous one.

He has his pick of the study rooms—as Mack says, *It's Saturday, man!* Simon's favorite is the one next to the Taft Rare Book Room; he likes being in such close proximity to all that ancient and arcane knowledge. The collection has no old editions of either Vicente or the *Cantigas*, so he has no legitimate reason to use the room, but a couple of times he's invented a reason, just so he could breathe in the funky scent of volumes that were printed or handwritten in a time when books were literal treasures.

According to Alec, his sometime sparring partner and a grad student in Chemistry, there's nothing particularly mystical or magical about that smell; it's simply caused by the breakdown of volatile organic compounds including toluene, benzaldehyde, and 2-ethyl hexanol. Well, Alec always has been kind of a jerk.

Really, if Simon had his choice, he'd take up residence in the Rare Book Room. He gazes longingly at the paneled walls, the delicate chandeliers, the oak tables, the burgundy velvet couch and chairs. If he ever manages to earn a doctorate and a faculty position somewhere, he'll furnish his office exactly this way.

In the meantime, maybe he could just live there in secret, like the Borrowers. It wouldn't be hard; as far as he can tell, the place is hardly ever used. Yeah, that could work . . . if, like the Borrowers, he were four inches tall. Of course, that might make it even harder to find a girlfriend. Grinning wryly, Simon starts to turn away, but something stops him. He catches a glimpse of a figure emerging from the stacks—a slim, dark-haired young woman in bell-bottoms and combat boots.

CHAPTER THREE

There's no sign of the baggy hooded sweatshirt; instead, she's wearing a snug V-neck sweater that nearly matches the wine-colored upholstery of the chairs. She takes a seat at one of the tables and props a bulky volume with gilt-edged pages in front of her, but she doesn't seem inclined to read it or to take notes. Instead, she flips through the index cards in the catalog tray next to her. She studies one particular card, frowning slightly, then opens the book and examines the title page.

She seems like a different person from the one he encountered this morning. The wary, skittish look is gone; so is the sense that she's stumbled into a strange realm where she doesn't belong. She's clearly very much at home here, surrounded by rare books rather than by ordinary people. And, though Simon wouldn't have thought it possible, she's even more appealing.

When she rises from the table, he realizes that, if he wants to get her attention, he'd better do it now, before she disappears into the stacks again. Ten years of practicing karate have taught him how to act on instinct, without thinking or analyzing. If he could just manage to apply that training to real life. It's probably a lost cause, though. Long before he took up martial arts, he had learned how to be careful, how to second guess himself, how to weigh everything he did and said to make sure he didn't do or say the wrong thing, the thing that would turn his mother against him.

By the time he's made up his mind to speak to Gabriela, it's too late. She's entered the maze of shelves. Maybe if he pounded really hard on the plate glass window, she'd emerge to see what all the fuss is about. But Simon can't bring himself to do something so rash and abandoned. With a sigh, he turns away and reaches for the handle of the study room door.

And then the girl unexpectedly reappears with another volume in her hands. He's been given a second chance. All right, no thinking, no analyzing, just *act*, the way a good *karate-ka* is supposed to. He descends upon the Taft and, with knuckles hardened by his sand-and-sawdust-filled punch bag, raps briskly on the glass—a little too briskly, maybe. The girl looks as startled as if he'd fired off a shotgun; she jerks her head around to stare at him, wide-eyed.

Wincing, Simon holds up his hands by way of apology, then beckons uncertainly to her. She frowns and shakes her head. "Please?" he calls. In the quiet library, his voice sounds almost as loud as Mack's. "I just—I just want to ask you something!" When she still hesitates, he says, "I'm not going to steal the books and sell them on the black market, I promise." This actually draws a hint of a smile. "I want to talk to you for a second, that's all."

Her comfortable, relaxed demeanor has vanished; she looks as edgy and cautious as she did this morning. With obvious reluctance, she moves to the door, but she doesn't unlock it; she just peers at him through the wire-reinforced window. "What?"

"It's Gabriela, right?"

"Yes?"

"I'm Simon. We met—sort of—this morning. At the self-defense class?"

She doesn't reply, just lowers her eyes and nods faintly.

"Right," says Simon. "I was wondering . . . well, why you left."

She clears her throat and, still not looking at him, says softly, "I just decided I didn't want to do it, after all." Though the glass muffles her voice, there's no missing the accent; it's a lot like that of Simon's favorite vocalist, Astrud Gilberto. "Didn't" comes across as "deeden" and "it" as "eet."

"Oh. That's . . . that's too bad." He's lost his momentum and is back to thinking and analyzing and fumbling for words. "Um, you . . . you don't like crowds, or what? Or you just didn't like the looks of me?"

"It's not that. I just . . . I just thought that . . . that you would be a woman."

"Uh-huh. Well, no offense, but the university might have a little trouble finding a woman karate expert. Besides, I work cheap." He's coaxed another semi-smile out of her. "Maybe you could come next Saturday and give it, say, a half hour? Then if you don't like it, you don't have to stay. *Está bem?*"

Her dark eyes go wide again. "*Você fala português?*"

Simon gives a self-effacing shrug. "*Um pouco.* I read it better than I speak it."

"What are you studying?"

"Comparative Lit. Working on my master's. Sort of. How about you?"

"Right now my major is History, but I may get a Library degree. I like books."

"So do I. Especially old ones. I know we're not supposed to trust anyone over thirty, but I don't think that applies to authors. So, you work here?"

She nods, with a little more enthusiasm. "The collection is kind of a . . . how do you say?" She flutters her fingers to suggest disarray.

"A mess?"

"*Exatamente.* Whoever catalogued the Spanish and Portuguese section didn't know much Spanish or Portuguese, I think. They asked me to see what I could do with it. I worked in the *biblioteca* in Recife, where I grew up. Have you been to Brazil?"

"Not yet. If I go for a doctorate, maybe I can get a Fulbright or something that'll pay my way. Um, listen, this seems a little awkward. Talking through a door, I mean. Is there any chance you could, you know, let me in, or . . ."

Her features, which had begun to relax, suddenly tighten again, and the look of wariness returns to her eyes. "No," she says bluntly. "I am sorry."

It's probably not allowed without staff approval, but if that's what worries her, why doesn't she just say so? She's acting more like she's *afraid* to let him in, like he might come on to her or something. "Um, all right. I guess I'll just . . . go next door, then. Or would you rather I went farther away? Some other building, maybe? Some other campus?"

Her mouth twitches upward, just a little. "You can stay here; I just cannot let you in."

"Ah. Well, I'll be right over here if . . . well . . . Can I just ask you one more thing?"

"*O que?*"

"Was that *okay* or *o que?*"

"Either one."

"Okay. Will you come to my class next week?"

She sighs. "I will try."

"Good. You won't be sorry. It'll be fun. Really."

"I am not looking for fun."

"Oh. Then it *won't* be fun. I'll be nasty and demanding."

She favors him with that lovely, melancholy smile again. "I do not believe you."

"Well, if you don't come, you'll never know."

He might as well have stayed in the Gas Chamber; though the study room is peaceful and all, he still can't concentrate on Gil Vicente. It's tricky to catch the nuances of sixteenth-century Portuguese, and the stodgy English translation doesn't help much. But that's not the real problem. The real problem is that his brain keeps dwelling not on Gil, but on Gabriela.

One thing he's thinking about is the fact that Portuguese is her native language. Not Renaissance Portuguese, granted, but still, maybe she could help him out, shed some light on the more difficult passages.

And maybe *porcos* could fly. In the first place, he'd never have the nerve to ask. In the second place, why would she even consider it? In the third place, even if she did, having her at such close quarters would be more distracting than several scantily clad Rhonda Horvaths with blaring radios.

No, he's just going to have to buckle down, that's all, really buckle down. As if he needed another distraction, now "Buckle Down, Winsocki" starts running through his head, the Broadway tune his mom used to sing at him when he was neglecting his homework. Oh, god, that's all he needs—to start thinking about *her*.

Jamming his notebook and the Vicente volume in his briefcase, Simon flees the study room and the memory of his mother, not to mention the presence of Gabriela, who is still at work in the Rare Book Room. Though he's not much of a drinker, he could use a shot of something about now. With any luck, Mack will still be hanging out at the Turtle Tap, and they can raise a glass and have a few mind-numbing games of pinball.

The Tap is only a block from campus, which is a good thing, since Simon has lost what little energy he had left after this morning's battle with the Visigoths. Maybe he's just hungry. When his mind is on his studies, he has a tendency to forget about food. Fortunately, the Tap serves gourmet quality onion rings at a poor man's price.

Though the building probably hasn't seen a new coat of paint since the last war—at which time, according to legend, it was also a whorehouse—it has a certain faded charm. The furnishings, too, have seen better days. Generations of students have engraved their initials in the tabletops—something Simon has considered but forgone, not wanting to chance being caught—but that, too, adds to the appeal of the place. It makes a fellow feel part of something enduring, something with a long and slightly seamy history.

The actual bar is practically a work of art, a massive horseshoe-shaped bulwark of mahogany that's been polished by an incalculable number of elbows and coasters. Simon perches on a bar stool, his long legs nearly reaching the floor, and surveys the place. There's no sign or sound of Mack, and he's hard to miss. "What can I get you?" says a smooth voice, and Simon swivels around to discover that Alec, his sparring partner, is manning the bar. "Hannay!" Alec has affected the habit of calling his friends, even his girlfriends, by their last names. "I didn't know you were a drinking man."

"And I didn't know you were a bartender."

Alec shrugs. "I'm just filling in for Boorman. He came down with the kissing disease."

"Mono? Bummer. You do know how to mix drinks, though, right?"

"I'm a man of many talents, my friend. Besides, we're not exactly making rocket propellant, here, just mixing an organic compound containing a hydroxyl functional group with various intermediates to synthesize a more complex compound."

"Ah. Well, I *was* planning to have a Slider, but you're making me reconsider."

"Hey, in the end, everything boils down to chemistry, right? Even sex."

"Just don't tell me what compounds are in the onion rings, okay?" When Alec returns with his Slider, Simon says, "Has Mack been in this afternoon?"

Alec nods and brushes his Robert Redford hair out of his eyes. "About an hour ago. He played a couple of games of pool and then he got to talking with some flower child and they split together."

"That's an oxymoron."

"I beg your pardon?"

"*Split together.* It's an oxymoron—combining two words with opposite meanings. Like jumbo shrimp. Or Living Dead."

"Oh. I thought for a second you were calling me a moron."

"If you were, they wouldn't let you fool around with dangerous chemicals."

"No, I'd have to study something harmless--like, say, Comparative Lit." Before Simon can think of a worthy reply, the bell in the kitchen pass-through dings. Alec grins maliciously. "Oops, there's your deep-fried thiosulfinates!" Simon is too hungry to be put off by this; as he digs into the crispy onion rings, Alec says, "So, how's the self-defense class going?"

"Okay." He's not really keen to discuss karate-related matters; their respective approaches to martial arts are just too much at odds. To Simon, it's a discipline; Alec considers it more of a sport. That's partly because of their training—or operant conditioning, as Mack would have it, something he picked up in Psych 101. But it's also due to their vastly different personalities. What it comes down to is, Alec is a hot dog; Simon is not.

"Just okay? Are those chicks giving you problems?"

"No, it's cool."

"Good, good. I told them you could handle it."

"Told whom?"

"*Whom*? The Athletic Department, that's whom. They asked me to teach the class, but I declined."

"Oh." Though Simon is a little hurt to learn that he wasn't their first choice, it's no surprise; he's never been anyone's first choice for anything requiring athletic skill. "You were too busy?"

"That was part of it. But I also don't like the idea of teaching women that, if a guy tries to cop a feel, they should knock his teeth down his throat with a flying side kick."

"I don't plan to get into flying side kicks."

"I know, I know; I'm exaggerating, but you see what I mean. Anyway, I convinced them that you were the man for the job. I told them you had the equivalent of a black belt, even if you don't wear one."

"Thanks. I think." Simon takes his change in dimes and heads for the pinball machines. There are only three. Moon Shot, his favorite, is out of order—probably from frustrated players pounding on it--and Monte Carlo is way too easy; that just leaves Beat the Devil. Great. He was hoping to forget about his Devilish thesis for a while.

In Vicente and the *Cantigas*, though Old Nick sometimes appears in the form of a bull, a lion, or an Ethiope, he usually has the good sense to disguise himself as an ordinary person--often a handsome young man. After all, he wants to win people over, not scare the shit out of them. The Devil pictured on the game's back rack isn't so subtle. He's fiery red, with horns and a wicked grin that exposes a set of shark-like teeth. His green cat's eyes glare malevolently at the puny mortals who dare to challenge him.

As Simon drops in a dime and presses the Start button, he recites the Soul's prayer from Vicente's *Auto da Alma*—one of the passages he's managed to translate pretty well: "*Anjo que sois minha guarda, tende sempre mão em mim porque hei medo de empeçar e de cair.*" Guardian angel, uphold me and sustain me, lest I stumble, fail and fall. You'd think the clatter of the ball, the clicking of numbers resetting to zero, and the Devil's tinny, maniacal laugh would drown out his incantation, but apparently Alec overhears it anyway, for Simon hears laughter from the direction of the bar; it's not quite as maniacal as Satan's, but it's not entirely benign, either. "What are you babbling about, Hannay?" Jeez. The guy must have ears like a bat.

"Just appealing to the angels," says Simon. "I need all the help I can get." Though the part about the angels is a joke, the part about needing help isn't. Beat the Devil is appropriately named; it's probably the toughest pinball game he's ever played--and he used to play a lot, back in Garden City, in the basement of the Legion.

That's where he met Frank Ávila, the summer before everything went to hell.

CHAPTER FOUR

When they met, Frank wasn't actually *inside* the Legion. Even though his father was a veteran—kind of a war hero, actually--it was understood that Mexicanos weren't welcome there. Or, for that matter, at the swimming pool or the bowling alley or the movie theatre. There was no law against it, of course, and nothing as overt as those "No Dogs, Negroes or Mexicans" signs they had in Alabama and Mississippi. It was just "understood."

He and Frank didn't exactly *meet*, either; it was more like Simon ran into him—literally. At thirteen, Simon was still on the gawky, graceless side; it was as if his body were getting ahead of him, anticipating the time when it would shoot up to six feet and finding it hard to deal with being nearly a foot shorter. As he was leaving the Legion, he rounded the corner of the building and walked right into a pair of outstretched legs belonging to one of five Mexicano boys about his age, maybe a year or two older. It was hard to tell; they tended to be smaller than Anglo boys of the same age. You couldn't judge by what grade they were in, either. Those who hadn't already dropped out by their teens were generally at least a grade behind, due to all the days they missed, working in the beet fields or the sugar refinery.

When they weren't in the fields or the factory, they were hanging around town. Lately there were a lot more hangers than usual. The past two summers had been so hot and dry that, even with irrigation, the sugar beet crop was about half what it was in a good year—which meant the farms and the refinery needed a lot fewer workers. Some of those who were let go packed up and went back to Mexico, where at least they had family. But some tightened their belts and took whatever sweaty, grueling, unskilled work came their way, work that the Anglos didn't want: replacing ties on the railroad, setting pins at the bowling alley, breaking up lime at the refinery. And some, like Frank and his friends, seemed to do nothing but hang around.

Main Street was one more place where they weren't welcome; the store owners didn't trust them. But the *muchachos* got as close to downtown as the police would let them, just to make a statement. Their favorite spot was the old basketball court behind the Legion; the place was so run-down that no one minded them claiming it.

Not that they played much basketball. They mainly lounged about, smoking hand-rolled cigarettes and exchanging bursts of rapid-fire Spanish. Simon's classmates speculated a lot about what was in those lumpy-looking fags. Simon wondered more about the content of the conversations; they sounded intriguing, mysterious, as if the Mexicanos were sharing some secret knowledge.

His Spanish was limited to a few phrases picked up from his dad, who was superintendent at the refinery. But when he stumbled over Frank Ávila and the boy growled *"Pendejo!"* Simon knew what it meant—literally "pubic hair," figuratively something like "dumbass."

"Sorry," he muttered. As he struggled to his feet he accidentally stuck one elbow in the boy's face.

"What are you, spastic?" said Frank, in heavily accented English.

Simon tried *"Perdóname,"* hoping that might earn him a few points, but it only made things worse.

"Oh, listen!" crowed one of the other boys. "The *gringo cabrón* can speak Spaaanish!" The four of them broke into mock applause. *"Bravo, gringo!"* Ducking his head to hide his flaming face, Simon scurried off, followed by a string of insults—presumably--and jeering laughter. For the rest of that summer, he didn't go back to the Legion once, not wanting to run the Mexican gauntlet again. But there seemed to be no avoiding Frank Ávila.

At the beginning of the summer, Peri Jurado had landed a job at the Five and Ten—apparently Latina girls were considered more trustworthy than the boys. Though Simon found some excuse to shop there almost daily, he seldom found the nerve to speak to her. Even if he'd been an extrovert like his father, it wouldn't have made mattered; Peri's English was on a par with Simon's Spanish. She rarely spoke up in class, and her conversations with customers were pretty much limited to "Fifty cents, please," and "Thank you."

Halfway through the summer she quit, and Simon feared her family had left town. But when school started, he was delighted to discover that she was still in his class. Unfortunately, so was Frank. He'd flunked eighth grade, and was forced to either repeat it or drop out, as most of his friends had done. For some reason, Frank stuck with it, despite the best efforts of the Anglo students--and several of the teachers—to make him feel unworthy and unwanted.

After school hours, he still hung out with the same bunch of boys. But as September waned, so did the size of their *pandilla*. Every week, at least one more family lost hope and headed South. Now that the beets were harvested and cold weather was on its way, the main provider of jobs was Carman Sugar. But according to Simon's father, the refinery was on the brink of bankruptcy. In fact, in Don Hannay's opinion, the whole sugar beet industry was doomed.

What he failed to foresee—or maybe just chose to ignore--was the fact that his marriage was also doomed. Though Simon's mother wouldn't have appreciated the comparison, it seemed to Simon that she had a lot in common with those Mexicanos who pulled up stakes as soon as the going got tough. As long as her husband was making good money at "the office," as she called it—it sounded so much classier than "plant" or "refinery"—and she could throw parties and dress fashionably and make improvements on the house and buy a new car every two or three years, Delia Hannay was content. When the bank threatened to foreclose, it was a different story, one in which she didn't care to play the plucky, steadfast heroine. Wally Butts, who was closing down his Ford dealership and moving to Tucson, offered her a much better role as his "secretary," and she took it.

Simon never managed to shake the feeling that it was his fault. Maybe she wouldn't have left if only he'd been a more dutiful son, a more outstanding student, if he'd helped out more around the house, gone out with more and classier girls, become the star of the basketball team or at least the debate team, gotten a part-time job—if, in short, he'd lived up to her expectations. The trouble was, her expectations kept changing. No matter how good he tried to be, it was never good enough.

And no matter how hard he tries to Beat the Devil, it's never hard enough. The worst part is, if you make under 5,000 points the Devil lets out that maniacal laugh, telling everyone what a loser you are. Anyone foolish enough to challenge the game has endured that small humiliation. Except for Alec, of course. Simon has seen him play only a few times, but each time he's racked up enough points to win a free drink—plus much acclaim, which for Alec is a far better high than alcohol.

When the Devil mocks Simon for the third time in a row, he calls it quits. He's hoping that, for a change, Alec will fail to offer his advice. But Alec is nothing if not predictable. "You know what I think your problem is, Hannay? You're pounding the flippers too hard. You need to use a little finesse. It's all in the timing."

Simon responds the same way he does when Alec gives him unwanted advice at Karate Club, as he so often does: he takes a deep, calming breath, bows slightly, and says "*Domo arigato*"—my humble thanks—with no attempt at irony.

The master's program requires at least three hours in some field besides Spanish and Portuguese Literature. Simon chose History of Books and Printing, figuring that, even if it didn't prove very useful, it would at least be interesting. He didn't count on Dr. Beebe. At every university there are professors who can make the most fascinating topic as dry as the High Plains in August, and Beebe the Booby is one of them. The nickname bestowed by his students is delightfully apt; with his wide-set eyes and beak of a nose, he actually does resemble that famously stupid seabird.

• • •

It's only the end of September, and already Simon has cut three classes, which really isn't like him. The only thing that keeps him coming back is his fear of failing—that, and the promise that they'll spend at least one class in the Taft Rare Book Room examining bindings and typefaces. He's beginning to suspect it was a hollow promise, designed to entice bibliophiles like him. But on Monday the Boob tells them that, come Friday, they're to meet in the entryway of the library. From there, the legendary Mrs. Pitman will conduct them to the *sanctum sanctorum*.

• • •

It's a long, slow week. Simon makes no real headway on the thesis, aside from giving it a moderately clever title—*The Devil is in the Details: Portrayals of Satan in Medieval and Renaissance Portugal*. He can't even gripe about it to Mack, who seems to have fallen off the face of the campus. But on Thursday afternoon, as Simon is passing the stadium, he spots his friend sitting all by himself in the stands, mournfully watching the Sliders' offensive line go through their speed and agility drills.

Simon's first impulse is to join him, maybe cheer him up a little, as Mack so often does for him. But he's not sure his company would be welcome. Though Mack cultivates a jovial, easygoing image, he has his melancholy moments--hours or even days during which he retreats into himself. Simon has learned that it's usually best just to leave him alone, let him work it out. But maybe that's just an excuse; maybe his friend really does need moral support, and Simon just doesn't know how to give it. God knows, his feeble efforts to coax his mother out of her blue funks never did any good; they only provided her with a handy target for her spite.

As Simon leans on the stone wall that surrounds the stands, debating his next move, a young woman approaches and hops onto one of the rows of bleacher seats. Arms spread, she does a balancing act over to where Mack is sitting and plops down beside him.

Simon doesn't like putting people in pigeonholes, but this girl seems intent on pigeonholing herself. She might have hitchhiked here direct from Woodstock, with her frizzy Janis Joplin hair, her bandanna headband, her tie-dyed skirt, her abundance of beads. No doubt this is the flower child Mack was hanging out with at the Tap.

Simon sticks around another couple of minutes, grinning a bit wistfully at the relaxed way Mack relates to the girl. You wouldn't think she'd be his type, but the truth is, Mack doesn't seem to have a type, especially when it comes to women; he gets along with everybody.

Well, no; that's not strictly true, as Simon discovered in their freshman year, when they were pledging Phi Alpha Xi. Simon was likely the only pledge to note the irony of the fraternity's acronym, PAX. Peace was one thing it didn't offer, particularly during Hell Week—and there was no irony at all in *that* term. Simon and the other damned souls underwent a dozen painful and humiliating ordeals, from being spanked to eating bugs to mopping up a foul stew of excrement and rotten food.

They endured it all stoically, not even griping to each other for fear of being branded a pussy. It wasn't easy. The frat boys seemed to have taken lessons from Simon's mother--or maybe just from their own mothers: No matter how hard you tried, it was never good enough. Simon had spent a lot of time and effort learning to control his anger, but more than once they pushed him close to the edge. Each time, Mack found some way of defusing the situation, by making a horrible joke or belting out some inane song—"Blue Moon," or "The Lion Sleeps Tonight"--so badly that it was impossible not to laugh.

Mack himself showed no sign of anger or resentment--not until the last day of Hell Week, when the Phi Alphs "dropped trou" and commanded the pledges to kneel and lick their asses. Three of the poor, demoralized frosh obeyed. If Mack hadn't been there, Simon might have swallowed his pride and joined them. But the two glanced at each other, and some unspoken message passed between them. As if they'd rehearsed it, they came to attention and shouted simultaneously, "Sir, no, sir!"

The astonished Phi Alphs rained down all manner of curses and threats upon them—but not for long. As his dad had taught him, Simon took his sails out of their wind; Mack followed in his wake. They were both blackballed, of course. Mack suffered more than Simon; after all, most of his teammates were frat boys. But eventually he won them over, as he does everyone.

He certainly seems to be doing okay with the flower child; they're sitting head to head, holding hands and chatting animatedly. But oddly enough, neither of them is smiling. It's not like Mack to be so serious for so long; it must be five minutes, now. What could they be discussing that's so sobering? Mack hasn't known the girl long enough to get her pregnant. Maybe she's breaking up with him—though, again, after a single week it can hardly qualify as a breakup. Anyway, it's none of Simon's business.

There are only six students in his History of Books and Printing class, and on Friday one of them is down with the flu. Like Simon, the others seem awed by the sumptuous but scholarly atmosphere of the Taft and they dial down their voices to a worshipful whisper. He half hoped that Gabriela would be here, working on the catalog, but of course she's not.

Mrs. Pitman gives a volume on the shelf next to her a familiar, affectionate pat. She has a lot in common with the books: Her skin is as translucent, fragile-looking and mottled with age as their pages, her spine as stiff as theirs, her scent also a little musty but pleasant, suggestive of vanilla and almonds. "As in the rest of the library," she says, in a delicate, breathy voice, "the books are shelved according to Library of Congress headings, with no regard to the age of the volume. So, you may have to do a bit of searching to find books representative of a particular time period. That's quite all right. We have the whole afternoon."

Carole Carter, a willowy History major, holds up a tentative hand. "Shouldn't we wear white gloves or something, to protect the books?"

Mrs. Pitman gives her a tolerant smile. "No, dear. The truth is, they can cause more damage than your bare hands. You can't feel the pages as well, you see, and are more likely to mishandle them." Her smile takes on a mischievous tinge. "I'm assuming, of course, that your hands are clean. If not, there's a sink at the rear of the room, and some lovely jasmine-scented hand soap."

Anxious to please as always, Simon scrubs his hands so thoroughly that he could safely perform heart surgery. The five of them fan out, taking different routes through the maze. Simon heads for the Spanish and Portuguese section. He's glanced over it before, but in a cursory fashion, with no particular purpose. He has a purpose now; he's thinking that, if he gets to know these books, it'll create some common ground with Gabriela, like sharing the same set of friends.

He passes over several editions of Cervantes, a collection of poems by the Generation of '27, a couple of novels by Machado de Assis. Nothing of note there. Then he spots, on the highest shelf, a volume that would draw a shout of delight from him if he were anywhere besides the Taft—not that he'd be likely to find it anywhere else. As it is, he limits himself to a subdued "Oh, man!"

Sometimes being tall is a blessing; he can reach the book without using one of those hazardous rolling step stools. Though he'd really like to keep his find to himself, it wouldn't be sporting not to share it with his classmates. He carries it to the nearest study table and, folding his frame into one of the lushly padded chairs, opens to the title page.

THE LUSIAD;

OR,

THE DISCOVERY OF INDIA.

AN EPIC POEM.

TRANSLATED FROM

The Original Portuguese of Luis de Camõens

By *WILLIAM JULIUS MICKLE.*

NEC VERBAM VERBO, CURABIS REDDARE, FIDUS

INTERPRES. Hor. Art. Poet.

THE SECOND EDITION.

**OXFORD,
PRINTED BY JACKSON AND LISTER.
M.DCC.LXXVIII.**

His assignment is to study the binding and the paper and the watermarks and such. Instead, he's drawn at once into the text itself.

Arms and the Heroes, who from Lisbon's shore,
Thro' seas where sail was never spread before,
Beyond where Ceylon lifts her spicy breast,
And waves her woods above the wat'ry waste . . .

Simon's concentration is disturbed—destroyed, in fact--by a whiff of something very unlike the scent of the book or of Mrs. Pitman, but exactly like the perfume his mother always wore, *L'Interdi*. It's also Audrey Hepburn's fragrance of choice, or so she says in the TV commercials.

Unfortunately it's not Audrey Hepburn who's leaning over his shoulder. But neither, thank god, is it Delia Hannay taking him to task for studying something so totally unsuited to "the job market." It's just Carole Carter. She's an attractive girl, in a sassy-smart sort of way, and her presence would be very pleasant if it weren't for the unpleasant memories provoked by her perfume.

"What'd you find, Simon? Ooh, eighteenth century, right?"

"Yep. 1778. How about you?"

"I'm so glad you asked. Take a look at *this*." Reverently, she places before him an ordinary-looking clothbound volume that can't be more than about twenty years old.

Simon reads the title on the spine. "*On the Road?*"

"Yes! First edition! 1957! Signed by *Kerouac!*" She lowers her voice conspiratorially. "I'm gonna have to steal this, you know."

"You're joking, right?"

"Not really. I mean, even if they caught me, I'd only get—what?—a couple of years, max. And I'd have *Jack*--" She hugs *On the Road* close to her chest. "—to keep me company in my prison cell."

"Um, I think they'd probably confiscate the book."

"Oh. Yeah. I guess you're right. So. Who's this Camões guy, anyway?"

"Camões, actually; they spelled it wrong. He was a sixteenth-century adventurer--the Jack Kerouac of his time."

"No kidding?" She plunks down in the seat next to him. "Tell me more."

Talking to the opposite sex isn't nearly as difficult when he's discussing something academic. Simon tells her what little he knows about Camões—that he was blinded in one eye fighting the Moors; that, as a government clerk in Macau, he was accused of stealing the property of dead soldiers; that he and his Chinese lover were shipwrecked off the coast of Cambodia and she drowned while he swam ashore, holding the manuscript of *Os Lusiadas* over his head to keep it dry.

"Wow," says Carole. But it's not Camões' exploits that fascinate her so much as the bigger picture, the historical context. "Isn't it incredible that the Portuguese were already a presence in the Far East clear back in the 1500s? Well, even earlier. While Columbus was still putzing around trying to reach India by sailing West, Vasco da Gama cruised on over and brought back a shipload of spices. That's *ship*load, by the way."

"'Illustrious Gama, whom the waves obey'd, And whose dread sword the fate of empire sway'd.' That's how Camões describes him."

Carole wrinkles her nose. "I like Kerouac better." With a sigh, she gets to her feet. "I don't suppose the Boob does, though. I'd better find something a little more creaky and crusty."

Simon knows he should explore the shelves further, too, but there's something about the *Lusiadas* that holds him spellbound. Not that the writing is all that riveting; like most 18th and 19th century translations, it's on the stiff and pompous side—or, as Carole put it, creaky and crusty. And yet that's what he likes about it: reading it is almost like reading a different language. Or like deciphering an encoded message—something he used to do a lot of.

It was all the Kellogg Company's fault. When he was ten or eleven, they started offering, inside specially marked boxes of Raisin Bran, a free Dick Tracy Magic Decoder. There was nothing magical about the device, of course. It consisted of a square of cardboard that resembled a slice of Swiss cheese. On the back of the cereal box was another square, printed with a mixed-up alphabet; when you placed the decoder on it, the letters that showed through the holes spelled out a mundane "secret message."

Simon quickly graduated to making his own punch cards and his own random alphabets, which he used to correspond with a couple of half-hearted classmates. The messages they exchanged were as dull as Dick Tracy's, but that wasn't the point. The point was, *no one else could read them.* His friends tired of the game after about three days, but not Simon; his interest in codes and ciphers just got stronger, became more of a passion.

Mickle's dense iambic pentameter may have nothing very profound to say, either, but again, that's not the point. There's something . . . substantial about it, something elegant and timeless and enduring, in the same way that the Briggs and the other brick-and-stone buildings on campus seem more enduring than, say, the uninspired Medical Sciences Center, which is constructed of cast-in-place concrete.

Mrs. Pitman said they had all afternoon; surely there's time to read a page or two of Camões. But two pages give way to three, then four, and before he knows it, a voice is saying, "I'm afraid that's all the time we have for today, boys and girls." It takes Simon's brain, which is grooving on Mickle's syrupy verse, a moment to make sense of Mrs. Pitman's crisp announcement. Groaning, he hastily jots down a few notes about the paper used in the book, which is dyed yellow on the edges, and the binding—marbled paper sides with spine and corners made of vellum—and then reluctantly escorts the book back to the stacks.

Oddly enough, the *Lusiadas* itself seems reluctant to be put away. When Simon tips it carefully onto the top shelf, the volume won't slide quite all the way in. Something is blocking one edge of it, making it go all crooked. "*Qué pasa?*" murmurs Simon. Though he can reach the shelf easily enough, he can't see the recesses of it, even on tiptoe.

With one long leg, he snags the rolling step stool and drags it to him. Perching precariously on it, he withdraws the Camões and peers into the empty slot. The shelving isn't open, like that in the regular stacks; there's a wooden backing, and pressed against it is a slim, grayish volume, lying on its spine. Most of it is hidden behind the bigger books that occupy the shelf; all that's visible is the bottom inch or so. Simon grips the tomes that have it pinned in place and pulls them out a few inches. Then he reaches one skinny arm into the gap and gingerly frees the captive volume.

By the Boob's definition, it's not a book at all, but a codex. It does have paper pages, and they are bound after a fashion, by a method known as stab sewing, which involves poking holes through the entire thickness—in this case, about half an inch--with an awl and then stitching it together with a large needle and coarse thread. The cover is made of what's called limp vellum, even though it's a little stiff with age, and has a flap that folds over to protect the pages.

It qualifies as a codex because the text is printed by hand, not by a press. The letters look a little shaky, as if the author was infirm from age or illness; still, they're well-formed and well aligned. Thanks to all the old Spanish and Portuguese manuscripts he's been studying, Simon has no trouble making out the words. And yet he gets no farther than the first sentence: *O meu nome é Vicente.*

CHAPTER FIVE

Simon blinks and shakes his head, thinking that maybe his eyes are tired and not seeing straight. He could have sworn the first line said "My name is Vicente." Sure enough, no matter how close or how far away he holds the book or how he turns it toward the light, it says exactly that.

He's a firm believer in synchronicity—*meaningful coincidence*, as Jung calls it. So many times in his research he's stumbled by sheer luck upon some book or some quote that relates directly to the topic he's writing about. But if the Vicente who penned this manuscript is *his* Vicente, it would be more than mere synchronicity. It would be a minor miracle.

Simon has been trying for months to scrounge up some solid information about Gil Vicente's life, with very little luck. What are the chances that he would suddenly unearth a journal written by the Troubadour himself, one that's not mentioned in any bibliography anywhere? Slim to none. Surely this is some other Portuguese writer who just happens to have the same name.

The only way to know for sure, of course, is to read the manuscript. But there's no time. He can hear the other students thanking Mrs. Pitman and being ushered out the door. He could probably get permission to visit the Taft another day, but he can't bear to wait that long.

What are the chances he could hide in here somewhere and go unnoticed? Again, slim to none. Well, then, what if he sticks the book under his sweater and casually strolls out of the room? It might work. But if he's caught, they'll never let him use the Taft again; he might even be suspended or, god forbid, thrown out of school and into Uncle Sam's greedy clutches.

While Simon is still thinking and analyzing, Carole Carter pokes her head into the aisle, startling him so that he nearly loses his balance on the stupid stool. "You planning to stay the night, or what?"

Simon feels himself flushing. "Um . . . actually, I was considering it."

"Cool!" she whispers. "Do it! I won't tell; I'll even keep you company!"

Now there's a tempting proposition. But that would get him—and her--in even worse trouble. Besides, she'd just ignore him and snuggle up with Jack Kerouac. Not to mention the fact that she smells like his mother. "Nah, only kidding. Go on, I'm right behind you."

As soon as she disappears, he heaves a sigh and sticks the codex back on the shelf—not upright and spine out, but just the way he found it, secreted behind the other volumes. Kind of a silly thing to do, but he's taking no chances; if synchronicity struck him, it could strike some other scholar. And if the journal actually was written by Gil Vicente the playwright, Simon is not about to let someone else be the first to find out.

He can't revisit the Taft on Saturday morning; he has a self-defense class to teach. He'd be tempted to cancel it if it weren't for the fact that Gabriela might turn up. It's a tossup whether he's more anxious to see her or to get another look at that journal. Of course, once he enters the wrestling room, he goes into karate mode and everything extraneous, including Gil and Gabriela, retreats to the back burners of his brain. He's ready to rumble.

At least he *was* ready, until the moment the first student walks through the door. It's not the Lawson's lady. Neither is it one of the Visigoths. It's Gabriela. She's wearing the same outfit she had on last week—bell-bottoms, combat boots, baggy hooded sweatshirt—and the same cautious, almost fearful aura.

"Hey," says Simon. "You made it."

She simply shrugs and nods, unsmiling.

"Good. Good. Um, do you mind removing your . . ." *Combat boots* sounds judgmental, somehow, like he's accusing her of hippie tendencies or, worse, of supporting the military. " . . . footwear?"

"Of course." Surprisingly, considering the bleakness of her other clothing, when she takes off the boots she reveals a dazzling pair of multicolored knee socks.

"Nice socks. A good way to distract your opponent." When she self-consciously pulls down the legs of the bell-bottoms, Simon says, "Sorry. Just joking." He holds out one of the enrollment forms. "Um, could you fill this out, please?"

She regards it as if it's an arrest warrant or a draft notice. "You said this would be a . . . how do you say? A trial run?"

"Sure, okay. You can always fill it out later. Speaking of which, would you, um, would you mind staying after class? Just for a couple of minutes? There's something I need to ask you."

Her look of wariness intensifies. "I would rather not."

"Oh. Um . . . okay. It's just . . . it's about the rare book collection, is all."

Her expression turns puzzled, maybe a little intrigued. "What about it?"

"Well, you see . . . yesterday I was . . ." His halting explanation is halted in earnest by the sound of clomping sandals and high-spirited chatter punctuated by laughter. Simon winces.

Just before the Visigoths storm the gates, Gabriela moves a step closer and says softly, "*Talvez pudéssemos encontrar-nos na* Gedunk?"

It takes Simon a couple of seconds to respond. It's not that he doesn't understand; it's just that the words are so unexpected. "At the Gedunk? Sure. That'd be . . . great." Now he has to calm and center himself all over again.

To his surprise, all the gabby girls have returned. He was sure that, after the workout he gave them last week, at least a couple would drop out. Lesson learned once again: it's not wise to categorize. The one who fails to show is the one who seemed the most eager—Felicia, the Lawson's lady.

She's left a legacy, though; last time, when the *karate-ka* were slow to follow his instructions, she quipped, "You forgot to say Simon Says," and it became a running joke. He keeps it going. "Simon Says--" A ripple of laughter. "Simon Says you will spend the first half hour practicing the four basic *kata* positions you learned last time. While you're doing that, I'll get our new recruit, Gabriela, caught up."

Wendy raises one neon-red-nailed hand. "Pardon me for saying so, but that's kind of . . . well, boring? When do we learn the cool stuff—you know, the kicks and spins and so on?"

Simon tries not to grin. He knew this was coming. "If you really apply yourselves . . . I'd say in about five years." A chorus of Visigoth groans. "But I'll tell you what: if you do well with the moves you've learned so far, I'll add a new one. You can also take turns kicking the *makiwara*, okay? Okay. First position— oops--*Simon Says* first position. *Yoi!* Remember, feet together, right fist pressing against the left palm. Deep breath; exhale. Now, on my count: *Ichi! Ni! San! Yon!* Rachel, right arm straight, left arm curled. Annie--"

"It's Amy," says Amy.

"Sorry, *Amy*--swing around a little farther, so you're at right angles to where you were. Good. Again. *Yoi!* Deep breath; exhale. *Ichi! Ni! San! Yon!* Good; keep it up. Wendy, you count, okay?" Her companions snicker, but Wendy silences them with a single glare. A natural leader, that one.

He beckons to Gabriela. Hesitantly, she follows him to a distant corner of the mat. "Okay. The *kata* you'll be learning are the same ones I started out with. They're part of a style called *shorin-ryu*. It's based more on speed than on strength, so it's better suited to women than *shorei-ryu*, which is what I study these days."

He demonstrates the *heisoku-dachi* stance, and she mimics him. "Close it up, okay?" When Simon reaches out to tap her left elbow, she shrinks back, almost as if he's threatened to hit her. "Um, sorry. I wasn't going to . . . Could you just . . . tuck your elbow in a little? Yeah, like that. Now take a deep breath and let it all the way out."

As they go through the *kata* positions, he's careful not to get too close. If she keeps being such a touch-me-not, it's going to make things difficult, especially when they start sparring. Maybe it's a cultural thing; maybe in Brazil girls aren't supposed to let boys touch them. Well, she'll likely loosen up as they go along. For all her nervousness or tenseness or whatever it is, she performs the moves with surprising grace. When he tells her so, she rewards him with a shy smile. "It is like dancing, isn't it?" she says.

"Yeah, it is, kind of. In fact, in *Kabuki* theatre, they call their dance moves *kata*. So. Are, uh, are you a dancer?"

"I studied ballet for a time, at the *conservatório*." She wipes the perspiration from her forehead with the sleeve of her sweatshirt.

"You could take that off." Well, that's a bit suggestive. "I mean . . . , if you're too hot." Even more suggestive.

"No. Thank you. I will leave it on." While she catches her breath, they watch Wendy giving the *makiwara* hell. Her feet are bare, and her toes sport the same garish nail polish as her fingers. With each strike, she shouts "*kiai!*" in an almost scarily vindictive way, as if the padded board has done her some grievous wrong.

"Wow," says Simon. "She's really getting into this."

"May I ask a question?" says Gabriela.

"Sure."

36

"Why do we spend our time learning to dance? Should we not be learning instead how to *hurt* an attacker . . . how do you say? *Disable* him?"

Simon is taken aback just a bit by the hard edge in her voice. Until now, she's seemed so reticent, so soft-spoken. He's heard this question, though, or one like it, more times than he can count, from the students at his dad's *dojo*. He's asked it himself, more than once. So he fully expected to get it from this group; he just didn't imagine it would be Gabriela asking it.

The others have stopped what they were doing and are listening in. All right, then; time to lay it out for them. "Actually, no. You see, that's why it's called self-*defense*. You're trying to defend yourself, protect yourself, not hurt the other person. If your goal is to defeat or disable your opponent, then it's called combat."

"I am sorry," says Gabriela, "but if someone attacks you, it doesn't seem to me that these moves would help very much, no matter how well you do them."

"Oh?" he says, feigning surprise, but he's not surprised at all, just disappointed. Talking is getting him nowhere; he's going to have to emulate Alec the Hot Dog and show off a little. "Well, why don't you try?"

"Try?"

"Attack me. Go ahead."

She ducks her head, embarrassed. "I can't *attack* you."

"No?" He turns to the Visigoths. "Would you ladies care to attack me?"

They glance at each other and giggle. "All of us?" says Amy.

"That might get a little crowded. No, three against one ought to be enough, right?"

"You promise not to hurt us?" says Rachel.

"I promise. Maybe a little temporary pain, but no broken limbs, no bloody noses. You can feel free to hurt me, though."

The girls look to Wendy, who gives a slightly nasty grin. "Let's do it!" The three of them converge on Simon.

The Visigoth attack lasts all of fifteen seconds. Rachel does a Norman Bates number, rushing at him with her arm uplifted as if holding a butcher knife. Simon steps slightly out of her path, blocks the knife arm, and, with a sweeping motion, traps it beneath his armpit and presses down, bringing the girl to her knees.

Amy opts for karate chops, the sort she's seen on TV. He grabs her wrist and, using her own momentum, pulls her off her feet. Wendy tries one of the kicks she's been practicing on the *makiwara;* Simon crouches, blocks it with crossed arms, and springs upward, sending her flying. He bows to each of his fallen opponents in turn. "Those are all moves that you'll be learning," he says.

To his relief, they don't seem resentful at all; in fact, they're laughing. "Okay," says Wendy, rubbing her trim butt. "You've made your point." She turns to Gabriela. "Don't you think?"

Gabriela smiles ruefully and nods. "Yes. But how do you move so quickly?"

Simon shrugs. "Practice," he says. "I've repeated those techniques thousands of times--so many times that I don't have to think about them; I just *do* them. It's automatic, like breathing. But it doesn't work if you're actively trying to hurt your opponent; that goal occupies your mind, and your mind needs to be empty."

"I have no trouble with that," says Rachel, and everyone laughs.

"Can I just point out one thing," says Wendy, "since we're talking about self-defense versus combat? The branch of the government in charge of making war is called the Department of *Defense*. Why is that?"

"Have you read *1984*?" says Amy. "It's called Newspeak. You know what I think? I think the military should adopt our *dojo kun:* 'Prepare for conflict, but pursue peace.'"

"Speaking of which," says one of the two girls who aren't part of Wendy's army and whose names Simon has forgotten. "There's a demonstration this afternoon in front of Taylor Hall, protesting the presence of Marine recruiters on campus. I think we should all be there."

"Or be square," puts in her friend.

Simon groans inwardly. Though he's not a big fan of the armed forces, he's always avoided any sort of protest. They have a tendency to get out of hand. At least twice in the past year, the police have waded into crowds of shouting students, leaving dozens of them battered by batons and smarting from tear gas. That doesn't worry Simon particularly; one of the things karate has taught him is how to block out pain. What does concern him is the fact that six of the ringleaders were put on probation and two were actually expelled. One of those, a friend of Mack's, was drafted a month later.

Simon gently steers his students back onto the karate track. His uncharacteristic theatrics have paid off; now that he's shown them what's possible, the women—Gabriela included--seem much more willing. Though they're worlds away from mastering the existing moves, Simon introduces a new one, just to keep them motivated—the *kiba-dachi* stance, complete with hook punch.

When their two hours are up, they're clearly exhausted, but most of them are smiling—a good sign. As they bow and exit, several of them call out "See you next week!" Not Gabriela, though. She slips out almost furtively, without so much as a wave, leaving Simon to wonder whether she'll be back. She seemed to actually be enjoying herself, at least some of the time. But maybe that's the problem. She said she wasn't looking for fun.

He can see her point; the possibility of being sexually assaulted is a serious and scary thing, no question. But karate is all about letting go of those feelings, learning to respond to a threat instinctively, without fear or anger. Simon's guess is that she's harboring some of each, and it's going to take a while to rid herself of them.

Well, he can't force her to come to the class. All he can do is wait and see what happens. If they meet at the Gedunk as arranged, he'll make sure not to mention the word karate; better to just stick to books. Of course, chances are she won't show up; that was probably just a polite way of putting him off.

On his way to the Gedunk, he passes Taylor Hall. Students are starting to gather for the demonstration, carrying an assortment of signs that range from flimsy and crude to amazingly artistic. Their slogans run the gamut, too, from a simple KILL? NOT ME, to a long list of grievances against the university administration, to a picture of a Neanderthal in uniform, with the caption MARINE BIOLOGY.

Simon spots one of the nameless girls from his karate class and makes an abrupt detour; if she tries to recruit him for the demonstration, he's liable to give in. Head down, he bucks the swelling tide of protestors and spectators until he meets a major obstacle in the form of Mack.

"Simon, my man! Glad to see you made the scene!" He wraps one arm around Simon's neck and the other around the flower child, who's wearing a Che Guevara beret and carrying a sign that reads GET THE HELL OUT OF VIETNAM (AND VAN DYNE). "Have you met Maisie?"

"Um, hi," says Simon. "I'm not actually here to . . . I'm just on my way to—to meet somebody."

"Aha. Somebody of the female persuasion, I hope?"

"Uh, yeah, in fact."

"Right on! Bring her back here, man! The more the merrier!" Mack makes it sound as if they're planning to party, not protest.

"Yeah, maybe. Listen." He pulls Mack aside--not an easy task, given the guy's size--and says softly, "Don't do anything dumb, okay? Like punching a cop, for instance?" Though Mack is easygoing, he's also a defensive tackle, and doesn't respond well to being pushed around. He can be impulsive, too. "Or burning your draft card?"

"Not to worry, man; it's cool. Maisie says everybody has pledged to keep this thing peaceful."

"Uh-huh. Has she ever heard of *agents provocateurs*?"

"Hey, if anybody starts making trouble, I'll just deck 'em." He laughs and claps Simon on the back, testing his ability to block out pain. "Kidding, man, kidding. Go meet your mysterious Miss, and come on back, okay?"

"I'll try," says Simon, lying through his teeth, and hurries off.

Due to the demonstration, the Gedunk is practically empty; it'll be easy enough to spot Gabriela. Or it *would* be if she were here, which she's clearly not. He should have straightened up the wrestling room more quickly and he shouldn't have wasted time talking to Mack. If she came at all, she probably got tired of waiting and split.

Simon isn't all that fond of the Gedunk. It has none of the Turtle Tap's atmosphere or history; it dates back only to 1954, when returning Korean War vets flooded the campus. They were responsible for the quirky name, which may be Chinese for "a place of idleness," or maybe not. The chairs are cold metal, the tabletops are glass—no old liquor stains or carved initials here.

Modernity does have its consolations, though. The place serves fruit smoothies, something the Tap hasn't discovered yet. Simon orders a Blueberry Blast and secludes himself in a corner to mope. Though Taylor Hall is halfway across campus, he can hear voices chanting "One, two, shame on you! Three, four stop the war!" and he feels a twinge of guilt, as if they're blaming him for not joining the protest.

It's not that Simon is unsympathetic to the cause. He knows that, like every war before it, this one is stupid and immoral. But he also knows that no amount of marching, chanting, or sign-waving has ever accomplished anything aside from getting the protestors beaten up or jailed—or, in some countries, thrown into a concentration camp or shot.

Many nights, when he's wide awake in the small hours, Simon finds himself wondering what he'll do if the lottery system kicks in and his number comes up. Will he be unable to say no, as he so often is? Or, as with the Phi Alphs, will he refuse to kiss the military's collective ass? He could always head for Canada; he knows of at least three guys who went that route.

Or, if he had the guts, he could follow in his father's footsteps.

That's another thing he often wonders about. Would his dad ever have opened up that particular can of worms if Frank Ávila hadn't beat him to it?

CHAPTER SIX

Simon still isn't sure when or how Frank learned about Don Hannay's service record. He certainly didn't hear about it from Simon, because Simon didn't know. He and Frank did talk once in a while, though. After that first encounter outside the Legion, they continued to run into each other--usually not so literally. They could hardly avoid it, since they were in most of the same classes—at least until Frank switched his focus to Mechanical Arts.

If someone had asked Simon to describe their relationship, he'd have been at a loss. Frank didn't exactly bully him, but neither did he act much like a friend. Once or twice a week, they happened to connect in the hallway or in the boys' bathroom--or maybe it didn't just happen; maybe Frank planned it. Sometimes he asked whether the refinery was hiring, or whether Simon's dad needed somebody to rake leaves or mow the lawn. Other times, he hit Simon up for money—not in a threatening way, but as if Simon owed it to him because his dad wouldn't hire Frank's dad.

Simon had trouble saying no, of course, but he also kind of agreed with Frank's logic, so he always handed over fifty cents or a dollar. Once, Frank even asked Simon to write an essay for him, so he wouldn't flunk World History. Simon agreed to that, too. The paper earned Frank his first B—well, Simon couldn't make it *too* good, or Mrs. McFadden would have smelled a rat for sure.

Outside of school, Frank was practically a stranger. Well into the fall, he was still hanging around with his *amigos*, but as more and more families gave up and went South, the brotherhood dwindled in size. When Simon passed by, they eyed him with amusement and traded scornful-sounding remarks. He knew they must be discussing something besides his clumsiness or his braininess, but he couldn't tell what—not until he was on Cassette Two of the Berlitz Basic Spanish Course.

He had ordered the course at his mother's urging but, even after she left, he kept at it, thinking that, when she came back--as she surely would--she'd be pleased at his progress. He had another motive, though: If he could say a few sentences to Peri Jurado in her native language, maybe it would break down the invisible barrier between them.

Her family must have been hurting for money, because in September they sent her back to work at the Five and Ten. Simon devised a devious plan: When she left the store some evening, he'd arrange to bump into her—he was good at bumping into people. He'd apologize profusely, impressing her with his impeccable Spanish--"*Lo siento mucho, señorita; soy san torpe*"—and they'd strike up a conversation.

Of course, it was probably best to wait until he got to, say, Cassette Three or Four and could say something more scintillating than "Do you think it will rain today?" or "Please speak more slowly." But he had a goal, at least, and it motivated him to work hard. By the end of October he could catch much of what Frank and his friends were saying—and quickly came to regret it.

One of their History assignments was to do a show and tell, and Simon had no trouble choosing a topic. He'd never lost his fascination with codes and ciphers, and lately he'd been reading about encryption methods used by the Greeks and Romans. For his project he created a modern version of the *scytale*— the wooden staff that Spartan commanders sometimes used as a device for sending secret messages. Simon carved a staff, then wrapped an old belt around it and scratched into the leather the words of an ancient proverb: WHATEVER IS GOOD TO KNOW IS DIFFICULT TO LEARN. When you unwrapped the belt, the letters looked like nonsense--until you wound it around another staff of the same diameter.

On his way to school on show and tell day, he spotted Frank and what remained of his gang—a single scrawny *compañero* with a sparse mustache and a Carman Sugar ball cap--leaning against the chain-link fence that surrounded the school grounds, surreptitiously sharing a smoke. As usual, they eyed him and made snide comments--only this time he understood most of the words. "*Todavía piensa que su madre va a volver*," said Frank. He still thinks his mother is coming back.

His companion gave a lewd snicker. "*Sí es asi,la visitaré. Escucho que es una puta.*" If she does, I'm going to pay her a visit. I hear she's a . . . . Simon didn't know the last word, but he could guess.

The anger and resentment he'd been holding inside ever since his mother left forced its way to the surface. Without considering the consequences, he stormed over and thrust his face close to that of the ball-capped boy, whose grin quickly faded. "What did you call my mother?" demanded Simon.

The boy held up his hands. "Hey, man, I didn't say *nada.*"

"The hell you didn't!" Simon poked his scytale into the Mexicano's scrawny chest. "Say it again! Come on, I dare you!"

"Leave him alone, Simon," said Frank. "He didn't mean nothing. We was just joking around."

"Joking?" shouted Simon. "You think my mother's a *joke?*"

Frank shrugged and gave a strained, sarcastic smile. "Well, you got to admit, it's pretty funny, her running off with a *fracasado* like Wally Butts."

He may have meant the remark to be conciliatory, but it only made Simon more furious. Still, he didn't really intend to hit Frank; it was as if his arm had a will of its own--or maybe it was the scytale, channeling the warlike spirit of the Spartans.

Maybe it's the same with the police who break up student protests—they don't really mean to hurt anybody, they just get carried away. As the old saying goes, *If you carry a stick, sooner or later you're going to hit somebody with it,* or words to that effect. Simon is tempted to backtrack to Taylor Hall. If the excrement is going to hit the air circulating device, as Mack is fond of saying, maybe he can see it coming and get the big guy out of the splatter zone.

He stands and gulps the last of his Blueberry Blast, but before he can make another move, he spots a sweatshirted figure weaving gracefully between the tables, heading straight for him. He almost chokes on the smoothie.

"*Boa tarde.* I am sorry to be so late. I—I could not make up my mind."

"Um, yeah, I know the feeling. I was just . . . just trying to decide whether to go to the . . ." He waves a hand in the direction of the voices, which are now chanting, "Bye, bye, Semper Fi! Don't send our students off to die!"

"Ah, *sim.* I thought about it, too. But if I got arrested or something, and my *padrinho* heard about it . . ."

"Your . . . godfather?"

"I call him that; he is the one who pays for my education. He is a teacher at the Joaquim Nabuco Institute."

"Wow; no kidding?"

"You know of the Institute?"

"Sure. I'm hoping to, uh, to study there at some point. So, um, you want to sit down? Would you like a smoothie?"

"A *smoothie*?"

"Well, or some tea? Or . . . I don't know, a *café com leite*?"

"That would be very nice. But you do not have to--"

"No, no, I asked you to come, so . . . I'll be right back. Don't go away, okay?"

"Okay."

He buys himself a coffee, too, not because he particularly wants one, just so he'll have something to do with his hands—and his mouth as well, in case he can't find anything sensible to say. Normally, he finds it easier to conduct a conversation involving books and research, but this time he has to be careful; if no one knows about the journal, he wants it to stay that way till he's had a chance to examine it. "So. What I wanted to ask was, uh, have you ever come across anything by Gil Vicente, the playwright, in the Taft collection?"

Gabriela seems a little more at ease than usual. Maybe she's getting used to him. Or maybe it's the coffee, which is advertised as Brazilian Dark Roast. She sips at it thoughtfully. "Vicente? I don't think so. Why?"

"I'm doing my master's thesis on him. Well, partly on him and partly on the *Cantigas de Santa Maria*. It's really hard to find any information about Vicente."

"Oh. That is too bad." She raises one hand, then, as if to prevent him from speaking—not that Simon had anything more to say, anyway. He can't help noticing that her nails are chewed to the quick and that the two carved silver rings she wears are far too bulky to suit her slender fingers. "*Espere um momento.* I *do* remember that name. There is a card in the drawer that does not match any of the books on the shelves. Where the title should be, it says *Journal*, and the author's name is listed only as Vicente, with a . . . how do you call it? *Um ponto de interrogação.*"

"Question mark."

"*Sim.* It gives no Christian name."

"Uh-huh. Does it . . . does it describe the book at all?"

"I think so, but I don't remember exactly. It has a PQ call number, but on the shelf where the book should be shelved, there is nothing. I hope it is not stolen. Perhaps someone only put it in the wrong place, and I will find it eventually."

"Maybe so. And maybe . . ."

"*Que?*"

"Well, I was just thinking that . . . that if I helped you look, we could find it twice as fast." Which, of course, is not what he's thinking at all. Nor is he thinking how much he'd like to be alone with her--at least that's not uppermost in his mind. He's thinking the same thing he thought on Friday, when he went straight to the Portuguese section: It would give them some common ground, something to explore together, to talk about. But only if she agrees to it, and, judging from her expression, that's not very likely. He'd probably have gotten a better reaction if he'd suggested skydiving or alligator wrestling.

Still, there's something more than just caution written on her face; there's curiosity, too. "I suppose that is true. When . . . when would you want to do that?"

"Um, well, you know what they say: *Carpe diem. Tempus fugit.*"

"*Aproveite o dia?*"

"*Exatamente.*"

Well, that was easier than he expected. It's even easier to get into the Taft; Gabriela just picks up the key at the reference desk while Simon stays out of sight. As they head upstairs, he whispers, "Shouldn't you tell them I'm coming in with you?"

She shakes her head. "You would need permission from your advisor. Just behave yourself, all right? If we do find the book, try not to steal it."

"I would never--" He starts to protest, and then sees the mischievous look in her dark eyes. "Oh. You're kidding. I always have trouble telling when people are kidding." Which is true, but it's especially true with her; this is probably the first time she's said anything resembling a joke. Maybe it's a sign that she's getting comfortable with him.

Not comfortable enough to take off the baggy sweatshirt, but maybe that's just due to the cool temperature in the Taft. Gabriela looks around thoughtfully. "It is probably going to be somewhere in the P section. If you will begin looking here--" She taps the end of the stacks labeled P-PF. "--I will search over here."

"Um, do you mind if we . . . you know, look at the card, first? I'd like to see what it says."

Gabriela leads the way to the card catalog, a bureau-sized piece of oak furniture whose varnish has turned chocolaty with age. Removing one of the drawers, she flips through the cards. "Here it is."

"They filed it under J?"

"For *Journal.* I told you, it is not very well organized. It would take me years to put it in proper order."

"Well," says Simon, "there are worse jobs." Personally, he'd relish the task, if it meant being this close to her for extended periods. Even though she may look a bit like Audrey Hepburn, thank god she doesn't feel it necessary to wear *L'Interdi.*

Despite his reluctance to classify people, Simon somehow expected Gabriela's scent to bear a sort of family resemblance to Peri Jurado's, which was sharp and spicy, like roasting chiles, and which he has never forgotten. But no, Gabriela has a fragrance all her own--a little earthy, a little minty, more than a little intoxicating. He wonders what she'd do if he buried his nose in her choppy, carbon-ink-hued hair and decides he doesn't really want to find out.

Just concentrate on the card, Simon. As Gabriela indicated, the author is listed only as **Vicente[?]** The description matches his codex: **Vellum bound ms. 60 p. 19 cm. 17th [?] century Foreword in Portuguese Text in Roman alphabet, Unknown Language** And that's it. Simon scratches his day's growth of stubble. *Unknown Language?* Unknown to whom? To the cataloguer, or to the whole of humanity?

"Um, do you mind if I do the PG through PZ's? Even if I don't find *this,* I might find something that'll help with my thesis." He adds, mostly to himself, "Like some motivation, for instance."

"*Que?*"

"Oh, nothing. Just griping. I think I should have picked a different topic; this one was mostly Dr. Espinoza's idea."

"He is your advisor?"

"Technically. I don't see much of him. Which is probably just as well."

Gabriela nods knowingly. "In the nineteen-forties, Gilberto--my *padrinho*-- studied here under Espinoza; he was a . . . a difficult man even then. Espinoza, I mean, not Gilberto, who is righteous."

Simon has never heard hip slang uttered in such an exotic accent. He can't help smiling a little, but only a little; he doesn't want to make her self-conscious. "Uh-huh. *Difficult* is one word for Dr. E. *Tyrant* is another one."

"Tyrant?"

"*Déspota.* In his class, every question was stupid, every answer was wrong. No matter how hard I worked, I never got anything better than a B."

"Gilberto says the same thing. But he also says there is a reason why Espinoza is so bitter and so angry. It is because of the war."

Simon thinks at once of Vietnam, but of course that makes no sense. "What, World War Two?"

"The *Guerra Civil Española.* I think his family were killed. So, do you want to find the book or not?"

Simon nods. "Right now, it's the only thing keeping me going—in terms of the thesis, I mean."

While Gabriela searches P through PF, Simon heads for the shelf where he found the codex yesterday. To his relief, it's still tucked away in the same spot and position that it's occupied for who knows how many years. He's dying to examine it, but he can't see much in this dim light. And he's promised not to steal it. That leaves only one option. "Um, Gabriela?"

"Yes?"

"I, uh . . . I think I found it."

"*Como?*"

"I say, I think I may have found the journal."

"*Putz grila!* Already?" She appears at the end of the aisle so abruptly that Simon almost drops the codex. "Where was it?"

"Tucked away behind some other books."

"May I see it?"

"Um, well . . ." Simon can't bear to hand it over. He climbs down from his precarious perch. "Could we look at it together?"

Gabriela considers this. "I--I suppose so." Awkwardly, they sit side by side at one of the tables. Simon folds back the protective flap and opens the slightly brittle vellum cover to reveal that initial, intriguing passage of Portuguese:

O meu nome é Vicente . Não irei revelar o meu apelido de família, não vão ela ter de sofrer pelos meus pecados. Não sei que olhos poderão estar a ler estas minhas últimas palavras, ou quando. Pedi a um dos poucos amigos que me restam que colocasse este diário entre os volumes da biblioteca do seu senhor, na esperança de escapar à atenção da Inquisição & que, daqui a alguns anos, ou décadas, ou séculos, quando o país & a Ygreja estiverem mais receptivos ao conhecimento que não saia directamente das páginas da Bíblia, algum sábio esclarecido venha a descobri-lo & seja suficientemente inteligente & determinado para desvendar os segredos que contém. Que ele - ou ela - seja melhor recompensado do que eu fui.

The page is creased and crumpled, and he has to smooth it out with his fingers. As he does so, the paper pulls away from the stab-sewn binding. "Agh!" Simon throws up his hands. "That wasn't my fault, I swear! It was already loose!"

"I know." Gabriela shakes her head in disgust. "Whoever handled it before was not very careful. I would like to crumple *him* up."

Simon gives her a worried glance. "Relax, okay? It's still readable." Though some of the spelling is archaic, he's used to that. He finds it easy enough to understand the words; obviously, so will Gabriela. She might have some trouble with the Chancery script, though, so he reads it aloud, automatically translating into English out of old habit. "'My name is Vicente. I will not reveal the name . . . the name of my family, so they will not have to suffer for my sins.'" Simon blinks in bafflement, not quite understanding after all—or maybe not wanting to understand. "What does he mean, the name of his *family*?"

"Let me see." Gabriela leans close to him in order to scan the page, and her scent makes Simon even more befuddled. "He must mean his *sobrenome*, his . . . how do you say? Surname?"

"Oh, shit." Simon claps a hand to his forehead. "Vicente isn't his last name; it's his *first* name!"

CHAPTER SEVEN

Simon gives a low groan of despair. "It can't be *my* Vicente, then, not Gil Vicente. I made the classic researcher's mistake: I saw what I *wanted* to see, not what was on the page."

"I am sorry, Simon." Gabriela lays a consoling hand on his arm--which, since it's the first time she's touched him, actually does make him feel better. Well, not much, but a little. It's also the first time she's spoken his name, which she pronounces *See-mohn*. A second later, she pulls her hand away, like a person who's accidentally touched a hot surface.

"Oh, well," sighs Simon. "I knew it was too good to be true. I guess we might as well read on, and see who the hell *this* Vicente actually is."

"Yes. At least then I can catalog the book more accurately."

"Okay. So. You want me to read? This script takes a little getting used to."

"Yes, *faz favor.*"

"I'll kind of translate as I go along, just for my own benefit. Feel free to jump in if I mangle it too much, okay?" Even though it makes him look like a first-grader, he finds it helps if he runs a finger along the line he's translating. "'I do not know whose eyes may be reading these, my last words, or when. I asked one of my friends who . . . '"

"'One of my last remaining friends,' I think."

"' . . . one of my last remaining friends to put this diary among the volumes in the library of his . . .'"

"His master."

"' . . . in hopes of escaping the notice of the Inquisition.'" Simon turns to Gabriela, his eyes wide. "The *Inquisition* was after him? I wonder what he did?"

Impatiently, Gabriela waves a finger at the codex. "Keep reading, please."

"Sorry. 'And in a few years, or decades, or centuries, when the country and the Church are more receptive to knowledge that does not come directly from the pages of the Bible, some . . . *sabio*?'"

"A wise person. A scholar, maybe?"

"' . . . some enlightened scholar will find it and be smart enough and determined enough to . . . untangle?'"

"Unravel, I suppose, or unveil."

"*Unveil*; I like that. '. . . to unveil the secrets it contains. May he—or she— be better rewarded than I was.' Hmm. What sort of secrets, I wonder? Obviously something the Inquisition wasn't going to be too happy about."

"Well, most of the people they persecuted were *hereges*--heretics—especially *Judeus* who converted to Christianity but kept on practicing their old religion."

"But they went after pretty much anybody who challenged the status quo, right? I mean, like Galileo, for instance. And witches. And sorcerers. And . . ." She's doing the finger wave again. " . . . and you want me to keep reading, right?"

"Please."

"That's all he wrote on this page. Let's see what else we've got." He gingerly lays the loose, crumpled sheet aside and examines the next page, which is definitely not written in Portuguese:

UIR EICADR NSA RA AAAC DSCU RIESUIUI EUI NARARGAAUNU IICI U CIDEU

DEDESN ISCLEUSRND S EUMTSM ND ASKND NU NSMLOISFEOEN RND TMSOEESD NU

TR RBIEUEORC OR EEIIRI IRB BR RE E SECRBBR RBIRIER RURNRB R EMEOEI

QST ITAI IT UUEAS TNTIVTV IUMT SAT VTTNU SATVUI UAVVUI IUUNUI T

CBTITAV QMV MMEAA TAEVMA I EQM FMANM VEI EIAA QIUAV FMIA A VEI

SCLIIL CEDE IDINED E NDIINI DIDUEUI I EEI E CEACE UE DIUNE CLUUICEL

STIISMHT SMSRASEPTTESMHS IPAES PI ESAI PEAEPI TPESHS AET SMPEES

OSMCEIDMDI DI UITMDDI I MEDCM DISD IFUEM-UDI MMD D SICAD "IFUEMC"

NVUSCVQS OAUUONU UE SOOASAIUVUAIDU AE UAFAOVS SIDAN UVTAO NEA UAFU

DTALAM TIM SISA S QAAEAVES UAMI UIV A NEVIA EEAA S AS AIMNIA

UUIAANIEUA DU IMAALU IIC U CIDEU UUCU ICIAEUU A NIMIIIU DI ADEUDEI

DRSM FULEN EMERLEN S UFS LODELEULESN EUE EOSLS TEDDNSD TSMS N EILMLN

TEE RB IEIIEIR EE RB TEREIR NR SEPEREIR BEIUMRBIRNIR UEI UIECEIRIRI

QU MTVIUIT UITIUV IT TU STA SUIU VTV TIVUIU MUIVUTVT STTUI ITITSUIU

CM EIAIEIM VM BIIVMVI VA VEI M EIAIEIM VA VTUNITIA VEI AAAA FET I

SEEI NLAL ILE CLD MEAMECIED ILMDI EIIEUNLI NEL EMINDENLI ME UEL

SEPIIP UTE-ES T SIIS SAEP

"*Fala sério!*" says Gabriela. "Now I see what they mean by *Unknown Language!*"

"Uh-huh." Simon scans the strange combinations of letters. "Only they were wrong. My guess is, it's not a language at all."

"Not a language? But what--?"

"It's a cipher. What some people would call a secret code."

"Really? Are you certain?"

If there's one area besides karate in which Simon feels confident, it's codes and ciphers. "Pretty much. I mean, no language has words that bizarre, right? BEIUMRBIRNIR? How would you even pronounce that? Be You Mister Burner? I Be Mister Hannay."

She rolls her eyes as if to say he's hopeless. But she's also smiling a little. "Can you . . . how do you say? *Uncipher* it?"

"*De*cipher. Well, if it's monoalphabetic--"

"Unknown Language," says Gabriela.

"Um, that means each letter is replaced with another letter, but always the same one. If that's so, it'll be easy to crack. But I'm pretty sure this is polyalphabetic. I mean, look at all the one-letter words. How many of those are there in Portuguese?"

"*A* and *E*. And *O*. And . . ."

"And that's about it, right? But he's got . . . what? Ten different one-letter words on this page alone? He must be using at least three or four different alphabets."

"But would he use such a complicated code? Is that not a modern thing?"

"Not really. In the early 1500s, a monk named Trithemius invented what's called a *tableau*. It's just twenty-six alphabets, lined up one under the other. The first one goes ABC and so on, the second one goes BCD and so on, and then CDE and so on and so on. It's not that tough to crack, either, if the person writing the cipher uses Alphabet Number One for the first letter, Number Two for the second letter, and so on. All you have to do is make your own tableau and reverse the process, *et voilà.*"

"So you think that is the method Vicente used?"

"If we're lucky."

"And if we are not?"

Simon likes how she says *we*, as if they're in this together. "Well, I guess we'll cross that bridge if we come to it. For now, let's assume he used the easy way. Do you have paper and a pen?"

"You are going to decipher it?"

"I'm going to try, if you don't mind hanging around for a while."

"I don't mind at all. I think it is *excitante*. I am sorry, pens are not allowed in here, but I can get you a pencil." She fetches writing implements from a small cupboard above the card catalog. "Are you certain you want to do this, Simon? If this is not *your* Vicente, will it not be a waste of time?"

"Hey, if I don't try, I'll always wonder if I got it wrong, if Vicente *was* his last name after all. I mean, maybe *apelido de família* meant something else back then."

"What else could it mean?"

"Well, *apelido* can mean a nickname, too, right? Anyway, you know how tricky Portuguese and Spanish names are. Lots of people used both their father's name and their mother's--like Miguel de Cervantes Saavedra. Nobody knows Gil Vicente's full name, or who his parents were; maybe he was Gil Vicente Something de Something."

Simon doesn't realize how emphatic, almost manic, he's starting to sound until he sees the slightly startled look on Gabriela's face. She cautiously places the paper and pencil in front of him. "Okay, okay. I was not suggesting that you should *not* do it; I was just asking."

Simon feels himself blushing. "Sorry. Like I said—"

"I know, you get carried away."

"Right. I'm also a sucker for anything that says it contains secret knowledge—in this case, so secret that he had to encipher it."

"And so dangerous that he could not let the Inquisition find out."

Glancing about furtively, Simon says, in a Boris Karloff voice, "Perhaps *too* dangerous. There are things that are best left alone!" For the first time since they met, Gabriela actually laughs. Then, as when she touched his arm, she seems to wish she hadn't. "So," says Simon. "Shall we live dangerously?"

"*Claro!* What do you want me to do?"

Put your hand on my arm again, he's tempted to say. "You want to make the tableau? Your printing has got to be better than mine. All you have to do is--"

"I know; you explained it."

"Right."

She snatches up the paper and pencil and begins printing rows of well-formed and neatly aligned alphabets. Simon sits watching for a moment, happy and a bit surprised to see her so relaxed and confident. She glances at him peevishly. "Are *you* not going to do anything?"

"Um, sure. I'll just . . ." He'll just make sure this actually is a polyalphabetic cipher. He must have cracked a hundred monoalphabetic ones, back when he still had lots of leisure time. Once you get the hang of it, it's a cinch, provided the letters are grouped the way they were in the original message—the plaintext.

First you figure out which letter appears most often. Say it's a Q; you assume that stands for *e*, the most common letter in English. Then you look for a three-letter block ending in Q; that's probably the word *the*. So now you have the ciphertext letters for *t* and *h*, and you go from there.

The same method should work with Portuguese; its most common letter is also *e*--though *a* runs a close second, and *o* is not far behind. But when he counts, he finds that the most-used letter in the ciphertext is . . . an E. Well, Vicente certainly wouldn't replace every *e* in his message with another E. So maybe all those E's are actually *a*'s? But that would mean that the two-letter word in line thirteen, EE, would be *aa*. Highly unlikely, unless they had Alcoholics Anonymous in the sixteenth century.

Gabriela slides the completed tableau in front of him. "All done."

"Wow. Your printing is a *lot* better than mine. You could have made a good living in the 1500s, as a scrivener."

She looks pleased. "The woman who taught us to write in *escolar primária* was a . . . how did you say it?" They speak the word simultaneously: "A tyrant." She looks over his shoulder at the cipher. "Have you had any luck?"

"Nope. Like I thought, it's got to be polyalphabetic. Let's try it with the tableau. How about if I say the letters and you write them down?"

"All right. I am ready."

"Okay. Assuming Vicente copied Trithemius' method and used the alphabets in order, we have . . . **uhp bexuwj**. Uh-huh. Well, that's obviously not right." He scratches his stubbly chin again. "So. Let's assume that he didn't start with Alphabet Number One."

"How do we know where he *did* start?"

"Well, what's a common three-letter word that you'd use to start a sentence?"

"*Que?*"

"I said, what's a common three-letter word that--"

She laughs. "I know. And I gave you one: *Que*."

"Oh. Sorry."

"You say you are sorry too often."

"Sorry. Just kidding. Okay, let's assume that first word—UIR—is really *que*. Which alphabet uses a U in place of a *q*?"

Gabriela counts down the rows. "Number Five."

"And which alphabet uses an I for a *u*?"

"Number . . . Fifteen. And Number Fourteen uses an R for an *e*."

"Five, Fifteen, Fourteen. If there's a pattern there, I fail to see it."

Gabriela gently turns the page and examines the writing on the verso side. "I think maybe I see a pattern, though. Look at the first letter of each line. They repeat themselves, don't they?"

"Do they? Let's see . . ." Simon jots down the initial letter of each line. After ten lines, the sequence starts over again--the same letters in the same order. "Holy cow. How did you happen to notice *that*?"

She shrugs. "I don't know; I just did."

Simon gives himself a mental karate kick. He's always thought he had a sharp eye for detail, and yet he's overlooked two fairly glaring things—the repeating letters, plus the first-name/last-name business. It's all Gabriela's fault, of course; she's just too distracting. He could probably make a lot more progress on his own.

But that suddenly seems like a rather cheerless prospect. In any case Gabriela, like his old classmates, will likely lose interest once the task gets tough or tedious, as it surely will. But maybe he's wrong. Maybe the solution lies in those repeating letters. "You know, I wonder if those first letters could be nulls."

"You are speaking the Unknown Language again."

"Sorry. And now I'm saying 'sorry' again. Okay, nulls are letters that aren't actually part of the message. What if they indicate the alphabet that Vicente used for that particular line?"

"The whole line?"

"Yeah. I mean, it'd be way faster than switching alphabets all the time, and he'd be less likely to make mistakes."

"Shall we try it?"

"Okay. The first letter of the first line is a U. If we use the U alphabet, we get . . . *ox koigjx.*" Simon sighs wearily. "Oh, boy. Clearly this is going to take a while."

"How long is a while?"

"I don't know. If Vicente used a keyword--"

"Unknown Language," says Gabriela.

"Sorr— Uh, a keyword is sort of like a password--like *open sesame* or something. The letters of the word tell you which alphabets to use."

"So if the keyword was his name, he would use the V alphabet, then the I alphabet, *et cetera.*"

"Right. But he could have used *any* word, you know, even . . ." Simon trails off. Gabriela isn't listening; she's too busy trying out the keyword *Vicente.* My god, he's created a monster. "Does that give you anything that makes sense?"

"Yes!" says Gabriela, breathlessly. "*zap!*"

"Uh-huh. And what does that mean in Portuguese, exactly?"

She gives a sheepish giggle. He never imagined she was capable of giggling. "Nothing. But maybe it meant something in the sixteenth century?"

"I'll bet. As I said, this could take a while. I don't suppose we can move into the Taft for the duration?"

"Probably not."

"And we can't take the book with us."

"Definitely not."

"So, what do we do? Meet here every Saturday afternoon?" That sounds a lot like he's asking her for a date. "I mean . . . you wouldn't have to. You probably have other things to . . ."

"I have a better idea," she replies. Oh, great. He's being too pushy, and she's going to say something like *Why don't you just work on it yourself, and let me know how it goes?* But, no, she's saying, "Why do we not copy the book and take it with us?"

"Oh. Um, we could do that?"

"*Claro.* There is a copy machine in the book repair room."

The machine is, in fact, a Xerox 3600; it's larger, faster, and a lot less idiosyncratic than the Language Department's old 914, which reportedly catches fire from time to time. "I'll let you do the copying," says Simon. "I don't want to pull out any more pages."

Gabriela places the loose first page on the scanning glass and smooths it out, but each time she starts to close the lid, the paper reverts to its crumpled state. "You want me to hold it in place?" says Simon. "I'll be careful."

"All right, but do not look at the light. It is very bright."

That's like the guy in the Isak Dinesen story telling the king not to think about the left eye of a camel. Simon can't help glancing at the paper as the exposure lamps pass under it, and he can't help noticing the pinpricks of light that pierce the paper where it's worn thin with age, like stars piercing the night sky.

The remainder of the pages—about sixty of them--present no problem for the copier; Gabriela just lays the open book face down on the glass, closes the lid, and presses a button. The whole process takes no more than half an hour. "Pretty slick," says Simon. "One of these days, they'll come up with a machine that can take a book like this and, in ten minutes, spit out a copy that's completely deciphered and translated."

"Perhaps," says Gabriela. "But how much fun would that be?" She hands him the stack of pages. "Now you may work on it wherever and whenever you please. How long do you think it will take?"

"Well, if Vicente used a keyword, it's useless to try and guess it. I'll have to look for combinations of letters that got enciphered the same way more than once. But if he used what's called an autokey, I'm probably screw—I mean, out of luck."

"This *autokey*—was it used in the sixteenth century?"

"Yep. By a Frenchman named Vigenère. He called it *le chiffre indéchiffrable*."

"The indecipherable cipher."

"Right. It's hard to explain; basically it uses the message itself as the keyword, so it never repeats."

"Will you have time to do all this?"

"Probably not," he admits gloomily, "considering I have a thesis to write." Then, like those tiny shafts of light shooting through the paper, a bright idea begins to pierce the gloom. "Unless . . . "

"Unless what?"

Simon hefts the pages, as if testing their weight. "Unless I make *this* my thesis."

CHAPTER EIGHT

"Do you think Dr. Espinoza will allow you to do that—change the topic of your thesis?"

"I imagine he'll like it about as much as the Inquisition would. I guess I could always change advisors if I have to. I'm just worried that, if I drag things out too long, I'll lose my fellowship." He sticks the loose page back in the codex and closes the flap. "What do we do with this?"

Gabriela studies the book thoughtfully. "I suppose I should shelve it in its proper place." Then she studies Simon's pained expression. "But perhaps that could wait for a while, until you have a chance to decipher it."

Simon heaves a sigh of relief. "Thank you. By the way . . . I mean, I don't want you to feel obligated or anything, but . . . well, if you thought you might like to . . . you know . . ."

"Yes," she says. "I do know. And I would be happy to help, if you need me."

"Really? That'd be great. You seem to have a knack for this stuff. It's kind of like karate; it takes a lot of practice to get good at it, but that's not enough. You want to reach a state of *mushin*, where you're open to anything and you see everything. I have trouble with that; I think and analyze too much."

While Gabriela returns the codex to its secret spot, Simon rolls up the copies and puts a rubber band around them. "I wonder how the demonstration turned out," he calls to her.

"We could go and take a look."

There she goes, using that term *we* again; it makes Simon smile. "Okay, sure."

Outside Taylor Hall, most of the protestors and spectators have dispersed. There are no belligerent policemen in sight, and no clouds of tear gas in the air. There is a small group gathered under one of the ancient oak trees, though, having a very heated discussion. One of the voices is unmistakably Mack's.

"Uh-oh," says Simon. "I'd better see what's going down. Maybe you should stay here." He hands her the rolled-up copies and approaches the group. He knows better than to barge right in; he needs to size up the situation first. Mack is arguing with a couple of guys--obviously fellow jocks. One is Bear O'Hara, the Sliders' running back. Maisie, the flower child, is standing between him and Mack, obviously trying to calm them down. The way his massive form looms over her, it's clear how Bear got his nickname.

While he tries to intimidate Mack and Maisie with his sheer size, his teammate--Duane or Dennis; something with a D, anyway--uses his mouth. "I thought you were one of *us*, McNaughton, but it looks to me like you're turning into some kind of a hippie faggot!"

Thankfully, Mack refuses to take the bait. "Oh, good," he says, cheerfully. "I don't have to worry about being drafted, then, 'cause the Army doesn't take faggots."

"No, but they sure as hell draft *peaceniks*. In fact I hear they give 'em rifles loaded with blanks and stick 'em right out there on the front lines for the gooks to use as target practice. And good riddance."

"Why don't you just settle down, boys?" says Maisie, her voice quiet and reasonable, almost sweet. "You say you're loyal Americans. Well, according to the Bill of Rights, we're all entitled to peaceably assemble and speak our minds."

"Not when you're spouting *treason*, you're not!"

"Treason?" Maisie laughs. "You want to know what *real* treason is?" Her tone is growing less quiet and reasonable. "Real treason is when Tricky Dick sabotages the peace talks."

This heresy prompts Bear to open his big mouth at last. "Are you calling the President of the United States a *traitor*?" With one huge hand he gives the flower girl a shove that almost knocks her down.

"Shit!" mutters Simon. He's seen how abruptly Mack can go from good-natured to murderous, and his friend behaves true to form.

"Son of a bitch!" Mack launches himself at Bear like the defensive tackle he is. If this were a football game, Bear would have been prepared, but it's real life and he's caught off guard. He backpedals and goes down with Mack on top of him. Mack is no longer a lineman; he's a boxer, now, pummeling Bear's head and chest mercilessly.

"Mack! Stop!" Simon springs forward, meaning to pull his friend off before he beats Bear to a pulp. Duane/Dennis sees him not as a peacemaker but as an enemy and takes a swing at him. Simon blocks the punch easily with one arm; with the other he delivers a knife-hand strike to the guy's bull neck. If he struck full force, it could do some real damage, so he pulls the punch a little. Duane/Dennis backs off, coughing and clutching his throat. Simon snatches the neck of Mack's sweatshirt and drags him off his victim.

No doubt Bear has taken worse beatings on the field, but this is different; this is personal. There's a look of panic--fright, even--on his blood-smeared face. Simon reaches down to help him up, but Bear contemptuously knocks his hand away.

As Simon straightens up, he feels a beefy arm encircle his neck and clamp down, choking him. At first thinks it's Mack, angry at him for interfering, so he doesn't react as he normally would—by driving an elbow into his attacker's gut.

But obviously it's not Mack, who's just now getting to his feet. By the time this registers with Simon, he's getting too weak to fight back. Luckily, Mack isn't. He jams a fist into the attacker's face and the guy lets go his stranglehold. Gasping for air, Simon turns to see who was trying to kill him. It's Duane/Dennis.

Holding his bloody nose, the guy shambles off with Bear close behind. But he can't leave without a parting shot: "You're gonna be sorry, Ho Chi Mack, and your little gooks, too!" a line so ludicrous that Mack just laughs.

While his friend checks on the flower child, Simon looks around for Gabriela. He's almost afraid to face her, after the pitiful fight he put up. She's got to be thinking, *He's teaching us self-defense, and he can't even defend himself?* But she can't tell him what she thinks, because she's disappeared.

Mack appears at his side, without Maisie. "You okay, man?"

"Yeah, sure. Thanks for coming to the rescue, Jim Dandy."

"No problemo. But if you don't mind my asking, why didn't you just cream the guy and put him out of commission? I know you could have."

Simon shrugs uncomfortably. "It's hard to explain."

"Hey, I'm a Psych major. I'm used to obtuse explanations."

"Obscure, you mean."

"Okay. Anyway, you know what always helps me understand them?"

"Um . . . a drink?"

"Right on."

As they head for the Turtle Tap, Mack is limping so badly that Simon says, "Are you sure you can walk that far?"

"I'll manage." He flexes his right hand. "Actually, my fingers hurt worse than my leg. You'd better teach me some of them karate punches."

"Hmm," says Simon, noncommittally, knowing that Mack would never have the patience to learn them properly. "So, how did the demonstration go?"

"Well, nobody got bludgeoned or gassed or arrested."

"Is that good or bad?"

"Both, I guess. I mean, we don't want anybody getting hurt, but it does win people over to our cause when they see the Man wailing on us."

"*Our cause? The Man?* When did you become part of the counterculture?"

Mack does his Stan Laurel move, rubbing his head sheepishly, and Simon notices that he actually seems to be letting his hair grow out. Though he's a long way from looking like a hippie, maybe it's a sign--as Mack says, the first step on the road to the depths of degradation. "I'm not. But I went to an SDS meeting with Maisie--"

"SDS? Is that the Self-Destructive Society?"

"Funny. It's Students for a Democratic Society, and they're not just a bunch of potheads—well, okay, a lot of them are, but they also make a lot of sense. You should come to one of the meetings."

"I don't think so. I'm not sure you should, either. The word is, the CIA's recruiting students to infiltrate groups they consider subversive. Anyway, if you start turning into Joan Baez, your coach isn't going to like it."

Mack once again behaves true to form, launching into a horrible rendition of "We Shall Overcome." Then he breaks off abruptly and stumbles to a halt, gripping his knee. "Damn. That hurts. I took a wrong step." But he's obviously feeling more than just physical pain. "The thing is, man, it doesn't much matter whether I piss off Coach or not; I'm not going to be playing this season, anyway--or probably any other season."

"Don't say that, Mack. If you go easy on the leg and get some physical therapy, by next year you'll—"

"Hey!" Mack interrupts. "Don't kid a kidder, okay?"

"Sorry."

They walk the rest of the way to the Turtle Tap in silence. The place is packed and noisy, as it always is on a Saturday evening, but they manage to get close enough to the bar to order a couple of Gin Sliders from Alec, who serves up a little sarcasm along with the drinks. "Hey, Mack," he calls, over the babble. "I hear you gave the Marine recruiters a little demonstration of your hand-to-hand combat skills. Did they sign you up?"

Simon glares at him. "Cool it, okay, Alec?"

"Okay. Just joking."

"Well, just don't."

Mack eases onto a just-vacated bar stool, downs his Slider, and orders another one. "So, you were going to explain to me why you didn't break Darrin's redneck neck."

"Is that his name? I thought it was Duane. Or Dennis."

"Don't evade the question."

"Sorry. It's kind of a long story."

"I like long stories. Unless they're about white whales or Okies or Russians with six different names."

So, under cover of the general din, Simon gives his friend a hesitant, halting, but very thorough account of what happened between him and Frank Ávila. It's the first time he's told it to anyone besides his father.

•   •   •

According to Don Hannay, sometime around the age of three or four Simon went through a "difficult" stage; every time something made him angry or frustrated, he threw a truly terrible tantrum. Simon doesn't remember much about those years. He recalls all too well, though, the years that followed, when his mother was the one prone to tantrums, when he learned to control his emotions, to weigh everything he did or said before he said or did it, to avoid setting his mother off.

His violent reaction to the Mexicanos' snide remarks surprised him as much as it did them. Their insults tapped into a reservoir of anger so deep and so toxic that it made him want to destroy something, and Frank was the closest target.

If Simon had struck an Anglo kid hard enough to break his cheekbone and ruin the hearing in one ear, there would have been the Devil to pay. But naturally the authorities—the police, the lawyer, the school principal--were of the opinion that, if a Mexicano got into trouble, he must be the one who started it. Simon got off scot-free--at least in the usual, obvious sense. He suffered far more punishment from his conscience, though, than he ever would have at the hands of the law.

For several weeks, he also lived with the certainty that Frank's friends and family were watching his every move, waiting for a chance to exact revenge. But, though he got a lot of hostile looks, no one actually threatened him. Maybe they were afraid of making their already shaky standing in the community even worse. Or maybe they concluded that Frank and his *compañero* were as much to blame as Simon—which perhaps they were. But not in Simon's mind . . . or his father's.

"Whatever they may have said about your mother," Don Hannay told him, "it was only words, and words are never an excuse for violence. You should have taken your--"

"--my sails out of their wind. I know, I know. It made me mad, though, the way they were talking about her."

"I can understand that. But did you ever think that maybe the one you're really mad at is your mother, and you just took it out on them? Anyway, I think you should do what you can to make amends."

"Make amends? How?"

"Well, you could start by paying me back some of the money I laid out for Frank's hospital bills."

"Oh. I didn't know . . . I guess maybe I could get a part time job?"

"I have a better idea. I'm thinking of opening a karate studio; there seems to be a lot of interest, and I have my eye on a building—the old IGA store. It's going to need a lot of cleaning up and fixing up, though."

"You want *me* to help you? I'm not very handy with tools, you know."

His father laughed. "I know. But you can push a broom and a wheelbarrow. And there's something else I think you should do."

"What's that?"

"Apologize to Frank Ávila."

"You mean . . . you mean face to face?"

Don Hannay nodded. "He's still not back to normal. His dad says every time he tries to stand up, he gets dizzy. It looks like he won't be going back to school until at least January."

"You want me go to his *house*? That's like going into enemy territory!"

"Mr. Ávila says you don't need to worry. But if it makes you feel better, I'll go with you."

Crossing the railroad tracks into Little Mexico was, Simon imagined, a lot like crossing the Rio Grande into actual Mexico. There were a few well-built, well-maintained bungalows with doors painted in bright colors, and a couple of the streets had more pavement than potholes, but they were the exception. The Ávilas' place was about the size of the Hannays' garage; it was sided, not with clapboard or asbestos shingles, but with heavy tarpaper that had torn away in several spots to reveal the dark wood beneath. At first, Simon thought the walls were made of logs; then he recognized the faint, acrid smell of creosote and realized that they were actually old railroad ties.

Frank's father answered the door. Simon had never seen him before without a hat; he'd never noticed the nasty-looking scar that traversed the man's forehead, as if someone had tried to take off the top of his head with a machete. "*Buenos días*, Ramón," said Don Hannay. "Is Frank feeling up to having a visitor?"

"I think so." Mr. Ávila regarded Simon not with malice, exactly, but with an intensity that made Simon avert his eyes. "Come in, please."

"You go ahead, Simon. Ramón, maybe it's best if you and I leave the boys alone?"

"*Sí*. Frank is in his room."

The interior of the house was dark and close and smelled a little of creosote, but it seemed neat and clean enough. Simon hesitantly passed through the living area to the two tiny bedrooms at the rear of the house. One was empty; the other had a blanket draped in the doorway. "Um, Frank?" Simon called softly.

"In here."

Simon lifted the blanket. Frank sat, propped up by cheap decorator pillows, on a white-painted metal frame bed that took up most of the room. Though it had been nearly two weeks since the incident, the left side of his face was still half covered by a gauze bandage held in place by adhesive tape. He stared at

Simon for several moments before he said, "What do *you* want?" He sounded less angry than baffled, as if he really couldn't imagine why Simon was there.

"I—uh—I just came to say I was sorry for . . . for what happened."

"I can't hear you," said Frank. "I think there is something wrong with my ear."

Did he mean it, or was this some kind of black humor? "I said—"

"I know. I was just joking."

"Oh. It's not very funny."

"I guess not. Neither was what we said about your *madre*, I guess."

"No. Even so, I shouldn't have hit you."

Frank shrugged. "If you had said stuff like that about *my* mother, I would have hit you. You want to sit down?"

Simon glanced around. The only spot available was the bed. "Uh, no thanks. I can't stay, anyway. My dad's waiting, and I . . . I just wanted to . . ."

Frank gave a sardonic, lopsided smile. "You didn't *want* to. He told you to, right?"

"Well . . . sort of, yeah."

"You do feel guilty, though?"

"Yeah. I do."

"Good. Then you'll do something for me."

"Do something? Like—like what?"

Frank lowered his voice. "Bring me some marijuana, man!" He waited until Simon looked suitably shocked before he said, "Seriously, could you bring me my school assignments, and maybe help me out with them *un poco*? I don't want to flunk ninth grade *again*."

65

CHAPTER NINE

"So," says Mack, "did you do it?"

Simon nods. "He actually ended up with a C average."

"No, I mean did you get him the *pot*?"

Alec materializes before them, as if magically summoned. "Did someone use the P word?"

"Why would you care about marijuana," says Mack, "when you can cook up any kind of mind-blowing thing you want in that lab of yours?"

Alec melodramatically puts a hand over his heart. "You wound me deeply, sir. We are not in the business of manufacturing drugs. Okay, we *are*, but not the recreational kind. We are creating magical compounds that will someday heal all of the miseries and maladies that plague mankind." Good alliteration, you had to give him that.

"Right," says Mack. "Nerve gas, for example, and napalm, and herbicides for the jungles of Southeast Asia."

Alec glares at him. "Where, may I ask, do you get your *mis*information? No, wait, don't tell me. The SDS, right? So Damn Stupid, as we call them. They've been spreading that kind of bullshit for years."

"Are you telling me the university doesn't have a contract with the military to develop chemical and biological weapons?"

"Certainly not."

"Okay, maybe you're not working directly for the Army, but the chemical companies *are*, and you're getting research grants from them. Right? *Right*?"

Alec gives a scornful laugh. "You don't know what you're talking about, McNaughton. You'd better stick to football." Luckily, at that moment another customer calls him away; if he'd hung around another second or two, Mack would likely have done something he'd be sorry for.

"Maybe what they should work on," says Simon, "is finding a cure for asshole-ism."

Mack rubs the fist that he bruised beating on Bear. "A good dose of knuckles would help."

"Hey, you don't want to rile the bartender. He's liable to lace your drink with LSD."

"Alec? Hah. He's too much of a pussy."

"I wouldn't be too sure. In Karate Club last semester, another guy made fun of him for shouting *Osu!* all the time, which is considered kind of pretentious. The next week, when they were sparring, Alec cracked one of the guy's ribs."

"No shit? Did he ever do anything like that to you?"

Simon shakes his head. "I'm too good at blocking."

"In all modesty."

"In all modesty."

"So, if you're so good, why didn't you just flatten Darrin?"

"I thought I explained that."

"Well, you know us jocks; we're kinda dense."

Simon stares into his Slider for a long moment, then says softly, "I just . . . I just don't want hurt anybody."

"Pardon me?"

"I don't want to do to anybody else what I did to Frank, okay?" snaps Simon, loudly enough to make Alec glance their way.

"Okay, okay," says Mack, making a *Down, boy* motion with his hands. "But why take up karate, then? I mean, isn't that kind of the whole purpose of it—to put the hurt on other people?"

"You develop that ability, sure. But you also develop discipline and control, so you don't *need* to hurt anybody."

"If you say so. It just seemed to me like you needed to hurt Darrin a little bit more. It would've made a better impression on your friend--whoever she was. I didn't get a good look; I was kind of busy."

"It was. . . it was Gabriela."

"Whoa. Really?" Mack wiggles his eyebrows. "Is she as wanton as Bear says?"

"No! She's very nice. She's helping me with my studies."

"*Studies*, huh? I never heard it called that before."

"Will you quit?"

"Sorry. Well, Bear isn't exactly a reliable source. What probably actually happened is, she told him to fuck off, and he's getting even by badmouthing her."

"And now he can badmouth you for a while."

Mack shrugs. "Let him. He's a moron. You know what he was saying just before you showed up? Maisie was trying to explain to him that what's happening in Vietnam is wrong, and you know what his answer was? 'My country, right or wrong.' He just kept repeating that, like some kind of mantra. Jesus."

"Hey, there's no shortage of people who agree with him—including some of the faculty, I'm sure."

"Well, they're all morons, then."

"Probably so. Just don't antagonize the Establishment too much, okay? If you get a reputation as a rabble rouser, they're liable to boot you out, and you know what that means."

"I'll get booted out anyway, if I lose my scholarship." He manages to get Alec's attention and holds up two fingers, which looks like a peace sign but is actually a request for more Sliders. Mack shifts position on his stool and winces. "Ow. Hey, maybe if I mess up my knee bad enough, the Army won't want me."

"I wouldn't count on it," says Simon. "They're pretty desperate for warm bodies. Frank never did get all his hearing back, and they still classified him 1-A."

"Bummer. Any idea what happened to him?"

"Actually, yeah. About two years ago, I got a letter from him, entirely in Spanish."

"You could read it, though, right?"

"Uh-huh. While I was tutoring *him* in math and science, he was teaching *me* to speak Spanish. He said he sent me the letter to keep my Spanish from getting rusty, but the truth is, I think he considers us friends, somehow--which is a little strange, considering what I did to him. Anyway, he told me that the Army doctors passed him in spite of his injury."

"So they drafted him?"

"Nope. He joined the Air Force and became an airplane mechanic."

"Did he go to Nam?"

"Yeah, but I guess he didn't see any combat. A couple of months ago I got another letter saying he got a medical discharge. He wanted to know whether I thought he should enroll in college."

"What did you say?"

"I said it was worth a try. His grades weren't good, but he was a smart enough guy--"

"Kind of like me," says Mack.

"Yeah, kind of like you, except a lot smaller."

"So no football scholarship."

"No, but he'll have the GI Bill."

"Speaking of scholarships, everything's still okay with yours, right?"

"For now. I don't know what'll happen if I . . . if I do what I'm thinking of doing."

"You're going to blow up the Marine Recruiting Office."

"No. But I might change my thesis topic."

"Uh-oh. Don't tell me; the Devil made you do it."

Simon laughs. "Well, I suspect that there'll be the Devil to pay, when I tell Dr. E." He glances warily around the room. It's getting on to suppertime, and the crowd has thinned out considerably. "The thing is . . ." Simon speaks so quietly that Mack has to lean in to hear him. Obviously, the fewer people he tells about the book, the better, but he's got to tell *someone*, and Mack is good at keeping secrets. "Promise me you won't breathe a word of this to anybody."

"Hey, man, you can trust me."

"I hope so. The thing is, I found this old book, a journal, written by Vicente Somebody."

"Sombadi? What nationality is that? Sounds kind of Italian, like sambuca, or spumoni."

"Har har. It looks like it dates back to the mid-1500s."

"Okay . . ." says Mack, waiting for the interesting part.

"The first page is in Portuguese, but get this: All the rest of it is written in *code*."

"Ah. That would explain your sudden interest in it. Any idea what it says?"

"Not yet. Whatever it is, Vicente didn't want the Inquisition to know."

"Whoa," says Mack, the former History major. "They were like the Gestapo of their day. So, the plan is to do your thesis on--"

He breaks off as Alec approaches and sets down a fresh pair of Sliders. "These are on the house, guys. My way of apologizing for being so snarky before."

Simon regards the drink doubtfully. "I don't know if I should have another one, on an empty stomach."

"Oh, quit over-analyzing, man," says Mack, with pretend irritation. "Just drink the damn thing." He clinks his glass against Simon's. "*Salud, amigo.*"

"*Amor, dinero, y tiempo para gastarlo,*" says Simon--approximately. He's beginning to feel the effects of the first two Sliders and losing control of his tongue just a little.

"What's this about your thesis?" says Alec.

"Um, well . . ." Simon doesn't really want to snub Alec; more than once, at Karate Club, he's listened sympathetically while Simon griped about how sick he was of his master's project. But neither does Simon want to reveal anything about the codex. Alec is not known for being tight-lipped; he'd tell tales on his own mother if he thought it would impress someone or get a laugh.

"He's decided on a new topic," says Mack. Alarmed, Simon starts to protest, but Mack can't be stopped. "The use of chemical and biological weapons by the Spanish Inquisition."

Alec blinks in surprise. "They used chemical and--? Oh. I get it. You're yanking my chain."

Mack grins and gives Alec's bartending apron a tug. "Yank, yank."

When Alec moves off to bother somebody else, Simon says softly, "We made a Xerox copy of the journal, but I gave it to Gabriela."

"She won't tell anybody, will she?"

"I don't think so. The thing is, I have no idea where to find her."

"You might try the student directory."

"Except I don't know her last name. I thought maybe you did, since you two had a class together."

Mack shakes his head ruefully. "If I ever knew it, I forgot. Didn't she have to sign up for your self-defense thing?"

"She hasn't got around to it yet."

"Well, you'll see her next Saturday, though, right?"

"If she shows up. Anyway, I can't wait that long; I need to figure out whether I can crack that cipher. If not, I can't very well do my thesis on it, can I?"

Mack raises a scraped and swollen finger to his lips. "Not so loud, man. I thought you wanted to keep this hush-hush."

Simon winces. "I do," he mutters. "I shouldn't have had that last drink. Liquor always makes me loud." He fishes a couple of bills from his wallet and plunks them down on the bar. "Well, Gabriela works at the library; they should know how to get hold of her."

"You gonna be able to make it home, buddy? You look a little wobbly."

"I'll be okay. I'm more worried about you, with that knee."

"Oh, well; maybe I'll just stay right here on this stool till it heals up. Gimme five." They slap hands and, for change, Mack is the one to say "Ow."

●   ●   ●

For about a year now, the sororities have been campaigning to have more and better lighting installed on campus, but the administration keeps pleading lack of funds—small wonder, considering how much money they poured into the new Medical Sciences Center. Well, at least the lousy lighting helps conceal how godawful ugly that building is.

Of course, it also means that in between the scattered lampposts lie vast pools of blackness that the students call Dark Shadows, after the Gothic soap opera. It's easy to imagine vampires or werewolves lurking in their depths—or, if you're a woman crossing campus alone at night, sexual predators. As far as Simon knows, no one has had an encounter with Barnabas Collins yet, but he has heard of several incidents of assault, and there are undoubtedly others that go unreported.

As Simon is walking—a bit unsteadily, still--through one of the Dark Shadows, from behind the hydrangea bushes comes a low female voice: "Take your hands off me, you beast!" He stops abruptly and stands there for a moment, listening, debating whether or not to interfere. There's the sound of clothing rustling, then a muffled gasp.

"Um," he calls, "what's going on in there?"

Several seconds of silence, then a few whispers, then a man's voice. "Who wants to know?"

"Just . . . just a student."

"Oh. Well, fuck off, Just a Student."

"Not before your friend says it's okay."

The woman's voice again. "Why don't you mind your own business, jerkoff?"

"Sorry. Just—just checking to make sure . . . " Simon trails off, then hurries away, followed by the sound of scornful snickering. So much for trying to be a Good Samaritan.

The Briggs is still open, but this late in the day it's staffed mostly by grad students, such as the pale, freckle-faced redhead seated at the reference desk; judging from her weary manner and the dark circles under her droopy eyes, she'd much rather be in bed. "Hi," says Simon. "I wonder if you could help me?"

"Probably not," says the redhead, "but I'll try."

"Okay. There's this girl named . . . uh, Gabriela who works here sometimes. I need to get hold of--I mean, get in touch with her."

"Last name?"

"Um, hers? Or mine?"

The woman rolls her eyes. "Hers."

"I—I don't know. All I know is her first name."

"Ah." She picks up a sheet of paper—a list of the library staff, Simon assumes. "What was it, again?"

"Gabriela."

She runs a pudgy finger down the list. "There's nobody here by that name."

"Really? Do you--do you mind if I look?"

"Yes, I do mind. This is personal information; we can't just go handing it out to *any*body, you know."

"Oh." Simon is still feeling a bit spacey from all those Sliders; he can't think of what to do next. He can't very well hang out in the library until she turns up; it could be days. If she'd just waited for him this afternoon, outside Taylor Hall . . . Why did she take off so abruptly, anyway? Because she didn't want to embarrass him after he made such an ass of himself? Because she can't stand violence? Or was there some other, more devious motive? He just handed her the copies of the codex pages without thinking; what if she's decided to keep them? Most people don't find codes and ciphers all that fascinating, and yet she showed a surprising interest in the book and in unveiling its secrets.

Simon hates to even consider that possibility, but he can't help it. Face it, what does he really know about Gabriela? She's told him practically nothing about herself, not even her last name. She did say she was majoring in History, which gives him pause. The codex might hold as much fascination for a history scholar as it does for a student of literature.

She also revealed that her *padrinho* was on the faculty of the Joaquim Nabuco Institute, and from what Simon has read, the Institute has a major collection of Portuguese literature. What if—he knows he's wandering into the realm of speculation, here, but it's the way his mind works—what if Vicente Somebody wasn't from Portugal, as he naturally assumed, but from Brazil? The Inquisition spread its long arms there, too, after all. And, going even deeper into Terra Spectativus, what if the Institute knows about the journal? Hell, maybe they sent Gabriela here for the express purpose of recovering it.

And maybe he's just being paranoid. Whatever the case, he'd be smart to make his own copy of the codex, just to be on the safe side. And, since Gabriela can't get him into the Taft, he's going to have to find some other means. He could ask Dr. Espinoza or The Boob to give him permission, but they might ask questions, and at the moment he doesn't have any answers.

He manages to get the attention of the redhead at the reference desk again— not an easy task; her droopy eyes are riveted on *Valley of the Dolls.* "Could you tell me when Mrs. Pitman will be on duty?"

Grudgingly, the girl consults another sheet of paper. "Monday and Friday afternoons."

•   •   •

Simon spends most of Sunday sitting around with the collected plays of Vicente—*his* Vicente—in hand, ostensibly studying but actually praying in both English and Portuguese that Gabriela will turn up, carrying the coveted copies. She may be hard to track down, but she should have no trouble finding him. Though he doesn't have a phone, his address is in the student directory. *Ah*, says his over-analytical mind, *but what if she doesn't know your* apelido de família, *either?* It's possible; as far as he can recall, he never told his karate students anything but his first name.

Every five minutes or so, he glances anxiously out the window, hoping to see her bell-bottomed, combat-booted, baggy-sweatshirted figure coming down the sidewalk. The only figure he sees is the more ample one belonging to Rhonda Horvath, who is raking leaves in the front yard—very resentfully, if he's any judge of body language. Despite the October chill and the menial nature of the work, she's clad in flip-flops, capri pants, and a form-fitting cashmere sweater that, when she bends over to pick up a fallen branch, hikes up in back to reveal quite an expanse of skin from which the bikini tan is beginning to fade.

When she pauses to pat down her hair--though she teases and sprays it mercilessly, it has a will of its own—she spots his face at the window. Simon ducks back at once, not wanting her to imagine that he's watching her. But each time he ventures another glance at the sidewalk, she somehow manages to catch him at.

He forces himself to keep his eyes fixed firmly on the text of *Tragicomedia Pastoril:*

> *The greatest slattern, I assert is she. . .*
> *And though she covered be with dirt*
> *Yet will she never comb her hair . . .*
> *She sweeps and lets the sweepings lie,*
> *She eats and will never wash the dishes.*
> *Her uncle beats her hourly,*
> *So laxly doth she flout his wishes.*

Simon laughs out loud; Vicente might be describing Rhonda, who seems bent on defying her parents as frequently and as far as possible. Just as he's finally managing to really concentrate on the play, he's startled by a peculiar noise; he hears it so rarely that it takes him a second to recognize it as the death-rattle of the faulty doorbell. He springs from the chair and scrambles to answer it.

It's not Gabriela. It's the teenaged slattern. "Um, hi," says Simon.

Rhonda surveys him critically, her eyes narrowed. "Aha. Just as I thought."

Simon shifts about self-consciously. "What?"

"You definitely need a haircut."

She sounds disturbingly like Simon's mother, and he automatically goes into apologetic mode. "Yeah, well, I was—I was planning to get one, I just—I haven't been able to--"

"Do you have a comb and scissors?"

"Uh, sure, but—"

"The scissors need to be sharp, if you expect me to do it right."

"*You?* I really don't—I mean, no offense, but—"

74

"I'll do a good job, I promise." Now she sounds less like Simon's mother than like a whiny five-year-old. "I'm studying to be a hairdresser and I need to practice, and Daddy refuses to let me work on him—not that he has enough hair left to be much use, anyway. You, on the other hand . . . " Circling him like a martial artist looking for an opening, she reaches out to tousle the shaggy locks at the nape of his neck, which makes him shiver slightly. "You're starting to look like a hippie."

"Well . . . maybe I'm turning into one."

She eyes him again and shakes her head. "Nahh. You're a straight arrow, and you always will be. I'll be careful, Simon. Come onnnn. You know you want me to." She should consider taking up acting, instead; now she's slipped into the role of seductress.

Simon's ingrained inability to say no is canceled out by the certainty that this girl is trouble, and if he encourages her in any way, he'll be sorry. "Um, I don't think so, okay? It's not that I don't trust you, it's just that . . ."

"Just that you're being a wimp." Smiling slyly, she walks her fingers up his arm. "If you don't let me, I'll te-ellll." She draws the word out, like a schoolyard taunt.

"Tell? What do you mean?"

"I'll tell my parents how you've been ogling me."

"*Ogling* you? I wasn't—I was just watching for a friend of mine--"

"Uh-huh. Right. So where is this friend?"

"She might show up any time," he says, a bit desperately, "and it'd be awkward if--"

"So, just let me cut your hair, and then I'll get out of your hair."

Simon sighs. Her threat may be just a bluff, but he can't take the chance. If her parents threw him out, he'd never be able to find another decent, affordable place in the middle of the semester. "I don't know. You might take off too much."

Rhonda gives a suggestive smirk. "How much would you *like* me to take off?"

Simon feels his face going red; to add to his embarrassment, he feels himself getting hard. "I—I meant my hair." Maybe the girl should study karate, not acting or hairdressing. She'd make a formidable opponent; she's both relentless and unpredictable. Simon takes a couple of deep abdominal breaths to calm himself. He's much better at deflecting and avoiding than he is at attacking, but this time he's going to have to take the offensive. As risky as it may be to chase her off, it's probably more risky to let her stay.

Just as he's about to get forceful, he's saved by the bell--literally. Rhonda's blue-shadowed, mascara-laden eyes go wide. "Oh, shit!" she whispers. "If it's my parents, tell them you haven't seen me!" With that, she plunges behind the sofa.

Simon's erection has magically wilted. He claws at his mussed hair and opens the door, fervently hoping to find Gabriela standing there, and not a vengeful Mr. Horvath. As it happens, it's neither one. "Mack! Hey! I'm glad to see you! Come on in!"

"Thanks, man. But you may not be as glad to see me as you think." Mack hoists some object that was hidden by the doorframe and shoves it into the room ahead of him. It's a faded olive drab duffel bag, crammed to capacity. "You mind if I move in with you for a while?"

CHAPTER TEN

"Um, okay," says Simon—as Mack obviously knew he would. "If you don't mind sleeping on the couch."

"Groovy," says Mack, a term undoubtedly picked up from Maisie the flower child. He flings his duffel bag onto the sofa, which groans and coughs up a cloud of fine dust. Like a character in a farce, Rhonda pops up from her hiding place, to Mack's astonishment. "Well, well! You should have told me you had company!"

"She's not company--" Simon protests, but Rhonda cuts him off.

"I'm the girl next door!" she announces gleefully. "I'm here to practice on Simon!"

"Oh, hey, I don't want to spoil your fun. Why don't I just--" He starts for the doorway, but Simon practically leaps into his path.

"No! No, it's fine! Rhonda was just about to leave!"

She goes into whiny five-year-old mode again. "Simonnn! What about your haircut?"

"Um, some other time, okay? Mack--Mack's in trouble, and--and he and I need to talk. Privately."

"Oh? What kind of trouble?" Suddenly she's turned into Ann Landers.

"Bank robbery," says Mack, soberly.

"Bank rob--!? Oh, you're kidding, right?"

"Maybe. But then again, maybe not. Anyway, you don't want to be an accessory, so why don't you go on home, like a good girl?" Rhonda scowls and starts to object, but when Mack breaks into the world's worst rendition of "Go

Away, Little Girl," the scowl turns to an incredulous grimace. Giggling and holding her ears, she hurries out the door.

"Works every time," says Mack. "So, what's the deal? Was Delilah really going to cut your hair, Samson? Or was that some sort of euphemism?"

"Come on, man. She's in high school, for god's sake."

Mack gives a derisive snort. "Do you have any idea what high school students are up to these days? No, of course you don't, because you grew up in Garden of Eden City. In East Cleveland, school was like a singles bar, without the liquor. Although some of us had that, too."

"Yeah, well, this isn't East Cleveland, and I'm not a high school student. Neither are you," he adds, pointedly, for Mack is at the window watching Rhonda sashay across the yard.

"Just anticipating. In a year or two she'll be a freshman, and then she's fair game."

Though Simon doesn't care for Mack's lecherous tone, he can ignore it. They've been friends long enough for him to know that Mack is not nearly the Lothario he pretends to be. Oh, he likes women, all right, and they like him, but he doesn't really see them as sex objects, or treat them as such, the way so many of his fellow jocks do. In fact, Mack has a tendency to put them on a pedestal, and when they inevitably step down or fall off, he's always disappointed.

"So," says Simon, "I take it you've been evicted from the field house?"

Mack just shrugs, as if it's no big deal.

"Because of what happened at the demonstration?"

"Probably. Although Coach says it's because I'm not an *active player*. You think it'll be okay with your landlord if I crash here for a while?"

"I guess so. If you keep your mitts off his daughter."

Mack grins. "I will if you will."

"Cut it out. I have no interest in her. She accused me of ogling her, but--"

"*Ogling* her?"

"Her word, not mine. But I was just keeping an eye out for Gabriela."

"Ah, you got hold of her, then?"

Simon shakes his head ruefully. "I'm hoping she'll get hold of me. No smarmy comments, please."

"I wasn't going to." Mack plunks down on the sofa, sending up another dust storm. "Bear O'Hara must know her last name, but me and him aren't on speaking terms right now." He props his injured leg up on the coffee table Simon constructed of concrete blocks and an old cabinet door.

"How's the knee?"

"Not too bad. Doc Savage gave me some Darvon for it."

"Doc *Savage*?"

"The team doctor. We call him that because he gets so worked up at . . . at games." Mack's voice falters, and his face takes on an expression of such sadness that Simon quickly steers them away from the topic of football.

"Where on earth did you get that duffel bag? It looks like it's seen some hard use."

"It was my dad's, during the war. According to him, a tank ran over it."

"Jeez. Well, better his duffel bag than him. Was he in the thick of things?"

"Nah, he was posted at Fort Knox the whole time. Your old man was on Okinawa, right?"

Simon nods, a bit hesitantly. When he steered the conversation, this wasn't the direction he had in mind.

"I've read about that battle," says Mack. "It was brutal. He was lucky to make it out in one piece."

"Yeah, well, he wasn't . . . He didn't see much . . . much actual fighting. He was more involved in the . . . you know, the reconstruction." Strange, how he still feels the need to be so circumspect about his father's role in the war. It's not like Mack is going to suddenly start despising him because of it, nor would most of the people he knows. These days, peaceniks are everywhere, like miniskirts or Peter Max posters. But in the decade following the Good War, if you had any objections to it, conscientious or otherwise, it wasn't a good idea to express them—not even to your wife or your son.

• • •

As a child, Simon encountered two sorts of veterans: those who would regale you with war stories until the cows came home and were milked the next morning, and those who never said a word about their experience, no matter how you begged them. Don Hannay was the second sort. For a long time, Simon assumed that, like Jimmy Johnson, who spent three hellish years in a Japanese prison camp, his dad just wanted to forget his ordeal.

He learned the truth from Frank Ávila during one of his Spanish lessons. They weren't lessons in the usual sense; he and Frank mostly just sat and talked, about the most basic things at first—the weather; food; TV shows. Simon had always imagined that, like codes and ciphers, foreign languages contained secret knowledge, mysteries known only to those who spoke them. If so, the secrets certainly didn't reveal themselves--at least not right away.

As the months went by and Simon's vocabulary started to expand, he and Frank explored more complex topics—politics; their dreams and ambitions; girls, of course—but still nothing particularly mysterious. Though neither of them ever mentioned Delia Hannay, Frank sometimes spoke of his own mother, who had stayed behind in Mexico with Frank's young sisters.

Then, toward the end of the school year, Simon's efforts finally paid off. He unveiled not just one secret, but two. And, as when he learned what Frank and his friend were saying about his mother, he almost wished he hadn't.

The first involved Peri Jurado. Just when Simon was starting to feel confident enough to speak to her, Peri quit showing up at school. No one seemed to know why. Worried that she might be ill, Simon stopped in at the Five and Ten, hoping to catch her there. But there was a new girl at the counter, an Anglo one. According to her, Peri had gone back to Mexico a week earlier, without any explanation; she hadn't even collected her paycheck.

Frank Ávila claimed to know the reason. "I'm only telling you," he whispered in Spanish, "because I know you have the hots for her--"

"I don't have the *hots* for her. I like her, that's all."

"Okay, okay. Anyway, you gotta keep this to yourself. If anybody finds out I told you, I'll be in deep shit. You understand?"

"Yes."

"Good. You remember when she quit her job, back in August? Her brother told me it was because her scumbag boss--what's his name?"

"Mr. Willis."

"Yeah. *Mister* Willis was always making suggestive remarks and trying to feel her up, and she was afraid he might do even worse if he got the chance. So, as you always say, she took her boat out of his wind."

"Why did she go back to work there, then?"

Frank shrugged. "Her family needed the money. They said that Willis was all talk, that he'd never actually molest her, because if he did people would find out, and he'd be run out of town." He let out a scornful laugh. "I can't believe they really thought that. I mean, her word against his? Who are they going to believe? Him, obviously; I mean, she's gone, right? And and he's still here."

"So you think-- You think he really did . . . molest her?"

"Sure he did. It's probably why he hired her in the first place. He knows how the rules work; if one of us gets in trouble, it's always *our* fault, right?"

He didn't learn the second secret until a week or so later.

When Frank finally took off his bandage, his ear was still red and kind of lumpy-looking, and there was a sizable scar on his cheek, where they'd cut it open to remove some bone chips, but Frank seemed pretty laid back about the whole thing. "Hey, I'll tell people I got it in a gang fight. It can be like in that book we read--a Badge of Courage." He laughs at the notion. "No. That's what my dad's scar is. Mine was just an accident."

"Your dad was wounded in combat?"

Frank nods. "The Battle of Okinawa. A Japanese bayonet."

"He was on Okinawa? So was my dad. I wonder if they met there?"

Frank gave him an odd look, as if that was a stupid question, or an embarrassing one. "I don't think so."

"We could ask him."

"No. No, you don't want to do that."

"Why not?"

"Because. He doesn't like to talk about it."

"Neither does my dad."

"I'll bet."

"What does that mean?"

"Nothing."

"Do you—do you know something I don't?"

"That depends," said Frank.

"On what?"

"On how much you know."

"Not much. So tell me, okay?"

Frank laughed humorlessly. "No way. You might hit me again."

"Don't even say that."

"Sorry. Look, I don't really know nothing either, okay? I've just . . . heard stuff."

"About my dad."

"Yeah."

81

"What kind of stuff?"

"I heard he refused to fight."

"Refused to fight? What do you mean? Oh. You think he was a--" They'd been speaking mostly in Spanish, but Simon didn't know the term for *conscientious objector*, so he used the derogatory English one: "You think he was a *conchie*?"

"Like I said, I don't know for sure; it's just something I heard."

"From who?"

"I don't remember. And if I did, I wouldn't tell you. They probably just heard it from somebody else. You know how rumors are. You want to know anything more, you'll have to ask your old man."

Well, there wasn't much point in that. Don Hannay had never spoken about the war before; why would he start now? Simon couldn't stand not knowing, though, any more than he could stand to let a challenging cipher go unsolved.

He wasn't worried that his dad would be angry; Simon had only ever seen him lose it once, when he chewed out the owner of Carman Sugar for taking advantage of the workers. But neither did he expect the kind of response he got. When Simon told him what Frank had said, his father didn't seem upset at all; in fact he seemed . . . well, relieved, as if he were tired of avoiding the matter.

"I never said anything to your mother because I didn't figure she'd really want to know. And I didn't tell you because I didn't think you'd understand. But after what happened with Frank, I think you probably will."

•   •   •

Don Hannay grew up in central Kansas surrounded by Mennonite farmers, the descendants of German-speaking Russian emigrants who settled there in the 1870s. Most of his boyhood friends were Mennonites and, though they didn't actively try to convert him, their beliefs and their way of life influenced his own—especially their commitment to nonviolence. Though he never joined their church, or any other, he came to consider himself a pacifist.

The Army didn't. Before he was even called up, he applied to the local draft board for Conscientious Objector status; they turned him down flat. But when he appealed the ruling, fifty of his Mennonite neighbors turned up at the courthouse to testify on his behalf. The judge approved his appeal, and the Army assigned him to a non-combatant role as a smokejumper in the Pacific Northwest.

Then, in the summer of 1945, they shipped him off to Okinawa. The island was recovering from three months of bloody combat that killed a quarter of the population and destroyed most of the homes, businesses, and farmland. The survivors were placed in refugee camps, where thousands more died of starvation and sickness. Those few men who were strong and healthy enough were hired by the military to dig ditches, clear away rubble, plant crops—and teach martial arts to the American GIs. Don Hannay was one of the first to sign up.

From the day he first applied for CO status, he'd had to run a sort of endless gauntlet of contemptuous civilians and resentful fellow soldiers and officers bent on breaking him down, making him betray his pacifist principles. They'd broken an unknown number of small bones, chopped off his hair, poured boiling coffee on him, cursed him and his family and his unborn offspring, stolen his blankets, stuck giant slugs in his boots and then berated him for murdering them.

After he proved his courage by parachuting into the middle of a dozen forest fires, the abuse had let up some. But in Okinawa, it started all over again. The combat troops--what was left of them—had been shipped home; to replace them, the Army had to scrape the bottom of the barrel. The occupying troops were the dregs of the military—the ones who continually challenged authority, regularly went AWOL, quarreled with the other soldiers, did hard drugs. But even losers have to lord it over someone. For the men posted on Okinawa, it was the COs, and they treated them like some subhuman species.

Tired of being insulted and beaten up, Don Hannay decided to do something about it. He had no desire for revenge and no intention of giving his tormenters a taste of their own medicine; he only wanted to protect himself. As he soon learned, that same philosophy was at the heart of Okinawan karate.

When the Japanese first conquered the Ryukyu Islands in the seventeenth century, they outlawed the use of weapons, so the locals developed a style of combat that made their hands into deadly weapons. But over the next couple of centuries, Okinawan karate became less aggressive; it stressed the art of *uke*--receiving, rather than attacking.

During the Second World War, many of the island's martial arts instructors refused to fight for either side. Some fled their homes and hid in the jungle. Others struck a deal: they taught their techniques to the Japanese soldiers and, in return, were allowed to remain civilians—for all the good it did them. Their *dojos* were destroyed along with everything else. Don Hannay and his fellow GIs attended *goju-ryu* sessions in what was once a rice paddy.

In the wake of the war, several of the most influential karate masters returned to the old, aggressive way of fighting; perhaps it was their way of proving that they weren't cowards. Chokei Chioyu was one of them. Though he could easily afford an assistant on the $300 a month the Americans paid him, he could never keep one for more than about a week. Even when he was just demonstrating a move, Chokei went all out and often left the assistant writhing on the ground, groaning.

He was almost as merciless with his students. Every week, at least one GI suffered a broken nose or a split lip or a cracked rib or, in one case, a dislocated elbow. Finally, the brass sent word that, if the instructors didn't lighten up, they'd be out of a job. Reluctantly, Chokei began emphasizing the *ju* part of *goju-ryu*-- which means, roughly, "hard-soft way." But he took out his resentment on his students, continually finding fault with them, making them practice the pigeon-toed *sanchin* stance until they collapsed, correcting their positions by whacking the offending body part with a bamboo stick.

He let his latest assistant do most of the instruction while he sat on a half-buried artillery shell—perhaps another way of showing his fearlessness--and smoked his *kiseru* pipe. More than once, Don Hannay found himself half wishing that, as dud artillery rounds so often did, Chokei's would suddenly decide to detonate after all.

The Army further angered the karate masters by insisting that they promote students as quickly as possible, so the GIs could return home boasting that they'd earned a brown belt, or even a black one. Simon's dad didn't care about belts or boasts; he just wanted to learn the techniques well enough to defend himself.

It didn't take much, usually; bullies tended to back off as soon as you went into the *sanchin* stance. But there was always some drunken dimwit who was sure he could take you. You might get by just blocking his blows until you wore him down. But sometimes you had to slip in a strike or two—not enough to really injure the guy or his pride, just enough to make him reconsider. Maybe not what a really committed pacifist would do, but if you let an attacker keep attacking, weren't you actually promoting violence, in a way?

If Don Hannay really expected his son to understand all that, he was wrong. Simon spent a couple of days mulling over the matter before he brought it up again. "So, you're saying it's okay to defend yourself, but not to attack somebody?"

"That's what I believe, yes."

"But wasn't that what the Europeans and the Americans were doing—defending themselves?"

To his surprise, his dad let out a laugh.

"What?" said Simon, irritably. "Isn't that a fair question?"

"Of course it is. It's just a very hard one to answer. There are entire books written about it."

CHAPTER ELEVEN

Eight years later, there are still books being written about it, and Simon has read a number of them. He still doesn't completely understand. He does see that his father was not a coward, that it took a lot of courage to do what he did, to stand up for what he believed no matter how many times he got knocked down. But Simon is still struggling with the conundrum of how to deal with something as illogical as violence in a logical, nonviolent way; though he's fond of riddles, this one is more like a Zen *koan*.

Sometimes he wishes he could be less analytical and more like Mack, whose solutions to problems tend to be very basic, very physical: a lineman gets in his way, he flattens the guy; someone pushes his girlfriend around, he beats the hell out of him. Ironically, it's Mack the fighter who's out there protesting the war, and not Simon.

There are a number of things about Mack that Simon would just as soon not emulate. For one thing, he snores—no doubt a result of having his septum deviated so many times on the football field. On Monday morning, Simon is so groggy from lack of sleep that he cuts Books and Printing yet again and heads down to Rexall Drug to buy some silicone earplugs; ironically enough, the brand is called Mack's Earplugs.

Once he's sure his class period is over, he wanders around campus for a while, hoping to run into Gabriela—and to avoid running into Dr. Beebe. He doesn't encounter The Boob, but neither does he spot Gabriela. It'd be just his luck if she were looking for him, too. She could be ringing the doorbell of the Gas Chamber right this minute. Well, chances are Mack is still in the apartment, but he's probably dead to the world. Though the Darvon is helping with the knee pain, it's also turned him into a bit of a zombie. Simon just hopes that the doorbell's death-rattle is loud enough to wake him.

He really should be working on his thesis, or at least studying, but all he can think about is the codex. He hangs around the Gedunk for a while, in case Gabriela turns up there. Around two o'clock he gives up and heads for the Briggs, hoping to catch Mrs. Pitman. Sure enough, she's at the circulation desk, sorting out books to be reshelved. Nice to know there's at least one person in the world you can count on.

"Um, hi, Mrs. Pitman. I'm Simon Hannay. You let our class use the Taft on Friday?"

She examines him as though he's a book that she's pondering whether to keep or throw out. "Yes, I remember. I practically had to drag you out the door."

Simon feels his face go red. "Uh, yeah. I'm kind of obsessed about books, I guess."

"Well, that's nothing to be ashamed of. You spent a lot of time with the *Lusiadas*, as I recall." Jeez, the old woman doesn't miss a trick.

"Right. There was another book that interested me even more, but I didn't have time to really study it. I wonder—do you think I could—you know, have another look at it?"

"Now?"

"If you wouldn't mind." He holds his breath, waiting for her to say that he needs faculty permission. But she seems to feel that being obsessed is qualification enough.

"All right. If you'll roll this cart of books upstairs for me."

As she lets them into the Rare Book Room and turns on the lights, she points to a small walnut table topped by a lace doily and an expensively bound guest book. "Sign in, please. We like to keep track of who our visitors are." When Simon has filled in his name and the time, she says, "Now. What book was it that you found so fascinating?"

Though he'd prefer to keep the codex a secret, there's no way he can avoid telling her. Anyway, as long as she's been here, she must know of its existence, at least. "The, uh, the Vicente journal?"

She blinks at him in puzzlement, or perhaps astonishment. "How on earth do you know about that?"

"Well, I—as I said, I spotted it on Friday, and--"

Mrs. Pitman gives an uncomfortable laugh "But that's impossible, my dear. It went missing . . . oh, it must be over ten years ago."

"I guess it wasn't actually missing, just hidden. I found it stuck behind a couple of other volumes."

"Really? Are you sure it's the Vicente?"

"Uh-huh. I'll show you." He leads her to the PQ9000s. Balancing on the stepstool, he pulls out the *Lusiadas* and the volume next to it and peers into the gap. There's no sign of the codex. "What the hell?" he starts to say, then switches to *heck* to spare her sensibilities. Thrusting his free arm between the books, he gropes around desperately. Nothing. "I—I don't understand. It was right here, honestly."

"I believe you," says Mrs. Pitman—though in fact she sounds pretty doubtful. "What did you do with it?"

"Nothing! I just—I just looked at it for a minute, and--"

"I wasn't accusing you of *stealing* it, dear. I only meant after you were done looking at it. Did you shelve it properly, or did you put it back the same way?"

Simon's mind is in a muddle. He's not much good at improvising. Should he tell her about Gabriela, about how they tried to decipher the manuscript and how they made a copy of it? He doesn't want to make trouble for his friend—if she actually is a friend--but the fact is, she was the last one to have the book in her hands. She said she was returning it to its hiding place. But what if she didn't? What if she . . . ? He can't even bear to finish the thought. "I, um, I didn't know what to do, so I put it back the way it was."

"I see. It's unlikely that the other gentleman found it, then."

"The *other* gentleman?"

"Yes. Isn't that the oddest coincidence? To my knowledge, no one has asked to see the Vicente for at least five years, and suddenly two of you come looking for it on the exact same day."

Simon is literally staggered; he has to grab hold of the bookshelves to keep from toppling off the stepstool. "Someone else—someone else asked for it? *Today*?"

"This morning, before I came in. He had a permission slip from one of the faculty, so Miss—*Miz* Harris let him into the room."

"Was it--I mean--was he—was he a student, or--?"

"I'm not certain. She would have had him sign in, though."

Simon hustles over to the ledger. There are only two names entered under today's date. One is his. The other is . . . Thomas Huxley? The name sounds familiar, but Simon isn't sure why. "Is Ms. Harris still here, do you think?"

She is, in fact, but she's not able to shed much light on the matter. She didn't recognize the visitor. He was older than most of the students, younger than most of the faculty, nothing remarkable about his appearance. He did have a slight accent, but she quite can't pin it down. His permission slip was signed by no less than the Dean of Arts and Science.

"There's no way he could have . . . you know, taken the book with him, is there?"

Ms. Harris gives him an indignant look. "Of course not. In any case, there was nothing to take. The book wasn't on the shelf."

"Oh. I'm sorry to be so insistent, but could I just—Did you—I mean, were you watching him when he--?"

"We're not in the habit of spying on library patrons."

"I didn't mean *spying*, I just meant . . . Never mind. Do you have—could I look at your campus directory?" There's no Thomas Huxley listed, either as a faculty member or as a student. While he's at it, Simon does a quick scan of the undergrads, hoping the name *Gabriela* will jump out at him. No such luck. "Um, sorry to bother you again, but do you by any chance know a student named Gabriela? She works in the Rare Book Room sometimes?"

Ms. Harris doesn't actually reply; she just gives him a look that's hard to read—Irritated? Angry? Suspicious?—and, without even stopping to think about it, shakes her head. Simon is as bewildered as he was by Vicente's cipher. This situation makes no more sense than those scrambled letters. He only hopes that Gabriela, wherever she is, has the key. He can't just wander around campus all day, looking for her; he may as well head back to the Gas Chamber and see whether she's been there.

•   •   •

Well, someone certainly has been there, and he's pretty sure it wasn't Gabriela-- unless a hurricane by that name swept through the area in his absence. The apartment has been turned inside out and upside down. Books and records are strewn about the room. The couch and chair cushions have been ripped open and the kitchen cabinet emptied out. A couple of loose floorboards are pried up.

The contents of Mack's war-worn duffel bag form an unruly pile in the middle of the room. Even Simon's framed *Lord of the Rings* poster has been yanked off the wall and flung aside, the glass cracked.

"Jesus!" he breathes. Is this Rhonda's perverse way of wreaking vengeance upon him? Surely she's not *that* crazy; besides, presumably she's been in school all day. It can't be Mack's doing, either. Granted that he's not the neatest guy in the world, but whoever created this chaos was more than just a slob. He or she was obviously *looking* for something. Everything inexplicable that's happened lately has been connected to the codex; he's willing to bet this is, too.

He needs to find Mack, to see whether he knows anything. *But first,* the voice of his mother is saying, *you need to straighten this place up.* By the time he has things squared away, it's almost five o'clock; if Mack bothered to go to his classes at all, he'll be done by now. The likeliest place to look for him is the Turtle Tap.

•   •   •

His friend is perched on a bar stool, halfheartedly playing Beat the Devil, a mostly empty glass of beer in front of him. Judging from the number of rings on the game's glass top, it's not his first one of the evening. As Simon approaches, the Devil lets out his maniacal laugh, and Mack laughs just as loudly, as if mocking Satan for mocking him. When he spots Simon, he delivers a sloppy high five. "Hey, Simon-and-no-Garfunkel. *Que pasa?*"

Simon is in no mood for their usual banter. "Listen, Mack, when did you leave the apartment?"

It takes Mack a minute to get his brain in gear. "When did I leave? I don't know, about twelve-thirty, I guess. Why?"

"Somebody trashed the place."

"Trashed it? How do you mean?"

Simon gives him a detailed account of the mess. "I presume it wasn't you."

"You presume correctly, Dr. Livingstone." He shakes his head, still trying to clear it. "Shit. You know, I wonder--"

"What?"

"I wonder if that note could've just been a ruse, to get me out of there."

"Note? What note?"

Mack pulls a crumpled sheet of paper from his pocket. Simon smooths it out on the glass top. It's a sheet of Athletic Department stationery with a brief message in childish block letters: COACH WANTS TO SEE YOU RIGHT AWAY.

"It was on the table when I woke up. I figured one of my teammates—*former* teammates--put it there. I got over to the field house as quick as I could. I mean, I thought . . . I thought maybe Coach changed his mind and was going to let me move back in, or maybe . . . Well, anyway, he hadn't sent for me at all. So then I thought, okay, it's just a shitty joke the guys are playing on me. But it's not very funny, especially if they wrecked the place."

"I don't think it was a joke, Mack. I think they were searching for something."

"Like what, for instance? My Darvon? If you take enough of them, they give you a nice high." He grins wryly. "Or so I've heard."

Simon leans in and says, practically in his ear, "I think maybe it was the codex."

"*Kotex*?" says Mack, incredulously.

"Ssshh! You know, the book I told you about? Apparently somebody wants to get their hands on it, and they think I have it."

"They must want it pretty bad. Any idea why? I mean, what's in it?"

"I have no idea. It's written in ciphertext, remember?"

"Oh, yeah." He downs the last of his beer. "God, my mouth is so dry it feels like beef jerky. Could you get me another one of these?"

"You sure it's okay to drink when you're taking painkillers?"

"Yeah, it's fine." He claps Simon on the shoulder. "Thanks for worrying about me, though, man."

For a change, Alec isn't behind the bar. Simon orders a beer and carries it carefully to Mack, spilling only a little foam on the way. "Well, I guess I'll head back. I'm worn out. Oh, I forgot to ask: Gabriela didn't come by, did she?"

"Nope. Unless it was while I was asleep. Hey, no offense, but is it possible *she* was the one that . . . you know . . ."

"Trashed the place? Why would she do that?"

"I don't know, man; just asking. I'm beat, too, but I promised Maisie I'd be at the SDS meeting." He beckons Simon closer and says, in his version of a soft voice, slurring his words a little, "Don't tell anybody, but they're planning a sit-in at the Marine recruiting office."

"You're not going to go, are you? That's just asking to get arrested."

Mack shrugs. "Yeah, probably. But, you know, what's the difference? If I lose my scholarship, I'm done for, anyway."

"Hey, there are other scholarships you can apply for."

"With my GPA? Hah!"

"We'll check it out, okay? There's got to be something. Look, why don't you just come back with me? You're not in any shape to--"

Mack sets down his beer so hard it threatens to crack the top of the pinball game. "I said I'm *fine*, man!" He sighs and waves a dismissive hand. "You go on, okay?"

•   •   •   •

When the days start getting short, it always takes Simon by surprise. They won't set the clocks back for another two weeks or so, and already it's looking like evening when it feels like it should still be afternoon. The gloomy, low-hanging sky doesn't help matters any; by the time he gets back to the Gas Chamber, it's practically dark. There's a light in Rhonda Horvath's bedroom window, silhouetting the Disney characters on her curtains—a strange contrast to the strains of The Doors'"Light My Fire" coming from her record player.

As he's about to cut across the lawn—something Mr. Horvath has asked him not to do, but he's feeling rebellious—there's a shock of pain just below his right shoulder blade, so sudden and so sharp that it makes him gasp. It's like being stung by a wasp—one of the giant wasps from H. G. Wells' *The Food of the Gods.*

With his left arm, Simon gropes around behind his back, trying to locate the source of the pain. His fingernails click against some object—something plastic, it feels like. He manages to get hold of the thing and yank it free, then lifts it up to the light of the street lamp that's just blinked on.

It looks like a hypodermic syringe for dolls, with a tiny feather duster attached. For several moments he just stares at it, unable to imagine where it came from and why it was sticking in his back. The longer he stares, the less sense it makes to his foggy brain. He knew he was tired, but not *this* tired. He really needs to lie down.

Simon shuffles across the lawn to the outside stairs that lead to the Gas Chamber. They look impossibly long and steep. He sinks down on the bottom step and puts his head in his hands, nearly poking himself in the eye with the needle in the process. He'll be able to manage those stairs if he can just rest for a minute or two; he's sure of it.

But, as is the case with so many things lately, he's wrong.

CHAPTER TWELVE

The first thing Simon is aware of is a smell; curiously enough, it brings to mind the Easter ham his mother used to bake every year. She wasn't the world's greatest cook, but one thing she took pride in was her Easter ham, glazed with pineapple and brown sugar and studded with cloves. Cloves. That's it; that's what he's smelling—that, plus an odor reminiscent of unwashed socks.

The second thing he notices is that he can't move his arms. They seem to be bound to his body by something stretchy—rubber tubing, maybe? In fact, his whole body is bound—to an office chair, apparently; he can feel the backrest digging into his spine.

The third thing is that he can't see. He tries opening his eyes, then realizes they're already open. The problem is, there's something covering his head— probably not an unwashed sock, but something else smelly and made of black cloth.

The strangest thing of all is that he's not particularly alarmed or upset about any of this. In fact, it strikes him as amusing, like some extreme version of blind man's bluff. He starts to giggle soundlessly—his voice box doesn't seem to be working quite right.

"Ah, good," says a brisk voice with a slight, undefinable accent. "You are awake." It sounds disembodied, as though it's coming from a loudspeaker or a walkie-talkie. This tickles Simon even more—well, the term *walkie-talkie* is pretty funny, isn't it? The giggles turn to snickers.

"In case you are wondering," says the voice, "the reason you are feeling so relaxed is that you have been injected with an antimuscarinic familiarly known as Devil's Breath."

This term is even more rib-tickling than *walkie-talkie*. Simon can hardly contain himself.

"Yes, I thought you would enjoy that. I am so glad you are having fun, but let's get down to business, shall we? I need to ask you a few questions. I know you will answer them truthfully—provided, of course, that you can manage to speak. If not, I am willing to wait a while. We have all night."

Simon clears his parched throat. "Could I--" he croaks. "Could I just have--"

"A drink of water? I am afraid not. It is best if you do not get a look at us, or at your surroundings. You might remember something later--though I doubt it."

"Oh, I have a very good memory," says Simon, still snickering. "Especially for my mother's cooking." He lowers his voice to a stage whisper. "That's because it was *terrible*! Naturally, we didn't dare tell her that. We acted as if she was Chef Boy-ar-dee!" The ridiculous name nearly sends him into hysterics.

The disembodied voice takes on an impatient edge. "That is very interesting, my friend, but not very productive. Let's get to the questions, shall we?"

"Oh. Okay. My first question is, why does it smell like cloves in here? Are we in a kitchen? Is it bigger than a breadbox? Oh, sorry, that's three questions, so I only have . . . what? Seventeen more? Let's see . . ."

"*I* will ask the questions; you just concentrate on answering them, all right?"

"Sir, yes, sir!"

"Good. Now. You have the codex, do you not?"

"Kotex? No, no, I never use them. That's because I'm a guy, in case you didn't notice. My mother had some, though. She tried to keep them hidden, but I found them when I was crawling around under the bed, hiding from the Communists, and I asked her why she kept a box of napkins under her bed-- because it said 'Napkins' right there on the box, you know--"

"The *journal*, then! The Vicente journal! Do you have it or do you not?"

"There's no need to shout," says Simon, pouting a little. "I was just trying to explain how my mother was always hiding things, pretending they didn't exist- -anything she considered unpleasant or distasteful or--"

"I can make things very unpleasant for *you*," says the voice, icily, "if you do not start answering my questions."

"Sorry. I'll try to do better, Mother—I mean, Mister—Mister Whoever You Are, Mister Walkie-Talkie Kawasaki." This prompts another snort of amusement, which he tries to suppress.

"Never mind; I know you must have it. Just tell me where it is."

"Where what is?"

"The *journal*."

"Well, I've never kept a journal, not as such. I tried to keep a diary for a while, but I always forgot to write in it--"

"Not *your* journal, you bloody idiot. The Vicente Marques journal!"

"Vicente *Marques*?" wails Simon. "Is *that* his name? Damn it all! I was hoping it was *Gil* Vicente!" He degenerates into pitiful sobs. "And there's no need to call me names! I'm doing the best I can!"

The voice heaves an audible sigh and switches to a more conciliatory tone. "I apologize. You are not a bloody idiot. You are a very clever fellow--so clever that you have hidden the journal where no one can possibly find it. Well done. But the game is over; you've won. Now you must tell us where your secret hiding place is, in order to claim the prize."

"Oh, there's a prize?" Simon would clap his hands together if his arms weren't bound at his sides.

"Indeed, and a very nice one, too."

"Really? What is it?"

"Well, it is . . . it is an all-expense-paid trip to . . . to wherever you would like to go."

"Brazil!" says Simon eagerly.

"Brazil it is. But first you must tell me where to find the journal."

"Oh, yeah." He feels tears welling up. "You see, the thing is . . . I can't."

"You can't? Or you won't?"

"I would if I could, honestly. It's just that . . . it's just that I don't *know* where it is. I'm sorry!" Simon breaks into sobs again.

"God damn it!" says the voice, more faintly, now, as if its owner has put down the walkie-talkie. "You said he would not be able to lie!"

"I didn't say that, exactly," comes an even more faint reply. "Scopolamine isn't a truth serum; it just lowers people's inhibitions, so they hold nothing back."

"Yes. I have noticed that. So why will he not tell us about the codex?"

"Well, perhaps he really doesn't know."

"I really don't know!" calls Simon. "In fact, I don't know much of anything. I enrolled in college to learn stuff—well, that, and because my mother wanted me to--but instead I just keep discovering more stuff . . . more stuff that I don't know . . ." He feels himself winding down, losing power, like a talking doll whose battery is getting low.

"Oh, do shut up!" says the voice.

Simon is only too glad to oblige. He's suddenly feeling very drowsy.

• • •

When he regains consciousness this time, the first thing he's aware of is someone shaking his shoulder roughly and slapping his cheeks. A voice says, "What are you doing out here, man?"

"Mack?"

"Yeah."

"Out--out *where?*"

"In the yard. I mean, you said you were tired, but surely you could have made it to the apartment before you crashed."

"Oh." With his friend's help, Simon sits up, shivering, and looks muzzily around. "Weird."

"You certainly are. Come on, let's get you inside. It's cold out here." He hauls Simon to his feet and, propping him up, steers him toward the stairs.

"Be careful," murmurs Simon. "Don't hurt your knee."

"No worries. Did you go back to the Tap for a few drinks, or what?"

"Um, I don't think so. Why?"

"You seem pretty woozy. You feeling sick?"

"Not exactly. I do have a splitting headache." Halfway up the stairs, Simon halts and leans against the handrail. "Just a second; let me catch my breath, okay?"

"Sure, man. Take your time."

"I was . . . I was having this really strange dream. I was tied up or something--"

"You can tell me later, Simon."

"No, no, I might forget. My mother was telling me it was time to go school, but I couldn't move, and then she started asking where my schoolbooks were, but I couldn't remember."

"Ah. A version of the classic Student's Nightmare. We talked about that in Psych class. You weren't naked, were you?"

"I don't think so. I had on a hooded sweatshirt or something, and the hood kept falling over my face." Simon shudders, making his head hurt even worse. "I need some aspirin."

"You want a Darvon?"

"No, I'd better not." Once they're inside, Simon sinks down on his bed and drapes a blanket around his trembling shoulders while Mack fetches him a cup of instant coffee and four aspirin. "Thanks, man. Did you go to . . . where was it you were going?"

"The SDS meeting." Mack sits on the couch and does his Stan Laurel head rub. "Just for a couple of minutes, just to talk to Maisie. I . . . ah . . . I decided you were right. The sit-in idea is too risky."

"Good thinking. Was she mad?"

"Maisie? Nah. She says we all have to decide stuff for ourselves. You know what else I've been thinking?"

"You're going to switch majors."

Mack chuckles. "Probably. But not right away. I was thinking I'd try to find a part-time job on campus. If you work for the university, they give you a break on your tuition, and maybe I could make enough to pay for the rest."

"Smart. And if you stay in the Gas Chamber, you won't have to worry about rent for a while."

"As long as your landlord doesn't mind. And you don't mind."

"I don't mind. I got these." He reaches in his pocket and pulls out the packet of Mack's Earplugs.

"Hey, sorry, man. I guess I snore pretty loud, huh?"

"No, no," Simon assures him. "These are to block out Rhonda's music."

In the morning, his head still feels like he took an elbow strike to the temple. When he heads to the bathroom, he's unsteady on his feet, and his limbs feel heavy, almost as if he's been drugged. He decides to take a page from Mack's playbook and just stay in bed a while.

But Mack himself seems to have turned over a new leaf in the playbook; by nine o'clock he's up and dressed and eating a bowl of Raisin Bran. Though Kellogg quit putting Dick Tracy decoders in the boxes ten years ago, Simon still buys the cereal due to some combination of loyalty and nostalgia. "Where are you off to so early? And so dressed up?" Mack is actually wearing a white shirt and khaki slacks, both a little wrinkled from being dumped on the floor.

"Student Services. Like I told you, I'm gonna look for a job." He shakes a couple of Darvon into his palm and regards them thoughtfully. "Maybe I better just take one. I don't want fall asleep during the interview." He washes one down with milk, then considers the second one. "On the other hand, I don't want my knee to start hurting. Nobody's going to hire a cripple."

"They're not going to hire somebody who calls handicapped people cripples, either."

"Yeah, yeah. Give me a break, okay?" He gulps the second Darvon and slicks down his hair; since he quit giving it a regular buzz cut, it's grown out and is now a good inch long. "Wish me luck, man."

"Luck, man."

Simon still feels chilled, as though lying on the cold ground last night sucked all the warmth out of him. He can't imagine why he would just collapse on the lawn that way. The area below his right shoulder blade is aching, as if something jabbed him there; he must have fallen on a stick or a stone.

He takes a couple more aspirin, grabs the *Todalas Obras de Gil Vicente*--like Mack's clothing, its pages are seriously wrinkled from being thrown on the floor—and crawls under the dingy down comforter. He may as well do some more research on his existing topic, in case he never recovers the codex—a dismal thought--or never manages to decipher it—an equally dismal prospect, but very possible.

As usual, Simon can't seem to concentrate on the plays. No doubt it's partly due to the unremitting ache in his head, but it's more than that. There's something nagging at the back of his brain, as if he knows he's neglecting some important matter but can't remember what it is. He's still concerned about Gabriela, of course, and about the Xerox copy, but those aren't at the back of his mind, they're right up front.

He has a hunch, though, that whatever's nagging at him has something to do with the codex, or with Vicente Marques. Vicente *Marques*? Where did that come from? He meant Gil Vicente, of course. Maybe he hit his head on a rock last night and knocked a few things out of place.

Oddly, just at that moment there's a knocking sound in his head. Well, no, it's in the wall, which he's using as a backrest. He leans forward and listens. When the knocking starts again, he realizes it's actually coming from the door. "Who is it?" he calls, praying that it's not the teenage slattern come to attack him with scissors and comb.

A soft voice says, "It is me, Simon."

Simon leaps out of bed. When he's halfway across the room, it dawns on him that he's wearing only a t-shirt and his Fruit of the Looms. "Just--just a second, okay?" He struggles into a pair of jeans and hurries to the door. It actually is Gabriela, and she actually has the rolled-up pages of the codex in her hand. Simon feels such a rush of relief, he's momentarily speechless. "Um . . . *bom dia,*" he says at last. "*Cómo está?*"

"Better than you, I think. You look sick."

"Yeah, I've got a headache, is all."

"I am sorry. I will not stay long." There's an awkward pause. "Are you going to invite me in?"

This throws Simon even more off balance. A week ago, she wouldn't even let him into the Rare Book Room; now she wants to come in his apartment? *Good thing you cleaned it up,* the spirit of his mother is saying. "Oh. Uh, sure. Come on in. I'll just—I'll just put a shirt on."

"I was here yesterday, and I rang the doorbell, but no one answered."

"You were? When? I mean, what time?"

"I am not certain. One or two o'clock, perhaps?"

"Uh-huh." So Mack would have been gone already, and Simon hadn't returned yet. "Did you—did you hear anybody moving around in here, or anything?"

"No."

"I don't suppose you looked in the window?"

"No. Why?"

"Well, apparently somebody was in here, right around that same time. They tore the place apart."

"*Nossa Senhora!* Who would do such a thing?"

"Your guess is as good as mine. I have a feeling they were looking for the codex."

Gabriela chews pensively at one of her already ragged fingernails. "That is very strange, Simon. I wonder whether . . ."

"What?"

"Well, there was a man in the Taft yesterday, asking to see it."

"I know. Two of them, actually."

"*Two?*"

"Uh-huh. Me and somebody named Thomas Huxley."

"You? When were you there?"

"About the same time *you* were *here*. But how did you know about this other guy?"

"I was in the Taft when he came."

"Really? You saw him, then?"

Gabriela shakes her head. "I was in the book repair room." She holds out the Xeroxed pages. "I had been looking at these, hoping I might uncipher--decipher something, and I noticed some of the letters were cut off. I think that, when we copied the pages, I didn't open the book wide enough. So, I went in to copy them again. I heard Ms. Harris and another person come into the room. They looked up something in the card catalog and then went into the stacks. After a few minutes, I heard him say 'It's not there' and Ms. Harris said something like, 'I'm very sorry. Perhaps it was mis-shelved.' He asked whether she could have someone search for it, and she said she would ask me to, and then they left."

"But--I mean--how do you know it was the codex he was after?"

"Ms. Harris forgot to return the drawer to the card catalog." She gives a disapproving scowl. "She does that a lot. As I was putting it back, I saw the card they had been looking at. It was the Vicente journal."

"So, what did you do with it--the book, I mean?"

"Well, I didn't want to put it on the shelf; if the man comes back, he might find it. So I hid it in the book repair room. None of the staff knows much about bookbinding, so no one ever goes in there except to make a copy."

"Good thinking. Listen, you want some tea or something?"

"I said I would not stay long. You are not feeling well."

Actually, he's feeling a lot better since she showed up, but he doesn't say so. He doesn't want her to know that he suspected her of making off with the copies, or the codex, or both. He also doesn't want to sound as if he's coming on to her. "Um, I'm okay; I think the aspirin is kicking in, now. But, hey, you don't have to stay if you don't want to."

"Well, I was hoping we might try to decipher these again. If you feel like it, I mean."

"Sure." The truth is, he's still feeling a little spacey, but he's not about to chase her off. Maybe a cup of strong tea will help. Though he doesn't have much in the way of food, he does have a huge tin of Tetley tea bags and a teapot designed to look like a VW van, complete with peace sign—a legacy of the previous tenant. "Before we tackle the cipher, though, there's something else I need to figure out."

"Oh? What is that?" Her voice has that familiar cautious, almost anxious sound again, as though she's afraid the thing he wants to figure out is *her*.

"Well, let's say this Huxley guy did come here looking for the codex. What would make him think *I* had it? I mean, nobody knew we discovered it, right? Unless you . . . you didn't—?"

"No, I didn't tell anyone, Simon," she says, a bit peevishly. "Did you?"

"Well, yeah--Mrs. Pitman. But by then the mystery man had come and gone. Oh, and I, um . . ." Simon busies himself with pouring the tea and doesn't look at her. "I also told my friend Mack. But he wouldn't tell anybody, I know he wouldn't."

"Mack? He was the one who quarreled with—with that other boy, outside Taylor Hall?"

Simon feels himself going red, remembering how inept he must have looked. "Uh-huh."

"I hope that Mack . . . how do you say? Taught him a lesson?" Her words are so unexpectedly vehement that it startles Simon. She seems a bit startled herself, as if she hadn't meant to sound quite so bloodthirsty. In a more subdued tone, she adds, "Well, he should not have pushed Mack's girlfriend."

"No; he's a jerk. I guess you didn't stick around for the fight." She shakes her head silently. Oh, good. "I didn't know where you got to," says Simon. "I tried to—well, to find out where you live . . . I mean, just to make sure--"

"I know. I am sorry. I had my name removed from the campus directory, and I asked the library staff not to give out any information about me."

"Oh. Can I—can I ask why?"

"I would rather you did not. Perhaps I will tell you sometime. But not now, okay?"

CHAPTER THIRTEEN

They sit at the tiny, rickety kitchen table and Simon unrolls the copies. He weighs down one curly edge with the sugar bowl and the other with the teapot.

"One thing I noticed," says Gabriela, "is that some words have the same letter two or three times in a row: EEI. NIMIIIU. Here is one with *four*: AAAA. What kind of cipher would do that?"

"Good question. The only thing I can think of is that, instead of using a keyword, Vicente--" He almost said *Marques* again; why is that name stuck in his head? And where did it come from? "--Vicente Whoever used a whole sentence as the key, or maybe a couple of sentences. Benjamin Franklin used a system like that to send secret dispatches."

"But how can we possibly tell what sentence he used?"

"Benjamin Franklin? Or Vicente Whoever?"

"Vicente Whoever."

"Well, he says--" Simon consults the Portuguese passage on the first page. "He says he hopes that some enlightened scholar will be smart and determined enough to unveil the secrets it contains. So he wanted the cipher to be difficult, but not impossible."

Gabriela chews on another ragged fingernail. "You don't suppose . . . "

"What?"

"You don't suppose this whole paragraph could be the key?"

"Hmm. It's pretty long for that. But, hey, it's worth a try. Let me get some paper and a pencil." He has Gabriela print the first few lines of the foreword in large letters on a sheet of paper, twenty-six letters to a line. "Franklin used a passage from a French essay as his key—something like *Voulez-vous sentir la difference?* He numbered all the letters in the phrase, and then he used those numbers to create the ciphertext. Vicente obviously didn't do that. But he could have done something similar, using the alphabet instead of numbers." He proceeds to demonstrate:

O m e u   n o m e e Vi c e n t e Na o i r e i   r e v
A B C D E F G H I J K L M N O P Q R S T U V W X Y Z

"So," says Gabriela, "that means the first letter in the cipher—U—is really an *r*?"

"Right. Unless the first letter is a null, like we thought."

"Ah, *sim*. I forgot. So the second letter, then. The I is really an *e*. And the R is really an *a*. Well, *ea* together doesn't mean anything, but *e a* separately does." Eagerly, Gabriela converts two more words to plaintext and then studies them skeptically. "*Ea neeoua noo*?" They glance at each other and shake their heads.

"Oh, wait!" says Simon. "You know what? We're doing this the wrong way around. Try using the *top* line as the ciphertext letters."

"Okay. If we do it that way, the *i* is really a . . . well, it could be either a K or a T or a W. And the *r* is . . . either a U or an X."

"But KX and TX and WX aren't actual words. Neither is KU or WU. So it has to be TU--"

"--which means *You*! Maybe this is going to work!"

It doesn't take long to discover that this path, too, is leading to a dead end. "Oh, boy," says Simon. "We have seven different choices for the *e*, and none of them makes any sense. And there is no *d*."

Undaunted, Gabriela prints an alphabet under the second line of text and tries again. The end that this path leads to is more than just dead; it has a stake in its heart and is buried at the crossroads. "*Vixe Maria!*"

"Hey, don't get discouraged, okay? Like I said, this could take a while."

"I am not discouraged."

"Good. Because I am. Not about the cipher; I think that, given enough time, we can crack it. The hard part is going be convincing Dr. Espinoza that we can."

"But, even if we do not, you could still do your thesis about it, couldn't you?"

"Well, I guess I'd have to include stuff about other books; I mean, it's supposed to be *Comparative* Literature. Maybe I could do something like Codes and Ciphers in Renaissance Manuscripts."

"Would you have enough research material?"

"Oh, sure. A lot of people used codes and ciphers back then: Da Vinci. Chaucer. The two Bacons—Roger and Francis. Galileo . . ."

Gabriela lays a hand gently on his arm. "I think you should do it, Simon."

Simon very nearly says, *I will, if you promise to help me.* But of course he doesn't. "Uh-huh. Too bad you're not my thesis advisor."

Their moment of intimacy is shattered by the door to the apartment flying open. Gabriela yanks her hand away; Simon twists about in his chair, sure in his muddled mind that it must be the mysterious Mr. Huxley, come back to steal the codex.

"Oh, sorry, man. Didn't know you had company." Mack starts to back out of the room.

"No, no, you don't need to--" As flustered as if they were caught in a compromising position, Simon gets to his feet, then abruptly plunks down again as a wave of vertigo washes over him.

"Whoa," says Mack. "You okay, man?"

"Yeah, I just . . . I'm just a little . . . dizzy, is all."

"Have you eaten anything?" asks Gabriela.

"Um, not lately."

"No wonder you are dizzy, then. You have to eat." It's the sort of thing his mother always said, but coming from Gabriela it sounds different. It's not just the accent, either; it's like she's really concerned, not just saying it because she thinks she's supposed to. "I will fix you something, okay?"

"Sounds good to me," puts in Mack. "I just moved in, so I don't know where anything is, and anyway I'm a lousy cook." He thrusts out a hand that's twice the size of hers. "I'm Mack. We were in Western Civ together."

She eyes the hand warily for a moment and then gives it a cursory shake. "Yes, I remember. You were the one who asked whether Napoleon was a homosexual, and the professor thought you were asking whether *he* was, and he said 'I don't believe that's any of your business, young man!'"

"Wow. You sound just like him. By the way, apparently he *is*. Not that it matters. Some of my best friends are homosexuals. Well, maybe not my *best* friends, but acquaintances, anyway. Definitely *not* Simon, though."

Simon groans and shakes his aching head. Luckily, Gabriela seems amused by Mack's heavy-handed attempts to transcend his operant conditioning—his East Cleveland roots and his years of associating mainly with jocks. "Well, that is good to know," she says, leaving Simon to wonder what she meant by that.

Nothing, most likely. After all, she's never given the slightest indication that she's attracted to him—or that she's aware of how much he's attracted to her, though how could she possibly *not* know?

She surveys the interior of his little cupboard, which bears a strong resemblance to Mrs. Hubbard's. "Well, you do not have much to choose from. Salt. Tomato sauce. Tang. Canned beets." Standing on tiptoe, she retrieves a lone box from the back of the shelf. "Ah. Macaroni and cheese. That should fill you up."

"Oh, god," says Simon. "That was there when I moved in."

"Hey, it never goes bad," says Mack. "It's like Hostess Twinkies. You know, I ought to go out and buy us something really good, to celebrate."

"Celebrate what?"

He spreads his arms wide, and forces a matching grin. "I've enlisted!" Simon is so stunned he can't even respond--which is just as well, because a second later, Mack adds, "In the Medical Sciences Center Cleaning Corps!"

"Jesus! Don't scare me like that. I thought you meant-- You mean you got a job as a janitor?"

"Yes! I'm following in my dear old dad's footsteps. He'd be so proud."

"Hey, it's nothing to be ashamed of, if it pays your tuition."

Mack shrugs. "Yeah, yeah, I know. It's just . . . if it wasn't for this damned knee, I'd be . . ." He manages another strained smile. "But, hey, I still get to wear a uniform--a nice white coverall. And no woman can resist a man in uniform, right?"

"I can." Though Gabriela says only those two words, Simon gets the feeling that there are a lot more left unspoken. Seeing that Mack is about to question her, Simon catches his eye and gives a subtle head-shake.

A long silence follows, which Mack finally breaks. "So, any luck with the Kotex?"

For some reason, that starts the nagging at the back of Simon's brain again, the sense that he's forgetting something crucial, but he has no idea what it is. "Um, not a lot. Listen, Mack, you haven't told anybody about the book, have you?"

"No!" he says, sounding indignant, injured. "I said I wouldn't, and I haven't."

"Okay, sorry; just making sure." Simon rolls up the copies and glances around the Gas Chamber. "We need to find somewhere to hide this, in case our mystery man comes around again. He may not care about a Xerox copy; he might just want the book itself, but we can't take any chances."

"I could keep it at my place," says Gabriela, "but then you would not be able to work on it."

"No, and it's obviously going to take a lot of work. Would you . . . um, would you be able to help me sometimes, do you think?"

"*Claro.* If you would like me to."

"Well, I don't want you to feel you *have* to . . ."

"Jeez, what a pair!" says Mack. "You sound like characters from *Marty*. 'What do you want to do tonight, Marty?' 'I don't know, what do *you* want to do?' In Psych class we call that *passive personality*. Trust me, he'd like you to, Gabriela, okay?"

She smiles. "Okay." Taking down a couple of mismatched plates, she serves up the macaroni and cheese and a sort of salad she's concocted of chopped beets with vinegar and oil and spices.

As she's about to toss the Kraft box in the trash, Mack shouts, "Wait! That's our hiding place!"

"*Que?*"

"Fold up the copies, stick 'em in the box, glue the top closed with rubber cement."

"Not a bad idea," says Simon.

Mack shrugs. "I do have one, once in a while. Hey, this stuff is good."

●　　●　　●

On Wednesday, Simon spends every spare moment in the library. He does drag himself to his Books and Printing class, but it might as well be taught in Greek, for all the good he gets out of it. His mind is too occupied with European cryptography of the fourteenth to seventeenth centuries, plus his head is still hurting on and off. He's had plenty of practice blocking out karate-related pain, but these headaches are a different matter. It's not just straightforward, physical pain; it's more like a severe cramp in his mental muscles.

Feeling the need to relax and clear out the cobwebs, he heads for the wrestling room. It's Karate Club night and all the usual suspects are there, including Alec. But to Simon's surprise, they also have some new members—Wendy and two of her Visigoths. The old familiar *karate-ka*—all of them guys—

look variously resentful, amused, and stunned by this unusual development. The Visigoths look the way she-wolves might look surrounded by mongrel dogs.

Though Karate Club has its own *dojo kun*—*To search for the old is to understand the new*--there's hardly anything else *dojo*-like about it; it's basically just a bunch of students of all skill levels and every conceivable discipline, each doing his own thing—or, starting now, *her* own thing.

Simon bows to the Visigoths, but he doesn't try to talk to them. He can manage it in self-defense class only because he's playing a role—the confident, knowledgeable karate master. He doesn't want to spoil that image by stammering incoherently at them. He retreats to a far corner of the mat to practice his *kata*. It feels good to let go of everything that's been preying on his mind and just act without thinking for a change.

The atmosphere at Karate Club has always reminded him of the weekly school dances back in Garden City, where the boys who lacked confidence—the majority, in other words—horsed around and tried to get up the nerve to ask a girl—any girl--to dance. Here, the higher-ranking *karate-ka* have long been the preferred dance partners, the ones that the less experienced guys want to pair off with but are half afraid to.

Now that the Visigoths have invaded, it's become even more like a school dance; all the boys are eyeing the girls, but only a few are brave enough to dance the *kumite* dance with them. Suddenly the brown belts and black belts don't seem so intimidating after all; at least they're guys. A green-belted high school student who has never sparred with Simon before approaches and bows. "*Onegai shimasu*," he murmurs. Please teach me.

Simon sighs; he was just starting to get into his groove. He tries not to show his irritation; the boy probably doesn't know any better. No doubt he studies with one of those half-assed instructors who don't bother to teach their students about politeness and respect. Simon stands erect and returns the bow. "*Hai.*"

The boy's instructor apparently hasn't taught him much about blocking, either. He's fast and strong, with a good snap kick, but he's all about offense; time after time he leaves himself open to a counterpunch. There's probably no point in telling him so. Boys that age tend not to listen; they need to be shown.

Simon watches his opponent's face; every time he's about to make a move, his eyes narrow. The next time he tries a kick, instead of dodging it Simon steps forward, so the blow catches only the back of his calf, and he elbows the boy in the solar plexus—perhaps a bit harder than he should have. The poor kid doubles over, gasping soundlessly, like a netted trout.

When he can breathe again, he backs away, looking seriously spooked and forgetting to bow. *"Sumimasen,"* Simon calls after him. "I'm sorry, I misjudged the distance." The part about being sorry is true; the part about misjudging isn't. He learned long ago how to gauge distance down to a millimeter, how to strike hard without injuring his sparring partner. So why didn't he, this time? He has nothing against the boy. Simon barely knows him; he doesn't even know his name, or has forgotten it.

His head is throbbing again. Sinking to the mat, he blots the sweat from his forehead and neck with a hand towel. Maybe he actually did hit his head the other day and it temporarily disabled the area of his brain that prevents you from doing rash things. Or maybe it stirred up the area that's *responsible* for rashness, the deeply buried part that once sent him a message telling him to whack Frank Ávila with the scytale.

• • •

Frank wasn't the only one who was scarred, or scared, by that experience. For a least a year afterward, Simon replayed it in his mind almost daily; sometimes he even had nightmares about it. He'd never thought of himself as a violent or impulsive person. In fact, he suspected he was too reserved, too cautious—a clear result of his operant conditioning. There was only room in their house for one impulsive person, and that was Delia Hannay.

Of course, she was gone by then, and they seldom heard from her, but something of her still lingered, like a ghost. For a time, Simon wondered how she would feel if she knew about the Frank Ávila incident. Would she be horrified, or would she be proud of him for defending her honor? Then he realized that, as was so often the case, it wouldn't have mattered how handled the situation; whatever he did would have been the wrong thing.

Don Hannay's attitude and approach were very different from his wife's. If Simon asked for advice, he was glad to give it, but he rarely criticized his son or tried to tell him what to do. Though he did insist that Simon help him set up the new *dojo*, which he called Wado-ryu Karate Academy—*wado-ryu* means 'the way of peace'--he never encouraged Simon to study karate. But he didn't discourage him, either. He seemed figure that, if Simon wanted to pursue it, he would.

In a town with a population—and a median income—as small as Garden City's, starting any sort of new business was a gamble. Starting a martial arts studio was more like a fool's enterprise. Karate lessons weren't exactly a necessity, like groceries or gas or clothing. If Delia Hannay had still been around, his dad wouldn't have dared do something so impractical; he had let his wife have her way in pretty much every aspect of their lives. There were times when Simon wished he'd stand up to her more--something Simon himself could never do.

Now, for better or worse, Don Hannay didn't have to care what she wanted. And the fact was, he really had very little to lose. He'd already lost his job at Carman, and the bank had foreclosed on the house. They needed someplace to live, anyway, and the old IGA building had a little apartment upstairs.

With the kung-fu craze still a decade away, young Kansans didn't have much exposure to the martial arts. They did, however, have plenty of exposure to Elvis, and Elvis was seriously into karate. On the set of *GI Blues*, he took every opportunity to demonstrate his board-breaking skills for the press. What's more, *The Adventures of Ozzie and Harriet* featured another karate-loving teen idol, Ricky Nelson.

Though the local boys didn't have much hope of becoming rock and roll singers or movie stars, they could emulate Ricky and Elvis in other ways. Most settled for sneering and styling their hair with Brylcreem. But some took up karate. Within a week, the Wado-ryu Academy sign—which took Simon many hours of painstaking effort to paint--had lured in half a dozen students.

Simon wasn't one of them. If his father had insisted, Simon would have gone along, because that was what he always did. But he really had no particular desire to take up martial arts. He'd played enough sports in gym class to know that it wasn't his thing. It wasn't due to his scrawny frame and clumsiness so much as to the fact that he just didn't have the motivation, the desire to excel, to wipe out the competition--the "fighting spirit," as their gym coach liked to call it.

Anyway, he didn't see much point in learning karate. Aside from the Frank Ávila incident--which wasn't exactly a case of self-defense--he'd never found it necessary to defend himself. Like every school, his had its share of roughnecks, but bullying wasn't nearly the problem that it was in larger communities. Not that the students were one big family, or anything, but there was a certain sense that they were all stuck in the same small boat and needed to row and bail together.

There was the same sort of feeling among the students at the *dojo*. Considering there were only six of them, they covered an astonishingly wide range of aptitudes and abilities and physiques, from Ronald Allgood, the beanpole star of the basketball team, to Matty Mays, who at the age of fourteen had played a Munchkin in the community theatre's production of *The Wizard of Oz*.

Simon watched the first couple of sessions from the shadowy safety of the stairs that led to their apartment. He expected to see more of the posing and pranks and put-downs that made gym class such a pain. Don Hannay was clearly expecting the same thing. His inaugural address to his motley group of *karate-ka* was pretty much the same one that Simon would later deliver to his self-defense class: "*Karate-do wa rei ni hajimari, rei ni owaru*. That means, karate begins and ends with respect. In this *dojo*, you will respect me, you will respect each other, and you will respect yourselves." And even though the students would subsequently fail to hear or to follow a hundred other instructions from their *sensei*, for some reason that one sank in. After a while, they seemed to grasp the fact that, no matter how foolish or inept or dense they were, no one would poke fun at them or lord it over them.

It was an appealing concept for somebody who had spent most of his young life feeling that nothing he did was right. But that wasn't enough to make him want to join the classes. What sucked him in was the same thing that made him so crazy about codes and made him want to learn Spanish: the siren song of secret knowledge.

First, there were the exotic Japanese and Okinawan words and phrases. Then there was the promise of learning special skills—how to break boards with your bare hand; how to wield *dim mak*, the fabled "Death Touch;" but above all, how to block out pain. He had done his best to bury the hurt of his mother's betrayal, but clearly he hadn't interred it deeply enough.

Three months after the Wado-Ryu Academy opened, Simon attended the weekly class for the first time; a month after that, he asked his dad to schedule extra sessions for the more serious students—which basically meant himself and Joe Wade, a stocky high school junior whose father had lost his job when the sugar plant closed but still managed to keep himself well supplied with tequila.

When Simon started training, he had no particular goal in mind; he just liked the way he felt when he was practicing *kata*—disciplined, calm, in control—and that was enough. Karate tournaments weren't a common thing yet, especially not in the Midwest, but even if they had been, he wouldn't have been interested, any more than he was interested in spelling bees or speech and debate or any other kind of competition. He didn't mind sparring with Joe, though; it wasn't like they were competing, more like they were cooperating, conducting an emphatic conversation, as it were, using only body language.

Though Don Hannay worked them hard, he was no Chokei Chioyu. He managed to strike a balance between the *go* and the *ju*, the hard and the soft. When he demonstrated a punch or a kick or a throw, he didn't hold back; occasionally he even gave one of the boys a charley horse, or knocked the wind out him. But there were very few bruises and no bloody noses, and no hard feelings.

However much their *sensei* demanded of them, Joe Wade never complained. In fact, the more rigorous and challenging the training was, the better he liked it. Simon put a lot of effort into it, too, but nowhere near as much as Joe did. The boy practiced every move as if his life depended on it. At the end of each session, Simon was ready to call it a day, but Joe always seemed reluctant to quit and go home.

If Simon had been paying attention, he would have guessed that there was some reason why Joe drove himself so hard, something more than just a desire to do well. But Simon was more concerned with improving his own skills—and, to some extent, with pleasing his father--than about what made Joe so gung-ho. Nearly a year went by before he learned that particular secret.

CHAPTER FOURTEEN

Feeling the mat give a little, Simon lifts his aching head to see Alec settling down next to him. "You certainly took him down a notch or two," says Alec.

Simon's mind is still on Joe Wade. It takes him a second to realize that Alec is talking about the green-belted boy Simon elbowed in the gut. "Uh, yeah. I don't know why I hit him so hard; I didn't mean to."

"No, no, it's a good thing. He thinks he's hot stuff because he's won a few competitions." Smirking, Alec swats Simon's arm. "I wasn't even sure you *could* hit that hard, Hannay. You never do when you spar with me."

Simon just shrugs. Ordinarily, he doesn't mind Alec's ribbing all that much, but today it's rubbing him the wrong way.

"You okay?" says Alec.

"Yeah, just a headache."

"Probably from all the stress."

"What do you mean?"

"Well, it's got be stressful, being in such close physical contact with those babes." Alec nods toward Wendy and her companions, who are learning some new moves—some of them are even karate moves--from a couple of the cooler Karate Club guys.

"Don't be crude," says Simon.

"Oh. Sorry," says Alec, and seems to actually mean it. "I guess it's just the academic stuff getting to you, huh? I'm glad we don't have to do a thesis for Organic Chem, just a directed research project." He leans in uncomfortably close to Simon and says quietly, "Don't tell anybody, okay, but we're *this* close--" He demonstrates with his thumb and index finger. "--to synthesizing an antihistamine that won't make you drowsy."

"Oh? You should tell Mack. He's convinced you're making nerve gas or something."

Alec laughs. "Mack's been spending too much time with the hippies. He's getting paranoid. How's his knee doing, anyway? I noticed it was bothering him."

"Yeah, he's taking Darvon—quite a bit of it. Sometimes I worry that he could get, you know, hooked on it."

Alec nods soberly. "He'd better not take any more than he absolutely has to. It's fairly mild stuff, but it is an opioid, so you can get dependent if you overdo it."

"Thanks. I'll tell him." Simon rubs the back of his aching head.

"Looks like you could use some, yourself."

"Nah, it'll go away. Like you said, it's probably just tension."

"Still fighting with that thesis, huh?"

"Yeah. Karate techniques don't seem work on it."

"Maybe you should consider changing your topic."

"Actually, I am thinking about it." As soon as he's said it, Simon wishes he hadn't. If he were thinking straight, he would have kept his mouth shut.

Alec grins wryly. "Oh, yeah. The use of chemical and biological weapons by the Spanish Inquistion, right?"

"Right." Simon gets unsteadily to his feet. "Listen, I'm not feeling so great. I think I'll just head home."

"Damn. I was hoping we could spar a little. You're the only one that presents much of a challenge."

"Not tonight, I wouldn't. You might try the babes. Watch out, though; they may not be experienced, but they're sneaky."

Well, so much for relaxing and clearing out the cobwebs. He'll have to come back when he has the place to himself and do a couple of hours of uninterrupted *kata*. Maybe Alec is right about his headaches being caused by stress. The thought of going up against Dr. Espinoza is enough to stress anybody out. The man tends to oppose on principle any idea that didn't originate with him; getting him to approve a new thesis topic is going to be a battle.

Simon wants to make sure he goes forth into the fray with plenty of ammunition. He spends the following week reacquainting himself with all the arcane enciphering methods he learned during his code-crazy phase.

There were dozens of secret writing methods used during the Renaissance but, since his major is Literature, he needs to concentrate on the ones that actually appeared in books of the period. As fascinating as he finds the Alberti disk and the Cardano grille and the pigpen cipher and the pinhole code, he ignores them and delves instead into Roger Bacon's shorthand and Shakespeare's sonnets—which, according to some scholars, contain hidden signs that their real author was Edward de Vere, Earl of Oxford. Simon even struggles vainly with a photocopy of that notoriously confounding codex, the Voynich manuscript.

He devotes far more of his time to researching than he does to sleeping, taking a break only on Saturday morning for his self-defense class. To his surprise, Gabriela comes early again and helps him set up. Not that it means anything; she seems a lot more interested in the codex than she does in him. "Have you made any progress with the cipher?"

"Not really. I've been so busy with research, I've hardly glanced at it. The mystery man hasn't shown up again, has he?"

"If he has, no one told me. Ms. Harris did tell me to search for the Vicente journal, and whenever she is around, I pretend to." Gabriela sets up the *makiwara* and, slipping off her bulky silver rings, practices her *seiken* punches.

"Where'd you get those rings, anyway?" asks Simon.

"At a . . . what do you call it? A flea market?"

"They're pretty cool."

She shrugs. "I suppose. I did not get them because they are cool." She delivers a fore-fist strike that makes the *makiwara* rock, then turns to him and abruptly changes the subject. "You know, I was thinking: When you talk to Dr. Espinoza, perhaps it would help if I came with you."

"You think so?"

"*Sim.* As I said, my *padrinho* was a student of his, and they have continued to correspond; Gilberto asked him to sort of watch over me. So if I tell him that you are my friend, perhaps he will be more *agradável.*"

"That's doubtful. But I'd settle for just not hostile. Anyway, I guess it's worth a try. And if he gives us any trouble, you can always hit him."

Gabriela throws him a peevish glance. "Funny, Simon. Very funny." She turns back to the *makiwara* and delivers a punch that would certainly settle Dr. Espinosa's hash, or anyone else's.

On Monday, as he's skimming the index in a worn Portuguese history text, looking for references to codes and ciphers, on a whim he scans the entries that begin with M. And synchronicity strikes again. There it is--the name that's been unaccountably popping up in his head for the past week or so: *Marques, Vicente,* 147. So he isn't dreaming it up; there actually was such a person. Simon must have come across him before in his studies and just forgotten. He flips to page 147, in the chapter titled "João III and the Inquisition." To his disappointment, Marques rates only a single sentence:

> Though most sources attribute João's death to apoplexy (severe stroke), some of his royal ministers suspected foul play; an adventurer and self-proclaimed *curandeiro,* Vicente Marques, was accused of poisoning the ailing king with an herbal decoction that Marques claimed was a panacea, or cure-all.

On the previous page, the author explains that a *curandeiro* was a traditional folk healer; apparently the Inquisition considered them little better than witches or sorcerers. There's no mention of Marques' fate. Did he manage to make his escape—and perhaps try to vindicate himself by writing the journal?—or was he brought up before the dreaded Lisbon Tribunal, from which there was no escape?

Simon consults every other book of Portuguese history he can find; none contains any reference to Marques or to the poisoning theory, let alone anything about a journal. But the Vicente who penned the codex and the Vicente accused of killing the king *have* to be one and the same. Don't they?

Well, maybe not. No doubt there were dozens of men named Vicente who came under the scrutiny of the Inquisition in during its 350-year reign. Maybe Simon is just falling into the classic scholar's trap again, seeing what he wants to see and not what the evidence really shows. But if the codex and "the secrets it contains" offer some new information about the death of a historical figure as important as João III, it could make Simon's academic career.

All he has to do is convince Dr. Espinoza that those secrets are worth unveiling.

It's not hard to schedule an appointment with Dr. E; given his reputation, who would want to face the man unless they absolutely had to? The only problem is that his office hours are so few and far between. But the administrative assistant, a cheerful, aggressively permed young woman named Marnie, pencils Simon in for Wednesday—at the same time as Books and Printing, but so what? His courses have long seemed like little more than busy work; now that he's on the trail of something really worth pursuing, it's even harder to take them seriously.

Now he just has to get hold of Gabriela. She didn't offer him her phone number or address, and he didn't want to seem pushy by asking. She did say that she usually works on the rare book collection on Tuesdays and Thursdays, so on Tuesday afternoon he stakes out the Rare Book Room, feeling a bit like a private detective--or a stalker. He takes along a single page of the copied codex and, while he's waiting, attacks it with various deciphering strategies. It's as impervious to his siege as a Renaissance star fortress.

His stakeout has better results. Around three, Gabriela turns up, wearing her usual uniform of combat boots and hooded sweatshirt. The shirt is unusually colorful, for her—blue, with an R. Crumb *Keep on Truckin'* graphic. Simon catches her just as she's unlocking the door. All he says is, "Um, hey," but it startles her anyway. "Sorry."

"It is all right. I just get a little . . . nervous up here, sometimes. It is so quiet and deserted."

"I, uh, I just wanted to tell you that I'm meeting with Dr. E tomorrow. I mean, in case you . . . you still want to . . ."

"Ah, *bom*! What time?"

"One o'clock."

"I will meet you there, okay?"

Though he was kind of hoping she'd invite him into the Taft, he nods and forces a smile. "Okay. Um, see you then, I guess." Feeling dejected, even a bit rejected, he meanders over to the Gedunk and drowns his sorrows in a smoothie.

As he's leaving, he can hear some sort of commotion going on in the general vicinity of Taylor Hall--another demonstration, it sounds like. Simon heads in that direction, hoping that, if there is trouble brewing, Mack will have the sense to stay out of it.

He arrives just in time to see a dozen students, some with bloodied faces, being carried or dragged from the building by cops who are forced to clear a path with their batons through the throng of protestors. Mack said the SDS was planning a sit-in; this must be it. To Simon's relief, his friend isn't among the sitter-inners, who are being crammed roughly into two paddy wagons. He does catch sight of Maisie, though; she's being hustled along by a policeman who has one of her thin arms levered up behind her back.

"Bastards!" says a voice next to him.

"Jeez, Mack; I almost didn't recognize you in your janitor uniform."

"Yeah, I'm supposed to be working, but I snuck out. Speaking of uniforms--" He jerks a thumb over his shoulder and Simon glances in that direction. Two Marine officers in blue trousers, white hats and khaki shirts gaudy with medals and ribbons are watching the show, smiling faintly, waiting for their chance to return to their post and resume recruiting naïve students. "Handsome devils, aren't they?"

"Uh-huh," says Simon. "In the *Cantigas*, that's how the Devil usually appears—in the guise of a handsome young man."

"I'd like to wipe those smug smiles off their faces."

"Not a good idea."

"You're right. Blowing up the recruiting office is a much better idea."

"Will you quit saying that? Somebody's going hear you and think you're serious."

"Who says I'm not?" For a moment, he actually sounds serious, and then he flashes a mischievous smile. "Hell, I can't even make macaroni and cheese; how would I ever manage to make a bomb?" Rubbing his head, he gazes after the departing paddy wagons almost longingly. "I wish I could have sat in on the sit-in, man. Those cops would've had their work cut out for them, dragging *me* out of there, wouldn't they?" He pulls a dust rag from his pocket and shakes it; the breeze carries a cloud of dust directly toward the Marines, who cast irritable looks in their direction. Mack shrugs innocently. "Sorry, gentlemen. Well, back to work."

"Same here," says Simon. "I have to present my new thesis topic tomorrow."

"Hey, you'll do fine. Just make sure you take the offensive, okay? Don't ask him if you *can* do it; tell him you're *gonna* do it." He punches Simon's shoulder hard enough to jar his aching head. "Right?"

Simon sighs. "I guess."

"What?" Mack is poised to strike again.

"Yes!" says Simon. "Right!"

•   •   •

By Wednesday, he has four typed pages of notes detailing his approach, plus photocopies of some of the research materials. After much debating with himself, he decides to take along a couple of the pages of the journal. He's not keen to tell Espinoza about the codex. What if the professor demands to see the original and then takes credit for finding it, or something? Simon wouldn't put it past him. But if he plans to make the journal part of his thesis, he pretty much has to tell his advisor about it up front.

He spends far too much time dressing for the battle; he wants to project an aura of studiousness without looking as if he's trying too hard. He finally settles on jeans, topped by a button-down blue shirt and his herringbone blazer. He can't help wondering whether Gabriela will show up in her usual outfit—or, for that matter, whether she'll show up at all. What if she can't find Dr. E's office? What if she gets the bright idea to bring the codex along? What if . . .?

Pull yourself together, Simon; you're thinking and analyzing way too much. He closes his eyes and does some *shin kokyu*. Dr. Espinoza has got to be one of the toughest opponents he's ever faced; he needs to stay calm, confident, in control. In an attempt to control his headache, he downs four aspirin before he sallies forth.

As is his habit, he arrives much too early and has to sit in the reception area for nearly half an hour, reviewing his notes and feeling the effects of his deep breathing slipping away. Marnie, who is having lunch at her desk, offers him an Oreo; Simon declines, not caring to have black crumbs in his teeth.

"I'm sure he'll be in any time now," says Marnie. Confidentially, she adds, "He tends to take rather long lunches." She makes a glass-tipping gesture with one hand and gives him a conspiratorial wink. He smiles weakly and nods. He's often suspected that the professor had a nip or two before class—his way of preparing for battle, no doubt. Simon wishes he'd thought of that tactic.

He hears a door bang out in the hallway, then sees movement behind the frosted glass of Espinoza's office door. "There he is now," says Marnie softly.

Uh-oh. And still no sign of Gabriela. "I'm, uh, I'm expecting another person, but she hasn't— I don't know whether-- Should I—should I go in, or--?"

"Better wait until he calls for you."

"Simon!" says a breathless voice that is definitely not Dr. Espinoza's. "I am sorry. Am I late?"

Simon glances up at Gabriela; to his disappointment, she's wearing the baggy Athletic Department sweatshirt—not the sort of studious attire he'd hoped for.

But a moment later, she's peeling it off, revealing a disturbingly slinky Twiggy-type shift and a large pair of hoop earrings. Simon is struck speechless. He found her disarming and distracting enough when she wasn't even trying to be; how will he ever manage to keep his mind on his thesis now?

"Am I late?" she repeats.

"No," Marnie answers for him. "You're right on time. It's Gabriela, isn't it?"

"Yes. It is nice to see you again, Marnie." She's wearing something else Simon has seldom seen on her—a more or less relaxed and confident smile. This isn't the Gabriela he knows; does she have a twin sister she hasn't told him about? "Is the *Maestro* in his office?"

Before Marnie can reply, the office door opens and the professor thrusts out his head, which has always reminded Simon of the grim bust of Beethoven his mother once kept atop her spinet piano. He even has an unruly mane of hair like the great composer's, though Dr. E's is retreating from his forehead and halfway gray.

Today he looks less Beethovenesque than usual; he's not exactly smiling, but neither is he scowling. In fact, he seems almost pleased—perhaps not by most people's standards, but in relative terms. Does he have a more outgoing twin as well? Or has Simon stumbled into some alternate universe?

"Gabriela! I was expecting--" The professor gestures toward Simon, whose name he appears to have forgotten. "—this young man. Are you with him?"

"Yes, *Maestro*. I have been trying to help him with . . . well, I will let Simon explain it to you."

"Oh." The scowl shows signs of returning. "Very well. I suppose you had better come in, then."

CHAPTER FIFTEEN

Simon's head is still aching and, beneath his herringbone blazer, he's sweating. He folds his long frame into one of the low upholstered chairs, which seem designed to seat grade schoolers—probably another of Dr. E's strategies for making his students feel incompetent and insignificant.

While the professor and Gabriela chat in Portuguese about Gilberto--her *padrinho* and his former pupil--Simon draws several deep but silent breaths and looks over his notes, which also seem to belong to an alternate universe; he spent days preparing them, but now they make no more sense to him than a page from the codex.

"So," Espinoza is saying, in a growl made even rougher by decades' worth of undiluted whiskey and unfiltered cigarettes. "What is the big idea?" It sounds like a line from an Edward G. Robinson gangster movie.

"Um, I'm not sure what-- You mean—you mean my thesis idea?"

"Is that not what you are here for? To propose a new topic? Though I fail to see what is wrong with the one you were working on."

"Well . . . nothing, I guess." Except that it's terminally boring, and if he has to translate one more word of the *Cantigas*, he's going to throw himself out a window. "It's just that—you see, I discovered this—this journal, written in the sixteenth century."

Espinoza looks at him as if he's lost his mind. "A *journal*. I hardly think that can be considered Literature. I hope it is in Spanish, at least?"

"Um, no; Portuguese, actually. That is, I—I assume it is."

"You *assume* it is? What does that mean? It either is or is not."

"That's true, but you see, I—I won't be sure until--"

Before he has a chance to melt down completely, Gabriela comes to his rescue. "It is written in code. We have been trying to decipher it, but so far all we are sure of is that it's pol—poly--"

"Polyalphabetic?" offers Dr. Espinoza. "So. In order to read this journal of yours, you would not only need to be fluent in Portuguese, you would also have to be an accomplished cryptanalyst."

"Um, yes, well, I'll have Gabriela's help with the Portuguese, and I--I used to study codes and ciphers a lot, back in high school, so . . ."

"In high school." Espinoza sighs and rolls his eyes. "I hope it is a very simple cipher."

"We have made a lot of progress already," Gabriela assures him earnestly. "We think the author used an autokey."

Simon groans inwardly. She's not helping their cause; he can only hope that Espinoza has no idea what an autokey is, or how problematic it could be. No such luck. The professor lets out a sarcastic laugh. "Oh, well, that *is* encouraging! I hope you are prepared to spend the next five years on this thesis of yours."

"No, *Maestro*," says Simon. "That is, I—I feel confident that we can crack it in--in a matter of months." He only wishes he could manage to *sound* more confident.

"Do you indeed? Very well, Señor . . . "

"Hannay."

"Very well, Señor Hannay, let us suppose for a moment that you are somehow able to decipher this journal. It might be an interesting enough project, but it certainly does not constitute a thesis, at least not in Comparative Literature."

"No, *Maestro*. But I've done a good deal of preliminary research--" He waves the sheaf of notes and the copies. "--and I've concluded that I can do an in-depth analysis of how Renaissance scholars used codes and ciphers to conceal ideas and discoveries that they knew could get them in trouble with the Inquisition." Talking to professors is a lot like talking to girls; once he gets past the awkward parts and into scholarly mode, he does a lot better. "I've brought--"

Espinoza interrupts. "And you feel that this journal falls into that category?"

"Yes, I do. It's written by someone named Vicente, and at first I thought it might be Gil Vicente, but now I'm pretty certain that the author is a man named Vicente Marques, an adventurer and self-proclaimed *curandiero*--" He's quoting straight from the history book, here. "--who was accused of poisoning King João the Third." Of course, he's not really certain of it at all, but it certainly is a great selling point.

Gabriela is staring at him, wide-eyed. "Really? You didn't tell me that, Simon!" She sounds as if she's chiding him for holding out on her.

Espinoza is staring at him, too. The scowl has disappeared again, replaced by what appears to be genuine interest. His body language has been transformed, too. Until now, he was tilted back in his swivel chair, regarding Simon skeptically, like a judge who doesn't believe a word the defendant is saying. Now he's leaning forward, his elbows propped on the desk, his deep-set, heavy-lidded eyes fixed on Simon's face. "If you are correct, Señor Hannay, this would be a significant discovery."

"*Sí. Yo sé eso.*"

"Where is the journal now?" asks Espinoza—a bit too eagerly, it seems to Simon.

He and Gabriela exchange furtive glances. "Um, well I--I don't know, exactly," says Simon, which is technically true.

"You do not *know?*"

For some reason, the dream Simon had a week or so ago has come back to haunt him, the one in which he was tied to a chair, being badgered by his mother. Or was it someone else? A man, maybe? He can't quite recall. He does recall that feeling of being bound and helpless, though, and it makes him squirm uncomfortably.

For a moment, he's worried that Gabriela will spill the beans, but she seems to realize that he's deliberately being vague, and she keeps her appealing mouth shut. "I think maybe it's . . . being repaired or something," says Simon, which is also sort of true; at least, it's in the book repair room. "But we did make a copy of it."

"The entire journal?"

Again, the man sounds uncharacteristically enthusiastic, which makes Simon characteristically wary. "Well, the first couple of pages, anyway." He produces the copies from among his notes and holds them up.

Espinoza leans even farther across his desk, with an expression so covetous that it's almost creepy; he reminds Simon of a jock lecherously eyeing a shapely coed. "May I see them?"

Simon and Gabriela trade glances again; she gives a faint shrug. Simon, as usual, can't bring himself to say no; he places the passage of Portuguese and the page of ciphertext in the professor's outstretched hand. Espinoza scans them silently for a minute or more before he says, grudgingly, "You are undoubtedly right. This has to be a polyalphabetic cipher, and very likely one that makes use of a keyword or phrase, perhaps even an autokey."

"You're familiar with codes and ciphers?"

Espinoza lowers the papers and regards Simon the way he always regards the students in his classes—as if the question is so stupid it barely deserves a reply. "Yes, young man, I am. Intimately familiar, in fact. During the *Guerra Civil*, I was a *descifrador de códigos*."

"A codebreaker? Really?"

"Do you suppose that I would lie to you about such a thing?"

"No, no, of course not, I was—I was just-- Why didn't you ever tell us this in class? A lot of us--the guys especially--would have found it fascinating."

"It was not a class about codebreaking, or about the *Guerra Civil*. It was a class about grammar."

"Um, I read someplace that Franco's army used an enciphering machine; is that true?"

"An enciphering *machine*?" echoes Gabriela; the cryptology buffs ignore her.

"*Sí*," says Espinoza. "The ciphers were nearly impossible to crack, but we had a little success--enough so that the British and the French came to us for help later on."

"I do not mean to be rude, *cavalheiros*," says Gabriela, "but do you think we could return to discussing Simon's thesis? He has worked very hard to prepare his presentation."

Espinoza sits back in his chair again. "I don't know that there is anything further to discuss. He has explained the approach he intends to take, and it sounds reasonable enough. He says he has enough research material, and I believe him."

"So, then it's okay--?" Simon starts to say, but the professor interrupts again.

"I am not at all sure, however, that I believe you can decipher *this*--" He brandishes the ciphertext. "--in a matter of months." Both Simon and Gabriela open their mouths to protest, but Espinoza holds up one blunt, hairy hand to cut them off. "Let me finish. I was about to say, *without some assistance*."

"Um, well, I admit neither one of us is exactly an expert," says Simon, "but where would we find somebody who--" He breaks off as the professor's face resumes its *How can you be so stupid?* look. "Oh. You mean—you mean *you'd* be willing to--? But wouldn't that invalidate my thesis?"

"That is up me to decide, is it not?"

"I—I guess so." Now Simon is really starting to worry. What motive could the man possibly have for making such an offer? Because he wants to see Simon succeed? Not likely; it never concerned him before, when he was handing out all those Bs and Cs. In order to please Gabriela, then? Well, maybe. Or maybe he recognizes the importance of the codex and wants to stake his claim on it. The thing is, Simon can hardly refuse the offer. If he does, Espinoza may reject the thesis proposal altogether, and Simon will be back to playing the literary version of Beat the Devil.

"You do not seem thrilled by the idea," says the professor.

Simon can't think of a reply that doesn't sound insulting. Luckily, his diplomatic friend comes to the rescue again. "It is very generous of you, *Maestro*, and I am sure it would be a great help, but you see, at the moment we have only the one copy of the codex, so you can understand that we are reluctant to part with it. Perhaps when the journal turns up, we could make a second copy for you."

Espinoza doesn't look exactly thrilled, either. "Oh, I understand well enough—better than you think. I have been in academia long enough, *minha querida*, to know when someone is anxious to keep his research to himself, to avoid having to share the credit. There is no need to worry, young man; I have no intention of trying to, as you would say, 'steal your thunder.' I would simply relish the challenge of trying to decipher this, to see whether I still have the gift. God knows teaching ceased to be a challenge for me long ago. Perhaps you will not object to my making a copy of these two pages only? I will not show them to anyone."

Gabriela looks to Simon; unable to find a good reason to refuse, he nods, wincing at the twinge of pain it sets off in his head. Espinoza shuffles to the door, looking distinctly weary, as if the whole experience--having to consider a new thesis proposal and, even worse, having to ask someone's permission for something--has taken a toll on him. He closes the door behind him, but Simon can hear him saying, "Miss Cameron, would you please make copies of these?"

Gabriela leans in so close to Simon that he catches her signature scent. "Do you think it is true, what he said? That the codex may be a significant discovery?"

"I guess so--assuming our Vicente is the same one who poisoned the king."

"Do you suppose it is also true that he will not—how did he say?—*steal your thunder?*"

Simon sighs. "I don't know. Sometimes people are harder to read than codes and ciphers. I do think we should tell him as little as possible. Thanks for doing that."

"You are welcome." She chews on one of her ragged fingernails. Simon notices that she's not wearing the chunky silver rings; presumably they didn't go with the dress and the earrings. "Simon, if . . . if the codex is so important, perhaps it is best if I do not help you?"

Simon can't hide his alarm. "No, no, I still want you to . . . I mean—I mean, unless *you* don't want to . . . "

"Oh, I would like to, very much. I just didn't want you to think I was stealing your thunder . . . whatever that means."

Simon laughs, partly at her puzzlement, but mostly with relief. "Well, I read someplace that, back in the 1700s, this theater manager came up with a really good device for creating the sound of thunder—metal balls in a bowl, or something--and another theatre manager copied his idea. Anyway, I know you'd never do that." Never mind the fact that, not so long ago, he suspected her of appropriating the codex.

He's still not entirely sure of her motives, but the fact is, she already knows about the journal, so what can it hurt to let her work on it? Once they've cracked the cipher, he can always take over, do the actual deciphering and the unveiling of secrets. "Listen, when we're done here, would you—would you maybe like to go have a drink or something . . . you know, to sort of celebrate?" She gives him such a startled look that he hastily adds, "I mean, you don't have to. I just thought . . ."

"I am sorry," she says. "I do not drink."

"Oh. Well, I didn't mean a *drink* drink necessarily. Maybe just a *café com leite* or something at the Gedunk? But like I said . . ."

"All right. Yes. That would be very nice."

As they head across campus, Simon starts singing, under his breath, "Someone to hold me tight/That would be very nice . . . " He's barely aware that he's doing it until, to his delight, Gabriela joins in. Like him, she knows all the words to "Summer Samba." They alternate between the English and the Portuguese lyrics and finish with a string of *doo-doo*s, just like on the record. "You know Astrud Gilberto?" says Simon.

"Well, not personally. Brazil is a big country."

"Oh, I--I didn't mean—"

"I am joking, Simon."

He blushes. "I knew that."

"To be serious, I do like her music. In fact, I have three of her albums."

"Hey, maybe if I go to Brazil to study, I'll get to see her in person. On stage, I mean."

Gabriela laughs. "One thing at a time, *Senhor*. First, we have a cipher to decipher."

"Someone to cipher with," sings Simon, mostly to himself, "that would be very nice . . ."

When they're seated in the Gedunk with their *cafés*, he lifts his briefcase onto the table, more motivated than ever to attack the cipher. Gabriela runs her fingers over the soft, scuffed leather, which is nearly the same shade as the vellum cover of the codex. "That is a very impressive . . . what do you call it?"

"Well, I call it a briefcase."

She snickers. "A *brief* case? That is funny."

"It is?"

"Is that not what you call . . ." She leans toward him and whispers, "Men's underwear?" When his face goes red, she stifles another laugh. "I am sorry; I didn't mean to embarrass you."

"No, I--I'm not embarrassed, I just--"

"Yes, you are. Look at you. Oh, I am not making fun of you, Simon. I think it is sweet. Most of the boys I have met here are . . ." She trails off, frowning, and takes a sip of her *café*.

"Are what?"

She shakes her head. "I don't want to talk about that. Tell me about the briefcase." She suppresses another snicker.

"Not if you're going to keep laughing."

"I won't. I promise."

"All right. It belonged to my father. And, no, he didn't carry his underwear in it. Well, maybe once in a while, when he was on a business trip." He wags a finger at her. "Uh-uh, you promised."

Gabriela pulls down the corners of her mouth. "Sorry. What did your father do?"

"Well, when I was growing up, he managed a sugar beet factory."

"Really? We had one of those in Recife, but it closed down a while ago."

"So did the one where my dad worked, and then--" He almost adds, *And then my mother abandoned us.* But, as Gabriela said, he doesn't really want to talk about that. "—and then he started a martial arts *dojo.*"

"And he didn't need the—the briefcase any longer, so he gave it to you."

"Well . . . not exactly. I sort of . . . I sort of inherited it, actually."

"*Inherited?*"

"*Herdado.*"

"Oh. You mean . . . *seu pai está morto?*"

"*Sim.* He was . . . he was killed by a drunk driver." Like his claim that he didn't know where the codex was, this is technically true. But it's certainly not the whole truth. The whole truth is a lot more complicated and a lot more painful to think about, let alone talk about.

CHAPTER SIXTEEN

Sometimes Simon isn't sure he even remembers the whole truth about his father's death. Maybe his memories have turned into something like a mental master's thesis; no matter how conscientious a scholar you are, when you write a paper you inevitably have some sort of bias, a particular point you want to make, and you gloss over or ignore everything that doesn't contribute to making that point.

Or maybe he never actually knew the whole truth. He didn't see it happen, after all; no one did except for Mr. Wade, Joe's father, and he was drunk, as usual. When the man testified in court, he didn't deny that he'd been drinking, but he did deny that the accident was his fault. According to him, Simon's dad stepped into the street right in front of his truck, swinging a baseball bat, like he meant to smash the windshield, or maybe Wade's head. Wade said he jammed on the brakes and tried to swerve, but it was too late. Since there were skid marks at the scene, a shattered side window, and a baseball bat lying in the gutter, the jury bought his story.

Simon's testimony didn't go over nearly as well. He told the judge and jury what had happened when Wade visited the *dojo*, a couple of months before his father's death. The man was drunk then, too; he went on and on about how Don Hannay had turned his son against him by teaching him karate. He couldn't discipline Joe any more, he said. The last time he tried, the boy nearly broke his collarbone; he couldn't lift his arm for a week afterward—though he could clearly manage to lift a tequila bottle.

Simon's dad had listened to the tirade calmly, without comment, which just seemed to infuriate Wade more. Even drunk, he knew better than to swing a punch at a karate master. Instead, he delivered a warning: "You keep on teaching my son this martial arts shit, and you're liable to end up in a world of hurt."

Simon's dad had simply shrugged. "I'm pretty good at defending myself, Mr. Wade."

"Against fists, maybe. But that wasn't exactly what I had in mind."

Simon's testimony would have carried a lot more weight if, like his dad, he'd kept his cool. But he let the defense attorney get to him. He was seething inside, as he had after his mother left, and the lawyer kept making unpleasant insinuations about his dad: Was it true that he was a conscientious objector? Wasn't it his mismanagement that caused Carman Sugar to go under? Did he ever behave inappropriately toward his karate students?

The defense attorney should have been called an attack attorney; he was obviously trying to rattle Simon--leaning against the witness box, his voice raised, their faces no more than two feet apart. When he leaned in a little too close, Simon instinctively thrust out a hand, trying to make the guy back off. But somehow it turned into an actual blow that sent the lawyer reeling backward— or at least he pretended to. Simon was sure he saw a self-satisfied smirk flit across the man's face.

Naturally, the defense used the incident to their advantage. They began referring to karate as a "deadly weapon" and made it seem as though Wade had been the one under threat of violence. He was found guilty of vehicular manslaughter, but the sentence was pretty paltry-- two years in a minimum security prison, of which Wade served only one.

Simon had never quit feeling that he was somehow responsible for his mother's leaving. Now he had a new layer of guilt to spread over top of the old one. Not that it helped to bury the old guilt; it just made the ground more fertile for producing hurt and anger. He was mainly angry at himself, for failing to defend his dad. But he couldn't help feeling resentful toward his father, too, for abandoning him, just as his mother had. It wasn't fair or logical, of course, but that didn't make it any less real.

He should have wanted nothing more to do with karate, either; after all, it was to blame for everything, in a way. But it was also the only means he had of keeping the misery and remorse at bay. To his surprise, the other students—with the exception of Joe Wade, who had dropped out of school and disappeared-- kept showing up at the *dojo* to practice their *kata* or do a bit of *kumite*. And they kept paying their fees regularly, even though they no longer had an instructor.

It didn't seem quite right to take their money, but Simon couldn't afford not to. Though his dad had an insurance policy, the beneficiary was still listed as Delia Hannay. She didn't seem to know that, and Simon never mentioned it to her; why should she benefit from his dad's death? Besides, she had enough money already. He didn't tell her about the funeral service, either, but she showed up anyway--just long enough to pay her disrespects.

He was afraid she'd insist that he come to live with her and Wally, the used car magnate, but she didn't. He would have refused, of course; still, it would have been nice if she'd at least offered. She did offer to send him a little money each month—not much, mind you; Wally wouldn't approve—but Simon said he didn't need it. Not exactly true, but close; when he turned eighteen, he planned to sell the building they'd worked so hard to fix up and use the money for college. In the meantime, there was enough in the bank for him to live on—barely.

The summer before Simon's senior year, Matty Mays's dad returned from a trip to Wichita with heartening news: He'd met a martial arts instructor who was willing travel to Garden City once a week to teach at the Wado-ryu Academy. *Sensei* Randy proved to be kind of cool, in a self-impressed sort of way, but his approach stressed style more than skill. Still, Simon learned some valuable stuff from him. For one thing, he learned just how good an instructor his father had been.

Randy spent a lot of time trying to break them of the "bad habits" instilled in them by Don Hannay, to make them more aggressive, more competitive. Most of the students, being teenage boys, were fine with that. Unfortunately, as they got more competitive, they got less tolerant. Randy's attitude didn't help; though he never actually poked fun at the less athletic *karate-ka*, he did tend to overpraise the hot dogs.

Eager to please as always, Simon did his best to follow the new *sensei*'s lead. At the same time, he hated himself for it; whenever he worked on perfecting a flashy kick or spin, he could hear his dad saying, *"Mime yori kokoro."* Heart rather than appearance. When Simon realized that he was taking out his frustration on his sparring partners, often striking so hard that he left them bruised and complaining, he stopped attending the regular sessions and just practiced on his own the *kata* he'd learned.

Since then, with the small profit he made from selling the building, he'd been able to spend a couple of weeks each summer at various *dojos* in Kansas and

Ohio, studying with Okinawan-trained *sensei*. Some were quite good, but none was a replacement for his father.

.   .   .

Simon reveals none of this to Gabriela. He hasn't even told Mack much about that part of his past; why would he dredge it all up for someone he barely knows? He says only that his father was killed by a drunk driver. "I am so sorry," says Gabriela. "You must miss him very much."

Simon simply nods. Though languages are a huge part of his life, none of them has words that can convey how much he misses his dad.

"What about your mother?"

"What about her?" says Simon, a bit belligerently.

"Well, is she . . . is she still alive?"

"As far as I know. I still get a Christmas card and a birthday card from her every year." He digs into the briefcase and pulls out the manila folder containing their copies of the journal pages. "Let's talk about the codex, okay?"

"Okay."

"I guess theoretically, even if we don't crack the cipher, I could still do the thesis. But it'll be a lot more impressive if I reference some primary source nobody's ever used before."

"And it will be much more impressive if we do it ourselves, without Dr. Espinoza's help."

"*Exatamente*. So. . . Oh, shit."

"What is wrong? Simon?"

He lifts the pages from the folder and shows them to her. Espinoza didn't give them back their copies; he gave them the copies of the copies, which are so dark and blurry that they're practically unreadable. Even worse, the Xerox machine cut off the last couple of letters on each line. Simon sinks his throbbing head into his hands.

Gabriela touches his arm lightly. "*Fique tranquilo*, Simon; we can make new copies."

"Oh. Yeah. I guess you're right. I'm just not thinking real clearly. My head's still hurting."

"I am sorry. *É so estresse?*"

"I thought so at first, but now I wonder. I mean, usually I can get *un*stressed by doing karate, but it just seems to make things worse."

"Forgive me for asking, but have you taken any . . . any *narcóticos*?"

"Well, just aspirin."

"I do not mean things to *fix* the headaches. I mean things that might have *caused* them."

"Oh. No, I don't really mess with drugs--well, except for a few drags on a doobie once in a while."

She blinks at him in bafflement. "*Adobe*?"

"No, no. A doobie. *Cigarro de maconha*."

"Oh. *Claro*." Though it's not so obvious with her caramel-colored skin, he suspects that she's the one blushing for a change. As Mack would say, What a pair.

"It never gave me a headache, though, and anyway I haven't had any recently. Maybe I should." Most of the students he knows have a pretty casual attitude toward marijuana and peyote and kinnikinnick and such, but the topic clearly makes Gabriela uneasy. "I guess you're not into that stuff, either, huh?"

She shrugs and shakes her head, as if she's ashamed of being so square. "Before I left home, I promised my *padrinho* that I would not drink too much or do any drugs. For a long time I kept my promise; if I went to a party I never had more than one drink, and if people were getting high, I just left. But at this one fraternity party . . . " She pauses and takes a sip of her *café*, as though fortifying herself for what comes next. "At this one fraternity party, someone . . . someone slipped something into my drink. I do not know what it was exactly, but it tripped me out—is that how you say it?--and for weeks afterward I . . . I had headaches like yours. Now I do not drink at all. And I do not go to parties, either."

"Sorry; I didn't mean to-- It was none of my business."

"You must stop saying you are sorry, Simon."

"I will if you will."

She sticks out a hand. "It is a deal."

He holds onto her hand a little longer than is probably required to seal the pact, but she doesn't seem to object. "Um, I guess—I guess we should go copy those pages."

"Yes, let's. We must make sure Dr. Espinoza does not steal our thunder."

"Yeah. He has way more experience than we do, though. We'll have to work really hard."

She smiles and, sounding surprisingly like Judy Carne from "Laugh-In, says, "Sock it to me."

•   •   •

"Ms. Harris is not in today," says Gabriela as she lets them into the Rare Book Room. "Neither is Mrs. Pitman; we should have the place to ourselves."

"Unless Mystery Man turns up."

"Oh, don't say that. Who do you suppose he is? And why does he want our journal? How does he even *know* about it?"

"I hope those are rhetorical questions." Simon glances at the visitor register and groans.

"What is it?"

"He was here again. Three days ago."

"Oh, no!" Gabriela rushes into the book repair room and, pulling the file cabinet out from the wall, gropes around behind it. She looks so distressed that, for a moment, Simon is sure the book is gone. Then she gives a sigh of relief and, with a flourish, produces it like a rabbit from a hat. *"Graças a Deus!"*

While the Xerox machine warms up, Simon examines the stack of books awaiting repair. "Wow. There's some really old stuff here. Nothing on Portuguese history, unfortunately. I keep hoping I'll find another reference to Vicente Marques."

"Well, you know, the Inquisition had a way of making people disappear." She gives a small, bitter laugh. "Not so different from what the military is doing now in Brazil."

"Really? I didn't know things were that bad."

"Your government does not want you to know, because they support the regime. It is one of the reasons my *padrinho* sent me here to study—so I would be safe." She laughs again, even more bitterly. "If only he knew."

"What do you mean?"

"Que?" She seems unaccountably flustered. "Oh, *não é nada*; I only meant that--that the military seems to be running your country, too." She spreads out the loose page from the codex on the scanning glass. "We should hurry, Simon, in case the mystery man shows his face again."

"Right." Simon places both hands on the brittle, wrinkled paper and gingerly smooths it out. "Okay, go." When the exposure lamps pass beneath it, he notices again how the light forces its way through the tiny fissures. But this time it dawns on him that they're not just spots where the page has worn through. They're actual holes—all in a row, all the same miniscule size, all perfectly round, as if . . . as if someone has repeatedly poked a pin through the paper. "Um, Gabriela?" he says softly. "Don't get too excited, okay, but I think—I think I may have found the key."

"To the cipher, you mean? *Vixe Maria*!"

"Like I said, don't get too worked up; I'm not sure yet." He nods toward the Venetian blinds on the small window at the rear of the room. "Could you raise those, please?" Gingerly he lifts the crumpled page and presses it to the window pane. It's a gloomy day, and late afternoon to boot, but there's still enough light to reveal the complete array of tiny holes. They're clearly not random; each has been deliberately poked through the carbon ink at the base of one of the letters. "Oh, man," breathes Simon. "I was right. It's a pinhole code."

"The letters with the holes--they spell out the words of the key?"

"Maybe. Or maybe they just tell us where to find the key."

"You read them," says Gabriela, eagerly, "and I will write them down."

"Okay. Ready?"

"Ready."

"T—U—E—S—D--"

"Tuesday?"

"I don't think so. E—U--S—O—M—N—I—A—N—O—S—T—R--A. That's it."

Gabriela studies the letters she's printed. "It looks like Latin."

"Uh-huh. I studied it in high school, but it's been a while. TU . . . ES . . . DEUS . . . OMNIA . . . NOSTRA?"

"'Thou art, oh God, our all.'"

"Right. I guess you studied Latin, too."

"I was raised Catholic, Simon; I could hardly avoid it. So, do you suppose each letter indicates an alphabet in the—the--"

"The tableau? Possibly. Do you by any chance still have the one you made?"

Smiling a bit smugly, she lifts the back cover of the journal and pulls out the sheet of paper. "Taa-daa!"

"Good, good." Simon opens the codex to the first enciphered page. "If I read off the letters of the ciphertext, can you find the plaintext letters?"

"*Com certeza*."

134

"All right. Assuming that U is a null, the first letter is I."

Gabriela runs her finger along the alphabet that starts with T—the first letter of the key. "An I would be . . . a *p*."

"Next letter, R."

"That is a . . . an *x. Px*? I don't think so. But suppose that U is *not* a null, and we start with it, instead. Then we get . . . *b . . . o . . . n*! *Bon*!"

"Hey, maybe we're onto something! Keep going!"

"*M . . . f . . . y . . . g . . . l . . . d . . .*"

"Uh-huh. Okay, that's no good. Switching alphabets with every letter is a pain, anyway.. What if he used each alphabet to encipher a whole *line*? What does that give us?"

"*B . . . p . . . y . . . l . . . p . . .*" She makes a disgusted face. "*Vira o disco e toca o mesmo.*"

"*Que*?"

"Different record, same song."

"Okay, okay. Let me think. There has to be some reason why those letters at the beginning of each line repeat themselves."

Gabriela scans the initial letters. "U . . . D . . . T . . . Q . . . *Ai meu Deus*! It is so obvious!"

"It--it is?"

"Yes! *Um, Dois, Trés, Quatro*--"

"*Cinco, Seis, Sete, Oito, Nove, Dez*! Gabriela, you're brilliant!" He can hardly restrain himself from hugging her.

She seems pleased, and yet she shrugs. "It was pretty simple. Anyway, I am not sure it helps very much. So they are numbers--but what is he numbering?"

"Hmm. Well, if he actually *is* using a tableau, then maybe--" Simon is interrupted by a sharp rapping sound from out in the main room. "What the hell?"

"Ssssh! Listen!"

"Could you let me in please?" calls a man's voice. Though it's muffled by the plate glass, Simon catches a hint of a European accent. "Hello? Is someone in there?"

"It is the mystery man!" whispers Gabriela. "I recognize his voice!"

CHAPTER SEVENTEEN

Strangely enough, the man's voice rings a bell with Simon, too, though he can't imagine where he's heard it before. Even more strangely, it summons up that disturbing dream about being tied to the chair.

"Simon?" says Gabriela softly. "Are you all right?"

He rubs the back of his aching head. "Yeah. Sort of. Um, what should we do?"

"He cannot get in without a key. We will just have to wait until he goes away."

"I'm going to get a look at him."

"Don't let him see you!"

"I won't." In order to make room at the copy machine, they had to push the door to the book repair room almost closed, so Simon is able to creep unseen across the room. When he peers through the crack where the hinges are, he gets a glimpse of a large, pale-skinned, pale-haired figure in a pale suit standing in the corridor, pounding again on the glass. Well, he certainly doesn't *look* familiar. But that voice . . . "Come, come," it's saying, impatiently. "You must let me in. I have a permission slip."

"Can you see him?" whispers Gabriela right in Simon's ear, startling him. Her warm breath on his neck makes him shiver.

"More or less. I don't think I ever saw him before."

"Let me have a look." When she squeezes in next to him, her nearness and her scent make him lightheaded, like when the Horvaths idle their car in the garage and the fumes seep into his apartment--only a lot more pleasant. "I do not know him, either," says Gabriela. "Surely he must be a professor or something, though. Who else would care about the codex?"

"Maybe he's with the Inquisition; maybe it never actually died out."

"*Muito engraçado.*"

"I wasn't trying to be funny. I mean, who knows? Maybe the government just took over where the church left off. Wow. That sounds pretty paranoid."

"Yes, it does. Oh, Simon, I think he is leaving!"

"That's good. We'd better wait a while, just to make sure." Besides, he'd like to stay this close for a little longer—say, a week or so.

To his disappointment, Gabriela returns to the window, where she holds up the crumpled page again. "You know, when you mentioned the church just now, it made me think of something. That phrase—*Tu es Deus omnia nostra*—it is the title of a prayer."

"A prayer?"

"*Sim.* In the *Liturgia Horarum.*"

"I've heard of that. They're prayers that mark the hours of the day, right?"

"Right. I do not remember them very well, but--"

Through the window, Simon spots a tall figure crossing the parking lot below. "Get down!" he whispers, and waves his hands frantically.

"*Que--?*"

Simon drops to his knees. "It's him! Get *down*!"

Gabriela hits the floor, too. "Are you sure?"

"Pretty sure. I think he was looking up here, too."

She lets out a nervous laugh. "I feel as if we are in a James Bond movie."

"I hope he didn't see us, or he may come back." Simon scoots over closer to her. "Sorry, you were saying?"

"Well, I think that the *Tu es Deus* is the one that starts out *Utinam me illuc dignares adsciscere ad illum fontem.* But I could be wrong."

"You think the Taft has a copy of the Liturgy?"

"We could look in the card catalog."

As they crawl on hands and knees from the book repair room, Gabriela starts laughing again. "What?" says Simon.

"We look like elephants." She waves one arm in front of her face like a trunk, and makes a trumpeting sound.

"Will you stop?" whispers Simon. But he can't help chuckling, too. He's never seen her act goofy before. First the slinky dress, now this; the woman is full of surprises. Simon has always liked surprises; they're like secrets suddenly revealed.

The card catalog reveals that there is indeed a *Liturgia Horarum* in the BX2000 section. They manage to infiltrate the area without being seen by the mystery man—if he's actually still out there. Sitting side by side on the floor, they prop the volume on their knees and rummage through it.

Though Simon has as many sexual fantasies the next guy, his all-time favorite scenario is not exactly raunchy: In it, he and some alluring woman are huddled together . . . reading a book. At last the fantasy has come to pass. And somehow the fact that they're being stalked by a shady stranger bent on stealing the codex only adds to the thrill.

"Here's the *Tu es Deus*!" says Gabriela softly. "And it starts out just the way I said!"

Simon scans the prayer:

Utinam me illuc dignares adsciscere ad illum fontem, Deus misericors, pie Domine, ut ibi et ego cum sitientibus tuis vivam undam vivi fontis aquae vivae biberem, cuius nimia dulcedine delectatus sursum semper ei haererem et dicerem: Quam dulcis est fons aquae vivae, cuius non deficit aqua saliens in vitam aeternam!

"I told you, you're brilliant."

"Do you suppose it is the key?"

"Well . . ." When it comes to ciphers, it's best not to take anything for granted. "It's a good possibility. Do you have anything to write on?"

"The tableau."

"That'll work." Simon pulls a pen from his shirt pocket.

Gabriela swats his arm lightly. "You bad boy. You know pens are not allowed in here."

He feels himself flushing yet again. "I forgot. Sorr—um, never mind. So. Could you copy down the prayer? Twenty-six letters to a line, please?"

She does so, rapidly but very neatly, on the back of the paper. "Oh, look, Simon!"

"Sshh! Not so loud!"

"*Sim, sim*! But look! It comes out to exactly ten lines! Now we know what those numbers one to ten mean!"

Simon is getting that familiar tingle that always comes when he's close to cracking a tough cipher; it's not unlike being slightly stoned. He takes a few calming breaths to keep his mind clear. "Could you print a regular alphabet under each line of the key?" Though the task probably takes her no more than five minutes, it feels much longer.

"There. I do not remember any of the ciphertext letters. Shall I go and get the codex?"

"Not yet. I remember the first several words. IR EICADR--"

"Wait, wait. Let me see what that gives us. It looks like the I stands for . . . oh."

"An *o*?"

"No, no. An *i*."

"An eye for an eye?" quips Simon. When she glances at him questioningly, he says, "Never mind. Go on."

"The R is an *a*. The E is also an *a*. Then we have another *i*. The C is . . . also an *i*? Simon!" she wails. "This is not making any sense!"

"I know. Take it easy, okay? I think we're just making the same mistake we made before--doing it the wrong way around."

"*Que?*"

"Try using the key as the ciphertext."

"I am getting confused. You do it." She thrusts the paper into his hands.

He takes another calming breath. "Okay. So. If we do that, the I could stand for several different letters: a *c*, or an *o*, or a *z* . . . or even another *i*."

"But how do we know which one?"

"Whichever one is most likely to form a word. The R can only be one thing—an *s*. And *cs* isn't a word. Neither is *zs*."

"But *os* is."

"Right. So let's assume the first word is *the*, okay? Okay. Second word. The E could be an *h* or a *t*. The I could be . . . " Simon jots down all the possible plaintext letters and juggles them until he gets an actual Portuguese word: "*Homens. Os homens*. The men. Phew; this may be a quick and easy method for *en*ciphering, but it's going to be the very devil to *de*cipher."

"We cracked it, though, didn't we?" says Gabriela, positively breathless with excitement.

"Yes, yes, I think we did." To his astonishment, and perhaps hers as well, she flings her arms around his neck—only for a moment, but even so. Now he's the one who's breathless. "But, um, it could—it could just be a fluke. We won't know for sure until we do at least a couple of lines."

She rubs her hands together in anticipation. "When can we start?"

"As soon we can get out of here, I guess."

"It has been a half hour since Mystery Man left. I think we are safe."

"What do we do with the codex? We'd better not take it with us; I mean, he might ambush us or something."

"*Ambush?*"

"Lie in wait for us."

"Oh, but you could take care of him, Simon."

"Hmm. I'd rather not have to. I think we should leave the book here. Someplace where he'd never think to look."

Gabriela's jumps to her feet. "I know!" She heads for the book repair room. When Simon catches up, she's standing on a small stepladder, lifting up one of the acoustic tiles overhead. "I saw this in a spy movie," she says as she sticks the codex into the space above the dropped ceiling.

"Uh-huh. Let's just hope Mr. Huxley didn't see the same movie."

When they exit the Briggs, Simon glances about furtively. There's no sign of the mystery man. They make it all the way to the Gas Chamber without being ambushed by him, only to encounter another dread figure—Rhonda Horvath.

She and Mack are sitting—practically snuggling, in fact--on the landing outside the apartment. Mack raises a coffee mug that bears the Van Dyne logo. "Hey, roomie! *Que pasa?* How'd your meeting go?"

Simon really doesn't care to discuss the matter in front of the teenage slattern. "Pretty good. How's work?"

"I'm really cleaning up," says Mack. He sounds loopy enough to make Simon wonder what's in the cup. "Standard janitor joke. Seriously, it's not bad. In fact, I'm learning some pretty interesting stuff. Hey, Gabriela. Are you two an item, now, or what?"

Gabriela does not look amused. "I might ask you the same thing."

Mack laughs as if this, too, is a joke, which doesn't seem to sit well with Rhonda; she scoots as far away from him as the stairs will allow. Does she seriously consider herself and Mack an item? "I was just soaking up some sun," says Mack, "and she stopped by to ask if she could . . ." He gives the girl a sly sidewise glance. ". . . borrow a cup of sugar."

"Uh-huh," says Simon skeptically.

Rhonda rises and descends the steps a bit unsteadily, gripping the railing with one hand and with the other pinning her Mod mini skirt to her thighs, as if she suspects Simon of ogling again--which he sort of was. "I'd better get home. My folks will be wondering where I am."

Simon moves out of her way. "Sorry we didn't have any sugar." She ignores him. He turns to Gabriela. "So. You want to come in?"

"If it is all right."

"Sure." As they squeeze past Mack, whose bulky frame takes up most of the top step, Simon gives him a look that says *Are you out of your mind?* Mack gives his trademark *Hey, it wasn't my fault* shrug.

A half-empty pint of Seagram's 7 Crown on the table answers Simon's question about what's in the coffee cup. Not good. When Simon moved in, he promised that he wouldn't keep any liquor in the apartment. He caps the bottle and sticks it under the sink, then takes down the mac and cheese box and the bottle of aspirin.

Gabriela, meanwhile, is making herself at home, heating up tea water, setting out cups for them. Smiling, Simon watches her covertly, contentedly for a minute or two, until she catches him at it and rolls her eyes, which makes him grin even more broadly. Isn't it funny, after all those years of agonizing over how to talk to girls, to discover that sometimes there's no need to talk at all?

As Simon retrieves the codex pages from the box, Gabriela says, "We don't have to do this now if you don't want to, Simon. It is nearly dinner time."

"I'd just like to know we're on the right track. But if you'd rather wait . . ."

She laughs. "Me? No, no, no, I can't wait! Let's do it!"

"Hey, you guys!" comes Mack's voice from the landing. "Behave yourselves!"

It's hard to say who is more embarrassed, Gabriela or Simon. "Um, why don't we try the second page," says Simon, "to make sure we weren't imagining things? You have the key?

"*Claro.*" To Simon's surprise, she pulls off the baggy *Keep On Truckin.'* shirt, as if stripping for action. He almost wishes she'd left it on; it's going to be harder to concentrate now. "Proceed."

"Okay. Remember, the bottom line is ciphertext, the top line is plaintext. Here we go. Line *número trés*. EE."

"*Ai,* there are five possibilities for an E. Can we try the next word?"

"Sure. RB."

141

"The R could be an *a* or an *e*. The B has to be an *s*."

"So either *as* or *es*. Next word: IEIIEIR. 'Old MacDonald had a farm . . . "

Gabriela gives him an exasperated glance, then lists all the possible plaintext letters.

"The most common letters are the most likely," says Simon. "So. . . *hornurs*?"

"I think not. *Norturs*? I have it! *Tortura!*"

"Torture. Sounds like the Inquisition, all right. Okay, EE again. Then RB again. Then TEREIR."

"*Vieita*? *Queire*? No, no, it must *queima*."

"Burn." Simon winces. "Kind of gruesome, but it fits."

After an hour and a half of concentrated effort, they have two complete lines of pretty credible plaintext: *Ou as tortura, ou as queima na fogueira, simplesmente por procurarem a verdade--apesar de, no meu caso, ter estado bastante menos dedicado.* Or tortures them, or burns them at the stake simply for seeking the truth—although in my case, I have been somewhat less dedicated.

To Simon's surprise, the painstaking task hasn't made the pain in his head any worse; in fact, it actually seems to have let up a little. He is, however, ravenous. "I move we go get something to eat. We've earned it."

"Yes, we have. It will be my treat."

"You don't have to do that—"

"Simon, you should never look at the teeth of a gift horse. Where shall we go?"

"How about the Turtle Tap?"

She makes a disapproving face. "Isn't that where the jocks hang out?"

"Not many of them, and not usually until later in the evening."

"Oh. Well, I suppose it will be all right. Shall we ask Mack to come?"

Though Simon would prefer to have her all to himself, he says, "Um, I guess so. Jeez, you suppose he's still sitting out there on the steps?" Simon takes a look; the landing is empty. "Maybe he's already down at the Tap. He probably didn't want to cramp our style."

"*Cramp our style*? What does that mean?"

"Um, you know . . . get in the way, sort of?"

"Because he thinks we are an *item*?"

Simon gives an awkward, noncommittal shrug.

"I do not like that term very much," she says. "It sounds as if we are not people, just *haveres*."

"Possessions? Yeah, I guess it does."

While Simon replaces the copies in their box, Gabriela struggles into the baggy sweatshirt and flips up the hood. "I am ready."

•   •   •

Mack is engrossed in a game of pinball and, judging from his gleeful look, is about to Beat the Devil. Not wanting to distract him, Simon guides Gabriela to his favorite table, the one next to the gas fireplace; the walk chilled them just enough to make the fire feel welcome. "Is this okay?"

"Yes, it is lovely!" Holding her hands out toward the flames, she scans the room, which is not at all crowded, only a trio of non-jocks playing pool and a cluster of undergrad girls who, with their chattering and giggling, remind Simon of the Visigoths. The boys are surreptitiously eyeing the coeds, who pretend not to notice. "I am glad we came," says Gabriela softly. "I do not go out very much."

Though Simon could use a *drink* drink, he orders a mint hot chocolate in deference to Gabriela, who gets the same thing. As the waitress—a Science major he remembers from his Freshman Comp class--is taking their dinner order, Mack approaches their table, limping less than usual, and plunks down in a chair.

"Okay if I join you guys?"

"Sure," says Simon, less than enthusiastically.

"I won't stay long, I promise. I just wanted to--"

"Can I get you anything?" the waitress asks.

"Another Slider, please."

"What is a *Slider*?" Gabriela wants to know.

"Sloe gin and hard cider," says Mack. "It's better than it sounds. Listen, I just wanted to explain about Rhonda." He's slurring his words a little; either he's had a couple of Sliders already, or a couple or Darvon, or maybe both.

"Please do," says Simon.

"Like I said, I'm just catching some rays and winding down after work, and here comes Lolita—I mean Rhonda—sashaying across the lawn in her itsy bitsy teeny weeny mini skirt. She plunks her little butt—okay, medium-sized butt--down right next to me, and you know what she says?"

"'Can I cut your hair?'"

"Good guess, but no. She pulls out a twenty-dollar bill and she says, 'Would you sell me some grass, please?' like she's at the drugstore buying cough drops or something. When I tell her I don't have any--which is true--she gets all put out, like she thinks that *I* think she's too young to be smoking pot--which is also true. So then she says she'll settle for a swig of whatever is in the coffee cup. Somehow she knew it wasn't coffee."

"You didn't let her, did you?"

"I had to. She said if I didn't she'd tell her dad. Apparently we're not supposed to have booze in the place."

"No."

"Jeez, you could have told me."

"I thought you weren't supposed to mix alcohol and Darvon."

"I'm probably not. But Darvon by itself isn't helping much, lately."

Simon sighs. "Let's not talk about this right now, okay?"

Mack does his abashed Stan Laurel thing. "Oh. Sorry, Gabriela."

"It is all right." She leans in close to Simon. "Should we tell him about the—you know?"

"The You Know?" says Mack. "Oh, you mean the Kotex?"

Simon grimaces at him. "Will you please keep it down? We don't want the whole campus in on this!"

"Yes, the journal!" whispers Gabriela. "We deciphered it!"

"Whoa! The whole thing?"

Simon, who is sipping at his hot chocolate, snorts, sending a little of it up his nose. "Um, not quite. We did figure out two lines, though."

"Well, it's a start. I guess Dr. Tyrant is okay with you doing your thesis on it?"

"He is more than okay," says Gabriela. "He is as obsessed with codes as Simon."

"I didn't know that was possible. So, what does it say, man?"

"Ou as tortura, ou as queima na fogueira, simplesmente--"

"Har, har. Never mind; don't tell me. When the Inquisition comes to get you, I want to be able to plead ignorance." He peers at his empty glass. "She never brought me another Slider, did she?"

"No," says Simon, "and maybe it's just as--"

Mack hoists himself out of the chair. "Well, I'm going to sit over there and give you two some privacy. Leave a light in the window, okay, so I can find my way home." Whistling "Show Me the Way to Go Home," he snags a stool at the bar, where Alec hands him his drink.

Simon turns back to Gabriela, who is peering into her cup of hot chocolate with a look of distaste. "What's wrong? Don't you like it?"

"No, no it is very good. Nothing is wrong, I just . . . I am sorry, Simon, I have to leave; I will see you tomorrow." Before he can protest or even ask why, she's out of her chair and headed for the door, pulling up the hood of her sweatshirt like a medieval monk hiding his face from the world.

CHAPTER EIGHTEEN

Simon's first impulse is to go after her, but he's not accustomed to following his impulses. If she'd wanted him to come, wouldn't she have said so? And if she'd wanted him to know what the trouble was, wouldn't she have just told him? Well, maybe not. Maybe she wanted him to coax her a little, to show that he was really concerned. She said there was nothing wrong, but maybe that's code for *There is something wrong, but you have to pry it out of me.*

Certainly his mother played that game often enough, sometimes sulking for days before she finally revealed the root cause: They had failed to notice her new bracelet, or they hadn't praised her pot roast enough, or she had really wanted to see *Spartacus* but no one had offered to take her. More than once, Simon suspected her of fabricating some far-fetched grievance because she'd forgotten the real one.

He hates to put Gabriela in the same class with his mother, but what does he know? Maybe it's a game that all women play instinctively. In any case, it's too late now. She said she'd see him tomorrow, and he hopes that's true; in the meantime, he's just going to have to wonder.

"Here you go!" says the waitress cheerily, startling him out of his mental muddle. "What happened to your friend?"

"Um, I don't-- She—she had to leave. She has a, uh, a big test tomorrow." Which is almost true, if you consider deciphering the codex a sort of test.

"Bummer. Me, too. *Geology*." She shudders at the prospect. "Well. I hope you're hungry."

He is, but not hungry enough to eat both Gabriela's Augustus Caesar salad and his own Spaghetti Rosetti. "Um, could you ask Mack to come over here?"

He assumes that it's not necessary to identify someone who spends as much time here as Mack does, and he's right.

The big guy wastes no time in returning to the table. "Where did Gabriela get to?"

Simon makes a "keep it down" gesture. "She had to leave. You want her salad?"

Mack eyes the big bowl doubtfully. "Salad? Well, hey, why not? Food is food. So," he says, around a mouthful of greens and hard-boiled egg, "did you insult her, or what?"

"No, no. I don't know what her problem was. She said she was glad we came."

"Maybe she just got her period." When Simon gives him a disapproving glance, he shrugs. "Well, I mean, it does tend to make 'em a little touchy, you know."

"Yeah, yeah, just don't make any Kotex jokes, okay?"

"I wasn't going to. So, you cracked the code for sure?"

"It looks like it."

"Way to go. Cheers, man!" He raises his glass. "Wait, wait; you can't drink a toast with *hot chocolate*, for Chrissake. Alec! Fix the genius a Slider, will you!" He turns back to Simon. "How'd you manage it, man? Did you have some kind of inspiration, or something?"

"Yeah. You might say I saw the light. The light from the copier, shining through pinholes in the paper."

"Pinholes? You mean as in holes made with a pin?"

"Exactly. People used to use that method a lot to send secret messages. In this case, it spelled out the title of a Latin prayer that turned out to be the cipher key."

"Sounds complicated."

"It is. But you know what they say: *Whatever is good to know is difficult to learn.*"

"I never say that." The waitress delivers Simon's Slider and Mack gives her a big grin. "Thank you, Angie, my dear."

"You're welcome, Mack, my dear."

Though the endearments are obviously playful, Simon senses an undercurrent of real interest. "What happened to Maisie?" he asks, when Angie has departed.

"Oh, they let her and all the rest of them go after twelve hours."

"I wasn't talking about the sit-in. I mean, I thought you two were a--" He almost said *an item*. "—sort of a couple."

"Oh, that." Mack drains his Slider. "No, we agreed that we should cool it for a while. The university tends to frown on its employees fraternizing with Subversives and Revolutionaries. Well, damn. We were going to raise a toast, and I finished off my drink. I guess I'll just have to—"

"Here." Simon pours half of his Slider into Mack's glass.

"Thanks, man. Here's to--"

"Careful!" whispers Simon.

"I know, I know!" says Mack indignantly. "I may be drunk, but I'm not stupid."

"Sorry."

"Here's to knowing things that are difficult to learn." They clink glasses. "Especially women." He nods toward the bar, and Simon turns to see Angie and Alec chatting very chummily, standing about as close as two co-workers can decently stand during working hours. Mack sighs. "Leave it to Alec."

"Yeah, I hear he's a real lady-killer. Mostly I hear it from him."

"It's true, though. He switches girlfriends the way I switch majors. Well, he can have her. I've got Rhonda."

"Mack!"

"Just kidding!"

"You'd better be. They have laws about contributing to the delinquency of a minor or something."

"Tell *her* that. Well, I better get some Z's. I work night shift starting tomorrow. You want to walk me home, so I don't get accosted by some rapacious coed?"

"You wouldn't joke about that if you were a woman."

"Yeah, you're right." As he's heading out the door, he turns back to call, loudly enough for the whole Tap to hear, "Oh, hey, man, I Beat the Devil! 7,000 points! Whoo!"

Simon carries his drink over to the pinball game. Sure enough, Mack's score is up there on the back rack. It seems to Simon that Old Nick's grin looks a little less gleeful than usual. Maybe if he plays while the Devil is still demoralized from the defeat, he can manage to make a respectable score, too.

As he's getting a dollar's worth of dimes at the bar, Alec says, "Hey, what happened to you, Hannay?"

For a couple of seconds, Simon just stares at him, speechless. So much has happened to him today. But how would Alec know about any of it? "What--what do you mean?"

"I mean, you missed Karate Club. What could you possibly have found to do that's more important?"

"Oh, um, just—just working on my thesis."

"Did you have some kind of breakthrough or something?"

This sets Simon back again. Is the guy psychic, or what? "No, no. Just the usual slog. You know."

"Yeah, I do. That's ninety-nine percent of lab work, too--slogging." He hands Simon the dimes. "Remember, don't whack those flippers so hard; romance them a little."

"Right. Thanks." Simon isn't quite sure how you romance pinball flippers, but he does his best. It's useless; his final score is a pitiful 4,800; the Devil jeers at him. Simon can hear Alec laughing, as well, and he turns to glare in that direction. But the laughter isn't directed at him; Alec is just responding to something Angie the waitress said—some arcane math or chemistry joke, no doubt, one that only a fellow Science major could appreciate.

Simon sighs and downs the last of his Slider. Though he's cracked the Vicente cipher, there are so many other secrets in the world that he will probably never succeed in unveiling—how to Beat the Devil, for instance. Or how to deal with women.

•

Thursday morning drags by without any word from Gabriela, and Simon still has no clue how to contact her. He dives headlong into the codex, hoping to distract himself, and to some extent it works. Despite Mack's snoring, which is a bit too much even for the earplugs, he manages to dredge up two more sensible sentences from the morass of letters. There was a time when he'd have found that sort of progress exciting, even exhilarating. And it is still satisfying, in an academic sort of way; it's just not nearly as much fun without Gabriela.

He fixes a quick lunch of Chef Boy-ar-dee cheese ravioli. For some reason, the brand name, which has always made him snicker, now seems slightly sinister. And he never noticed before how much the mustached Chef resembles Hitler. At a quarter to one, he slouches off to his Contemporary Spanish Lit class.

The instructor, Señor Reyes, has either not heard the cliché about Spaniards being hot-blooded, or is determined to disprove it. He manages to suck all the magic out of magical realism, and make One Hundred Years of Solitude seem like a Thousand. At one point, Simon actually dozes off, something he almost never stoops to. When class is over, the prof calls, "Señor Hannay? I'd like to speak with you." Simon shuffles down the aisle, prepared to apologize, but before he can utter a word, Reyes says, "Dr. Espinoza is your advisor, *sí*?"

"*Sí. Por qué me lo preguntas?*"

"I thought you might like to know: He was taken to the hospital last evening."

"Really? What happened? Is he sick?"

"I'm not sure. I spoke with Miss Cameron; she seemed to think it might be his heart."

A reasonable assumption, considering his fondness for alcohol and cigarettes. "*Gracias, Profesor.* I'll see whether he's allowed to have visitors." A week ago, Simon probably wouldn't have bothered, but since their conversation about codes in general and the Vicente journal in particular, he feels more of a connection with the man. Of course, he also has a purely selfish motive: If the *Maestro* is seriously ill or even dying, Simon needs to know; it'll likely mean that his thesis is doomed, too. After all, what other professor is going to approve such an off-the-wall topic?

As he heads across campus, he's so preoccupied with these gloomy thoughts that he doesn't even notice Gabriela until she calls his name. He turns to see her hurrying toward him, her sweatshirt hood flapping in the breeze, her combat boots clomping on the sidewalk. "Hey. I'm, uh, I'm glad to see you. I was afraid that—well, that you were . . . I don't know."

"I am fine, Simon. I just . . . I was tired, that's all. I am sorry if I made you worry. And the dinner was supposed to be my treat, too."

"Oh, that's okay. Mack ate your salad. I think he actually liked it."

"Can I buy you something at the Gedunk, to make up for it?"

"Okay. But, um, right now I'm on my way to the hospital."

Her eyes go wide. "Are you ill?"

"No, no. It's Dr. E. He had a heart attack or something."

"Oh, no! May I go with you?"

"Yeah, sure."

The Research Hospital is a lot more attractive than its squat concrete neighbor, the Medical Sciences Center. It was constructed in the 1880s of limestone from the Bluestone Quarries in northern Ohio and, seen from the outside, it still seems to belong to another century. The interior, though, has kept up with the times. The reception area is all clean lines and bright lights and Norwegian furniture.

The receptionist informs them that Dr. Espinoza is in fair condition and able to receive visitors. Whether he's *willing* to receive them is another story, according to the nurse on the ward. "He is not one of our more cooperative patients, I'm afraid."

"Why am I not surprised?" murmurs Simon.

"Could you tell him that Gabriela would like to see him?" When the nurse goes to convey the message, Gabriela whispers, "I wish I had worn something more attractive; he is liable to tell my *padrinho* that I have become a hippie." She wrestles off the sweatshirt, revealing a sweater that Simon considers quite attractive. "There; that's a little better." Simon is tempted to ask why she keeps wearing her usual outfit, if she knows how unflattering it is—but of course he doesn't.

The nurse returns and leads them to Espinoza's rather claustrophobic double room. At least he has the place to himself; well, who could bear to share it with him? He's propped up with pillows, his shaggy mane spread out on the white linen like a dark halo; an oxygen tube dangles from his nose, along with a good deal of gnarly nasal hair. Ignoring Simon, he fixes his heavy-lidded gaze on Gabriela. "Had I known I would have such a lovely visitor," he rasps, "I would have insisted that they shave me."

She sits on the edge of the bed and takes his hand. "How are you feeling, *Maestro*?"

"My head hurts. Did they tell you what is wrong with me?"

"No. Have they not told you anything?"

"The physician—who was here for approximately thirty seconds--seemed convinced that it was a drug overdose." He gives a feeble, sardonic laugh. "The only drug I am accustomed to use is whiskey, and I had very little of that . . . as far as I can recall." He grimaces and puts a hand to his head. "They say I called for an ambulance, but I cannot remember doing so. I cannot remember anything, really, after . . . "

"After what, *Maestro*?"

Espinoza squeezes his eyes shut in concentration. "I was in my office, marking papers—a task which needs a glass of whiskey and soda to be bearable—when there was a knock at my office door. The visitor said he had been a student of mine, some years ago. I did not recognize him, but that is not surprising; I make it a point to forget my students as quickly as possible."

In fact, Simon says silently, *you're often not quite aware of them in the first place.*

"What *was* surprising was his claim that he very much enjoyed my class. Indeed, he said it *inspired* him to continue his studies, and he had come to thank me and to give me a gift—a bottle of Calisay liqueur, which we wasted no time in sampling. And . . . and that is the last thing I remember."

"Do you suppose . . . ?" says Gabriela hesitantly. "Could the liqueur possibly have been drugged?"

"I suppose it is *possible*. But why?" He laughs humorlessly again. "Perhaps the man was lying; perhaps my class actually ruined his life and he is taking his revenge."

Simon speaks up for the first time. "Um, do you mind if I ask. . . what did this man look like? Do you remember?"

Espinoza casts him a withering look, as if Simon has questioned his sanity. "Of course I remember. He was quite large, with skin and hair almost like that of an albino--or *un fantasma*. Both his Spanish and his English were spoken with a slight accent—German, I suspect."

Simon exchanges glances with Gabriela. She's clearly thinking the same thing he is: It's the mysterious Mr. Huxley; it has to be. He doesn't give her a chance to say it aloud. "Um, I guess we should go; we don't want to wear you out, *Maestro*. Can I—can I just ask one other thing?"

The Professor sighs. "I suppose so."

"Did you—did you put the copies of the codex somewhere safe?"

"In my desk drawer." He manages a small, sly smile. "Next to my bottle of 1960 Saburomaru."

As they're leaving, Gabriela whispers, "Why did you not tell him about the mystery man?"

"I didn't want to worry him. I don't think we should tell him about the cipher key, either. I have a feeling that, at this point, the less he knows, the better."

When they enter the Language Department office, Marnie is on the phone. "No, I'm sorry; I don't know anything more than that. Yes, sir; as soon as I find out anything, I'll let you know. Yes, sir." As she hangs up, she gives a weary sigh. "If you're here to see Dr. Espinoza, I'm afraid—"

"Yes, we know," says Gabriela. "We have just come from the hospital."

"Oh! How is he? Is he--"

"He says that his head hurts, and he can't remember what happened; otherwise, he is his usual disagreeable self."

"Did they say what's wrong? Is it his heart?"

Gabriela gives Simon another sidewise glance. "I think they are not quite sure yet. I suppose they will need to run tests or something. He asked us to bring him a few things from his office. Would that be all right?"

"Yeah, sure, go right ahead. The door's open."

As Gabriela closes the office door behind them, she says softly, "I wonder whether she has a key for his desk?"

"It doesn't look as if we'll need it," says Simon. The drawer has been forced open, the cam on the lock snapped in two. The bottle of Saburomaru is there, just as Dr. Espinoza said. The pages of the codex are not.

CHAPTER NINETEEN

Simon sinks into the professor's swivel chair and holds his aching head. "Oh, great! The mystery man must have taken the copies."

"But how could he even know that Dr. Espinoza *had* them?"

"Maybe . . . maybe Marnie told him? Or maybe he's shadowing us."

"*Shadowing*?"

"Watching us. Keeping track of our moves."

Gabriela shivers. "This is getting creepy, Simon."

"Kind of scary, actually. I mean, this guy wants the codex bad enough to drug somebody."

"But why bother? Why not just break in when no one was here?"

"Maybe . . . maybe he wanted to question Dr. E, find out whether he's cracked the cipher."

"How would it help to drug him?"

"Well, what if it was some kind of truth serum or something? Like Devil's Breath."

"*Devil's Breath*?"

"Uh-huh. I guess it breaks down your inhibitions, so you tell people whatever they want to know." Simon has no idea where that arcane bit of knowledge came from. It's like with Vicente Marques: He doesn't recall ever reading about Devil's Breath, or any truth serum for that matter, but obviously he must have. "Listen, Gabriela, if you don't want to keep doing this, you don't have to."

"No, no, I would like to, please."

"I just don't want to put you in any kind of danger."

She shrugs. "I have been in danger before, Simon. It does not frighten me. Especially now that I am studying karate. I know, I know, I am not very good at it yet. But I will be."

"Okay, I guess," says Simon, with a reluctance in his voice that he doesn't really feel. The truth is, if she'd backed out, he'd have been devastated. "We've got be more careful, though. I mean, suppose Huxley turns up while we're working on the cipher? We need to find some safer place."

"The library? There is usually someone there from Campus Security."

"Okay. Not the Rare Book Room, though; that's the first place he'll look. How about one of the study rooms? They lock from the inside."

"That is a good idea." As they're leaving, Gabriela stops to speak with Marnie. "Do you remember the copies you made for Dr. Espinoza yesterday?"

"Which ones? He has me make a *lot* of copies."

"These were in *Português*."

The girl gives an apologetic grimace. "I'm sorry, Gabriela; I'm afraid I don't pay much attention to what I'm copying. Were they important?"

"Oh, no, not really. He just wanted to see them; I am sure it can wait until he is feeling better." As they exit, she whispers to Simon, "I think she is telling the truth. Can we go get our own copies now? I am worried about them."

So is Simon, of course, but he's almost equally worried about Rhonda Horvath. Obviously part of her plan for becoming a full-fledged woman is to snag herself a college jock--even a disabled one. To his relief, she's not hanging around the Gas Chamber—nor, as far as he can tell, is the mystery man.

It's also a relief, considering how much time Mack spends in bed, to find him fully awake and dressed for work. He's chowing down on Wonder Bread and canned baked beans; in fact, he's combined the two in a gross, lopsided sandwich with bean juice seeping from it like blood from a scraped knee.

"Speaking of knees--" says Simon.

"Were we?"

"Well, no. I was just wondering how yours is doing."

"Not good," says Mack grimly. But when he heads for the door, Simon notices that he's barely limping at all. "Stay out of trouble, you two."

Gabriela gives him a semi-serious frown. "And you as well."

"Listen, Mack," says Simon. "If you see anybody lurking around outside, let me know, okay?"

"Like who, for instance?"

"Like Rhonda, for instance." Though Simon meant it as a joke, Mack doesn't look amused; in fact, he looks distinctly guilty. Great; so she *has* been hanging around. "Seriously, I meant the mystery man. We think he's stalking us."

"Whoa. He must really want that Kotex. What does he look like?"

"Big and blond. When I saw him, he was wearing a white suit."

"Obviously he has no fashion sense. Nobody in the know wears white after August. If I see him, what should I do? Punch him out? He's not armed, is he?"

"No, no. Just let me know, okay?"

"Roger that. Good luck with the deciphering."

"Thanks. Good luck with the janitoring."

"Yeah. Man, you wouldn't believe the stuff those lab rats leave laying around."

"What do you mean?" asks Gabriela.

Mack wiggles his scarred eyebrows and says, in a conspiratorial whisper, "I'll tell you sometime when I'm not in a hurry. *Adiós.*"

"He asked whether the mystery man is *armed,*" says Gabriela. "What did he mean?"

"Um, you know, with a gun or a knife or something? Don't worry, I'm sure he's not."

"If this were Brazil, he would be." She takes down the mac and cheese box and pries the top open. "Ah, the copies are just as we left them. Let's get them out of here while we still can, okay? I think we should split up, Simon, like they do in spy movies. That way, Mystery Man will not know which one of us to follow."

Simon studies her face, which doesn't look worried or scared so much as just excited. "You're enjoying this whole thing, aren't you?"

"*Sim!* Aren't you?"

"Not especially."

She gives him a skeptical smile. "Not even a little bit?"

"Well, okay, a little bit, I guess. At least I'm enjoying being with . . . I—I mean . . ."

Her smile fades. "Do not say it, Simon. Please? Let us just think about the codex for now, all right?"

"Okay. Sorry. So. We split up and meet at the library, right? Should we synchronize our watches?"

She giggles. "I do not have a watch. Which one of us should take the copies?"

"Um, I guess I will?"

"I agree. You can defend yourself better. For now." Her combat boots perform a clunky tap dance step. "And you can probably run faster, too. I will see you soon."

Simon gathers up his bulky research books; he won't be needing them anymore, thank god. And they make a handy camouflage for the codex copies. He sticks several pages inside each of the volumes and crams everything into Mack's Van Dyne Sliders bag, which he's inherited now that Mack is, as he puts it, just an ordinary shmoo—by which he means *schmo,* as opposed to the cartoon creature from *Li'l Abner.*

Simon takes a roundabout route to the Briggs, stopping several times ostensibly to tie his shoe or shift the gym bag, but actually in order to glance surreptitiously over his shoulder. If anyone's following him, it must be The Invisible Man.

He and Gabriela agreed to meet near the reference desk, but there's no sign of her. Simon sits with the gym bag in his lap--one arm through the straps in case someone tries to snatch it--for a quarter of an hour before she turns up, also carrying a gym bag. "I am sorry to be so late, Simon!" she says breathlessly, then leans in close to whisper, "I brought us food from the Gedunk! Do not tell anyone!"

As they hurry upstairs, Simon says, "Did anybody follow you?"

She shakes her head. "Twice I hid in a doorway and waited to see, but there was no one."

"Don't tell me—you saw that in a spy movie."

"Yes. A very bad one."

They claim a vacant study room on the second floor—best not to get too close to the Rare Book Room—and settle in. Gabriela tapes notebook paper over the windows so no one can spy on them and pulls their lunch from her gym bag. "I got a fruit smoothie for each of us, and some cheese enchiladas. Okay?"

"Terrific. I'm starved."

"So am I. But we can work while we eat, can we not?"

Simon grins and shakes his head. "Spoken like a true cipher fanatic."

They puzzle out an entire paragraph of Portuguese plaintext before they grow punchy and start making too many mistakes.

*Os homens que se veem numa situação tão desesperada como a minha
estão habituados a culpar os Fados, ou o alinhamento dos planetas, ou a
estupidez de outrém, mas se eu o fizesse estaria apenas a iludir-me. Deus,
se algum existir, sabe que tenho muitas outras falhas e vícios, mas a auto-
ilusão é uma falha que, pelo menos, faço o que posso para evitar. A triste
verdade, é que a culpa da minha condição assenta inequivocamente sobre
os meus ombros. Cometi uma enorme variedade de pecados, e agora devo
expiá-los.*

Gabriela smiles wearily but proudly. "I can't wait to wave this in Dr.
Espinoza's face. He didn't think we could do it."

"Well, I'd prefer to wave a lot more. I mean, obviously we'll have to show
him *something*, to prove we're making progress. But let's wait till we have a couple
of pages, okay?"

"Okay. What do we do with this in the meanwhile?"

"I've been thinking about that." Simon starts to reach into the gym bag, but
Gabriela clamps a hand on his arm.

"No, wait, Simon. Perhaps it is better if you hide it and do not tell me
where."

"Why? I trust you."

"Thank you. Of course I would never give anything away--not willingly. But
what if . . . what if the mystery man does to me what he did to Dr. Espinoza?"

"Jesus, Gabriela; don't even say that."

"But it is possible. As you said, what if he used some sort of truth serum?
What did you call it? Devil's Breath?"

"Shit. I wish you'd never gotten involved in all this. I'm sorry."

"I am not. Don't worry, Simon; I will be careful. I already am, in fact; I go
out only when there are many people around." Except for last night, Simon
almost says, but doesn't. She stuffs their paper plates and cups and napkins into
her gym bag. "I will meet you downstairs. Take your time and find a very good
hiding place."

"I will." When she's gone, he pulls out the oversized volume of the *Cantigas
de Santa Maria* and opens the back cover. The endpaper has come partially

unglued and the binding has pulled loose, revealing the rags that were used for padding, back when padded covers were the rage.

He pulls out the padding, replaces it with the copies of the codex pages, and sticks down the endpaper inconspicuously, using folded-over strips of Scotch tape. Then he carries the volume to the PQ9000 section and shelves it—not in its proper place, but in the adjacent aisle, just in case some crazed scholar comes looking for it. Not very likely, considering that, according to the due date card, the last time it was checked out was May 1941. In any case, the pages are bound to be safer here than in a macaroni and cheese box.

As they're leaving the library, Simon glances about cautiously, almost fearfully, the way he's seen Gabriela do so many times—the way she's doing right now. "This feels kind of silly," he says softly. "Obviously nobody's following us."

"Just because you're paranoid doesn't mean they aren't after you."

Simon lets out a surprised laugh. "You've read *Catch-22*?"

"*Sim*. In American Lit. Well. I suppose we should split up again."

"Um, okay. If you want to."

"I don't *want* to, exactly. But it is probably best."

"I just thought maybe you'd want to go to the Turtle Tap or . . . or someplace."

"No."

Simon was kind of hoping that, if he mentioned the Tap, she might tell him why she took off the night before; instead, it's made her clam up. "I, um, I thought maybe I'd look in on Dr. E again tomorrow morning, see how he's doing."

"Should we tell him about the missing copies?"

She said *we*; that's encouraging. "I guess we'll have to. Maybe he'll remember something more."

"I have a class at ten o'clock; we could meet after that. At the Gedunk?"

"It's a date. I—I mean, not like a *date* date, just—"

She smiles and nudges him gently in the ribs. "I know, Simon. I will see you tomorrow."

"Be careful!" Simon calls after her, and she waves her silver-ringed hand in acknowledgement.

•   •   •

Sometime during the night, Simon is treated to a rerun of that disturbing dream, the one where he's bound to a chair, unable to move, being tormented by someone. He can't quite make out who it is, but this time he's sure it's not his mother. There's no scent of *L'Interdi*. Instead, his tormenter gives off a rank, repulsive smell, something like sweaty socks.

The figure leans in closer. Though its face is still indistinct, its foul breath is overwhelming; it envelops Simon like a cloud of poison gas, making him cough and gag. The Devil's Breath.

He sits up in bed, gasping, and knocks heads with the dark shape that's looming over him—a flesh and blood person, not the figment of a dream. "Ow! What the hell--?!"

"Jeez, man; take it easy, okay? It's just me."

"Mack? What time is it?"

"I don't know. Three-thirty or so, I guess. I just got off work."

"And why are you hanging over me like a vulture?"

"I gotta tell you something."

"Can't it wait till morning?"

"No." He switches on the bedside lamp, temporarily blinding Simon. In the nearest thing to a whisper Mack can manage, he says, "You know that guy you told me to watch out for? The mystery man?"

"Yeah?"

"I think I just met him."

Simon shakes his groggy head and rubs the sleep from his eyes. "You *met* him? Where?"

"In the Ratitorium."

"The *what*?"

"Sorry, that's what we call the Medical Sciences Center. It's my job to go around and clean all the offices, right? Well, usually they're empty by that time, but there's this one guy who's working late. I've gotten know most of the staff, but I don't remember ever seeing this cat before. He's not wearing a lab coat, like most of them; he's dressed like you said, in a white suit. He's almost as big as me, and has short blond hair and a little accent of some kind."

"He spoke to you?"

160

"Yep. Hang on a second." Mack retrieves the bottle of Seagram's from under the sink and pours himself a shot, which he uses to wash down several Darvon. Seeing the look of disapproval on his friend's face, he says a bit defensively, "It helps me sleep, okay?" Before he puts the whisky bottle away, he pours a second dose.

"So, anyway, the guy asks me if there's any place in the building where he can get some coffee. I tell him there's a vending machine on the third floor that dispenses something they *call* coffee, though I think a more accurate term would be horse piss. He laughs and says isn't it ironic that his colleagues can synthesize all sorts of lifesaving drugs, but they can't make a decent cup of coffee."

"His colleagues? So he works there?"

"Well, apparently not. I tell him I'm going to go clean another office and I'll come back and do his later. He says there's no hurry, since he's not going to be using it any more. I don't want to sound too nosy, so I just say, 'Oh, you're leaving?' He nods. 'Going home tomorrow morning. Unfortunately.' 'Where's home?' I say, real casual, and just as casual he says, 'Delaware.' I say, 'I didn't know anybody actually lived in Delaware,' and he laughs. 'I certainly would not, if I had my choice.'

"Well, I move on, but as soon as he goes upstairs for his coffee, I slip back into the office to see what I can see, which is not much. *But* . . . there is this Telex message on the desk from a company called AllChemi, sent to the attention of a Dieter Weiss. It says they've made airline reservations for him for tomorrow. Which is today. So. I guess now we know your mystery man's name."

"But he signed into the Taft as Thomas Huxley."

"Obviously an alias. Huxley was the guy that got people to take Darwin seriously."

"Oh, yeah. I thought it sounded familiar."

"So does the name AllChemi."

"It's a pharmaceutical company, right?"

"It's a lot more than that. Just like the name implies, anything that involves chemicals, they've got their big old nasty tentacles in it: drugs, herbicides, chemical weapons, fertilizer, paint, explosives, synthetic fabrics, you name it. And guess what? They also fund most of the university's medical research."

"How do you know all this?"

"I told you, those lab rats leave all kinds of stuff just laying around. And their wastebaskets? Man, they're like little treasure troves of information."

161

"You search their *wastebaskets*? Mack, you're going to get yourself fired."

"Suits me. I mean, it's not like I really wanted to work there."

"So why are you? There were other jobs you could have applied for." Instead of replying, Mack gives his familiar *Hey, it wasn't my fault* shrug. Simon stares at him for a long moment, as the truth sinks in. "Oh. I get it. The SDS put you up to this, right? You're their inside man."

Mack still doesn't say anything; he doesn't need to. The abashed Stan Laurel head rub says it all.

CHAPTER TWENTY

Though Mack conks out within minutes, Simon lies awake until dawn, mulling over the crooked pieces that Mack has added to the puzzle, trying to figure out where they fit. When it's light enough, he gets dressed and heads down to Dad's Restaurant for breakfast.

On his way back to the Gas Chamber, he spots the teenage slattern and two of her friends flouncing down the sidewalk, on their way to school. Simon crosses the street and keeps his head down, but he can't escape Rhonda's roving eye. When she catches sight of him, she makes little pointing motions in his direction and murmurs something secret and snide to her sidekicks, who let go a barrage of giggles. It's almost like Frank and his *compañeros* all over again; good thing he doesn't have a scytale.

Simon spends the morning doing what he always does when real life gets too muddled--he buries himself in a book, specifically a facsimile of Samuel Pepys' original diaries. Unfortunately, it turns out they weren't written in cipher at all, just an early and very unwieldy system of shorthand. Apparently Pepys didn't actually have anything to hide; he just wanted to write quickly.

Simon also keeps a close eye on his father's watch; when eleven o'clock approaches, he hurries to the Gedunk, hoping Gabriela hasn't changed her mind. No, in fact, she's actually beat him there, and has even ordered a Brazilian Dark Roast for him. "Are you all right, Simon? You look *exausto*."

"Yeah, I am, kind of. I didn't get a lot of sleep." Between sips of coffee, he recounts Mack's encounter with the mystery man. Naturally he tells her nothing about Mack being a spy for the SDS; Simon only wishes that *he* knew nothing about it. He has a feeling that, whatever the lab rats are up to, it may be one of those secrets he's better off not knowing—like the fate of Peri Jurado, or his father's service record, or the things the Mexicano boys were saying about his mother.

"But that makes no sense, Simon. What would a drug company want with our codex?"

"That's what I keep asking myself. But myself isn't giving me any answers."

"Perhaps we should tell this to Dr. Espinoza; it might—how do you say?— jog his memory?"

The professor looks a bit more civilized today—he's lost his whiskers and his oxygen tube--but his attitude is uncivil as ever. "I hope you brought the bottle of Saburomaru," he growls.

"You are joking, right?" says Gabriela.

"Not at all. What is the point of your coming if you don't bring whiskey and cigarettes? I don't suppose you brought the codex pages, either? I need something to occupy my brain. I refuse to watch the *caja boba*." He nods contemptuously at the television on the wall.

"Um, actually," says Simon, "the copies are gone, *Maestro*. Somebody broke open the drawer."

"*Mierda*! It must have been my pale-faced visitor! I *knew* there was something suspicious about him, the moment he said that my class inspired him."

"Did he ever tell you his name?"

Espinoza shakes his shaggy head and winces with pain. "If he did, I have forgotten it."

"Does the name Dieter Weiss sound familiar?"

"No. Should it?"

"I don't know." Simon gives Gabriela a questioning look.

She nods. "Tell him."

"Tell me what?" demands the professor.

"Um, well, it sounds like your visitor is the same guy who's been asking about the codex. Apparently he thinks we have it."

"And *do* you?"

"No." Not literally, anyway. "But he searched my apartment, and we're pretty sure he's been . . . well, following us. Okay, that sounds kind of far out. But, I mean, how else would he know that we came to see you?"

"And what did you say this man's name is?"

"Well, we think it's Weiss; Dieter Weiss. Again, this sounds a little strange, but it seems he works for--for a big chemical company."

"A *chemical* company?"

"Yeah, I know; why would he be interested in the codex, right? We thought maybe you could tell us."

Espinoza gives a scornful snort. "Well, you thought wrong. I can think of no conceivable reason. Perhaps you are working too hard on the cipher, young man, and your fevered imagination is running away with you."

Before Simon can protest, Gabriela says sweetly, "Perhaps so. And perhaps you only imagined that this man drugged you, *Maestro*, and stole your copies of the codex."

The professor's face forms a Beethovenesque scowl. "Yes, yes, very well. Let us suppose, then, that you are right. Let us suppose that--god only knows why--he does want the codex. What good will it do him if he cannot decipher it?"

"Well, maybe he doesn't want to," says Simon. "Maybe he's just a--a rare book collector or something."

Espinoza shakes his head again, and again the pain makes him wince. "No, no, no," he says, and sighs heavily. "*Jesucristo*, I would kill for a cigarette. All right, listen. I told you I remembered nothing that happened after I drank the liqueur, but that is not quite true. You see, last night I had a dream—a nightmare, really--in which I was being interrogated. I have had similar dreams ever since the war, when Franco's men worked me over, trying to learn what I knew of their codes and ciphers. But this time was different. This time my interrogator mentioned a truth serum--Devil's Bread, or something like that."

"Devil's Breath," says Simon, almost to himself.

"That may have been it."

Gabriela casts Simon a startled glance. "That is the same term *you* used."

"So it is a real thing?" asks Espinoza.

"Um, I—I think so. I think I read about someplace. But maybe--"

"Maybe *what?*" demands Espinoza.

"Well, I--I've been having that same sort of dream. But nobody's drugged me or anything."

"Are you certain? Perhaps you just do not remember."

Simon holds his head, which has begun throbbing again. "I--I don't know. My mind's all mixed up."

Gabriela gently strokes his shoulder. "It is all right, Simon. It does not matter."

"But it *does* matter," insists the professor. "If this Weiss *tipo* drugged you, too, then perhaps he got you to reveal something—the location of the codex, or the key to the cipher, or both."

When Simon can't manage a reply, Gabriela jumps to his defense. "I am certain that he did not, *Maestro*. For one thing, Simon didn't *know* where the codex was. Also, he had not cracked the cipher. That is why the mystery man came after *you*."

"All right, all right. I am not thinking very clearly, either. So. What do we do now?"

"Well, we could tell the police--have *Senhor* Weiss arrested."

"It's probably too late," says Simon. "He flies back to Delaware today. That's where the company's headquarters are."

"Does that mean that he has given up?" asks Espinoza.

Simon shrugs. "Your guess is as good as mine."

"Well, he now has two pages of the codex. My guess is that he will try to decipher those."

"He will not be able to," says Gabriela. "Not without the key, and it is--" She breaks off as Simon throws her a warning glance.

"Yes?" prompts the professor. "It is *what*?" When she doesn't reply, he smiles grimly, knowingly. "So. You have found the key, eh?" Still no reply. He makes a weary dismissive gesture. "Never mind; you do not need to answer. I learned long ago how to read my students' faces--my own version of a truth serum, you might say. I only hope that, if you decipher it, you find a good hiding place—both for the plaintext and for yourselves. Somehow I doubt that the mystery man is done with you."

Sighing again, he lies back on his pillows and closes his eyes. "I will not offer my help. I doubt that you either want or need it--or that I would have much to contribute, in any case." His eyes open a little and he turns his head toward them. "May I offer one word of advice, though?"

Gabriela takes his hand. "Of course, *Maestro*."

"You will want to publish as soon as possible, before this Weiss person steals your thunder. In that respect, at least, I *can* be of help. I have contacts at some of the best scholarly journals; in fact, some were students of mine. I would also advise you to translate into English, so you do not limit yourselves to Portuguese-language journals. Of course, that will make it even easier for the mystery man to read. I wish I knew why he is so eager to get his hands on it."

"Well, Vicente does say that it contains dangerous secrets."

"Thank god for that. There are enough dull old diaries in the world already." He slips into a surprisingly spot-on British accent. "'Today I dined with Lord and Lady X; over a glass of very satisfactory Madeira we discussed the deplorable state of the economy.' What we really need is a rousing tale of vice and corruption--and, if possible, blood and guts." He raises one hand and points a finger at Simon, the way he did so often in class when he wanted to put a student on the spot. "You will bring me something soon, *sí?*"

Simon lowers his eyes and nods. "As soon as we have enough."

"Good. I should be out of this *lugar infernal* by then."

•   •   •

As they exit the *lugar infernal,* Simon pauses and thoughtfully eyes the ugly facade of the Medical Sciences Center. "I wonder . . . "

"*Que?*"

"Mack didn't say what time Weiss' flight left. I wonder if there's any chance he's still around."

Gabriela shrugs. "There is only one way to find out."

"You really think we should?"

"How else can we be sure that he is our mystery man?"

"Suppose he is; what do we do then?"

"That is a good question. I know one thing we should *not* do."

"What's that?"

"Well, if he offers us a drink, we should not take it."

The entryway is as unlovely the building's exterior. Even the floor is concrete, though it's dyed dark red and polished to a sheen. Several circular planters—concrete, of course—contain trees that look fake but could conceivably be real, rather like the flawlessly dressed and coiffed woman behind the white marble reception desk.

Something about the receptionist reminds Simon of his mother; maybe it's the arch look she gives them, as if challenging them to account for their presence in the building, or perhaps in the world. Probably no explanation he gives will be quite good enough. Once again, Gabriela comes to the rescue. "Excuse me. Can you tell me where we might find Dr. Weiss?"

The woman flashes a fake, flawless smile. "I'm sorry. Dr. *V*eiss--" She pointedly stresses the V sound. "—left this morning."

"Oh, no! I had an appointment with him. I was to interview him for the *Tatler*—the student newspaper, you know—about the work he has been doing here." Clever girl; she knows how to fish for information.

Unfortunately the woman doesn't take the bait. Raising one plucked eyebrow, she says, "And how, may I ask, were you aware that Dr. Weiss was on campus?"

Her accusatory tone doesn't faze Gabriela. "I met him in the Rare Book Room of the library. He was looking for a particular volume, but we were not able to find it."

This bait doesn't get taken, either. "I see. Well, as I said, I'm afraid you've missed him."

"Um, will he be coming back, do you know?" puts in Simon.

"I really couldn't say."

"Well," says Gabriela. "Thank you for your help."

"My pleasure." If this is her pleased look, Simon would hate to see her displeased one.

Leaning in close to Gabriela, he whispers, "Just a second." He clears his throat and the woman glances up, seemingly surprised to find him still there. "Um, do you have any idea where I could find Alec Lowe? He's a grad student in Organic Chemistry. He works in one of the labs."

The receptionist gives a small but very audible sigh, as if to make it clear that keeping track of grad students is not part of her job description. "I suppose I could buzz that department for you."

Gabriela tugs at the sleeve of Simon's jacket. "I need to be going, Simon. I will see you tomorrow at class."

"Oh. Um, okay, I guess. I just thought maybe . . . " He trails off as she hurries across the entryway and through the revolving door.

"Shall I call that department for you?" prompts the receptionist.

"What? Uh, no, thanks; that's okay. I'll—I'll talk to him later."

Gabriela's abrupt exit is like a replay of the Turtle Tap episode. He's tempted to go after her but afraid that, if he does, she'll resent it. At least she did say she'd see him in the morning. It's just that he was hoping they'd spend the afternoon together, teasing out the message of the cipher one letter at a time, sitting side by side, breathing the same air, sharing the same secret language and feeling no awkwardness, no need to fill up the silences with small talk.

Well, no use sitting around feeling sorry for himself; he's perfectly capable of deciphering the thing by himself. It *is* his thesis, after all, not hers. And the sooner it's done, the sooner he can publish, without worrying about competition.

As he wends his way through the book-lined paths in the library's P section, Simon feels a frisson of anxiety; what if, like the codex, the *Cantigas* isn't where he left it? Suppose, when he shelved it yesterday, the mystery man was spying on him? He picks up the pace and, as he rounds a corner into the PQ9000's, he nearly collides with another student—no, actually, *not* a student. "Marnie! I'm sorry, I--I didn't see you."

"That's all right. No harm done."

"Um, looking for a little light reading, are you?"

"Ha. Not me. I'm more of a murder mystery sort of girl. Dr. E asked me to bring him a book."

"Ah," says Simon, trying not to sound alarmed. "Any, uh, any particular one?"

"Well, it's kind of hard to read his writing; it looks like *Tiempo de Silencio* by . . . Sartos?"

Simon lets out a laugh, mostly of relief. "I think it's supposed to be Santos. And I think you wrote down the wrong call number. It should be in the 6000s somewhere. Come on, I'll help you find it."

The book's easy enough to locate; getting rid of Marnie proves a little more difficult. "So," she says, coyly, "what's going on with you and Gabriela?"

"Going on? Um, nothing. I mean, she's helping me with my thesis, that's all."

"I doubt that."

"No, she really is."

"Okay, but you said that's all. I'm not sure I believe that." She nudges him. "Come on, Simon. I've seen the way you look at her." When Simon doesn't reply, she lets the subject drop, thankfully. But she takes up one that he's even more reluctant to discuss. "How's the thesis coming along, anyway? I hear you changed your topic."

"Oh? Uh, where did you hear that?"

"I guess Dr. E must have mentioned it."

That's a little strange. He only got Espinoza's permission a couple of days ago, and for most of the time since then, the professor's been in the hospital. "I hope—I mean I guess he didn't say what the new topic was?"

"No, not that I recall."

Well, that's good, anyway. "Listen, Marnie, I'd better get to work."

"Oh, right; sorry. Thanks for helping me find this."

"Yeah, sure."

As she walks away, she calls over her shoulder, "Good luck with your love life—I mean your thesis!"

When he's certain that she's good and gone, Simon hastens to the PQ9000s. *Graças a Deus*, the *Cantigas* is right where it's supposed to be—well, technically not where it's *supposed* to be, but where he left it. He holes up in a study room and slips the copies out of the book's binding.

He tries to Buckle Down, Winsocki and concentrate on the cipher, but there are too many unanswered questions taking up brain space. He has no hope of reaching that mindless state of *mushin*, but he forces himself to slog away at it until, through sheer doggedness, he's sweated out two more paragraphs of plaintext.

Downing several aspirin to ease the throbbing in his head, he switches to the slightly less grueling task of translating to English—just to further demonstrate that he doesn't need Gabriela's help.

Thanks to all the centuries-old books he's been studying, his translation assumes a sort of formal, stately quality that mimics—pretty feebly, to be sure—the succulent prose style he's come to relish so much.

Though he has to consult his Portuguese/English dictionary from time to time, for the most part the process is pretty painless. No doubt it helps that he spent all those tiresome months slaving over the *Cantigas;* nice to know it was good for something, anyway. Occasionally he comes across a word that's totally unfamiliar and that doesn't appear in the dictionary; all he can do is hazard a guess at the spelling—and sometimes at the meaning.

Dr. Espinoza will be gratified to learn that the codex is not some dull old journal that records mundane events from an uneventful life. In fact, it becomes apparent early on that Vicente's story is far from mundane--and that he's really more concerned with death than with life:

Men who find themselves in a situation as hopeless as mine are accustomed to blame the Fates, or the alignment of the planets, or the stupidity of others, but if I did so I would be deluding myself. God--if there is one--knows that I have many other failings and vices, but self-delusion is one, at least, that I do my best to avoid. The sad truth is, the blame for my condition lies squarely on my own shoulders. I have committed a vast array of sins, and now I must atone for them.

No, the word atone implies regret or repentance. I should say instead that I must pay for them, and dearly, too, with my life and, if the Church is to be believed, with my immortal soul. It is hard, though, to put much stock in an institution that exiles folk, or tortures them, or burns them at the stake simply for seeking the truth—though in my case, of course, I have been somewhat less dedicated to seeking truth than to seeking money. Foolish of me.

And foolish of me to go on about such abstract matters; I no longer have that luxury. Even if the King's men fail to find me here, in this cramped, dank room in this out-of-the-way little inn, the festering wound in my arm will surely do me in before long. I have always appreciated irony, so I take grim amusement from the thought that, if I still had that marvelous plant that is responsible for my being in such dire straits, or even a portion of it, I could easily heal myself. But the Inquisitors have deemed it an invention of the Devil, and have burned it, as they have burned so many so-called witches and sorcerers.

Simon is feeling a bit dopey; he has to reread those last two sentences several times before their significance sinks in. A plant with marvelous healing powers? Suddenly the connection between the codex and the pharmaceutical company seems a lot less tenuous. Dozens of drugs are derived from plants, after all— atropine, morphine, digitalis, quinine, aspirin—and more are being discovered every year. Most of them, though, seem to come from the depths of some remote rain forest, not from well-settled places like Portugal.

Of course, who's to say that Vicente didn't spend some time in the jungle? By the time the Inquisition was in full swing, Portuguese explorers and merchants had been knocking about India and Southeast Asia for decades, and they were in Brazil even earlier. Maybe Vicente was one of them. The only way of finding out is to grapple with the ciphertext again, and Simon is just too exhausted.

It's all he can do to reshelve the *Cantigas*—or rather mis-shelve it--and drag himself back to the Gas Chamber, where he downs a bowl of Raisin Bran doused with orange juice—they're out of milk--and collapses into his sagging armchair. But there's no rest for the weary. A couple of minutes later, there's a knocking— actually, more of a pounding--at the door. Though Gabriela is not usually the sort to pound, Simon can't help hoping.

And he can't help groaning when he opens the door to find the teenage slattern on the landing--wearing, of all things, Mack's letter jacket. "Where did you get *that*?" Simon demands.

She holds out her hand, which contains some odd-looking object. "I found it at the bottom of the stairs, when I was raking leaves. I thought it might be yours."

Simon meant the jacket, of course, but when he gets a closer look at what she's holding, it commands all his attention. He picks it gingerly from her palm. It looks like a miniature hypodermic needle with a little clump of feathers on one end. He has the feeling he's seen it before, but can't quite pin down the time or the place. "Um, okay. Thanks."

"You're welcome." She peers around him, surveying the apartment. "So, is Mack here?"

"No. He's at work."

"Okay, bye." Before Simon collects his wits enough to ask again about the letter jacket, she's gone. Well, no matter; he can interrogate Mack about it. But the next morning, when he heads out to his self-defense class, Mack is still sound asleep, and Simon doesn't want to wake him.

CHAPTER TWENTY-ONE

Each week, Simon has been adding a new move to the *kata* routines, but his students are still griping about how boring they are, so this week he spices things up by assaulting them. Not in earnest, of course; he just plays the part of a villain who grabs his victims from behind. He'd like to use Gabriela as his partner, but she's such a touch-me-not, he chooses Wendy the Visigoth instead.

The defense he teaches them is the one he *should* have used against Duane/Dennis/Darrin. You drive your head backward into the assailant's face, then whack him in the balls, then elbow him in the throat or the solar plexus, depending on how big he is. Luckily, Simon had the foresight to wear a crotch cup, because Wendy really gets into the spirit of the thing. She's so aggressive that he can't help wondering who she's *really* elbowing and whacking in the balls; surely not him.

For an hour or so, the women take turns being victim and attacker. Though Simon warns them not to overdo it, inevitably some of them get carried away and grab or strike a little too hard, which elicits a whole new set of complaints. There's just no pleasing some people.

To calm things down, Simon has them pair up and perform some *kakie* exercises, which are less about creaming your opponent than about reading her. You place the backs of your wrists together—sort of like arm wrestlers but without gripping hands--and take turns pushing and resisting in a constant flow of motion.

He deliberately matches up Gabriela and Wendy; at first they seem almost hostile, each trying to shove the other away, but after a while they get into the give-and-take groove, and their moves become more graceful, more like a dance.

A very sensual dance. A hula; a hoochie koochie; a Dance of the Seven Veils. Just watching them, Simon gets so turned on that he has to do some abdominal breathing to get himself under control. Once again, he's thankful that he wore the groin protector.

When the session ends, he's afraid Gabriela will run off again, but she actually hangs around after the others are gone. She's gotten comfortable enough at last to remove the baggy sweatshirt; her black leotard has dark, damp patches, and there's a dew of perspiration on her forehead and her neck, which somehow makes her more alluring than ever. "I think," she says breathlessly, "that I understand the purpose of the . . . what do you call them? The pushing exercises?"

"*Kakie.*"

"I thought that was a kind of pants."

"Well, you're panting, aren't you?"

She ignores the awful pun. "It shows how important it is not just to act, but to *react, não é assim?*"

"*Muito bom*. You suppose Wendy figured that out, too?"

"Yes, I think so." She dabs at the sweat with her hand towel, then says softly, "She seems angry to me, Simon. She has not said so, but I suspect that . . . that she may have had a bad experience."

"Um, you mean maybe she was assaulted?"

Gabriela shrugs and slips into her sweatshirt. "Perhaps," she murmurs, her voice muffled by the cloth. "I think it happens more often than anyone realizes." As she's dragging the *makiwara* into the storage room, she calls, "If you get dressed, I will buy you a smoothie."

Simon grins. "You're starting to like those, aren't you?"

"No, I just don't want you to have to drink alone."

Though Simon changes speedily into his street clothes, he's in no hurry to get to the Gedunk. "Could we talk for a minute first?"

Gabriela eyes him a bit warily. "About what?" So much for her feeling comfortable. Is she expecting him to hit on her, or what?

"Um, I just—it's—it's about the codex, is all. I--I thought we should discuss it someplace where nobody could, you know, overhear us."

"Oh. Okay. Sure." She sinks down onto one of the mats and pats the spot next to her. "Did you decipher some more?"

174

"Yeah, quite a bit. And then I translated everything we've got. I would have had you help me, but . . ." *But you ran off,* he doesn't say. "Anyway, I found out some pretty interesting stuff. Vicente mentions a plant that, according to him, has miraculous healing powers. That might explain why Mystery Man and his company are so interested in the journal."

"Oh, Simon! I bet you are right! What sort of plant?"

"I don't know yet; that's as far as I got."

"People have been discovering medicinal plants in the Amazon for a long time. Do you suppose Vicente was in Brazil?"

"I don't know that yet, either. I'm only on page two."

Gabriela springs to her feet. "So why are we sitting here? We should be deciphering!"

"Okay, okay. Only, um, could we get some food on the way? All I've had for the past two days is Raisin Bran."

"Oh, you poor boy. Doesn't your mother ever send you a Care package?"

Simon makes a scoffing sound. "I'm not sure the word *care* is in her vocabulary."

• • •

While Gabriela is at the Gedunk, filling her gym bag with food, Simon retrieves the *Cantigas* from the shelves, keeping a sharp eye out for spies. It's hard to imagine who would be tailing him now that Mystery Man is gone; still, he's not taking any chances.

Though Simon is the experienced cryptographer, he's learned to let Gabriela handle most of the deciphering. She's such a natural. Her approach is less plodding and analytical than his, more instinctive. Often she's able to correctly guess a plaintext word on the basis of only two or three letters. The fact that Portuguese is her native language helps, of course, but not really all that much. Modern Brazilian Portuguese, after all, is a far cry from Renaissance European Portuguese.

Simon's job is mostly just to back her up, help her out when she gets stuck. When it comes to translating, they switch roles. Simon does the lion's share, and Gabriela is the backup. They make a good team. Simon has always enjoyed the codebreaking process, in the same way he enjoys performing *kata* or working out on the punch bag. It's exhausting and repetitive, sometimes literally a headache, but ultimately satisfying. Now, with Gabriela working alongside him it's become . . . well, *fun*. Even when he irks her by trying to help a bit too much, neither of them gets too bent out of shape.

A half hour or so in, she runs up against a baffling block of letters: CIDIGIUII. Though she tries to seem all nonchalant and in control, he can tell she's struggling, and no wonder; there are four possible plaintext letters for those I's. Leaning over, Simon points to the first line on their chart of alphabets. "We can probably assume that most of those I's are really *o*'s," he starts to say, but she brushes him off.

"*Sim, sim*," she mutters, and pushes his hand away. He pushes back. She turns to frown at him, then realizes what he's up to and responds with a push of her own. "*Kaiei!*" she exclaims with a giggle.

They keep it up for several minutes, acting and reacting, laughing at first, then getting caught up in the ritual of give and take, looking into each other's eyes, reading the opponent's intentions. Simon isn't quite sure what her intentions are, but he certainly knows his own. This is the most physical contact they've had, and he can't help wishing for more. He doesn't dare make the first move, though, and risk scaring her off.

And then whatever chance he may have had is gone; still smiling, she takes her hand away so suddenly that his nearly falls before he catches himself. So much for reading the opponent. As usual, he's doing way too much thinking and analyzing.

"All right, now, let me see," says Gabriela. "**Yonopoaoo**? I don't think so. **Monopoaio**? Ah! **Monopolio!** Monopoly. Was that a word back then?"

"Well, I don't think the board game was invented yet--"

"Ha, ha."

"—but I've seen the term used to refer to the *Casa da Índia* trading company."

By suppertime, she has an entire page of Portuguese plaintext, and he's converted it all into pseudo-sixteenth-century English. "Read it to me, please, Simon? My eyes are so tired."

"Okay. Remember, he's talking about the Inquisition getting rid of the plant because it's an invention of the Devil." Simon clears his throat and, a bit self-consciously, begins to read:

Well, perhaps they're right about it; perhaps man is meant to suffer, to fall ill and die in misery. Perhaps it is all part of God's plan—again, assuming there is a God—and to try to defeat it is blasphemy.

But I suspect the only plan at work here is that of the medicós, those university-trained physicians —many of them in the employ of the Inquisition--who wish to keep their monopoly on the treatment of illness . . . if you can call it treatment to drain half the blood from a patient or make him vomit his guts out.

And here I am vomiting bile myself, when what I really need to do with the little time left to me is to give an account of how and where I found the plant, how best to make use of it—and how it brought about my downfall--so that others may profit from my experience. Conveying this information in code is a time-consuming task— ["Not as time-consuming as trying to decipher it," sighs Gabriela] *--but necessary, I think. Only a seeker of truth—or perhaps money—will be clever and motivated enough to decipher my message. There are plenty of dedicated scholars, of course, who glean the gospels and twist the words to mean whatever they wish, but none with the necessary desire to look beyond the boundaries set by the Church. Lover of irony that I am, I have used their own words as the key to my cipher--which you of course know, since you have used that key to open up this little book of mine.*

Enough philosophizing. I must begin my story now, before it reaches its end.

Gabriela's bulky rings make a loud clack as she smacks the tabletop peevishly. "Oh, I wish we could do this more quickly! I can't wait to see what happens next!"

"I know. It's like one of those serials they used to show at the movies on Saturday mornings. Did you have those in Brazil?"

"Yes, and I hated them!" She makes her voice low and dramatic. "*No episódio da próxima semana. . .* I didn't want to wait until next week, I wanted to see it *now!*"

"Well, we can keep going if you want to." He's tired, too, but only of deciphering, certainly not of Gabriela's company.

"No, I suppose it's best to quit now. Even the plaintext is starting to look like an Unknown Language. Tomorrow is Sunday, so we'll have all day to work on it."

Simon can't help grinning. "Sounds good to me."

She studies him, as if trying to decide how to take this. "How is your head? Is it still hurting you?"

"Sometimes. But not like it was before." For some reason, thinking about the headaches brings to mind the little feathered syringe that Rhonda discovered. He fishes it out of his shirt pocket. "Um, have you ever seen one of these?"

"*Certamente*. It is a *dardo tranquilizante*."

"A tranquilizer dart?"

She nods. "My uncle is a veterinary doctor; he sometimes has to use them on big animals."

Simon has a fleeting but vivid flashback, or vision, or something in which he's trying to pull the dart from his shoulder. He can even feel the stab of the needle. "You know what?" he murmurs. "I think somebody shot me with this thing."

"*É mesmo*?! Did it . . . how do you say . . . knockout you?"

"I guess it must have; I don't remember anything after that . . . unless . . ."

"*Que*?"

"Well, I keep . . . I keep picturing myself tied up in a chair, being asked a bunch of questions. I thought it was a dream."

"That is just what Dr. Espinoza said! Maybe you were drugged, too, Simon!"

"By the mystery man."

"*Claro*. And I bet he used that stuff you spoke of--Devil's Breath."

"Uh-huh. Wow. He must have wanted me to tell him where the journal was. Except I didn't know, because you hid it."

"Was I not smart to do that?"

"Brilliant. And so modest, too."

"Just call me Modesty Blaise."

Simon stares at the dart. "I can't believe he *did* that. Why is he so desperate to get his hands on this?" He gives the enciphered pages a proprietary pat.

"Perhaps he already has some idea of what it contains. I mean, think of the money his company would make if they found this plant of Vicente's--a plant with miraculous healing powers."

"Good point." Simon shakes his head, which is suddenly aching again. "I'm sure glad he's gone."

"So am I. But you know, in those spy movies, the criminal mastermind always has minions."

"*Minions*?"

"Is that not the right word?"

"Um, sure. It's just not one you hear very often. So. I guess we need to watch out for minions. What do they look like?"

"Simon. You are making fun of me."

"No, no, I'm serious. How do we know who's a minion and who isn't?"

"If they drug us, then they are minions, okay?"

"Okay." He examines the little syringe again. "Maybe we should check out the Veterinary Medicine department, see if they're missing a dart gun."

Gabriela grins. "Now you are thinking like a spy. I will do that."

"And I'll ask my friend Alec if he knows anything about Dr. Vice."

Gabriela's smile abruptly vanishes, as if he said he was planning to commune with the Devil. Now that he thinks about it, her quick departure yesterday happened right after he mentioned Alec's name, too. Does she have some kind of history with the guy? If so, it's no big surprise. According to several reliable sources, Alec has left a trail of broken hearts all across campus. It's just that Simon would have thought Gabriela had better taste.

CHAPTER TWENTY-TWO

He doesn't ask Gabriela about her obvious aversion to Alec, of course, nor does he bring it up when they meet at the Briggs on Sunday afternoon. It's her business. It's not like he has any kind of claim on her--as much as he might like to have. They're just colleagues. Fellow laborers in the groves of academe. Fellow minions of that evil mastermind, Dr. Espinoza.

"I guess we should show our efforts to the Tyrant sometime soon. Surely he's out of the hospital by now."

"Let's not leave copies with him this time," says Gabriela.

"I doubt he'll want them; he seems convinced that the mystery man will come back."

"Then we had better get to work, in case that happens."

Though Gabriela seems as keen as ever, for some reason Simon's heart isn't quite in it. Several times, when she gives him the little sidewise glance that means she could use some help but doesn't want to say so, he fails to notice, and she has to nudge him and say, "Wake up, *dorminhoco*," or "What do you make of this word?" Finally, she turns to him with a look that's both puzzled and peevish. "We don't have to do this today, if you don't feel like it."

"No, no, I want to. I'm just--" Just what? Worn out? No more than usual. Worried? A little, maybe, about the mystery man and his minions. Sulking? Aha. Though he doesn't really like to admit it, that's closer to the mark.

He doesn't know for sure that Alec and Gabriela ever were an Item, he's just guessing. But even the possibility of it makes him cringe. He feels betrayed, somehow, as if she's cheated on him. It's ridiculous, of course, but probably no more ridiculous than the other feeling he's been having for some time now--the scary sense that he's falling hopelessly, helplessly in love with this woman.

Though Gabriela is clearly aware. that's something's eating at Simon, she doesn't push him. Maybe she figures it's his business. Or maybe she just doesn't want to know. All she says is, "Well, if you do feel like quitting, tell me, okay?"

He nods silently. For the rest of the afternoon he continues to say no more than necessary. Gabriela doesn't seem to mind particularly; in fact, she seems just as happy to keep things on a strictly businesslike basis. She's not unfriendly or anything, but there's none of the usual joking and banter. Thanks to Simon's stupid sulking, the deciphering process has turned into a rote, repetitive chore-- hour after hour of *kata* with no free sparring and no *kakei*.

Simon even finds the usually enjoyable job of translating a bit of a pain. He's good at ignoring pain, though, and by the time they're ready to call it day, he has another two pages of passable prose. As he did the previous day, he reads it aloud:

I will not bore you, reader, with the details of my life before I traveled to Malaca. ["Malaca?" says Gabriela. "It's in Southeast Asia," says Simon, "and these days it's spelled with two *c*'s."] *It has little bearing on anything and is, in any case, so familiar a tale that you know it already: the older brother inherits the family's estate, leaving the younger—myself--with no real recourse but to become a soldier.*

Not long after I enlisted, I was shipped off to the Portuguese garrison in Goa, where I made the acquaintance of several delightful, dusky ladies-- [Simon stumbles a little over that sentence; it hits too close to home] *--and, more importantly, the acquaintance of Dom Alvaro Atayde de Gama. He had been appointed Captain-Major of the Fortaleza de Malaca and was recruiting soldiers to protect the tiny colony there, which had been under assault by various armies ever since Alfonso de Albuquerque conquered the island in 1511. Though hostilities had died down somewhat, it was only a matter of time before the Mahometans or the Chinese launched another offensive. It was too important a location to ignore, for whoever controlled that narrow passage in the Malacan Straits controlled the lucrative trade in spices and silk and opium and pearls and other such treasures of the Orient.*

I had heard stories of daring and enterprising young men who grew rich by engaging in that trade. Well, I was as enterprising as any, and more daring, if I may say so, than most. I had an opportunity to prove it when, during the voyage from Goa to Malaca, our vessel was attacked by Turkish pirates. Dom Alvaro was a clever enough fellow, but not much account as a swordsman; he would have been gutted by a Saracen's scimitar had I not stepped in and dispatched his assailant--not to mention a dozen or so others. So grateful was Dom Alvaro that he made me his aide-de-camp, the man who formerly occupied that post having lost his head.

Once on Malaca, I set about making myself indispensable. I plied the crews of visiting vessels with palm wine and learned from them all I could concerning the various kingdoms that encircle the Cham Sea, including a little of each language. In less than two years, I gained Dom Alvaro's confidence so completely that he appointed me unofficial ambassador to the kingdoms of Camboja and Siao. My mission was to win their friendship and, more importantly, their trade. I accepted the position eagerly--although admittedly I had a somewhat different agenda.

The most intriguing information provided by those foreign sailors concerned a small kingdom that lay between Siao and Camboja, a kingdom called Lanchang, which means Land of a Million Elephants. It was not the elephants that interested me, however; I had seen plenty of those in Goa. No, it was gold I was after—specifically a golden Buddha called the Pra Bang that was said to weigh as much as a good-sized person of flesh and blood. A man who claimed such a prize had no need of a paltry inheritance.

"*Ah-ah!*" says Gabriela. "Perhaps Mystery Man cares nothing about the miraculous healing plant after all! Perhaps he is after the golden Buddha!"

"Hmm. Now it really *does* sound like a Saturday morning serial. *The Curse of the Golden Buddha.*"

Gabriela taps his translation. "That is good writing, Simon."

"Um, thanks."

"I wish you could write my Western Civ paper for me. Actually, I wish I were taking *Eastern* Civ; it would be more useful right now. Are you going do some more tomorrow?"

You, she said, not *we.* Simon's heart sinks like a golden Buddha dumped into the Mekong River. "Um, yeah, I guess so."

"My paper is due on Wednesday. I can help you again after that."

Her words perform a salvage operation on his sunken heart. "Oh. Okay. Good."

"In the meanwhile, please get some sleep. You look very tired. And eat something besides Raisin Bran."

But Raisin Bran is about all the Gas Chamber's cupboards contain, and on a Sunday evening the food stores will be closed. Well, he was too beat to fix anything, anyway. Though his funds are running low, he can still afford a plate of onion rings—or thiosulfinates, as Alec would have it. The jerk.

When he slouches into the Turtle Tap, he's gratified to find that Alec isn't behind the bar. Mack, predictably, is in front of it; Simon waves to him and then collapses into one of the worn leather armchairs next to the gas fireplace. A few minutes later, his friend claims the other chair, which groans pitifully under his weight. He hands Simon a Slider. "You look like you can use one of these, buddy."

"You're right. Thanks." As he takes a big dose of the drink, he peers over the rim at Mack, who is either happy or drunk or both, maybe with some Darvon thrown in. "You're in a good mood."

"Hey, it's my day off. Besides . . ." He glances around furtively, then scoots his protesting chair closer to Simon's. "I found some really good stuff yesterday."

"What kind of stuff?"

"Information."

"In the wastebaskets, I suppose."

"No! Just sitting there on the department head's desk!" He ducks his head and rumples his already rumpled hair, which is looking even less conservative and more counterculture. "Well, okay, in a *drawer* of the department head's desk. But it wasn't locked or anything."

"Jeez, Mack!" hisses Simon. "You're going to get yourself in trouble!"

"It'll be worth it." He leans even closer. "Get this. I find this memo that makes it pretty clear their labs are working on a new herbicide—a *defoliant*, they call it. What do you bet the U.S. is planning to use it in Nam?"

"The last I heard, chemical warfare was illegal."

"So is bombing neutral countries, but they're doing it anyway."

"What neutral countries?" says Simon, skeptically. Mack is not known for his grasp of current events.

"Cambodia, for one."

"Says who?"

"Says the *New York Times*. Front page, May 9th."

"Oh. I wasn't aware of that."

"Most people aren't. Maybe you should go to a few SDS meetings."

Simon shifts uncomfortably, making the leather upholstery squeak. "I don't know, Mack. I don't want to get expelled or anything."

"Hey, no big deal; they've suspended the draft, remember?"

"Only till the lottery kicks in, which is about a month from now, remember? If I stay in grad school, I'm okay until June, at least."

Mack shrugs, palms upward. "Your call, man. I don't blame you for wanting to play it safe; this is some scary shit."

"I just wish *you'd* play it a little safer."

"That's what Coach was always telling me. He said there's a difference between being aggressive and being a maniac, and that I was no good to him if I got injured out there." He rubs his bum knee. "I guess I always have to learn the hard way." He downs the last of his Slider. "You want another drink?"

"No, thanks. And--"

"And don't say I shouldn't have one, either."

It's Simon's turn to shrug. "Your call, man." There's no point in saying anything, anyway. Mack wouldn't listen; he'd just resent it. When the big guy returns from the bar, this time with a Screwdriver, Simon says, "Hey, there's something I wanted to ask you."

"I hope it's not about women."

"No. Well, sort of. How did Rhonda Horvath get hold of your letter jacket?"

Here comes the abashed head-rubbing move. "I gave it to her. I know, dumb, right? But she blackmailed me again; she said if I didn't, she'd tell her folks about the booze, and I figured, what the hell, I've got no more use for the thing; if it makes her happy, she's welcome to it."

"So now she can tell all her friends that she's going steady with a Van Dyne jock."

"*Former* jock. Again, if it makes her happy, why not?"

"I would think her parents would be more concerned about *that* than about a little whiskey."

"She promised not to wear it in front of them."

"Oh, well, then, I guess there's no problem."

"Are you being sarcastic?"

"Yes."

"Let's change the subject, okay? How are you and Gabriela hitting it off?"

Simon stares glumly into his half-empty glass. "She hasn't asked for my letter jacket yet."

"Hey, there *should* be letter jackets for outstanding scholars. So, have you gotten to first base yet?"

Simon avoids his friend's gaze. "I haven't tried," he mutters.

"Why not?"

"Because. Because I . . . I like her, and I don't want to her to think I'm just . . . you know."

"After her bod? Okay, I can understand that. Sort of."

Simon considers asking Mack whether he knows anything about Gabriela and Alec, but he's afraid of what the answer might be, so he just sits staring into the fire for a while.

It's not like Mack to stay silent for long, though. "So, if you're not making out with her, how are you making out with the Kotex?"

"Pretty well. We've got several pages deciphered and translated. It sure is hard work, though."

"Well, as you always say, and I don't: Anything worth knowing is hard to learn. Or something like that."

"Close enough."

Mack digs in the back pocket of his jeans. "Oh, speaking of translating, you got a letter from your Mexican buddy, it looks like." He hands it over. Sure enough, the return address is Frank Ávila's.

"Where was this? In our mailbox? I never think to check it."

"No, it got delivered to the Whoremongers--" Mack's pet name for the Horvaths. "--and they brought it over."

"*Rhonda* brought it over, you mean."

"Well, yeah. Listen, how about I order us some onion rings while you read that?"

"Good idea."

Frank's letter is brief, as usual, and for a change it's in English. He's coming to Ohio over the Thanksgiving holiday, and he's hoping to find a cheap place to live while he takes classes at Van Dyne. If anyone else had written it, Simon would figure they were subtly asking to share his apartment, but Frank generally says what he means. Presumably the GI Bill will cover his rent as well as his tuition.

"Does he still want to be *amigos*?" asks Mack, as he plunks down the hefty plate of onion rings and then his hefty self.

"I guess. He's coming here; he got accepted for next semester."

"No kidding? Maybe grades don't matter if you're a veteran."

As Simon leans over to dig into the rings, the tranquilizer dart digs into him. Pulling it from his pocket, he shows it to Mack and explains where it came from.

"Whoa!" says Mack. "When I found you passed out on the lawn, it was from *this*?"

"Apparently."

"So, the mystery man is playing dirty."

"Uh-huh. You haven't found out anything more about him, have you?"

"Nope, sorry. I'll keep looking."

"Thanks. Just don't do anything foolish, okay?"

Mack gives him an injured look. "Who, *me*?"

CHAPTER TWENTY-THREE

Over the next three days, Simon spends as much time as he can bear to in the study rooms—a different one each day, just to be safe--chipping away at the ciphertext, all alone. It's a cheerless task without Gabriela by his side. But, as she said, if the mystery man or his minions are still after the journal, they need to get the thing deciphered and published.

He attacks the text as he would a karate opponent, maneuvering around the words of the Unknown Language, searching for an opening and, when he finds one, pressing his advantage.

By Wednesday afternoon, he's forced the journal to give up three whole pages of plaintext. This new chapter resembles even more an episode from an exciting movie serial, complete with cliffhanger:

With the fortress under constant threat of attack, Dom Alvaro could spare no more than eight men to accompany me—which suited me well enough. Surely even such a small force of experienced, well-armed soldiers would have no trouble carrying out a raid on a backward little kingdom. After all, Cortes had conquered the whole of the Aztec empire with only 400 conquistadores. Besides, the smaller my army was, the bigger each man's share of the gold would be.

We needed sailors, too, of course, but not many; our vessel, a two-masted jurupango, was a mere 60 spans in length, and easy enough to handle. Naturally we had no intention of sharing our spoils with our Asian mariners or with our sole passenger, a Dominican friar charged by his church with the unlikely task of converting the Cambojan heathens to Christianity.

We set off early in the dry season, when the sea was calm—a mixed blessing. While the friar, Dom Gaspar--who suffered cruelly from seasickness-- thanked his God, the sailors begged their gods to send them a good stiff breeze. It took us five dull days to reach the mouth of the river that our navigator called Song Cu Long, which means River of Nine Dragons, though it was more in the nature of one very long dragon with nine mouths. Each was lined with yellow teeth in the form of bamboo huts on stilts, and each held a mouthful of fishing boats so narrow and shallow that they seemed in constant danger of being swamped.

Using the Cambojan tongue, Dom Gaspar hailed one of these, which ferried him to shore and to whatever fate awaited him there, while we continued upriver. Even in the dry season, the water was so swift that we made little headway using only our sails; we had to resort to the oars. As there were not nearly enough sailors to man them, my soldiers were forced to row. Though they complained and cursed, when I reminded them of the riches that awaited us in Lanchang they put their backs into it.

The boat was heavily laden with trade goods, though, and our progress was painfully slow. After two weeks, our food supply began to run low. Luckily, we came upon a village of some twenty or thirty thatched stilt houses surrounded by tilled fields. As the inhabitants seemed more curious than hostile, we took a small party ashore. I had learned enough words in the Lao tongue to conduct a bit of business, trading some of our iron goods for yams, coconuts, papayas, and rice.

I tried to determine how far we had yet to go to reach Lanchang, but my vocabulary was not up to the task. There was another matter, too, about which I was curious: I had noticed that most of the menial labor in the village—hauling water, weeding crops, repairing the palm-leaf thatching--was carried out by men and women quite different in appearance from the majority of the villagers, both in their physical features and in their attire, which for the men consisted solely of a loincloth; the women added a band of fabric over the breasts for modesty's sake. Through a combination of words and gestures, I gathered that these were slaves, captured from another tribe called, apparently, Kha. They did not seem to be badly treated, though we saw one man receive a rather severe beating—a punishment, I gathered, for attempting to escape.

As we were getting underway again, our navigator gave a shout and pointed downstream. Another vessel was approaching, a three-masted junk so massive that she resembled a floating castle; her bamboo sails were the size of windmill blades. She flew no flag, which I took to be a bad sign. She could certainly have overtaken us had she cared to; instead, she reefed her sails and dropped anchor before the village. We laid on our oars and put as much distance between us as we could.

For most of that day, we saw no more sign of the junk and we breathed easier; in unknown waters—in fact, in any waters at all--a ship carrying valuable cargo cannot be too careful, and our trade goods were of considerable worth, though nothing compared to that golden Buddha.

Our relief was short-lived. Just before dusk, the other vessel loomed suddenly around a bend in the river. She had no need of oars; those immense sails caught so much wind that she descended upon us like an avenging angel--or, more aptly, a devil, for as she drew near we recognized her crew as belonging to that notorious tribe of sea gypsies, the Orang Laut. Our sailors cried out in despair.

I had heard many stories of how fierce and merciless the Orang Laut were, and the tales proved true. Our little band stood no chance against fifty pirates armed with bows and cutlasses and faulconers. We were able to fire only one round from our muskets before the brigands overwhelmed us. Our poor sailors, with only their keris to defend themselves, were cut down at once.

We soldiers fared little better. Though a few of us flung ourselves overboard, it was a case of leaping from the pot and into the coals, for most of my men were unable to swim. Fortunately for me, I had always been a strong swimmer and I gained the muddy shore and the safety of the forest without any cannon shot or arrow finding me.

So I had leapt not into the coals, but only from the pot to the frying pan. I was marooned in a trackless jungle with no food or shelter--and, I now discovered, with a gaping cut on my upper arm; in the heat of battle, I had scarcely been aware of it. I wasn't entirely helpless, however; somehow—by instinct, I suppose—through it all I had kept hold of my sword.

I had no hope of making my way to Lanchang on foot, of course; my only real option was to head back to the Lao village—an easy enough journey in a boat, but I had no boat, only a few dead tree trunks. Though I was, as I have said, daring enough, I was not a fool. Only a fool would have tried to float downstream on a log or a flimsy raft. If the crocodiles did not seize me, the sharks would. Perhaps even more to be feared were the little pa pao fish, whose favorite trick was to nip off the tip of a swimmer's male member.

Well. This Vicente certainly makes for more compelling reading than the other one, whose work, even though he's called the Troubadour, doesn't exactly sing. Simon can't help wondering, though, how much of Vicente Somebody's story is actually true. Sixteenth-century chroniclers—Fernão Mendes Pinto, for example, who explored the East Indies a decade or two before Vicente—had a bad habit of exaggerating their exploits, or flat-out making them up, in order to glorify themselves or to boost sales, or both.

Everything Simon has read so far, though, has the ring of truth. The man even admits to fleeing in fear from the Orang Laut, which might make him seem a coward. He doesn't mind sounding unpatriotic or disloyal, either; he makes no secret of the fact that he's less interested in being a good soldier than in being a rich one.

Simon is so brain-weary that he almost crams the ciphertext and the translation into his gym bag instead of into the binding of the *Cantigas*. "Smart, Simon," he mutters. "Real smart." As he's tucking the sheets into their proper place, he hears, or imagines he hears—with the throbbing in his head, it's hard to tell—a noise just outside the study room; it sounds like the squeaking of tennis shoes on tile.

Since he neglected to mask the windows with notebook paper as Gabriela always does, he can peer out into the hallway—which of course means that someone could peer in. He doesn't see anyone lurking about, though. It was probably just a med student headed for the R section; most of them wear Converse All-Stars to make themselves appear more With It. Still, when he re-shelves the *Cantigas*, he's even more cautious than usual.

He feels about as eager to go to Karate Club as he was to tackle the ciphertext without Gabriela's help. But it's his chance to connect with Alec and bring up the topic of Dr. Vice. He downs a quick chili dog and some aspirin and plods on over to the field house. The chilly air perks him up enough so he doesn't look like a total zombie out there on the mats. Alec, as usual, shows no sign of fatigue after his long, hard day of dropping stuff into test tubes and Petri dishes.

Wendy and her fellow Visigoths are apparently regulars now. They're practicing their newly learned techniques on the poor, unsuspecting guys, one of whom backs into Simon, grimacing and holding the general area of his groin. "Should've worn your crotch cup," Simon murmurs sympathetically.

He barely manages fifteen minutes of *kata* before Alec comes around, wanting to do some serious sparring. They start out fairly subdued, with Alec doing nearly as much talking as striking. "Looks like your girls are learning some nasty moves."

"Uh-huh," says Simon, effortlessly blocking a snap kick.

"You think they could disable a real live attacker?"

Simon shrugs. "I wouldn't want to find out. Anyway--" He deflects a *shuto* strike. "--disabling is not the point; the point is to break free."

Alec gives a skeptical smile. "Whatever you say." Simon sneaks in a side kick that catches his opponent off-guard. "Oho! A tricky kick, Tricky Dick!" Alec steps up his game, and they engage in a sustained sequence of blows and kicks and grabs so fierce and so rapid that, when they stop to catch their breath and bow, they find half the club staring at them. Wendy is wiggling her eyebrows and silently clapping. Though a good *karate-ka* tries to keep his ego in check, Simon can't help feeling a little pleased and proud. He also can't help wishing it were Gabriela applauding him.

He sinks onto a bench and takes a few gulps from his water bottle; Alec follows suit. "My, my, Hannay; you're unusually feisty this evening."

"Yeah, well, it's been a frustrating week."

"Your thesis still giving you problems?"

"Sort of." Simon wipes the sweat from his face and neck and, without looking at Alec, says offhandedly, "What about your project? Did you get a chance to work with Dr. Weiss?"

Simon has seldom seen Alec at a loss for words. No doubt he's wondering how Simon knows about Weiss, and why he's interested. If so, he doesn't let it show; he says, just as casually, "Not really. He didn't spend much time in the lab. He was here for the same reason the Marines are."

Simon gives him a puzzled glance. "The *Marines*?"

Alec grins. "Recruiting, old boy. Recruiting."

"For his company, you mean?"

"Exactly." He leans uncomfortably close to Simon. "Can you keep a secret?"

"Um, sure."

"He offered me a job, doing basically the same stuff I'm doing for my project."

"Which is . . . ?"

Alec gives a laugh not unlike the pinball Devil's. "If I told you that, I'd have to kill you." He gets to his feet. "Speaking of which, how about a little more *kumite*?"

Simon is tempted to ask about the defoliant Mack mentioned, but Alec would have no trouble guessing where *that* information came from, and Simon doesn't want to get his friend in trouble. However, he can't resist bringing up another insidious chemical compound: "Did you, uh, did you ever hear of Devil's Breath?"

This time, Alec is clearly taken aback, so much that he momentarily relaxes his guard. Simon knocks his arm aside and delivers a left-handed *boshi-ken* strike to his neck; it doesn't actually connect, of course, but it comes close enough to startle Alec. "Who wants to know?" he counters. "You? Or your girlfriend?"

Now Simon is the one who's caught off guard. He barely manages to deflect a hook punch aimed at his head. He takes his time in replying. One of his instructors introduced him to a tactic called *Feign madness, but keep your balance*— in other words, play dumb—and he falls back on it now. "My girlfriend?"

"Oh, don't act all innocent, Hannay. Everybody knows you have a thing for Gabriela."

This time Simon doesn't reply at all. Better to let his opponent take the initiative and try to read his intentions. Alec's words come out in short bursts, punctuated occasionally by a show-offy "*Osu!*" as he attempts a strike that Simon effortlessly blocks. "I think . . . it's my duty as a friend . . . to warn you . . . about her."

"*Warn* me?"

"Right. It sounds like . . . she's still insisting . . . that she was drugged. She wasn't. She was just . . . plain . . . drunk. *Osu!* And Bear didn't . . . take advantage of her. She was . . . ready . . . willing . . . and able."

Though Alec hasn't tried any more snap kicks, Simon feels as if his legs have been knocked out from under him. Once again, he's unveiled a secret that he really would rather not know. He makes no attempt to deflect Alec's next strike and, even though it's delivered with more force than necessary, he barely feels it when it lands. "Sorry, man," says Alec; it's unclear which blow he's apologizing for, the physical or the verbal one. Simon disengages and turns away without even bowing.

But Alec isn't done yet. He moves up behind Simon and puts a hand on his shoulder. "You need to be careful, Hannay," he says, panting. "The woman is seriously unstable. She's liable to accuse you, too."

For once, Simon doesn't think or analyze; he does what he's been teaching his students to do when attacked from behind. No, he doesn't whack Alec in the crotch, but he does thrust an elbow into the guy's solar plexus, making him double over, gasping for breath.

Simon doesn't apologize; he doesn't say a thing, in fact. He just changes into his street clothes and goes home.

CHAPTER TWENTY-FOUR

The next day, he mopes around the apartment like someone who's been drugged--but certainly not with a truth serum. Though Mack asks him half a dozen times what's wrong, Simon doesn't divulge a thing; he just shrugs and pretends to be suffering from a headache, when it's actually his heart that hurts.

Mack offers him a Darvon, a shot of whiskey, an abysmal version of "Hey, Jude" that ordinarily would have Simon groaning and grinning. Nothing. "How about if I skip work today, man, and we go shoot some pool?"

"No, no, you go dig through some wastebaskets. I'll be fine."

He's not fine, of course; not even close. He really needs to go grocery shopping, but it seems like way too much trouble. So does eating. So does going to Spanish Lit. So does working on the codex. Gabriela promised to join him again today, but she'll probably forget. He's not sure he even wants to see her, anyway. If she wants him, she knows where to find him. Not that she's likely to bother.

By mid-afternoon, he's surrendered to his hunger pangs and is scarfing down the last of the Raisin Bran straight from the box when the anemic doorbell sounds. Great. Just what he needs—a visit from Rhonda. Unless, of course, it's one of the mystery man's minions.

It's neither, in fact. "I thought you would be at the library, Simon. Are you feeling sick?"

"Um, sort of, yeah." Seeing her usually makes him feel better instantly, but not today. Today he feels the way he did when Alec dropped his little bomb— as if his legs are about to give way under him.

"Oh. I am sorry. Maybe we can get together tomorrow?"

"Maybe."

Her dark eyes meet his, trying to read him, but he drops his gaze. "What is the matter, Simon? Did I—did I do something wrong?"

"I don't know. Did you?"

"I—I don't understand what you mean. Is it something about the codex? Simon?" When it's clear that he's not going to reply, she sighs and starts to turn away.

He can't bear to let her leave like this. "No," he says, "It's, uh, it's not about the codex."

"What, then?"

"It's something . . . something Alec said."

"Oh." Her lovely face transforms into a kabuki Omen Mask, the one with a set mouth and glaring eyes. "I knew that this would happen sooner or later. I am not certain what he told you, Simon, but I am fairly certain it is a lie."

"Um, well, he didn't say anything very specific, just—just hints. Like he assumed I knew what he was talking about."

"And you do not?"

"No!"

She gives a sardonic smile. "I thought surely everyone on campus must know. Perhaps I am not as notorious as I thought. *Bem*. I suppose I should tell you."

"You don't have to tell me anything if you don't want to."

"I *don't* want to. But I will, anyway. I think you should know the truth."

"Um, okay. You, uh, you want to come in? I'll make us some tea."

She takes a seat at the rickety table. Simon assumes she'll hold off until he can join her, but she clearly prefers to have him busy with the tea-making, so she doesn't have to look him in the eye. "You remember the fraternity party I told you about? The one where someone slipped something into my drink."

"Uh-huh."

"Well, it—it wasn't a party, exactly. I was told it would be, but it turned out to be at Alec's apartment, and there were only . . ." Her voice quavers a little. She pauses and swallows hard, then continues. "There were only four of us: Me, Alec and his girlfriend, and . . . and Bear O'Hara. He was supposed to be my date. He should have taken care of me. Instead, he drugged my drink and then he raped me."

"Jesus, Gabriela! Did you report it?"

194

"*Claro*. To the doctor at the infirmary, to the police, to the Dean of Women. They all tried to make it seem like it was *my* fault, like I had done something to . . . how do you say? Lead him on?" She gives something halfway between a laugh and a sob. "Well, they could not accuse a big football player of such a thing, could they? It would make the university look bad."

Simon aches to comfort her, to put his arms around her, but he doesn't dare. All he can do is set a cup of tea before her and murmur, "I'm sorry."

"So am I." She swipes at her eyes with one coat sleeve and gets unsteadily to her feet. "I should go."

"You don't have to--"

"Yes. I do. I do not like to cry in front of anyone. And I do not want anyone feeling sorry for me." Before Simon can protest, she is out the door, leaving it hanging open behind her.

He feels like crying, too, for her and for himself. He had hoped that, by now, she would consider him not just anyone, but *someone*.

•   •   •

Except for an agonizing hour in the Boob's Books and Printing class, he spends all day Friday at the Briggs, plugging away at the ciphertext. He leaves the windows unmasked again so that, if Gabriela should come looking for him, she can spot him easily. Not that he's really expecting her to turn up. He's probably more likely to be visited by the mystery man's minions, but he can't bring himself to care very much. He's tired of worrying about them.

He's tired of deciphering, too; it's no longer a challenge, just a chore, the way translating the other Vicente and the *Cantigas* was. It's the same sort of feeling he had after his father died and *sensei* Randy took over. Simon no longer got any real pleasure or satisfaction from the karate lessons; he was just going through the motions. And that's what he's doing now, going through the motions. Still, it's better than sitting around brooding.

He takes it one slow word at a time and by suppertime—he skips lunch so he can feel more like a martyr--he's wrestled another couple of pages into submission. It's a hard section for him to translate—not because the words are especially difficult, but because it introduces a slim, dark-haired, dark-eyed, brown-skinned woman to whom our hero is very attracted.

On land I had to contend only with snakes, leeches, and mosquitoes. The leeches could be pried off and the snakes avoided or beheaded; the mosquitoes could not. My only defense against them was to plaster my skin with mud from the riverbank. When it dried to a crust, it was nearly as maddening as the mosquito bites, but it did help to stanch the bleeding from the sword cut. And it proved to be a boon in another, quite unexpected way.

The following day, as I hacked my way through the undergrowth along the river bank, I came upon a narrow trail that, in one direction, led downriver and in the other headed uphill, toward the mountains. Though the dense foliage hid the peaks from my sight, when we'd been aboard our ship I had seen them rising in the distance, their tops shrouded in mist.

I was grateful to have a clear path to follow—that is, until I heard the tramp of feet on the uphill portion of the trail, accompanied by voices barking orders, a sound that, to me, suggested only one thing: enemy soldiers. I barely had time to scramble behind a stand of young bamboo before the party came into view.

There were seven of them. Four were armed with bows and spears, but they did not appear to be warriors, only ordinary villagers like those we had met the day before. The others were undoubtedly newly captured slaves, for they were linked together by a fibrous rope tied loosely around their necks. Two of these were young men with loincloths and shoulder-length hair; the third had straight dark tresses that, though they hung to her waist, only partly concealed her small breasts.

I, too, was only partly concealed; I was certain the armed men would spot me and perhaps take me prisoner. But my second skin of dried mud mixed with grass must have made a chameleon of me, for no one noticed my presence—no one except the woman. She was glancing about furtively as though searching for some means of escape. When she looked my way, our eyes met. Though the contact lasted but an instant, I seemed to read a multitude of things in those dark eyes: fear, bravery, intelligence, determination, curiosity, sensuality.

But perhaps I exaggerate; perhaps I recall it that way only because I came to discover those qualities in her later. In any case there was a connection of some kind between us, one so profound that I knew I had to rescue her.

Call it daring or call it foolish, but the moment the party were out of sight, I rose and followed them, treading as softly as I could. As luck would have it, the guard who brought up the rear stopped to relieve himself and fell behind. Without a moment's hesitation, I sprang forward and, before he was even aware of me, lopped off his head as I might a snake's. It was all done soundlessly, without alerting the others.

Swiftly, I caught up to the captives and, with a single sweep of my sword, severed the rope that tied the woman to the others. Seizing her wrist, I plunged off the path and into the undergrowth. Though we ran headlong, I soon discovered that there was no need; the remaining guards hadn't bothered to pursue us. No doubt they assumed that my comrades were close by; they had no way of knowing that I was all alone.

I had ruined for myself any chance of returning to the village, of course. My only hope now was to accompany the woman to where her people lived and trust that they were friendly. She seemed to understand this and took the lead, beckoning me to follow. Her fine, muscular legs showed that she was well accustomed to climbing hills; I, however, was not. What's more, I was weak from hunger and thirst and loss of blood. Though my pride suffered considerably, I could not keep up with her.

She repeatedly urged me on, in some guttural, staccato tongue that bore little resemblance to Lao, until at last I sank down on a log, unable to continue. For a moment, she stood regarding me with hands on hips, uttering something like Juque-cre-rei, which seemed to convey both impatience and concern. When I did not reply, to my dismay she turned away and stalked on up the hillside. I simply sat there, stunned. How, I wondered, could she abandon me after I had risked my life to rescue her?

Tune in next week, when our hero will discover whether he truly has been abandoned.

For a long while, Simon sits staring at the page. If only he'd been given the chance to rescue Gabriela when she was duped and drugged. He probably wouldn't have lopped off any heads, but he would have taught that big bastard Bear a very painful lesson. In fact, he still may.

He doesn't have to wait a week to find out whether Gabriela has abandoned him. To his surprise, she shows up at self-defense class the following morning. She doesn't arrive early to help set up, as she had been doing, but at least she does come. And she doesn't exactly avoid him, but neither does she seek him out. She bows in his direction and then focuses on her *kata*.

After class, as she's pulling her street clothes on over her leotard, she approaches and says softly, so the others won't hear, "How is the deciphering going?"

"Um, okay. I guess." He doesn't want to make it sound like he can't manage without her, but neither does he want her to think that he wouldn't welcome her help.

"Does he find the miraculous plant yet?"

"Not yet. But he does find a beautiful woman."

She glances away awkwardly, as if they're getting into uncomfortable territory.

Simon tries another topic. "So, how did your, uh, your Western Civ paper turn out?"

"I will find out on Monday."

"Uh-huh. Um, let me know, okay?"

She nods and gives a faint smile, then flips up her sweatshirt hood and hurries off. Simon feels as if they're back where they started, a month ago.

He's anxious to find out what becomes of our hero, but not anxious enough to spend the afternoon battling the cipher. Though he's always hated grocery shopping, especially when he has so little to spend, right now it sounds as good as a trip to Disneyland—which actually isn't saying much; he's never found the Magic Kingdom very appealing.

He can't bring himself to buckle down on Sunday, either. Instead, he whiles away most of the day playing pool and pinball with Mack at the Turtle Tap. Ordinarily, Mack would try to strike up an acquaintance with a couple of likely coeds, but he seems to sense that his friend is not in the mood. Though Simon hasn't told him exactly what's going on with Gabriela, he can't hide that fact that he's seriously bummed about it. Mack settles into his familiar role of cheerful companion, keeping the conversation light and the drinks coming.

Simon would be a lot more bummed if Alec were on duty; luckily for both of them, Bobby Boorman has recovered from his bout with mono and has reclaimed the bartending job. Simon's melancholia lifts a little when, with Mack's enthusiastic coaching (and a few well-timed bumps from the big guy's hip) he manages to score a respectable 5100 points on Beat the Devil—not great, but enough to keep Old Nick from filling the room with his scornful laughter.

On Monday, Simon dutifully returns to the Briggs and settles in with the ciphertext, but he can't keep his mind on it. Well, he tells himself, there's no big hurry, in any case. It's not like Dr. E is going to kick him out of the master's program if he takes a little longer. He could turn in the completed pages, but he'd rather wait until he's uncovered something of real significance. Vicente hasn't even discovered the miraculous plant yet, let alone poisoned the king.

There's a lot more to his thesis than just the codex, anyway. He may as well concentrate on research for a while, until he feels more like tackling the cipher—which is to say, until Gabriela rejoins him. Surely she will, if he just gives her a little time. Of course, that's what he thought about his mother, too.

He can only guess at what Gabriela is feeling. All he can compare it to is the way he felt after Wade's attack attorney raked him over the coals—as if he were the one on trial and had been judged guilty. Maybe if he can show her somehow that he understands, that he knows it wasn't her fault, that he's not judging her . . . That should be easy, right? Sort of like finding the key to the cipher.

He doesn't get much chance to show her anything, except for a few new self-defense techniques. Over the next couple of weeks, the only time they cross paths is at the Saturday morning class, and their conversations are mostly about karate. She does ask about the codex, and when he says he's put it aside for now, she's obviously disappointed. Simon also senses an undercurrent of guilt, as if she feels responsible for his loss of interest—which in a way she is, though Simon would never say so. As usual, he just doesn't know what to say.

He comes up a bit short in the research department, too; the Briggs doesn't have as much material on Renaissance codes and ciphers as he hoped. After getting permission to skip a few classes, he catches a bus to Ohio University, where he spends most of a week rooting through the collection at the new Alden Library, scribbling notes and making Xerox copies of relevant pages.

It's a cheap trip; one of the Karate Club guys has a friend at OU who puts Simon up and feeds him. In return, Simon teaches a few new tricks to his host and half a dozen other martial arts enthusiasts. He welcomes the workout; he hasn't been to Karate Club since the unpleasant face-off with Alec.

He doesn't make it back for that week's self-defense class, either. He has no idea what the women will do in his absence. Will they go ahead and practice dutifully without him, or will they give a Visigoth cheer and descend upon Dad's Restaurant for brunch? Probably some of each. If he knows Gabriela, she'll put in a full two hours, anyway, performing her *kata* and attacking the *makiwara* with her usual intensity. But of course he doesn't know her, not really.

To Simon's surprise, the change of scene and routine work like a dose of the marvelous healing plant—a small dose, admittedly, but when he returns to his own campus he's feeling refreshed, recharged, ready to attack the cipher again.

His upbeat mood doesn't last long. Back at the Gas Chamber, he finds Mack sawing logs—not on the couch, for some reason, but in Simon's bed. When the big guy wakes up, he mumbles an apology and, after much head ducking and rubbing, proceeds to tell the sobering story of all that went down while Simon was away.

It's not quite as dramatic as Vicente Somebody's tale, but almost.

CHAPTER TWENTY-FIVE

When Simon sees that familiar shamefaced look, he figures that his impulsive friend must have joined an SDS demonstration and punched a cop or something. Or maybe he's been caught rummaging through the Medical Sciences Center's wastebaskets. But, no, the story seems to revolve around Mack's injured knee, and it actually starts out pretty hopefully. He's been cutting back on the Darvon lately, he says. The leg was hurting a lot less, and he was getting around with hardly a trace of a limp.

Now things start to get grim: Mack being Mack, he decided to put the leg to the test. He had the brilliant idea that, if he started exercising again, maybe he could get himself in good enough shape so that, come summer, he'd be ready for football preseason camp.

"Oh, no, Mack," groans Simon.

"Hey, I didn't overdo it, I swear. No running up the stadium steps, or skipping rope, or anything. Just a little easy jogging, a few deep knee bends, that kind of stuff."

But as he was jogging easily down the sidewalk, he encountered Rhonda and one of her classmates on their way home from school. In gentlemanly fashion, he side-stepped to make way for them. As he did, his foot slipped off the walk and into the gutter. There was a burst of pain in his knee so fierce that he shouted "Jesus Christ!" and collapsed onto the curb.

The teenage slattern—who was wearing Mack's letter jacket—and her friend draped his massive arms over their puny shoulders and, with no small effort, managed to hobble him back to the Horvaths' garage and up the stairs to the Gas Chamber. Her parents were away for the weekend, visiting relatives in

Pennsylvania, but Rhonda had refused to go; she had a ton of schoolwork--or so she told them. To Mack she revealed the real reason: She didn't like the creepy way her older cousin had been leering at her lately.

If she actually did have schoolwork, she let it slide, preferring to play the role of full-time nurse to her poor sidelined athlete. She brought him coffee and canned soup and grilled cheese sandwiches. She fetched a deck of cards and they played game after game of gin rummy, most of which she won.

After Mack's small supply of Seagram's 7 ran dry, she stole a bottle of her dad's Scotch. She doled out Darvon when he needed it, which was more often than ever, and in larger doses. She may have popped one or two herself, just for kicks, he wasn't sure. She had a couple of giggling fits, but it may have just been due to the Scotch, which she definitely did sample.

Some part of him knew that letting her hang around might not be the best idea, but he really did need her help. He could barely make it to the bathroom, let alone make meals for himself. Besides, it was kind of nice, being waited on hand and foot; he'd never had that luxury. Even when he was laid up with mumps as a kid, there was no one to take proper care of him. His dad, who often worked twelve-hour shifts, had to beg the cranky neighbor lady to keep an eye on him.

The Gas Chamber was never very warm this time of year, but it seemed colder than usual, probably thanks to the Darvon, which in large doses always gave him chills. Even with the comforter and a couple of other blankets piled on him, he kept shivering. Just as he was about to suggest that Rhonda bring some blankets from her place, he felt her crawl under the covers and snuggle up next to him.

He should have kicked her out, he knows that, and he probably knew it even then, though he wasn't exactly thinking straight. But again, it was kind of nice, and besides it worked; with her skin right up against his, he felt a lot warmer. Oh, did he mention that she was wearing nothing but a bra and panties? At some earlier point—he had lost all sense of time--she had helped him out of his clothes, to make him more comfortable, so he was wearing only his tee shirt and boxers.

Mack gives a defeated-sounding sigh. "Well. You can guess what happened next."

"Oh, great. Jeez, Mack, I warned you. That's like statutory rape, or something!"

"Actually, no. The age of consent in Ohio is sixteen." He gives one of his sheepish shrugs. "I looked it up once. Just out of curiosity. I mean, it's not like I planned the whole thing. It just sort of . . . happened. At least I think it did. Maybe I just dreamed it." He pulls back the covers and eyes the stain on the sheet. "Okay, no."

"You just better hope she doesn't get pregnant. *And* you'd better hope she doesn't tell her parents."

Mack squirms uncomfortably, then gives a grunt of pain and clutches his knee. "I don't see how I can I go in to work. What day is it?"

"Wednesday."

"Oh, man. I've missed two days already. You think you could you find a phone and call in sick for me?"

"I guess. Anything else I can get for you?"

"Yeah. A cheap lawyer."

"A *lawyer*?"

He nods ruefully. "Her parents say they're going to sue the shit out of me."

"So she *did* tell them?"

"Apparently."

"Why would she do that?"

"The same reason we did stupid stuff at that age—to show that she doesn't have to follow their rules."

"At that age," says Simon, "I didn't have anybody to show."

"Oh, yeah. Sorry, man."

"It's okay. Anyway, I don't think they can actually sue you for . . . for . . ."

"Deflowering their daughter? Maybe not. But they can make my life miserable. They already are. They say I have to move out as soon as I can walk. They talked about getting rid of you, too, but I convinced them not to. Plus, I think they need the rent money."

"Aw, Mack. Where are you going to go?"

"Some of my old teammates will put me up if I give them a sob story."

"I hope so."

"Hey, look on the bright side. You won't have to wear those damn earplugs. Listen, could you just do one other thing for me?"

"Strangle Rhonda?"

"Ahh, it wasn't her fault. Like I always say, us jocks are irresistible. No, just stop by the field house get me a knee brace, would you?"

Simon uses a pay phone in the Student Center to call the head of maintenance, then solaces himself with a Brazilian Dark Roast at the Gedunk. The brew seems to have summoning powers: No sooner does he sit down at a window table than he sees his coffee-colored Brazilian friend hurrying down the walk. Beneath her coat she's wearing her Athletic Department sweatshirt, with the hood half-concealing her face. Simon is about to rap on the glass to get her attention, but as always he hesitates, and then she's gone past and the opportunity is lost.

Or maybe not. She rounds the corner of the building, pushes through the entrance doors, and heads for the Gedunk. Simon is tempted to wave to her, but if he catches her eye, she might just beat a hasty retreat, so he just sits there like a lump. She spots him anyway and, to his surprise, makes straight for him, or as straight as the tables allow. "Simon! *Olá!* I was just on my way to your apartment!"

"You--you were?"

"Yes; I wondered what became of you."

"Oh. I, uh, I was just doing research at OU."

"OU?"

"Ohio University."

"Oh."

"This is a strange conversation. Lots of ohs and yous. You look cold. You want a sip of my *café?*"

"No. Thank you. I have something to tell you."

Uh-oh. Though Simon doesn't know much about women, he knows that when they say they have something to tell you, it's not likely to be anything good. "Um, okay."

She glances about furtively, then leans across the table, as close as she can get. "One of the minons attacked me," she whispers.

"*What?*"

"Sssh!"

"But—but what do mean *attacked* you?"

"Be quiet, and I will tell you!"

"Okay, okay."

"I went to the Veterinary Medicine department and I showed the tranquilizer dart to some man in a lab coat--a graduate student, I think. He said it looked like theirs, so I asked if anyone had borrowed one of their tranquilizer guns. He said no, they always kept them locked up. But you know, he seemed to me to be very . . . how do you say? Uptight?"

"Like he knew more than he was saying?"

"*Exatamente*. I could not get any more out of him, though. By the time I left, it was getting late. I don't like to go out after dark, but I wanted to speak to you. You were not at the Gas Chamber, so I thought I would try the library. As I was passing the field house—that area with no lights, you know?--I heard someone behind me. I walked more quickly, but not quickly enough. He grabbed hold of me and wrapped one arm around my neck." She raises a hand to her throat. "He was a big person, and strong—like a football player—and he squeezed so hard I could barely breathe. He stuck his face up close to mine and he said, very quiet but very rough, "If you know what's good for you, bitch, you'll stop poking your little nose in where it doesn't belong."

"Holy shit! What did you *do*?"

Unexpectedly, her face forms a self-satisfied smile. "Just what you taught us, *sensei*: I flung my head backward, then I hit him in the *testículos*, then I elbowed him in the stomach."

"And he let you go?"

"Oh, yes. To tell the truth, I felt a little sorry for him. Not much, but a little."

"Any idea who it was?"

She shakes her head. "He was wearing a . . . how do you say . . . a ski mask? I didn't recognize his voice, either."

"So it wasn't Bear?"

"No. I thought there was no use reporting it to the Campus Police, after . . . after what happened before, so I just went on to the library. You were not there, either, of course. But-- May I still have a drink of your *café*?"

"Uh, sure. Finish it off."

"*Obrigada*. As I was leaving, Ms. Harris called to me. She wanted to know if you and I were friends. I said yes--"

"I'm glad."

She smiles faintly. "—so she asked me to give you this overdue notice." She digs a paper out of her jeans pocket and passes it to him. "She mailed one a week or two ago, but she never heard back from you."

"Oops. I don't get much mail, so I always forget to check, except when my NDEA payment's due--which it is, come to think of it." He scans the notice.

"Ah. The *Cantigas*. I didn't realize I'd had it that long. I guess I'd better renew it, or she'll be wondering where it is."

"I don't think you can, Simon; someone put a hold on it."

"Really? Who on earth would want it?"

"It is funny you should ask. I glanced at the hold request; the person's name—or at least the name he gave them—is Thomas Huxley."

"Oh, great! The mystery man is back."

"Perhaps. Or perhaps it is like a code name, and his minions use it, too. Whoever it is, why would they be interested in the *Cantigas*?"

Simon nearly says *Because it contains the copies of the codex?* But how would Dr. Vice or his minions know that? Why would they even suspect it? In any case, Gabriela asked him to not to tell her where the pages are hidden, so he doesn't reply, just stammers a little and shrugs.

"Simon?" She eyes him suspiciously. "I think that now *you* are the one who knows more than he is saying. Why will you not--" She pauses a moment, then nods knowingly. "Oh. I see. That is where you hid the copies, *não é assim?* No, do not answer. But if it is, they would have no way of knowing that, would they?"

"I don't see how. Unless maybe they're still spying on us and saw me with it."

"But if they knew where it was, they would not need to put a hold on it."

"Well, it'd be a little hard to find. I shelved it in the wrong place."

Gabriela chews at a ragged fingernail. "I think we should make sure it is still there, Simon."

"Good idea."

⋅ ● ⋅ ● ⋅

On their way to the third floor stacks, they manage to avoid Ms. Harris; Simon doesn't care to explain to her why he hasn't returned the *Cantigas*. There's only one other person in the P section—Susan, one of the library interns, is wheeling around a cart filled with books. It's not likely that she'd be one of the mystery man's minions, but you can't be too careful. Simon waits until she's several aisles away before he heads for the spot where the *Cantigas* is tucked in among titles on Indo-European philology. "You don't have to look, if you don't want to know where it is."

Gabriela grins mischievously. "I like to poke in my little nose where it does not belong."

"Okay. I just hope they don't--" He breaks off and stands staring blankly at the shelf.

"What is it? Simon?"

"Um . . . it's not there."

"Are you sure?"

"*Claro.*" He sits on a rolling stepstool and puts his head in his hands. "This makes no sense. I don't see how they could possibly . . ." He gives Gabriela a look of despair. "What are we going to do?"

"Let me think." There's a long moment of silence, except for the faint rumble of the book cart's wheels rolling along some distant aisle. Gabriela gives a small gasp. "Do you know what? I will bet Susan was reading the shelves!"

"And putting the out-of-place books back where they belong?"

"*Exatamente.* What is the number of the *Cantigas*?"

"PQ9189.A44. But don't get your hopes up."

"And don't you get *your* hopes down." She disappears into the PQs and emerges a minute later with a huge smile on her face and the *Cantigas* in her hands. "See? I was right."

Simon refuses to feel relieved until he's pried up the endpaper and made sure the copies are still there. "You're brilliant, as I always say sometimes."

"Thank you. Shall we do some deciphering?"

We. She said *we.* "Um, yeah, okay."

"Your head is not hurting?"

"It was," he says. "But it's feeling a lot better now." He thinks but doesn't say: *It's not only plants that have the power to heal.*

CHAPTER TWENTY-SIX

Before they tackle the cipher, Simon reads aloud the new pages he's translated. Gabriela is as rapt as an audience watching a serial at a Saturday matinee. "You have done a lot, Simon!" she exclaims.

"We'd have done more as a team," he says, and immediately regrets it. "I mean . . . I--I wasn't trying to make you feel bad, or . . . "

"I know. I should have kept helping you. It was just . . . a little awkward, after . . . "

"It's okay. We don't have to talk about that."

"Good. So. Let's find out whether the woman abandoned Vicente. I think she did not."

"I don't know; I hope you're right."

"I am always right."

"Says Modesty Blaise."

For a change, Simon doesn't wait until they have a page or two of Portuguese plaintext to start translating. He takes it one sentence at a time. "'She had done no such thing, of course; she soon returned, carrying an armful of small coconuts.' Yay. She came back."

"Of course."

It doesn't take long for them to slip back into their old rhythm. They've learned not to waste time on words that resist deciphering; they breeze through the easy ones and the ones that repeat, such as *she* and *her*, and then they infer the tough ones by the context in which they appear. By suppertime—well, more like bedtime, really--they've churned out an astonishing four pages of English plaintext. Even better, they've uncovered the first hard evidence regarding the miraculous healing plant.

She had done no such thing, of course; she soon returned, carrying an armful of small coconuts. With my sword, she pierced them so that I might drink the contents, which did me much good. Meanwhile she examined my wound, which had begun to fester. From a small hemp pouch at her waist, she drew what appeared to be a root of some sort. She bit off a portion and chewed on it for several minutes, then applied the sticky pulp to the sword cut and bound it in place with a strip of bark.

The poultice stung like a jellyfish, and I was tempted to tear it off, but she guarded it with both hands and shook her head emphatically, saying something like Gee-mon. Since she had no conceivable reason to want to poison me, I decided to trust her. It was a good decision. Within hours, the pain had subsided. When she exposed the wound the following day, it was no longer inflamed; in fact, incredible as it seemed, it had practically healed.

After climbing for half the morning, we reached our goal: A small, primitive settlement occupied by a tribe of thirty or so who, I later learned, called themselves ma-bri—meaning People of the Forest. They seemed quite alarmed by my presence; the women and children retreated into the trees, while the men snatched up palm-stem spears and threatened me with them—not very fiercely, to be sure, but more in the manner of Please do not make me use this.

My new friend indicated that I should put down my sword; with much reluctance I complied. She then she made a small speech to the others that seemed to reassure them. The men laid aside their spears and called to the women and children, who crept into the clearing and regarded me with a curiosity akin to awe. Probably they had never seen anyone so pale-skinned before, or so hairy, or so large. None of them was over seven spans in height; their spears were twice as long as they were. Their complexion was the shade of a ripe mango, and the men's faces were beardless.

In an effort to appear harmless, I approached a fellow who seemed as much in charge as anyone, holding out my hand. Gee-mon! cried the woman, which I had determined meant no. Snatching my sleeve, she led me away a few paces and signified that I should remain there. From this I understood that I was not to enter the living area until invited.

It took the tribe, women included, at least an hour of heated discussion to make up their minds. Meanwhile, I sat on a stump and surveyed the settlement—one could hardly call it a proper village. Nor could one apply the term house to their crude shelters; they were mere lean-tos, each smaller than the poop deck of our captured ship, constructed of bamboo poles and thatched with yellowing banana leaves.

There were no areas of tilled soil such as those in the Lao village. These people were clearly hunters and gatherers, not farmers. No doubt when they depleted the nearby resources, they would move on to new territory; that explained the temporary nature of their shelters.

At last the woman signaled that I might join them. I sat with a dozen of the men in the shade of the largest shelter while the women served us a variety of foods. Some I could identify—papayas, bananas, yams; others I had to guess at, such as the roasted carcass of an animal that resembled a deer but was no larger than a Podengo dog.

Acclimating oneself to new surroundings and society is like navigating unknown waters: One is almost certain to hit an obstacle or two. In addition to barging in uninvited, I managed to commit several other sins. As a soldier, I was naturally interested in weapons of any sort so, with a questioning look, I pointed toward one of the palm-stem spears. The men reacted with considerable alarm, shaking their heads vehemently.

As I later learned, the ma-bri believe that all animals and plants and many objects are possessed of a spirit that must be respected. This is one reason they do not till the earth—to avoid offending it. And because a spear has a spirit, only the man to whom it belongs may touch it. How they managed to distinguish one spear from another, I have no idea.

It is also forbidden to reveal one's name, lest it give the bad spirits power over you. When I began repeating "Vicente" and tapping myself on the chest, they didn't understand at first; when it dawned on them what I meant, they were appalled. I proceeded to make matters worse by insisting they tell me their names. Before they could flee in horror, my friend stepped in and made an impassioned plea to them on behalf of the poor benighted barbarian.

I never learned her name, either, of course. Since she often said to me something that sounded like Alaela, I took to calling her that. Eventually I deduced that it is their word for hello. Over a period of what I suppose was three months or so—one day was so like another that I quickly lost track of time—under Alaela's guidance I learned a little of their language, which contained a smattering of Lao words, and a good deal about their simple existence.

I was right in assuming that the ma-bri were nomadic. When I had been there perhaps a week, they gathered up their few belongings and, abandoning their crude shelters, moved to a new site half a day's walk away, near a spring. There we constructed a whole new array of lean-tos. It took us only a few hours, thanks in part to my sword, which could sever a stalk of bamboo as thick as a man's arm with a single swipe. I offered the use of the sword to several other men but they all declined—feeling, no doubt, that the spirit residing in such a powerful weapon demanded even more respect than that of a simple palm-stem spear.

Once we were settled in, the never-ending task of obtaining food began. The women were in charge of the gathering; the men, for the most part, were the hunters, though the women and children sometimes acted as beaters to flush out game.

One might expect that I would spend my time hunting with the men, but I already knew how to kill; instead I accompanied Alaela on her foraging expeditions. She gave me a thorough education in recognizing and harvesting wild foods and medicinal plants—knowledge that would serve me well in Malaca, assuming I managed to find my way back.

Ironically, one of the things I learned from her was another method of killing: She pointed out a fig-like tree called kok nong whose poisonous sap the men sometimes daubed on their spear points if they were after some particularly fierce prey such as wild boar.

But she taught me far more about healing, particularly about the plant she called o-dai, which had worked such wonders on my wounded arm. It is a thorny vine that apparently is found only in that one area of the mountains—a realm that, as I later discovered, the Lao call Dong Ling, or Monkey Forest. I believe the term monkey is an insulting one, used to refer not to those abundant animals but to the ma-bri themselves. Kha, the other name they have for the ma-bri, means simply slave.

I saw ample evidence of o-dai's healing powers. When one hunter's leg was torn open by a wild boar's tusk, Aleala pounded a large chunk of the root into a pulp and plastered it onto the ugly wound. Within two days, the man was up and about and cheerfully recounting his adventure. Not only did the plant speedily mend injuries and infections and bruises, the people drank a tea made from the bark to ease the pains of childbirth, to bring down fevers, and as a means of warding off malaria. Apparently it worked, for I followed their example and never did fall prey to that debilitating disease. Such a tonic, I thought, would be a godsend for the soldiers at the fortress.

Though I had no hope now of capturing the Golden Buddha, I realized that I had discovered something of far more value, something that, for centuries, physicians and alchemists had been seeking and falsely claiming to have found—the cura-tudo or panacea. If I could take cuttings of the vine back to Malaca and propagate them successfully, I would make my fortune.

"I will bet that is exactly what Dr. Vice is thinking," says Gabriela.

"Maybe. I just keep wondering how he knew what was in the codex in the first place."

She shrugs. "Just because *we* never heard of Vicente, it does not mean that other people do not know of him, people who have studied the history of . . . what do you call them?"

"Pharmaceuticals. Good point."

"Thank you. And I have another one."

"Okay."

"Would this not be a good time to show our efforts to Dr. Espinoza, before he is overwhelmed with term papers and exams?"

"No," says Simon.

"No?"

"This would be a good time to get something to eat. The Tyrant can wait until tomorrow."

They run off copies of both the Portuguese plaintext and the English translation on the Taft's Xerox machine. Simon is about to tuck the originals back into the *Cantigas* when he has second thoughts. "Um, you know, if the minions are looking for this book, maybe we should find another hiding place."

"But Ms. Harris thinks *you* have it; no one will expect to find it here."

"Hmm. I guess not. And if they just finished reading these shelves, they won't do it again for a couple of months, right?"

"Right."

"Okay, then." Simon sidles down the aisle, surveying the shelves. "Let's stick it . . ." He zeroes in on a row of raggedy oversized Norwegian picture books. "Here! I mean, who's going to be looking at these?" He slides the *Cantigas* in among them, with the spine facing to the rear. "Now. Let's go eat."

There's no need to avoid Ms. Harris--she's gone home long ago—but they do keep an eye out for minions as they make their exit. "Is Dad's Restaurant okay with you?" asks Simon.

"It will be the only place open."

"Yeah, unfortunately. I mean, it's not bad, but I wish we had a Mexican restaurant."

"Well, if you will be on campus during Christmas break, then perhaps . . . "

"Perhaps what?" Though it's too dark to see her face clearly, Simon gets the sense that she's flustered, uncertain whether or not she wants to finish the thought.

"Perhaps," she continues, softly, "I will make you a nice Brazilian meal."

Simon is struck dumb. Surely she can't cook a whole dinner on the Gas Chamber's single burner hotplate. Does this mean he'll actually be invited to her place? At last he manages to mutter, "Um, sure. That'd be great."

CHAPTER TWENTY-SEVEN

Simon doesn't bother making an appointment with Dr. Espinoza; he's pretty sure the Tyrant will make time for him. In fact, he'll undoubtedly be eager to hear every little detail about how they cracked the cipher.

On Thursday, the two of them show up unannounced at Dr. E's classroom just as the few students brave enough to take his Spanish Morphosyntax are shuffling out, most of them looking either bewildered or disgusted or both. For a change, Gabriela has dressed to impress, foregoing her *I'm unattractive, pay no attention to me* outfit in favor of a red sweater, a pleated skirt, and black tights.

Espinoza seems pleased to see her. In fact he actually gives her a half-hearted hug. "*Bom Dia, minha querida.*" Simon, as usual, barely rates a nod.

"How are you feeling, *Maestro*?"

"Like I need a drink." He fishes a flask of something from his briefcase, pours a capful, and downs it in a single gulp. "Is it only my imagination, or are students becoming more idiotic with each year that passes?"

Gabriela gives him a mock frown. "You are supposed to say *Present company excepted.*"

Espinoza shrugs indifferently. "Perhaps I shall . . . if you give me some reason to."

Simon holds out the Portuguese plaintext. "Is this reason enough?"

The Tyrant snatches the papers and sits on the edge of his desk perusing them for a good five minutes before he speaks. "Perhaps I underestimated you," he says grudgingly. "So, it was not an autokey after all?"

"Nope. He used a Latin prayer as the key. Each line of text was enciphered with a different line of the prayer."

"But how did you discover the key?"

Simon exchanges a guarded glance with Gabriela. "Um, I'd rather not say, *Maestro*."

"No, no, of course not," the professor growls. "I should not have asked." He leafs through the plaintext. "Have you translated this yet?"

Simon waves the rest of the pages. "I have."

"I do not see any reference here to João o Terceiro. Am I missing something?"

"We are only halfway through, *Maestro*," explains Gabriela. "Perhaps there will be something later on." She moves up close to Simon and says softly, "I think we should tell him about . . . about the other thing."

"You do?"

"*Sim*. He deserves to know why the mystery man drugged him."

"Okay, I guess so." Simon clears his throat. "We, um . . . we found out why Dr. Weiss is so keen to have the codex."

"And why is that?"

"Well, as you probably gathered, Vicente travels to Southeast Asia. While he's there, he finds a plant called *o-dai* that has miraculous healing powers."

"Ah. And Dr. Weiss--he would like to find this *o-dai* before some other company does."

"That would be my guess."

Dr. Espinoza fixes Simon with the same withering stare he uses on his students when they're being particularly dense. "*Señor* Hannay. Has it never occurred to you that you might *sell* the information to him? I am certain it would fetch a high price."

Simon shifts about uncomfortably and stammers, "Um . . . actually, no. I never thought about it."

"And why not?"

"Well, I—uh—I guess . . ."

"I think that if the *o-dai* still exists," says Gabriela, "and if it is as miraculous as Vicente claims, then it should *not* be controlled by men who do not care about how much good it can do, only about how much money it will make for them."

Dr. Espinoza does something Simon can't ever recall seeing him do before—he smiles, openly and genuinely. "An excellent answer, *minha querida*. You have scored one hundred percent on my little test. So. You need to publish this as soon as possible, in a journal that is as influential as possible. My suggestion would be the *JRL.*"

Simon's jaw literally drops. "Um, *really?*"

"What is the *JRL?*" Gabriela wants to know.

"Oh, nothing; just the most prestigious journal in the field. But, I mean, shouldn't we wait until we've deciphered the whole thing?"

"No," says the professor. "Since the *JRL* is a quarterly, it has a long lead time. The editors can decide on the basis of this--" He taps the papers in Simon's hands. "--whether or not they want to publish it. And I can promise you they *will* want to."

Simon shakes his head incredulously. "Okay. If you say so."

"I do. Come to my office; I will telephone the editor and give him what you call a *hard sell.*" He shakes his shaggy head. "I am not fond of English as a rule, but you do have some very apposite phrases."

"You know the editor of the *JRL?*!"

"*Claro.* He was a student of mine."

And you're still on speaking terms? Simon wants to say but doesn't.

Marnie is at her desk typing furiously, but pauses long enough to say, "How are you feeling, Dr. E?"

"Discouraged," the professor grumbles. "Are there no intelligent students on this campus?"

She rolls her eyes in Simon and Gabriela's direction, as if to say *Here he goes again.* "I know a few," she says.

"Could you convince them to major in Foreign Languages?"

"I'll try."

"Good. In the meantime, please get me the contact information for Mitchell Reid at the *JPL.*"

Simon winces and notices Gabriela doing the same. Apparently Espinoza has noticed, too, for as soon as they're in his office he says, "Is there some problem?"

When Simon hesitates, Gabriela picks up the gauntlet. "Not exactly. It is just that . . . well, I think that the fewer people who know about this, the better."

The professor gives one of his Beethoven scowls. "I do not think we need worry about Miss Cameron."

"I am sure we do not. But--to use one of those handy English sayings--better safe than sorry."

"Well, if you do not trust her, you may mail the manuscript yourselves, *está bem?*" There's a rap on the office door. "*Sí?*"

Marnie peeks in. "I have the information you asked for, Dr. E."

While the Tyrant chats on the phone in Spanish with his former student, Simon and Gabriela hold a whispered consultation. "How cool would that be," says Simon, "if I had a paper in *JRL?* Your name should be on it, too, though; you did half the work."

"You do not need to do that, Simon."

"Maybe not. But I want to."

"*Obrigada.* Do you suppose that, once it appears, the mystery man will leave us alone? Or," she adds, a bit breathlessly, "will he take revenge on us for foiling his plans?"

Simon laughs. "You've been watching too many spy movies, *minha querida.*" The endearment just sort of slips out, but Gabriela doesn't seem to object.

Espinoza hangs up the phone and swivels in his chair to face them, wearing a smug sort of smile. "It did not require a very hard sell. Dr. Reid is, as you would say, licking his chops." He hands Gabriela the paper with the editor's name and address. "Be sure to send it *por avión*. He would like it as soon as possible."

•　　•　　•

Now that the paper seems almost certain to be published, they're even more motivated to finish deciphering and translating. Armed with a bag full of snacks and drinks, they sequester themselves in a study room the whole of Friday and end up, punchy but proud, with four more pages of English plaintext. Simon begins his reading with the final sentences of the previous segment:

Though I had no hope now of capturing the Golden Buddha, I realized that I had discovered something of far more value, something that, for centuries, physicians and alchemists had been seeking and falsely claiming to have found—the cura-tudo or panacea. If I could take cuttings of the vine back to Malaca and propagate them successfully, I would make my fortune.

I had also begun to consider the possibility of taking Aleala back with me. There was no shortage of attractive and willing local women around the fortress, of course, but none was as appealing or clever or spirited as Aleala. Surely she would welcome the chance to live a more comfortable, civilized existence. But how could I convey to her the advantages of such a life? Their language had no words for such luxuries as shoes and gowns, hot baths and feather beds and Madeiran aguardente.

There was a way of winning her without words, of course. Despite the unmistakable attraction that existed between us, I had so far made no advances, [Simon stumbles a bit over this passage; Gabriela pretends not to notice] *wary of committing another blunder that might turn her people against me. But one afternoon while foraging, we became separated from the others; it seemed an opportune time to try my luck, so to speak.*

When I embraced her, [more stumbling from Simon] *she did not resist, but neither did she respond as warmly as I hoped. I might have pressed my suit more insistently except that, at that moment, we heard shouts and screams nearby. We hurried toward the sound, to discover two young ma-bri women struggling to free themselves from the grasp of Lao villagers.*

I had nearly forgotten about the slavers. I suppose I assumed that, after I beheaded one of their number, it gave the others second thoughts about raiding the ma-bri settlement. But I think now that it just took them a while to find the spot in the Monkey Forest where the monkeys had resettled.

Drawing my sword, I descended upon the men, who had laid their bows and quivers of arrows aside; with no effort at all I struck them down. If I had expected the women to be grateful, I was disappointed; they seemed, in fact, as frightened of me as they had been of their attackers, and scurried for the safety of the settlement.

Though Aleala appeared rather stunned by the sudden violence, she did not run off. Instead, she approached the corpses and examined their faces. Pointing at the larger of the two men, she indicated through a combination of words and gestures that he was one of her former captors and that, before I came to her rescue, the villain had had his way with her. [Simon does more than just stumble over this bit; he can barely get the words out. Gabriela places a hand on his arm as if to say *It is all right.*] *I understood now why she might not welcome my attentions.*

When we rejoined the tribe, the two women were relating what had happened. Again, no one thanked or praised me; instead they regarded me with astonishment or incredulity, as though I had done something unheard of, when I had only acted as I supposed any man would in such circumstances. I was astonished as well when I saw that they had no intention of sending out an armed party to search for other slavers. They took no action at all, in fact; they merely shook their heads sadly, as if what had happened was regrettable but inevitable.

Why, I wondered, did they refuse to defend themselves? I demanded to know how often these raids occurred. Though the ma-bri seem to have little sense of time, I gathered that the slavers came perhaps twice a year and made off with several captives each time—it wasn't clear just how many, for the ma-bri also have a limited grasp of numbers.

Though I had begun to grow restive and to long for my own life again, at the same time I felt compelled to improve the sorry lot of these people. It is what we Europeans always do. By improving their lot, we of course mean imposing our own values upon them. I decided that, before I left, I would at least teach the men how to fight. The Lao villagers were clearly not much account as warriors; I was convinced that, if they met with real resistance, their raids would cease.

The ma-bri went along with my plan--more or less. I think they worried that, if they did not, I would be upset and, whether out of fear or out of politeness, they did not wish to upset me. I knew that trying to school them in the art of archery would be useless; I settled for teaching them that it is possible not only to thrust and jab with one's spear, but to actually throw it. I also helped them construct heavy bamboo shields for warding off arrows. I had no notion of how to go about infusing the shields with the appropriate spirit.

To my surprise, several of the women, including Aleala, took part in the training. In fact, they were my most enthusiastic pupils. ["Just like the Visigoths!" says Gabriela.] When we faced off with bamboo staves and shields, they laid on with a will, while the men tended to hold back, as though afraid of hurting their opponent.

I also implemented a second strategy: During daylight hours, I posted a guard in a tree overlooking the trail. If a stranger approached, the guard was to blow a warning signal on a bamboo flute. I suspected that the Lao would send another raiding party soon, to determine what became of the first one, and I was right.

Several days later, as I was taking a cutting from one of the o-dai vines, I heard the guard's shrill signal, which was abruptly cut off, no doubt by an arrow. Wrapping the cutting in a banana leaf packed with damp soil, I thrust it into my shot-bag and ran for the clearing, shouting às armas!—the only Portuguese phrase I had managed to teach my recruits.

Waving my sword, I commanded them to follow me. A few of them did so, with obvious reluctance. Aleala was only the one to show any real spirit. She grabbed her shield and the spear she had fashioned and sprang to my side, which shamed several more of the men into joining us.

I had expected to encounter perhaps half a dozen Lao; instead, we found ourselves facing at least twenty, all of them armed with bows and bamboo quivers full of arrows. Desperately, my men and women flung their spears as I had taught them; not one found its target. The enemy archers were far more accurate. Panicking, my poor little army dropped their shields and ran, but they could not outrun the flock of arrows that flew after them.

The few of us who remained retreated to the settlement. I was certain that the Lao would not be so bold as to pursue us. Once again, I misjudged them. Many of the ma-bri managed to escape into the forest, but just as many were slain or were rounded up, roped together, and herded off like animals.

Aleala and I stood our ground as long as we could and did our share of slaying, but at last we, too, were forced to flee. We holed up in a bamboo thicket until darkness fell; then Aleala indicated that we should return to the settlement. Gee-mon, I replied. She was clearly puzzled; surely the enemy would be gone by now? But of course it was not the Lao I was afraid to face. It was the ma-bri. I had insisted that they learn to defend themselves, and it had led to their slaughter.

I explained as best I could why I did not wish to go back. Juque-ga-lang? she asked. Where will you go? To my own land, I told her. I was confident that, if I could make my way to the coast of Camboja, I would eventually find a trading vessel willing to deliver me to Malaca for a price. Though I doubt that she fully understood, she did grasp the fact that I was leaving and she replied, like Ruth, that whither I went she would go.

"Ah, how sweet!" exclaims Gabriela. "And how sad, that so many of her people were killed and enslaved."

"It might have been better," says Simon, "if he hadn't tried to teach them to fight."

"I do not believe that. People have to defend themselves." She smiles impishly. "Perhaps he should have taught them martial arts."

"Yeah, he could have had them make *salawaku* shields; Indonesians used them both for protection and as a weapon. They're also quite beautiful."

"Oooh, I want one!"

"You *are* one," says Simon, before he can stop himself. He feels a blush coming on.

Gabriela gives him a bemused look. "That is a strange compliment. Simon. At least I *think* it is a compliment."

"Um, it was meant to be, anyway."

"Thank you." To his astonishment, she leans into him and presses a soft kiss on his stubbly cheek.

On the way home, Simon is feeling a bit giddy, but somehow he remembers to check the Gas Chamber's mailbox. It contains both his monthly stipend from the NDEA and the original overdue notice from the Briggs. How long, he wonders, can he manage to put Ms. Harris off? He could always tell her he lost the *Cantigas*, but she might suspend his library privileges or something. Or he could stash the pages in some other volume, but, aside from those in the Rare Book Room, there aren't many with padded covers. They'll just have to finish off the codex as fast as possible. That means spending even more time with Gabriela; gee, what a shame.

He can't help wishing Mack were around, so he could brag a little about the kiss, but the big guy is busy sweeping floors and rummaging through wastebaskets. Or so Simon supposes.

CHAPTER TWENTY-EIGHT

As he's fixing a grilled cheese for himself, the doorbell gives a half-hearted growl. He opens the door to find the girl next door standing outside, shivering in pajamas, a bathrobe, and bunny slippers.

"Rhonda? What the hell?"

"Can I c-come in for just a second? I've g-got a message from Mack."

"From *Mack*?"

"Please, Simon, b-before they see me!"

Reluctantly, Simon lets her slip inside and quickly closes the door. "Before *who* sees you?"

"Our n-neighbors, the Allens. They're the ones that t-told my parents I was here with Mack while they were g-gone."

"Oh. Well, um, what are you doing dressed like that?"

"I was g-getting ready for bed when he called."

"Mack called *you*?"

"Uh-huh. He didn't know how else to get hold of you. He wants you to bring him a few things."

"What kind of things? Where is he?"

"In jail," she says, as if he should have known.

"In *jail*?"

"Yeah. Look, I've g-got to get back, before my parents notice I'm gone. D-Don't hate me, Simon, okay? I didn't want to tell them about . . . you know. They forced me to."

"I don't hate you. It was stupid, that's all. That's not why Mack's in jail, is it?"

"I don't think so. I've gotta go. Bye." She scrambles down the stairs, across the yard, and through her open bedroom window, from which issue the strains of "This Girl is a Woman Now."

Simon wishes she'd been a little more informative. He has no idea what sorts of things Mack wants him to bring. Bail money, maybe? He sprang his friend from jail once before, when the big guy was arrested for punching out a football fan who was taunting him. The trouble is, at the moment Simon is broke. Well, he does have the NDEA check, but there's no place to cash it this late in the day.

Or is there? Unless Felicia the Lawson's lady has quit or changed her schedule, she'll be on duty, and he might just be able to persuade her. Of course, he's going to need the money for rent at the end of the month, but he can't worry about that now; he's got Mack to worry about.

He's relieved to find Felicia behind the counter. She's watching some sitcom on a tiny TV; the sound is turned too low for Simon to identify the show—not that he's well-informed about the latest TV fare, anyway, dwelling as he does in the sixteenth century most of the time. Afraid that he may have misremembered her name, he just says, "Um, hi."

She seems half pleased, half embarrassed to see him. "*Sensei!*" She performs an exaggerated bow, nearly poking her eye out with the TV antenna, which embarrasses her even more. "I haven't seen you for a while! But I guess that's because I quit coming to your class. I'm sorry; I just felt kind of, you know, out of place. All the other girls were so much younger and more . . . you know." With her hands, she describes a svelte figure.

"You shouldn't let that bother you."

"I know. But it does. Do you think you'll ever have a class for adults? I mean, not that those girls aren't *adults*, but you know what I mean. I could probably get some of my friends to sign up."

"Uh, yeah, maybe, if the university will let us use the room."

"Oh, that'd be great!" She claps her hands, and then puts them over her mouth. "I'm sorry; here I am, babbling away, and I haven't even asked if I could help you." She pats her hair, assumes a businesslike expression, and clears her throat. "May I help you, sir?"

"Well, um, I was going to buy some milk, but I also wondered if, uh, you might possibly be able to cash a check for me. A pretty large one." Hesitantly, he places the NDEA check on the counter and gives an apologetic shrug. "My, uh, my friend Mack is in jail, and needs me to bail him out."

"The Mack who plays defensive tackle for the Sliders?"

"That's the one."

"What's he doing in jail, for goodness sake? I mean, if you don't mind me asking."

"Uh, well, I'm not sure yet."

Felicia leans over the counter and whispers, "What do you bet he just had too many beers and got a little rowdy? It *is* Friday night, after all." She glances at the amount on the check, then flips it over and hands him a pen. "Would you sign your name right there, please?"

The holding cell at the police department does contain a couple of students who are drunk and rowdy, but Mack isn't one of them. He's slumped in a corner by himself, still wearing his janitor's coverall and looking weary and dejected. He's removed the knee brace Simon obtained for him and is rubbing his bad leg. When he spots Simon, he brightens a little and limps over to the bars. "Simon! You came!"

"Of course I came."

"Well, I wasn't sure whether Rhonda would get the message to you." His voice is more subdued than usual; Simon can barely hear him over the loud talk and laughter coming from the two revelers. Mack turns to glare at them. "Hey! You bozos want to keep it down?" That does the trick.

"So what are you in here for?" asks Simon.

Mack sighs. "You'll never guess."

"You blew up the Marine Recruiting Office."

"I wish." He leans in as close as the bars will allow. "Get this. They found a brick of hash in my locker at work."

"*What?*"

"My sentiments exactly. One of the security guards was doing a search. He said somebody tipped him off. You can probably figure out who."

"Rhonda's dad."

"Bingo. My guess is, he paid the guard to plant it there."

"Jesus, Mack. This is serious. What are you going do?"

"Well, first I'd like to get out of this place." He glares at his cellmates, who are still snickering over some secret joke. "I don't like the neighbors."

"I didn't know how much the bail would be. I cashed my NDEA check."

Mack does his abashed head-rub. "Hey, thanks for the thought, buddy, but I'm afraid we'll need a little more than that."

"Like how much?"

"Like five thousand smackers."

"Whoa!"

The big guy shrugs. "The judge says I'm what they call a flight risk. Apparently a couple of the guys they've booked for possession were also draft dodgers, and as soon as they made bail they made tracks for Canada."

"Wow. I don't see how I can raise that kind of money."

"I don't expect you to. The lawyer says it won't be more than about a week until the hearing. It won't be so bad if they give me a private cell. Could you just bring me something to read, and a toothbrush and so on? Better forget about the Darvon; that'd just help convince them that I'm a druggie. I'll have to make do with aspirin."

•   •   •

Simon pays his friend another visit on Saturday afternoon, right after self-defense class. Mack doesn't look good at all. He's hunched over as if his stomach is hurting; there's a cold sweat on his forehead and he keeps swiping at his nose with one sleeve. "Withdrawal symptoms," he says. "From the Darvon."

"Jeez, what a bummer. I left your bag of stuff at the desk. There's a bottle of aspirin in there. And a copy of *Moby Dick*."

"You're kidding, right?"

"Right. Actually, it's *The Sterile Cuckoo*."

"Thanks, man. How'd your class go?"

"Good. They're learning fast. A couple of days ago, some jerk grabbed Gabriela, and she made him wish he hadn't."

Mack smiles weakly. "Good for her. How about the Kotex?"

"We're making a lot of progress--" Simon starts to say, but breaks off as the big guy stumbles to the toilet and heaves up his latest meal.

"Sorry, man," says Mack, as he sinks down on his cot. "Come see me tomorrow, when I'm not so out of it, okay?"

Gabriela is waiting for Simon at the Briggs. When he tells her about Mack's fate, she's nearly as distressed as he is. Somehow they manage to focus on the codex enough to produce another two pages of plaintext. That's as far as they get before the story takes an unexpected turn, one that's even more disturbing and depressing, in a way, than Mack's fate.

As Gabriela teases out the plaintext, Simon notices that she's struggling with it, but he figures it's just an unusually difficult passage. It's not until he tackles the translation that he understands why it's such a problem. It has nothing to do with the deciphering process. "Oh, shit," he says.

"Go ahead and read it," says Gabriela grimly.

"Um, okay."

We dared not descend from the hills to follow the river, lest we fall into the hands of the Lao. Had I still had my eight soldiers, we would have staged a raid of our own and freed the captive ma-bri. But there is only so much one man can do, no matter how daring he may be. So in the morning we set out along the crest of the mountains, keeping the rising sun on our left.

On the first day, Aleala led the way, for the surroundings were still familiar to her, but on the second day, she let me take the vanguard. Time and again I turned to see that she had fallen behind. She assured me that she was simply weary, but that evening I noticed her tugging at her loincloth as if it were chafing her. I asked to examine her, and at first she resisted—perhaps she suspected me of having some more lewd motive.

At last she let me untie the cloth and fold it back to reveal a festering wound. During the battle, an arrow had glanced off her hip, leaving little more than a scratch, which she ignored. But it did more damage than she thought.

I had seen wounds like this in India, caused by arrows whose heads had supposedly been thrust into a putrefying corpse. I suspect that was only a legend, that in fact the heads were coated with some slow-acting poison. Whatever the method, it seemed that the Lao had copied it.

Pointing to Aleala's hemp pouch—I dared not touch it and offend its spirit—I said o-dai, o-dai. She shrugged and shook her head, which I took to mean that she had used up her supply of the vine and not yet gathered more. I did not tell her of the small cutting that lay, wrapped in a banana leaf, in my shot-bag. I am ashamed to say that I did not even consider it. Surely, I thought, there must be some other healing herb she could use, one that did not constitute my best hope of becoming something more than a scurvy, sweating, scurrilous soldier.

Her pouch did indeed contain a quantity of brittle, dark green leaves, and she used them to make a poultice for the wound. I prayed that it would draw out the infection, and at first it did seem to help, but not nearly enough. By the afternoon of our third day, she had developed a blistering fever. On the fourth day she died. I dealt with her body according to the ma-bri custom, cradling it carefully in the limbs of a sunda oak tree.

Toward the end she was often in delirium, but there was one lucid moment during which her fever-bright eyes locked on mine. She placed a feeble, trembling finger on her breast and whispered Riam—her real name, I supposed. It didn't matter if she revealed it now; the spirits could no longer have any power over her. Then she beckoned me to draw nearer. When I did, she murmured something that sounded like o-mok-mon.

I was never able to learn the meaning of the phrase.

Simon is so choked up, he can barely get the words out. He glances at Gabriela, who is wiping her eyes. "Oh, Simon!" she wails. "How could he *do* that? How could he let her die?"

"Um, I don't know. I guess . . . I guess the *o-dai* was just more important to him than she was."

"*Ele é um idiota!* He did not even know that she was saying *I love you!*" She flings the Portuguese plaintext across the table and several pages flutter to the floor. "I do not want to know what else he has to say!" She rises and slips into her coat. "I am sorry, Simon. I cannot do this any longer. I am too upset. You do not need me, anyway."

Before Simon can protest, she's out the door. Once again, he's left wondering whether he should go after her, and once again his inability to decide is a decision in itself. For several minutes he sits staring at the translated pages without really seeing them. Finally, he gets up and, moving as mechanically as the robot from *Lost in Space*, gathers the fallen pages and stacks them neatly on the table. Then takes a seat again and tries to focus on the few pages of ciphertext that remain.

It's a lost cause. What Gabriela said is true, of course; he could finish the task without her. He's just not sure he wants to. Which, when you think about it, is pretty dumb of him. After all, getting his paper published in *JLR* is a lot more important than trying to hang onto a relationship that seems to be going nowhere, right? Right. And that sounds an awful lot like the rationale Vicente used when he decided that the *o-dai* was more valuable to him than Aleala's life.

Maybe it's not too late to catch Gabriela. He crams everything into Mack's gym bag and heads for the door without even bothering to pull down the sheets of notebook paper Gabriela used to mask the study room windows. That can wait.

Just as he's reaching for the handle, somebody raps on the door. Gabriela. It's got to be. She decided it wasn't fair to leave him in the lurch and she's going to see the project through to the bitter end. Though the door is locked from the outside, it opens from the inside when the handle is turned. As Simon swings it inward, he performs a low bow. *"Konnichiwa."*

"Gesundheit," says Alec.

CHAPTER TWENTY-NINE

Simon stumbles backward. "What the hell? What are *you* doing here?"

Alec smiles, obviously relishing the effect caused by his appearance. "I might ask you the same thing--except I know the answer." He steps into the study room and closes the door behind him. "Well, well," he says, glancing at the gym bag. "So *that's* where you're stashing it. Pretty risky, isn't it, lugging it around like that? Not very imaginative, either. I was just sure you stuck it inside that other old book and shelved it in some strange place."

Simon resorts again to the *Feign madness, but keep your balance* strategy. "What are you talking about, Alec? This is research for my thesis. Why would I need to hide it?"

Alec raises his eyebrows. "You're getting pretty good at that innocent act, Hannay. I'd almost believe you, if I didn't know better. Okay, you're not exactly *lying*. I'm sure you do plan to use that material in your thesis. But you see, I have other plans for it."

Let him go on talking, Simon; let him reveal his intentions. "Really?"

"Yeah, really. Like I told you, Dr. Weiss offered me a job with AllChemi. The thing is, the offer comes with a contingency clause."

"A contingency clause?"

Alec laughs humorlessly. "You're also pretty good at acting dumb, aren't you? Or maybe you're not acting. Okay, I'll spell it out for you. In order to get the job, I have to deliver the Vicente journal—preferably all deciphered and translated, which I understand most of it now is?"

"What makes you think that?"

"A little bird told me."

228

Simon groans inwardly. He should have known. "Marnie."

"Ah. So you're not so dumb after all." He shrugs in mock modesty. "Hey, she's a lonely lady; it hardly took any effort at all to win her over."

"You know, I've always thought you were kind of a jerk; I didn't realize you were an out-and-out bastard."

Alec's smile is starting to look a bit strained. "Let's get down to business, okay? How much do you want for it? A couple hundred bucks? Five? That should be enough to bail out your buddy, right?"

"Not even close. Anyway, it's not for sale. *My* career depends on this, too, you know."

"Oho, your big career in *Comparative Literature*? So you can be what--an assistant prof at some Podunk college, making eight or nine thousand a year? You know how much I'll make at AllChemi?"

"No, and I don't care. I also don't care how much Dr. Vice and his company stand to make off this information. Like I said, it's not for sale."

Once again Alec lets out a nasty laugh reminiscent of the pinball Devil's. "Oh, man. You think they want to find Vicente's secret formula and make some kind of miracle drug out of it, right?" He shakes his head and sighs. "Hannay, Hannay. You don't understand how it works. They don't want to *develop* it. They want to deny its *existence*. I mean, think about it: If AllChemi or some other company creates a pill that cures whatever ails you, what happens to all those other pills that just alleviate the symptoms--beta blockers and antihistamines and antibiotics and antacids and laxatives and pain pills—all the stuff that's making a fortune for them?"

While Alec is talking, Simon is doing some *shin kokyu* breathing to keep himself calm and in control. "So they're all bastards, too. You should fit right in."

"Funny." Alec sighs again, as if his patience is wearing thin. "Come on, Hannay; Let's Make a Deal."

"No, thanks, Monty."

"So I was right the first time; you really *are* stupid. You know what this means, don't you?"

"It means you're going to try and take it."

"Good guess."

"I don't think you can, Alec. And even if you could, it won't do you any good. It's all going to be published soon, so anybody can read it."

"In the *JRL*, right? Oh, don't look so surprised. My little bird again. But I wouldn't be so sure about the publication thing if I were you."

"What do you mean?"

"Hey, I don't want to spoil the surprise." He takes a tentative step forward, reaching out for the bag. "Come on, Hannay. Give it up."

Simon glides backward and then sideways, putting the table between them. Dropping the gym bag, he raises his arms to waist height and forms each hand into a *seiken*, or fore-fist—not as a threat, just as a way of showing that he's ready. He's waiting for Alec to make the first move.

He doesn't have to wait long. Alec grabs one corner of the table and shoves it out of his way. The chairs topple over with a crash that makes Simon wince slightly, but he stays calm and keeps his eyes on Alec's face. It's not hard to read the bastard's intentions; he's going to attack. Alec returns his gaze, coming on all capable and confident, trying to intimidate him, but Simon senses that it's partly a pretense. When they sparred at Karate Club, neither one of them was going all out; no doubt Alec is wondering how things will play out if they really do mix it up.

Simon is wondering the same thing. "Maybe you should've brought the dart gun," he says.

"Maybe I should have." Alec cautiously closes in. "You sure you want to do this? One of us could get hurt."

"I'm not doing anything. Just standing here."

"All right, then." Alec is smart enough not telegraph his moves; his right leg lashes out suddenly, and he shouts "*Osu!*"

Simon steps to one side a little and blocks the kick, using his right palm and his left elbow, which he jabs sharply into Alec's calf muscle. Alec looks more injured emotionally than physically, as if he feels betrayed somehow. He expected to be blocked, but he didn't figure on a counterstrike. Neither did Simon, really; he just sort of did it.

"Could you spare us the *Osu*?" says Simon. "It sounds stupid."

"Maybe I'm just doing it to irritate you." In mid-sentence, Alec delivers a strike at Simon's gut. It doesn't connect, but it wasn't meant to; it was just a feint. He follows up with a rapid-fire series of blows aimed at other areas of Simon's body, all of which Simon deflects without attempting to strike back. There's no need; surely Alec will realize that trying to beat him into submission is as useless as offering him money, and he'll just let it go.

But no. He must be really desperate to land that job with AllChemi. Instead of backing off, he engages Simon again, even more fiercely. You've got to give the guy credit; he's not all about flashy kicks and spins. He has a good command of the basics, and he's quick and strong, probably stronger than Simon.

For the first time, he considers the possibility that Alec might be able to win out, just by wearing him down. He obviously can't take his sails out of the guy's wind; he can't stay on the defensive forever, either. If he wants to end this thing, he's going to have to strike back, actually try to disable Alec, to hurt him. He's not sure he can bring himself to do that.

If he even hopes to put up a decent defense, he's going to have to quit thinking and analyzing and just rely on his instincts, but he can't seem to focus. There's something preventing him, some distracting noise, and it's not Alec's cries of "*Osu!*" It's a persistent pounding on the door of the study room, and a voice calling, "Simon! What is happening? Open the door, please!"

Alec grins crookedly and, without slackening his onslaught, shouts, "He's busy right now, Gabriela!"

"Alec? Why are you in there? Let me in!" There's another flurry of pounding, and then she cries, "I am going to get a key, Simon!"

Simon feels a stab of panic. He doesn't want her getting involved in this, maybe getting hurt. Nor does he want her to see him putting up a half-assed fight again, the way he did against Duane/Dennis/Darrin—or, even worse, to see him getting creamed by Alec. "No, Gabriela!" he calls. "Don't--!"

His words are cut off by a *seiken* strike to his ribcage. He can feel one of the ribs give way, but he doesn't let it faze him; he just accepts it, then ignores it. What he can't ignore is the old toxic anger that's rising up from whatever place he banished it to; it's beginning to burn in his gut, like a chunk of habanero pepper or a shot of tequila. It heats up even more when Alec starts throwing verbal jabs along with the physical ones.

"You didn't listen to me, Hannay. I told you . . . she's *trouble*. Whatever you're getting from her . . . it's not worth it."

Simon knows well enough what Alec is doing: Trying to psych him out, get him to lose his cool so he'll do something dumb, something reckless, so he'll strike out blindly, the way he did when Frank Ávila taunted him. But unlike Frank, Alec will be ready; he'll use Simon's emotions against him. Simon is not about to play that game. He's spent too many years learning to control the anger to give in to it now. As much as he despises Alec, he doesn't really want to murder him; he just wants to stop him.

"She's a slut, man," says Alec. "Forget about her." He follows this verbal jab with another fore-fist to Simon's ribs and again it finds its target.

One good thing about pain: It drives everything else out of your head. No more thinking; Simon is acting purely on instinct now. He snatches the sleeve of Alec's bulky sweater and yanks him off balance. At the same time, he pivots and delivers a palm heel strike to his opponent's face.

Alec staggers backward, clutching his nose. "Jesus Christ, Hannay!" He takes his hand away and gapes at it incredulously; it's drenched in red. "Look what you did, you asshole!" he wails, his lips bubbling with blood, sending a shower of droplets into the air.

His legs look shaky, as if they're about to give out; Simon snatches up one of the fallen chairs and shoves it beneath the guy's sinking rear end just in time. "Hey, I'm sorry. You gave me no choice, man." And he really is sorry--though not terribly. It's not like he's going to agonize over it for weeks to come, the way he did after the Frank Ávila incident. What else could he do, after all? Let Alec take the codex? He fishes a couple of napkins out of the gym bag and hands them to Alec. "Tilt your head back and pinch your nostrils."

Alec glares at him. "I know, damn it! I've had nosebleeds before!"

"Okay, okay. Just trying to help." He hears the key in the lock, and a moment later Gabriela bursts in, her dark eyes wide.

"Are you all right, Simon?" she asks breathlessly.

"Um, sure. Alec's not doing so great, though."

"Oh, quit gloating, Hannay!" snarls Alec, his voice nasal and muffled. "This isn't over yet!"

Gabriela gives a harsh laugh. "That sounds like a line from a bad spy movie." She turns to Simon. "What was he doing, trying to get the codex?"

"Yeah." He picks up the gym bag. "I'll tell you all about it. But first, let's get out of here, okay?"

"Should we not call the police, or something?"

While Simon considers this, Alec eyes him with equal amounts of resentment and anxiety. "Um, I don't think so," says Simon. "Like you told Dr. E, the fewer people who know about this, the better."

• • •

As they head across campus, Gabriela says, "So, *he* was one of the minions?"

"Uh-huh. Dr. Vice promised him a job if he'd get the codex. He was using Marnie as his source of information."

"*Vixe Maria!* What a scumbag!" When Simon lets out a nervous laugh, she glances at him quzzically. "What? Is that not the right word?"

"Um, yeah, it's the right word; I guess I just didn't expect you to know it."

"It is another of those useful English terms. I am glad you taught him a lesson. I hope you broke his nose."

"I hope I didn't." Simon gingerly prods at his ribs and gives an involuntary gasp. "Don't tell anybody, but I think he cracked a rib or two."

"Oh, I am sorry."

Simon shrugs. "No big thing. I'll just tape them up. What really worries me is something Alec said. He said, 'I wouldn't be so sure about the publication thing if I were you.' I asked him what he meant, but all he said was 'I don't want to spoil the surprise.'"

"Surely there is no way they can stop it from being published. Is there?"

"I don't see how. Maybe he just figured that, if he kept us from finishing the thing, the *JRL* wouldn't want it."

"Perhaps he is right. I think we had better get it done *rapidamente*. Are you feeling up to it?"

"Oh, sure. But what about you? You said--"

"*Sim, sim.* I was being emotional, not logical. Vicente is a scumbag, too, but I suppose we should give him a chance. Maybe he will change."

"Uh-huh. I wouldn't count on it."

"Well, anyway, there will always be scumbags in the world. We cannot avoid them, so we must find a way of dealing with them."

"You know, that's pretty much what I was thinking when I was busy blocking Alec's moves. I knew the only way I could salvage the situation was to stop *re*acting and just *act*. Engage. Commit. Whatever you want to call it. I wasn't trying to hurt him, just to keep him from taking the papers."

"Well, it worked. Now that he's found our hideout, we should get a new one."

"Any suggestions?"

"Well . . . what about my place?"

CHAPTER THIRTY

Her place, it turns out, is a huge old Victorian house just off campus, complete with turrets and dormers and gingerbread trim and a vast veranda that extends across the whole front of the building and wraps around one side. "*This* is where you live?"

"It is where Mrs. Pitman lives. But she was kind enough to rent a room to me, and to let me use her kitchen. She is glad for the company, I think. Her husband died many years ago, on an expedition to South America. And before you ask, no, he was not looking for miraculous healing plants; he was an archaeologist. When Gilberto, my *padrinho*, was at Van Dyne, he actually stayed here, too, in that same room." She glances up and down the block. "I think it is safe to go in. I didn't see anyone following us."

They enter through a side door that opens directly into the kitchen. Simon, who was expecting the interior to look Victorianish, too, is surprised by the Formica countertops, the chrome and avocado gas stove with double ovens, the dishwasher, the stainless steel sinks. The only thing in the place that speaks of an earlier era is Mrs. Pitman herself, and even she is looking, if not exactly Mod, at least pretty modern, in slacks and a sweater.

She turns from her task of filling a huge copper teakettle and holds up a slightly shaky hand in greeting. Nothing shaky about her memory, though. "You're the young man who was looking for the Vicente journal."

"Yes, ma'am." Simon holds out a hand. "Simon Hannay."

She places one hand in his; it feels dry and fragile, like the pages of the codex. "Did you ever manage to find it?"

"Um, well . . . "

"Yes, we did, Evie," says Gabriela. "But now it seems to be gone again."

"Oh, my. You don't suppose the other gentleman took it?"

"I hope not. If he happens to come around again, could you please let us know?"

"Of course, dear. Would you and your . . . friend--" She smiles knowingly. "--like a cup of tea? If you want coffee, you'll have to make it yourselves."

"Tea would be lovely, Evie. Do you mind if we use your library? Simon is working on his thesis, and I am helping him."

"I see." She's still wearing that sly smile. "You may take him to your room if you like; I don't mind."

Simon glances at Gabriela just long enough to determine that she's as embarrassed as he is. "No, no," she says hastily. "It will be more comfortable in the library."

"Suit yourselves. I'll bring the tea when it's ready."

"You don't need to--" Simon starts to say, but Gabriela elbows him in the ribs and it turns into a groan.

"I am sorry," she whispers, as they head down the hallway, "but she likes to be . . . what is the word? *Hospitaleiro.*"

"Hospitable."

"*Sim.* And she likes to do things herself if she can."

"You did a good job of dodging her question about the codex."

"I did, didn't I? It is better, I think, if she does not know what we are up to."

Unlike the kitchen, the library looks just the way Simon expected: A sturdy oak table, plush chairs, brass reading lamps, a twelve-story tenement of shelves that houses books of every color, creed, and language.

"Wow," says Simon. "I wonder if I'll ever have a place like this."

"*Claro.* You will be a world-famous scholar. But only if we finish this paper."

Once Mrs. Pitman delivers the tea—plus a plate piled with shortbread cookies—they unload the gym bag and set to work. After an hour or two, they have to turn on a table lamp in order to see. By the time their stomachs call a halt, they have three full pages of deciphered and translated plaintext. When Simon reads it aloud, he doesn't lead in with the end of the previous passage; they remember it all too well. He jumps right into the new stuff:

I will not dwell on the rest of my journey to Camboja; in truth, I recall very little of it. I know that, for most of the time, I felt as though I were delirious myself, suffering from some previously unnoticed wound. But though I closely examined my entire body, I could see none. I found barely enough food and water to sustain myself, but at least I was able to keep my precious cutting from shriveling up into a brittle, worthless stick.

A week or so later, mostly by luck, I stumbled upon the very village where Dom Gaspar was preaching the gospel in a fairly civilized-looking chapel fashioned from thick tubes of bamboo whitewashed with water buffalo milk. A week after that, I was aboard a trading vessel that was headed for India by way of the Malaca Straits.

My old comrades at the Fortaleza de Malaca were astonished to see me; word had reached them that our vessel was captured and its entire crew slaughtered. I dreaded the prospect of facing Dom Alvaro; he had put his trust in me, and I had failed him miserably. But he was a reasonable man; he knew the risks that my mission entailed. Besides, he had more grave matters to concern him.

During my absence, he had incurred the wrath of no less a personage than the Pope. I never learned the exact details, but apparently Dom Alvaro had seized the cargo of a ship whose captain owed him money. Unfortunately, one of the ship's passengers was the renowned Jesuit missionary Francis Xavier, who had been sent to preach the Lord's word to the heathens, and much of the cargo consisted of gifts for the Chinese emperor.

Xavier had continued on to China, but had fallen ill and died, and his body was shipped back to Malaca. According to some, the corpse was perfectly preserved—a miracle, they called it. I cannot vouch for the truth of that. Though Dom Alvaro and I sailed for Europe on the same vessel with Xavier's casket, I never managed to look inside it. I could not help wondering whether, if he had carried a supply of o-dai, he might have survived.

As a result of the Captain-Major's actions, he had been relieved of duty and ordered home to face a papal enquiry. Dom Alvaro insisted that I accompany him and testify on his behalf--never mind the fact that, when the incident occurred, I was marooned in the Monkey Forest. He told me exactly what I was to say; I merely had to say it convincingly enough and all would be well.

I agreed to do as he asked, provided he would do something for me in return—introduce me to influential people who might vouch for my character and for the efficacy of my cure-all.

Upon reaching Malaca, I had planted the cutting in a pot; during the voyage home I kept it always at my side and tended it as if it were a sick infant, sharing with it my small daily ration of drinking water. The sea air seemed to agree with it; it took root and flourished. By the time we docked in Lisbon, it was two spans tall and decked with glossy leaves.

Dom Alvaro was as good as his word. Due largely to my wholly concocted but very convincing testimony, he narrowly escaped excommunication; he repaid me by arranging a demonstration of the o-dai vine's miraculous healing powers. Our test subject was a young cavalheiro named Alfonso, who had caught a musket ball in one leg and contracted gangrene. The army physician wished to amputate the limb, but Alfonso refused. He would rather die, he said, than become an object of pity, begging for handouts in the street.

Fortunately for him and for me, he was forced to do neither. I had taken several cuttings from the vine in order to propagate new plants; what remained was barely enough to make one poultice a day for five days, but it was all that was needed. Our audience had seen the original condition of the leg; when, less than a week later, I unwrapped it in their presence, they were astounded to see that the putrid flesh had melted away, leaving healthy tissue that would soon heal completely.

Not caring to raise the hackles of the medical establishment, Dom Alvaro had neglected to invite any of the city's university-trained medicos. Instead, he had recruited lawyers and scientists and grandees, including some who held positions at the royal court. With a single sortie, I had won for myself a host of powerful allies.

"He still has made no mention of King João," says Gabriela.

"Well, we have five pages to go. Should we pull an all-nighter?"

She regards him a bit warily. "An *all-nighter*?"

"Um, yeah. You know, like . . . like when you're cramming for an exam."

"Oh. I thought . . . never mind."

"I mean, we don't have to, if you're tired."

"You should be the tired one. You had to do battle with Alec, not to mention the Visigoths. You lie down for a while, and I will fix us some sandwiches."

"What? You promised me a full Brazilian meal."

She laughs. "During Christmas vacation, I said."

"Well, okay. Could you get me some aspirin, too?"

Though the sofa in the library is soft and nearly long enough to accommodate his lanky frame, Simon has trouble finding a position that doesn't make his ribs hurt worse. And yet it seems he's capable of dozing off. When he opens his eyes, Gabriela is hunched over the codex pages with an empty glass of milk next to her and a half-eaten sandwich in one hand. Simon sits up, groaning softly as his ribs shift.

Gabriela glances over her shoulder. "You were supposed to *rest*, not fall asleep."

"Um, I'm sorry," he murmurs. "I guess I was . . . "

"Simon, I am joking, okay?"

"Oh. Right. Did you save me a sandwich?"

"Three of them. I hope you like peanut butter and jelly."

"Love y—uh--*it*." He's so groggy, he almost said *you*. When she replies, "Me, too," it sort of feels as if she knew that. "Mrs. Pitman won't mind if we keep working?" he says.

"As long as we're quiet."

The aspirin don't do a lot for his aching ribs, but he's able to block the pain and focus on the Portuguese plaintext. It's a bit harder to block out his awareness of Gabriela, especially when she asks for his help every five minutes. Not that he minds.

Not long after they resume work, they see the first reference to João III. "Thank god," says Simon. "I was getting worried."

By two a.m., they're so exhausted that they're acting goofy, making deliberate mistakes just for the hell of it. "*To cure Percy*?" reads Gabriela. "Who is Percy?"

"What?" Simon gapes at the line of plaintext she's indicating. "Oh, *per se*." He lets out a laugh. "You dope!"

"Ssshhh! How is the translation going?"

"You want me to read it?"

"*Sim*. Softly, please."

"Just let me finish this paragraph about Percy, okay?" Now she's the one laughing and he's the one shushing.

In the two years that followed, I treated perhaps a hundred patients who had learned of my panacea. Though their complaints ranged from boils to gout to syphilis, they all had two things in common: One, they were all cured. Two, they were wealthy enough to reward me handsomely.

Forgive me; I forgot to mention the one man I failed to cure. He was a notorious womanizer whose wife had fed him rat poison. By the time he came to me, he was too near death for the o-dai to be of any use. I am not certain it would have helped, in any case. While all the other illnesses and injuries were of a naturally occurring sort, most poisons are an unnatural thing. I came to understand that the power of o-dai lay not in some innate ability to cure per se, but in its ability to aid the body in healing itself.

During those two years, I had done my best to block out any memory of Aleala, for it pained me to think of her. But when I found that my miraculous plant could do nothing to counteract poison, it brought me a little comfort. She had been wounded by a poisoned arrow, I was sure, so even had I used my precious cutting of the o-dai vine to prepare a poultice for her, it would have made no difference.

"Well, well," says Simon. "It seems he *does* have a conscience after all."

"Perhaps. It seems to me that he now sees the *o-dai* as something more than just a source of money and fame. I think that he is actually committed to curing people. Or is that just . . . how do you say? Wishful thinking?"

"Hmm. Let's see what else he has to say."

"Okay. You go ahead; I am just going to close my eyes for a moment. They are tired."

Simon suspects it's more than just her eyes that are tired. As he digs doggedly into the cipher, silently cursing Vicente for using such an unmethodical method, he feels a slight pressure against his left shoulder; he turns cautiously to see that Gabriela's head has drooped sideways and come to rest on his arm. Simon does what he's longed to do so many times, but never dared: He lowers his face so it's barely touching her close-cropped hair and breathes in her intoxicating scent. Then, as tentatively as a person tasting an exotic dish for the first time, he plants the lightest of kisses.

Though he sits as still as humanly possible, eventually she shifts restlessly and her head sinks onto her folded arms. Simon heaves a sigh that holds a little disappointment but mostly contentment. They don't need to be in close contact; it's enough just to be in her presence and to have her let down her guard so completely that she can drift off to sleep next to him. Granted that they're just sitting at a desk, but still.

He should be worn out, too; instead, he feels strangely energized. Gabriela has provided them with a pot of coffee; though it's lukewarm now, he uses it to wash down another couple of aspirin, and then he buckles down like Winsocki . . . whoever that is. A football player, he seems to recall his mother saying. Oh, god, Simon; don't let your mind veer off in that direction. No thinking about Delia Hannay, or about Mack, either. Just focus on Vicente.

With no distractions except the soft sound of Gabriela's breathing—which is somehow more soothing than distracting—Simon drifts, almost without trying, into something resembling that mindless state of *mushin*. Vicente ceases to be just a disembodied voice from the distant past; he becomes an almost physical presence. And Simon no longer regards him as a sort of adversary, a challenge to be overcome. He's more like a sparring partner, one whose moves Simon can read and anticipate before he makes them.

What's more, the cipher itself no longer seems like an unknown language; it's come to feel familiar, the way Latin and Spanish and Portuguese do. Back when Simon was conversing regularly with Frank Ávila, he reached a point at which he no longer had to mentally translate each word from Spanish to English or vice versa; he understood their meaning without having to think or analyze. He's reached a similar point with the ciphertext; he seems able to grasp the gist of the words instinctively. Of course, he still needs to write down the plaintext and then covert it to English, but the process is far faster now--almost effortless, in fact.

By the time daylight finds its way into the room, he's converted into English the final line of Vicente's journal. "Holy smoke, Batman!" he croaks, his voice feeble from exhaustion. "That's it. It's all done."

Gabriela stirs, peers at him through half-open eyes, and murmurs, *"Que?"*

"Está terminado."

In the blink of an eye—both eyes, actually—she's wide awake. "You finished it without me?" she cries.

"Um, yeah. I was on sort of a roll. Is--is that okay?"

She squeezes his arm lightly. "Of course. I was surprised, that is all. So tell me--did he really poison the king?"

Simon hands her the English plaintext. "Read it for yourself. I'm going to lie down."

"Please do. You look . . . what is the word? Haggard?"

"Oh. Thanks a lot." With a groan, he stretches out on the sofa. "You want to read it out loud? I was kind of on automatic pilot, so some of it may not make much sense."

"Okay." Stretching and yawning extravagantly, she glances toward the window. *"Meu Deus,* it is morning already!" She pours half a cup of cold coffee and downs it.

241

"I could make us a new pot," offers Simon.

"No, no, I am too anxious to see what happens! Where did we leave off?"

"I marked the spot."

"Ah, *sim*." She yawns again, then begins to read.

CHAPTER THIRTY-ONE

Naturally, I made certain that no one learned of my sole failure. I was hailed as a miracle worker. The medicos bitterly resented me and even threatened me, but there was little they could actually do to a man with so many influential fiends. ["I think you mean *friends?*" "Good guess."] *All the same, I thought it wise to hire a bodyguard: Alfonso, the cavalryman with the formerly gangrenous leg.*

In the summer of 1557, my fortunes reached their peak. I was summoned to the Paço da Ribeira to work my herbal magic on the king himself, ["Ah, ah!" says Gabriela. "Then he is Vicente Marques after all!" "So it would seem."] *who was suffering from frequent headaches that often incapacitated him. The stakes were high; the hall outside the king's chambers was crowded with cortesãos. Most of them, I was sure, were anxious to see me succeed. But among them were the very medicos who had been cursing me for years, and I knew that they were praying fervently for me to fail. I felt nothing but confidence, however, for I had on my side the most powerful ally of all—the o-dai vine itself.*

With Alfonso standing guard, I made my secret preparations. There was nothing mystical about them, of course; all one had to do was peel off a quantity of the vine's inner bark and steep it in boiling water. Still, the less the public knew about the process, the more miraculous it would seem. Just when my infusion was nearly ready, one of the king's attendants appeared with a message from the monarch himself: His Majesty wished to speak with me before I began.

Leaving Alfonso to watch over the brew, I wormed my way through the crowd--smiling graciously at those who wished me well, and smugly at those who wished me ill--only to be told that the king was in no condition to converse and that I should proceed with the treatment at once.

That was a simple enough matter, too; once the infusion had cooled, His Majesty was propped up and, with my help, drank it all down—well, most of it, at any rate. He did splutter and spew a bit, for the taste was not pleasant.

Naturally, I was not permitted to leave until the results of the treatment were known. They put me in a small sleeping room, under guard. I had no objection, for I was sure the medicine would work its usual miracle. Only one thing gave me cause for concern: Alfonso had unaccountably disappeared.

Nevertheless, I was relaxed enough to fall asleep, only to be startled awake again when the door to my room flew open and the guards burst in, armed with pikes. They were accompanied by the king's head physician, who informed me that, not long after I left, João was seized with convulsions; in a matter of minutes, His Majesty lay limp and lifeless.

Though I was now a celebrated curandeiro, I had not lost the skills I learned as a soldier. I wasted no time expressing astonishment or pleading innocence. Instead I sprang upon the nearest guard, seized his pike, and plunged the point of it into his unprotected neck, then jammed the butt of it into the groin of the second soldier, who collapsed in agony. The physician turned and fled; so did I, in the opposite direction.

I smashed the leaded windowpane and climbed onto the sill. The paved courtyard lay four varas below me—too far to jump safely, but I had no choice. Fortune chose to smile on me, however. At the base of the wall lay a row of decorative shrubs; I aimed for them, and my aim was true.

But as Fortune will do, she also played a little joke: Within the shrub on which I landed was a broken, jagged branch that skewered my upper arm as handily as any sword or spear. Fickle fate then blessed me again, by placing in the courtyard a messenger about to mount his steed; to his dismay, I mounted it instead. What's more, most of the castle guard had been summoned to the room I had just departed, so I was able to gallop away unhindered.

I know the seamier sections of Lisbon well, from my days as a raw recruit, when my duties consisted mostly of drinking and carousing, so I went to ground there. I sold my mount for enough to keep me in food and lodging for a long while—provided they were cheap.

The gaping puncture in my arm needed tending, but I could scarcely avail myself of a reputable physician; they all knew me, and most hated me. I did find a midwife who was willing to dress and bind the wound, but it did little good. What I really needed was someone to fetch me the o-dai vine.

I did not think I could rely on Dom Alvaro; I had outlived my usefulness to him. But I had become close friends with another grandee, whom I had cured of gout--I dare not reveal his name, of course. I sent a street urchin with a message to him. That same afternoon he came to see me—alone, thank God, or Fortune, or whoever is responsible for how the world works. He brought news both of Alfonso and of my precious plants.

The former had been executed—supposedly because he was my accomplice, but more likely in order to keep him quiet. Quiet about what? I wanted to know. My friend was not certain, but he had heard rumors. Some said that an enemy of the king--or of me, or both-- had added a large amount of opium to my infusion, after paying Alfonso a large amount of money to look the other way. I could hardly condemn Alfonso, considering all the things I myself had done in pursuit of wealth; it was a pity, though, that he never had the chance to spend it. I did not need to ask who could be responsible for such a scheme; the answer was obvious.

As for the o-dai, when the Inquisitors—who had judged me guilty of sorcery--searched my apartments, they burned all my vines and cuttings, along with my notes concerning the many hopeless cases the herb had cured. The only record that survives is the book you hold in your hands.

I cannot know, of course, what the world may be like decades or centuries from now. Perhaps in your time, men will be able to cross the oceans in mere weeks, or even days; if so, it may be a simple matter to travel to the Monkey Forest and collect new cuttings of the o-dai vine.

Then again, perhaps your men of science will have discovered other, even better means of healing. Perhaps they have found a way to manufacture medicines, and have no use for those provided by nature, nor for the natural ability of the body to heal itself—a process that seems to me even more miraculous than the o-dai.

If by some miracle my own wound should mend, I would lead an expedition to harvest the vine--and perhaps free the captive ma-bri as well. But of course miracles are not granted to sinners. I know well enough that I will die here in this shabby room, and soon. I think that I grow delirious already, for I find myself imagining a time in the future—perhaps it is your time--when there is little need for a panacea, when the world has become more civilized, when mankind has reduced or eradicated the sources of suffering, when disease has been conquered and we have found more reasonable ways of dealing with our fellow humans, ways that do not involve killing or enslaving them.

When Gabriela finishes reading, she's silent for a long moment. Finally she says, "He did change, after all. I think, though, that he is too optimistic. I am not sure the world will ever become that civilized."

"It doesn't seem like it," murmurs Simon.

"It is a shame that João died. I have read about him, and I think that he subscribed to the same rule as our *dojo—Prepare for conflict, but pursue peace.*"

"Uh-huh. Too bad about the Inquisition thing."

"Ah, well, no one is perfect, I suppose. Most sources say that he died of a stroke, yes?"

"Yes. I've only found one book that mentions poison."

"So your paper will receive much attention."

"I hope so--and not just because it'll help my career. I mean, wouldn't it be cool if people rediscover the *o-dai* and start planting it all over the place, like Johnny Appleseed?"

"It would be wonderful—if the vine still exists."

"I don't see why it shouldn't. They just have to find the Monkey Forest." Simon stretches and groans. "And I have to tape up these damn ribs."

"I will find the tape. And then I will make us some breakfast. *You--*" She pushes a finger into his chest—a sort of non-lethal version of the Touch of Death. "--lie down and relax. You have done enough."

Despite his exhaustion, Simon is too keyed up to just lie there. He sits at the table and examines the final page of his translation, certain that he must have omitted something, barely able to believe that the task that seemed so monumental is actually finished, wondering what he'll do with himself now. Of course, he still has loads of research for his thesis, but it'll seem like mere busy work compared to the codex.

Gabriela cracks open the library door just enough to toss him a roll of adhesive tape, then disappears again. Once he's repaired his ribs, Simon gobbles the last remaining half-sandwich and surveys Mrs. Pitman's considerable collection of books. There must be at least a thousand volumes, and it looks like a fair number of them deal with European history. Who knows; maybe he'll find one or two that will help with his research.

When he examines the titles more closely, he discovers that about a two-foot section of one shelf is devoted to the work of a single author--somebody named Pitman, in fact. Mrs. Pitman's husband, maybe? No, Gabriela said he was an archaeologist, and these are all eighteenth and nineteenth century history: *Prudence, Intrepidity, and Perseverance: George Anson's Circumnavigation of the Globe; The Curious Mind of Ben Franklin; Restless Spirits: Swedenborg, Mesmer, and the Fox Sisters;* and so on.

Simon pulls out a volume titled *Seeds of Discontent: Poor Farms in Post–Colonial America* and opens it to the title page. The author is listed as Dr. Evelyn Pitman, Senior Lecturer in American History, Cambridge University. Mrs. Pitman's sister, then? Surely it can't be the old lady herself? Gabriela did call her *Evie*, which could be short for Evelyn, but he's never heard anyone address her as *Dr. Pitman.*

He sticks the book in the gym bag, along with all their codex-related papers—he's not about to let them out of his sight—and follows his nose to the kitchen, where Gabriela is buttering thick slices of homemade bread and softly singing a sort of bossa nova version of "Chelsea Morning." She smiles as if she's actually glad to see him. "Did you get some rest?"

"Um, sort of. Wow, something smells good."

"*Mugunzá*. Sit down and I will give you some." She ladles something resembling brownish Cream of Wheat into a bowl and sets it in front of him. "At home we make it with coconut milk, but I could not find any here."

"It's scrumptious," he says, in between panting breaths meant to cool down the big spoonful he's rashly stuck in his mouth. "And hot!"

She hands him a welcome glass of orange juice. "I think we should make copies of the plaintext right away, in case the *JRL* wants to see the whole thing."

"Yep. Although I don't imagine they'll look at what we already sent until after Thanksgiving. Then they'll probably send it off to a couple of referees."

"*Referees?* Like in football?"

Simon laughs. "Not exactly. They're other scholars in the field, and they say whether they think the paper is valid and worth publishing." He pauses and dips into the gym bag. "Speaking of scholars . . . " He opens the book and turns it to face her. "Who's Dr. Evelyn Pitman?"

"Oh. That is Evie. When she retired, she quit using the *Doctor*. She says that students have enough authority figures already; the library should feel friendly and welcoming, not like another classroom."

"Wow. I had no idea she was a professor. At Cambridge, yet."

"That is where she met her husband. But when he started going away on long expeditions, she came back here, to her *alma mater.*"

"Hmm." Simon stares dreamily out the window. "I wonder where *I'll* end up."

"I think that when your paper is published, you will have your choice of positions."

"What about you? I mean, um, are you planning to—to go back?"

"To Brazil?" She shrugs. "I am not sure. I would like very much to attend graduate school up here, provided Gilberto can help pay for it, or I can get an assistantship."

Simon can't hide his pleased smile. "Ah. That's good. I mean, it'll *be* good. For you."

•   •   •

While Gabriela goes over the latest pages of plaintext, checking for accuracy, Simon conks out on the couch again. When he comes to, they stuff the pages of cipher and Portuguese into the cover of the *Cantigas* and cram the volume in among the oversized books in the Pitmans' collection.

"I wonder where the codex was concealed all those years?" says Gabriela.

"In the library of the grandee he mentions, I assume. There's no telling how it got to the States. Probably some unscrupulous scholar made off with it. That happened a lot in the seventeenth and eighteenth centuries." He laughs ruefully. "It still does, as far as that goes."

After downing more sandwiches and some homemade smoothies, they bundle up for their trek across campus. "Oh, wait!" says Gabriela. "I have an idea!" With a paring knife, she cuts a few of the stitches that secure the lining of her coat, then she folds the pages of the translation and slips them through the little gap. "There! Just in case we are ombushed."

"*Am*bushed." Simon grins and shakes his head. "*Spy vs. Spy.*"

"*Que?*"

"Oh, it's just a comic strip in *Mad* magazine."

They take a roundabout route to the Briggs, keeping an eye out for minions. Under the pretense of doing some cataloguing, Gabriela gets the key to the Rare Book Room. The first thing she does is climb the little stepladder and check the space above the ceiling tiles. As she gropes around, a dismayed look comes over her face. "Oh, Simon! I cannot find it!"

"Um, that's because you lifted up the wrong ceiling tile. It's the next one over."

Blushing with embarrassment, Gabriela scoots the ladder sideways and tries again. "Ah, *Graças a Deus.*" She takes the precious volume down and examines it, as if making sure it wasn't replaced by some other, totally useless codex, then hides it away again.

They make quick work of the copying, half afraid that Alec will turn up, or the mystery man, or Marnie, or the guy in the ski mask or who knows who. It seems unlikely, but then so does the whole situation. Simon always knew that the academic world could be competitive, even cutthroat, but this is ridiculous. And Alec did say that it wasn't over yet. He was probably just being a sore loser, but maybe not; he's definitely the sort of guy who holds a grudge.

Gabriela slips the originals and the copies inside the lining of her coat, then they cautiously make their way back across campus to Mrs. Pitman's. *Dr.* Pitman's. Once the papers are safely stowed in the binding of the *Cantigas*, they head out again, this time to visit Mack.

CHAPTER THIRTY-TWO

The big guy is still suffering from Darvon withdrawal, though not as acutely. He looks pale and sort of hunched over, but at least he's not throwing up--not at the moment, anyway. "Are they feeding you okay?" asks Gabriela.

Mack shrugs. "No worse than the campus dining hall. Not that it matters; I can't keep anything down yet. I better get my appetite back by Thursday; I hear they serve a real fancy Thanksgiving dinner."

"You are joking, yes?"

"Yes."

"Well, don't worry. We will bring you something nice."

"Have they set a date for your hearing?" asks Simon.

"A week from Monday. The judge wants to clear his calendar before the holidays. Apparently he's going to spend Christmas in the Caribbean."

"Did they assign you a decent lawyer?"

"Isn't that an oxymoron? I don't know how decent he is, but he *is* a lawyer. I think he specializes in real estate."

"Wonderful. Jeez, Mack, I wish we could hire a better one for you."

"Hey, it's not you guys' problem. I brought this on myself."

"No, you didn't!" protests Gabriela. "You were framed!"

"Tell that to the judge. My fingerprints were on the package."

"They were?" says Simon.

Mack does his familiar head rub. "The security guy tossed it to me, so of course I caught it. Hey, I'm a football player. Okay, not anymore, but old habits die hard. Anyway, enough about me. How's it going with the Kotex?"

"Well, we finished deciphering it."

"No shit, man? That's great!"

"If you think *that* is great," says Gabriela, "wait until you hear about Alec."

•

On Monday, they pay another visit to Dr. Espinoza—in his classroom, not his office. Considering what they've learned about Marnie, having to face her would be embarrassing for all of them. After some debate, they've decided not to reveal her transgressions to the professor, at least not yet. With any luck, she'll have nothing more to do with Alec, and the problem will be solved.

Besides, Dr. E has all the surprising revelations he can handle. First, there's the news that they've finished deciphering the codex. Then they inform him that Simon's theory about Vicente was correct: He was, in fact, the same Vicente who was accused of poisoning João III.

"*Increíble,*" Espinoza murmurs. "*JRL* cannot possibly turn down your paper now. I will call and let them know about this." He retrieves the little flask of liquor from his valise, takes a swig, and hands it to Simon. "Let us drink to your success." When Simon hesitates, the professor says, "Do not worry; it is not drugged. I am sorry; that is not a very amusing joke, is it?"

"No." Simon ventures a sip and passes it to Gabriela, who follows suit.

"There is just one thing that concerns me," says Dr. E.

Gabriela coughs a little as the whiskey goes down. "What is that, *Maestro?*"

"They will want to be certain that your source is genuine, that it is not some sort of hoax."

"*Hoax?*"

"*Um embuste.* It has been known to happen. Do you have any idea what became of the original codex?"

Simon and Gabriela exchange wary glances. "Um . . . well . . . sort of," stammers Simon.

"I thought I knew where it was," says Gabriela. "But I was wrong." Which is sort of true.

When they're clear of the classroom, Simon says, "That was a clever answer to his question."

"Thank you."

"He didn't look too happy. Maybe we should have just told him."

"We will have to show it to him sooner or later, of course. But I think that later is better than sooner."

"You don't trust him?"

"I don't like to say so, Simon, but at this point I do not trust anyone." She lays a hand lightly on his arm. "Except you, of course."

•

When Simon visits Mack the next day, the big guy is looking better and is eager to hear what's been happening on campus in his absence. "Maisie sent a note saying it wasn't a good idea for any SDS people to visit. It might make me look like some kind of dangerous radical. I mean, the cops know all their faces by now."

"Uh-huh. Well, I'm not exactly on top of things, but the word is they're planning a big demonstration for December first."

"The day of my hearing? Awww."

"The day of the *draft lottery*, you bozo."

"I knew that. So, are you gonna join? The demonstration, I mean, not the Army." When Simon hesitates, Mack waves a dismissive hand. "Never mind; like I said, that's your business. I just wish *I* could be there. Oh, hey, did your old *amigo* turn up yet?"

"Not yet," says Simon.

•   •   •

When he gets back to the Gas Chamber, there's an unfamiliar figure sitting on the steps. Simon slows to a halt, worried that it's another of the mystery man's minions, come to grill him about the codex--perhaps at gunpoint this time. Then the stranger waves and calls, "*Olá*, Simon!" and it becomes clear that he's not a stranger at all. But neither is he the same Frank Ávila that Simon remembers.

Frank was always slender; now, in spite of his bulky sheepskin jacket, he looks practically emaciated. His cheekbones are more prominent than ever, his legs even scrawnier than Simon's, his skin ashy and blotchy-looking—the part that's visible, anyway. He's sporting a Pancho Villa mustache and a sparse beard, and his hair is hippie-length. Simon can still make out the scar left by the scytale, though, and he feels guilty all over again. "Um, hey, Frank. How'd you get here?"

"I drove. That's my car over there--the Corvair. Nobody wants them anymore, so I got it real cheap."

"Uh-huh. It, uh, it didn't give you any trouble, I hope?"

Frank lets out a laugh that turns into a brief coughing fit. "Nothing I couldn't fix. You know I'm a wizard when it comes to cars."

"Right. Um, it's cold out here; why don't we go inside?"

With his jacket off, Frank looks even skinnier, almost fragile. Beneath the wispy beard, the skin of his face resembles that of an adolescent with a nasty case of acne. He catches Simon staring, but doesn't seem offended; maybe he's used to it. "I guess I look a little different, huh?"

"Yeah. You said you got a medical discharge, but I didn't know what . . . "

Frank gives another coughing laugh. "The VA docs say they don't know, either. But *I* know, and so does everybody else that messed around with Agent Orange."

"Agent Orange?"

Frank sighs and shakes his head. "You don't want to know. You got any coffee?"

"Just instant."

"That'll do. Mind if I sit down?"

"No, no, go ahead. *Mi casa es tu casa.*"

"Don't worry, I'm not going to move in or anything. I'm staying at the Slider Inn till I find a place. Hey, what the hell is a Slider, anyway?"

"Some kind of turtle. The team mascot is kind of scary, but I think the real thing is actually pretty harmless."

Frank seems surprisingly at ease, as if they're old buddies who meet up every week or so, and not two guys with an uncertain relationship who haven't seen each other for five years. Though Simon would like to know more about the Agent Orange business, Frank doesn't seem inclined to talk about it. He wants to discuss school stuff: where he goes to register, what classes he should sign up for, what professors he should avoid, what are the chances of getting a part-time job on campus. He also doesn't seem inclined to speak Spanish; it's as if he wants to put his Garden City days behind him.

"Um, any idea what you might major in?" asks Simon.

"Art," says Frank, very matter-of-factly, though it couldn't have come as more of a surprise if he'd said he was planning to be a linebacker. Simon figured him for something more . . . well, practical, like maybe engineering. Frank grins, clearly relishing Simon's reaction. "I know, weird, huh? But I've been fooling around with old auto parts, welding them into sort of sculptures, you know? I thought maybe if I studied, I could get really good at it, be the next David Smith or something."

Simon doesn't know the first thing about David Smith or, for that matter, about Van Dyne's Fine Arts program. "I could show you where the department is, though. Then if you want to, we could go get some food—my treat. I just got my NDEA check." God knows, Frank looks like he could use a good meal.

As they make a brief tour of the campus, Simon does most of the talking, giving his friend—or whatever he is--a rundown of the various buildings and what's in them. Frank stays pretty much silent, as if awed by his new surroundings.

When they're sitting in the Turtle Tap with Sliders and onion rings in front of them, Simon finally gets the nerve to ask what he's been dying to ask ever since Frank turned up. He doesn't want to just bring it up out of the blue, though; he has to lead into it. "So, um, how are things in Garden City these days?"

Frank shrugs. "About the same. Seems like the Chicanos are getting to be more a part of the community, which I guess is a good thing."

"I, um, I don't suppose you've heard anything about . . . "

"About Peri Jurado?" Franks asks slyly.

"Yeah."

"Not much. I heard she got married to some farmer in Chihuahua and has a couple of kids."

Simon nods glumly. He's not sure what he expected; just something a little more, a little better. There's a long silence while they concentrate on the onion rings—Simon does, anyway; Frank apparently doesn't have much of an appetite. When he finally speaks, he seems to have caught Simon's chronic tendency to hesitate and fumble his words. "Uh, listen, Simon . . . there's something I . . . something you ought to know about. I . . . I wasn't gonna bring it up this soon, but . . . well, I don't know how much we'll see of each other, so . . . "

"What do you mean? Something about Peri?"

"No," says Frank. "Something about your dad."

Like Simon asking what became of Peri, this is not something you can just throw out there. It takes some leading into.

For some reason, Frank starts by telling about his *Tía* Delfina, who also lived in Little Mexico. When she was dying of lung cancer, he visited her in the hospital almost every day. Near the end, she made a kind of deathbed confession. She had seen something happen years before--something bad. But she never told anyone, afraid that if she did, they'd consider her somehow guilty and arrest her or send her back to Mexico. Now that she was dying, it didn't matter.

As she was walking home one evening with a sack of groceries from the *tiendita,* she heard loud voices out in front of the Wades' house. That was nothing new; the father, who was a drunk, was always yelling at the boy for something—or, more likely, nothing. But this time it sounded like real trouble, and looked like it, too.

There were no street lights in that part of town, but a beat-up Ford truck sat at the curb with the driver's door open, and the dome light illuminated the two forms. The boy was trying to get into the truck, to escape; the father was holding him back and threatening to hit him with something—a baseball bat, maybe.

To get home, the aunt would normally pass by their house, but she didn't dare; instead, she crouched down in the shadows next to a tree to wait until the trouble was over. A moment later, she heard someone running down the walk—a policeman, she supposed. But no--it was the man who once ran the sugar refinery and now ran the martial arts academy. He was calling out, "Stop! Stop it!"

The boy must have heard, for he turned to look. As he did, the father swung the bat and struck him in the head. It must have been a hard blow; even at a distance, the aunt could see blood flowing down the boy's face, half blinding him. The boy pushed his father away, climbed into the truck, and slammed the door; there was a grinding noise as he tried to put it into gear. Before he managed it, the father smashed in the side window with the baseball bat.

When the martial arts man reached Wade, he yanked the bat from his hands and tossed it in the gutter; then he stepped in front of the truck, holding up his hands, calling out, "Joe! Joe, wait! It'll be all right!" The boy couldn't have seen much through all that blood, and probably couldn't hear over the racing engine. He finally found a gear and the truck leaped forward, knocking the man down. *Tía* Delfina had to stifle a scream.

When the truck stalled, the father flung open the door and dragged the boy out from behind the wheel. He shook him, the way you would to wake someone up, and shouted, "Joey! Listen to me! Go in and call the police! Go!" As the boy shuffled toward the house, wiping the blood from his face, the father climbed into the Ford, closed the door, and just sat there. No doubt he was still there when the police came--the aunt didn't stick around long enough to be sure. She hurried back the way she had come and took a different route home.

"Jesus!" breathes Simon. "It was *Joe* that ran my dad down, and Wade was covering for him?"

"According to my aunt, yeah."

"Then he sent Joe away, so he wouldn't testify and maybe reveal the truth."

"I guess so."

"So my dad didn't attack Wade at all; he was just trying to stop him." Simon is feeling dizzy, as if he's downed a whole slew of Sliders and not just half of one. Across the room, the Devil is mocking some poor sucker, but this time Old Nick isn't content with a single manic laugh. He does it a second time, then again, and again; the machine must have gone haywire.

Simon gets unsteadily to his feet. "I—I've got to get out of here, man, and get some fresh air." He tosses a couple of bills onto the table. "You stay here and finish your rings," he says, and heads for the door.

"Hey, I'm sorry, *amigo*," Frank calls, over the Devil's din. "I just thought you ought to know."

"No, no, it's okay. I'm just—I've just got to process this, you know?"

Frank allows him plenty of processing time. Maybe he's feeling remorseful, the way Simon did after the scytale incident. Maybe he's just busy finding his way around and looking at apartments and signing up for classes. Or maybe he's feeling as ill as he looks. Whatever the reason, Simon sees no sign of him the rest of the week.

The day after Frank's visit, Gabriela stops by to invite Simon to Thanksgiving dinner at Mrs. Pitman's. He considers asking whether he can bring

Frank; it would be the friendly thing to do, but Simon isn't feeling very friendly. Granted, it's sort of a case of killing the messenger—after all, it wasn't Frank's fault that things turned out the way they did for Peri and for Don Hannay--and yet Simon can't help feeling a certain resentment. He's spent the last five years learning to deal with his father's death, only to have to start over at the scrimmage line, as Mack would say. In the end, only he and Gabriela and Evie share the dinner —and, a bit later, Mack, when they take him a warming tray full of leftovers.

On Saturday, Simon holds his self-defense class as usual, not so much for the benefit of the students--most of whom have gone home for the holiday—as for himself. He needs to get back in the *goju-ryu* groove after devoting so much of his energy to the codex. He also needs to get back in the academic groove. He's skipped so many sessions of both Spanish Lit and Books and Printing that he's way behind, and finals are coming up way too fast. It's not going to look good if he has a paper accepted by *JRL* and then flunks his course work.

To his delight, not only does Gabriela spend much of the karate class sparring with him, she also suggests that they cram for exams together. They don't pull any all-nighters, just a couple of pleasant afternoons in Mrs. Pitman's library, with breaks for tea and sandwiches. In addition to relishing Gabriela's company, Simon is happy to have something besides his father's fate to occupy his mind. He doesn't say anything about it to Gabriela; like her, he doesn't want anyone feeling sorry for him. Or even *someone*.

Returning to the lonesome Gas Chamber in the evenings feels like a punishment, like solitary confinement—which, admittedly, is a stupid way to feel. Compared to what Mack is going through, his plight is pretty pathetic.

When Simon visits the big guy on Sunday morning, he asks whether he should come to the hearing the following day, for moral support. "I'd just as soon you didn't," says Mack.

"Really? Why? I mean, I'm not a dangerous radical."

"I know, but you said there's going to be a demonstration tomorrow."

"Yeah. So, what; you want me to be part of it?"

"Not if you don't want to. But I was hoping maybe you could sort of hang around on the fringes and let me know how it goes. Like, for instance, whether they bring up the topic of defoliants and stuff."

"Oh. I guess you didn't hear?"

"Hear what?"

"A couple of days ago, Tricky Dick made a statement renouncing the use of chemical and biological weapons."

"No shit? Of course, what he says and what actually happens are two different things. Thus the nickname."

Simon nods thoughtfully. "I don't really want to be in the thick of things, but I could observe from a distance. You'll probably want to know how the lottery goes, too. When's your birthday? April, right?"

"The twenty-sixth. I hope I get a big number." Unexpectedly, the big guy lets out a laugh.

"What?"

"Well, if they slap a felony charge on me, it ain't gonna matter, is it? That's one thing about being behind bars; Uncle Sam can't get you."

CHAPTER THIRTY-THREE

The anti-draft demonstration takes place on the main quad—a good thing, since it draws twice the number of students who gathered for the sit-in at the former Recruiting Office--the Marines have since beat a discreet retreat to a new location downtown. When Simon shows up after his Books and Printing class, things are already in full swing.

SDS has rigged up a rickety speaker's platform out of packing crates and 2X4s. A student with an enormous Afro is shouting something into a megaphone that badly warps his words; as far as Simon can tell, he's saying something about a how a disproportionately high percentage of combat troops are black or Hispanic.

When the speaker is done and the applause dies down, Maisie climbs onto the shaky stage and takes possession of the megaphone. She speaks more softly and calmly, and her words are actually intelligible. "We had hoped to convince some of the faculty to join us today; unfortunately, we couldn't find anyone brave enough." A chorus of boos. She holds up a hand to still them. "*However--*! We are honored to have on our side a *former* member of the faculty, one you all know and respect--Dr. Evelyn Pitman." A riot of cheers and clapping.

The black student helps Evie mount the platform; Maisie keeps hold of the old woman's arm to steady her as she raises the megaphone. Simon has never heard her voice sound so strong, so confident; it does tremble, but only a little. He's never seen her smile so broadly, either. It's as if she's traveled back in time a decade or two. So have her thoughts.

"The last time I addressed a peace rally, it was on this same spot, twenty-five years ago, at the height of the Second World War. You may have heard it called the Good War. I can assure you, it was not. Neither was the rally a good one, not like this one. We had perhaps two dozen protestors—and three times that many who were protesting the protestors." A wave of appreciative laughter.

"On that occasion, I recited a very powerful anti-war poem by Edna St. Vincent Millay—whom I once met, by the way, just before the U.S. entered the War. She was no longer such a staunch pacifist; like so many others, she felt that Hitler had to be stopped, by whatever means necessary. Whether or not she was right, her poem has lost none of its power and none of its relevance, and I shall recite it again now . . . if my memory will cooperate." Astonishingly, considering the size of the crowd, it goes utterly quiet. "The poem is called . . . 'The Conscientious Objector'."

Simon feels suddenly dizzy, disoriented, the way he did last night when Frank dredged up a part of the past that Simon had tried hard to forget. Now he's assailed by a memory from even farther in the past, from when he was six or seven years old and Don Hannay read this same poem to him and he was too young to understand.

He understands it now.

"I shall die, but that is all that I shall do for Death.
I hear him leading his horse out of the stall;
I hear the clatter on the barn-floor.
He is in haste; he has business in Cuba,
business in the Balkans, many calls to make this morning.
But I will not hold the bridle while he clinches the girth.
And he may mount by himself:
I will not give him a leg up.

Though he flick my shoulders with his whip,
I will not tell him which way the fox ran.
With his hoof on my breast, I will not tell him where
the black boy hides in the swamp.
I shall die, but that is all that I shall do for Death;
I am not on his pay-roll.

I will not tell him the whereabout of my friends
nor of my enemies either.
Though he promise me much,

I will not map him the route to any man's door.
Am I a spy in the land of the living,
that I should deliver men to Death?
Brother, the password and the plans of our city
are safe with me; never through me shall you be overcome."

There's no applause this time, only a sober, reverent silence. When they help Evie down from the platform, Simon doesn't see it. He's blinded by something wet and warm coursing down his cheeks. For a moment he imagines that it's blood, that he's been struck by some object--though the pain is in his chest, not his head.

He puts a hand to his face--the way Frank Ávila did when the scytale struck him; the way Joe Wade did when the bat split his forehead open; the way Alec did when Simon whacked him in the nose. But when he takes his hand away, it's not drenched in red. He's not bleeding, only weeping. It's been so long since he let himself cry that he almost forgot what it felt like.

By the time he pulls himself together, the crowd is on the move, brandishing signs and chanting, "Hell, no, we won't go!" Simon trails after them, wondering where they're headed. Ah, the Military Science building.

The R.O.T.C is clearly expecting them. A couple of dozen cadets in uniform are lined up in front of the building, gripping their wooden rifles in port arms position. They're backed up by an equal number of campus security and police bearing batons.

For ten minutes or so, it's a standoff, with the demonstrators doing nothing more threatening than holding aloft a burning draft card or chanting, "One, two, three, four; we don't want your fucking war!" and the cops and cadets standing as stiff and stony-faced as statues. Then some unidentified person—an *agent provocateur*, maybe?--flings a stone, shattering a window on the second floor, and it's like firing a starter pistol at a track meet. Suddenly the uniforms surge forward and wade into the crowd, swinging batons and fake rifles.

The front ranks of protestors try to retreat, but the mass of bodies behind them makes it impossible. Dozens of students are knocked to the ground, many of them battered and bleeding. Some are hauled away in handcuffs.

As the rally breaks up and disperses, Simon turns away, cursing the police and cadets and cursing himself for staying on the sidelines. Not that he would have wanted to actually cream anybody, but if he'd been where the action was he might at least have disarmed a few of those shithead pseudo-soldiers and kept some peaceniks from getting their heads broken.

Simon only hopes that the SDS managed to keep Mrs. Pitman out of harm's way. He's tempted to stop by the house and check on her and Gabriela, but he doesn't really care to explain what he was doing--or not doing--when it all went down. He heads for the Turtle Tap instead, hoping to grab some food and a drink or two before the place starts filling up with anxious guys herding around the big color TV to watch as their futures are determined by the draft lottery.

It's still early, and the Tap is mostly empty. As he sits down at the bar, Simon glances warily in the direction of the pinball games, fearing that the Devil might break into another unprovoked paroxysm of laughter. To his surprise, the play board of Beat the Devil is propped up like the hood of a car, revealing the game's wiry innards. The mechanic who's tinkering around beneath the hood is none other than Frank Ávila.

Drink in hand, Simon approaches, clearing his throat a little to avoid startling Frank. *"Que pasa?"*

Frank doesn't look up from his task, which seems to involve unplugging a series of colored wires and plugging them in somewhere else. "Hey, Simon. Apparently, in order to repair these things, they usually bring in somebody from Pittsburgh; I told them I could do it a lot quicker and cheaper. Remember, I used to fix the ones at the Legion?"

"Oh? I never knew that."

"Well, I did." He emerges from the maw of the game, lowers the play board back into place, and screws it down. "There. That ought to change the Devil's tune." He nods at the backboard, where Old Nick still leers malevolently. "Don't tell anybody," he says softly, "but I also reset the scoring mechanism. You want to give it a try?"

"Sure." With Frank watching, Simon is so self-conscious that he manages to rack up only 3,500 points; he winces, anticipating that infuriating, mocking laugh. Instead, there's a brief, almost benign-sounding chuckle that's nearly drowned out by Simon's own laughter. "How did you *do* that?"

Frank shrugs. "I just made a few little adjustments," he says modestly, though he looks pretty pleased with himself.

"That's great, man. So, you gave the Devil his due."

"Huh?"

"Never mind. Are you going to fix Moon Shot, too?"

Frank pats that machine. "Already did."

"Wow. You're a genius."

"Hey, compared to working on a C-123, this is nothing."

"C-123? Is that an airplane?"

Frank's expression turns grim. "Yeah. The one they used to spray Agent Orange." Reflexively, he scratches at his ravaged skin.

"Ah," says Simon, still not sure exactly what Agent Orange is. "Um, listen, let me buy you a drink, okay? I'm going to get some food, too, if you . . ."

"No food for me; I don't have much of an appetite these days. I'll take the drink, though."

Over Sliders and the Tap's newly christened Chief Justice Burger plate— from which Frank snags a few of the fries—Simon gets a quick and dirty course on the use of defoliants in Vietnam: how Operation Ranch Hand dumped millions of gallons of toxins over the jungles and croplands, and sometimes over population centers and water sources. How the chemical companies assured everyone that the stuff was harmless. How the soldiers were stupid enough to buy that line and used the orange-striped barrels as barbecue pits, as storage bins for gasoline and potatoes, as water reservoirs for their showers. How, when men started getting sick and scientists started asking questions, the government scoffed at the notion that Agent Orange was responsible. How the military kept right on spraying—occasionally drenching their own troops by accident—until they realized that it was basically doing nothing to hinder the Viet Cong.

When Frank got his discharge, they were starting to phase out Ranch Hand. But of course it was too late for him and for all the other soldiers who had been exposed to the defoliant--not to mention the Vietnamese civilians whose land and water had been poisoned. And of course the chemical companies and their buddies at the State Department were still denying that there was a problem.

Simon shakes his head sadly, incredulously. "So the VA isn't doing anything to help you?"

Frank gives a bitter laugh that turns into a racking cough. He takes a swig of his Slider to stem it. "How can they help, when there's nothing wrong?" Pushing back his chair, he gets to his feet. "I'm tired of talking about it, *amigo*. How about I beat you at a game of Moon Shot?" He leans in and whispers, "I rigged it so we can play for free!"

The draft lottery is scheduled to start at eight. By seven, the place is filling up; by seven-thirty, it's standing room only. There's barely enough space to move, let alone play pinball or shoot pool. To get a drink, you have to jump up and down and yell out your order, then hope that, by the time it's relayed to you via a sort of bucket brigade, there's some of it left.

When eight o'clock comes, an anticipatory hush falls over the mob, followed by a chorus of groans and curses when it becomes obvious that all three networks are running their usual programs. Still, nobody stirs, except to make their way to the bathroom—a Herculean task, unless you're a football lineman or the girlfriend of one. Finally, when nine o'clock rolls around, the words "CBS News Special Report" fill the screen and a cultured voice says, "Because of the CBS News Special Report that follows, 'Mayberry RFD' will not be presented tonight--"

A smattering of smart alecks give cries of mock anguish—"Oh, no! That's my favorite show!" and "What, no Goober?" and the like—but they're quickly silenced. With the brio of an emcee at a beauty pageant, The Voice announces, "The Draft Lottery! A live report on tonight's picking of the birth dates for the draft!"

While Roger Mudd gives a brief and solemn history of the draft, in the background a couple of well-fed, gray-haired and bespectacled government minions read out a series of dates and stick them up on a board that's already mostly full. "Shit!" shouts someone. "How are we gonna know--!" A hundred other voices shush him, barely in time to hear Roger say, "The famous first pick tonight is September fifteenth."

At least that's what Simon hears, and he's hit by a jolt of panic; that's *his* birthday. But then the cameraman zooms in on the board, and he sees that the slip next to the number 001 in fact reads "Sep 14." "*Graças a Deus!*" he breathes. It's lucky he got here early enough to claim a bar stool; he's not sure his legs would hold him up.

Number 002 is April 24, and Simon panics again, because he can't remember the date of Mack's birthday—April twenty-something, Mack said. But was it the twenty-fourth? No, no, the twenty-sixth, that's right. Simon is forced to do some *shin kokyu* to calm himself. He also orders another Slider.

Slowly, the camera moves down the list of numbers and dates, while Roger reads them off. At first, the only responses from the students are soft sighs of relief. Then, somewhere around number 009—Nov 22—the sighs begin to sound more defeated and hopeless.

Simon is really more worried for Mack's sake than for his own. According to the current rules, Simon's student deferment is good until he finishes grad school; since he changed his thesis topic, that might not happen until this time next year. Unless, of course, he does something to get himself kicked out of the program. Or—the thought strikes him suddenly—unless someone *else* gets him kicked out. Alec, for instance, or Dr. Vice. No, surely that's not possible.

He shakes his head hard and forces himself to focus on the dates and numbers. Still, when the camera glides by his birthdate, he almost misses it. Number 113. Not good, but not that bad, either. According to Roger, the top third of the list are the most likely to be drafted, which would include him, but the youngest men will be the first ones called up, and that wouldn't include him.

Mack's birthdate hasn't appeared yet. But, to Simon's surprise, the big guy himself has. Somehow he's persuaded the sea of students to part for him--once again, the advantages of being a defensive tackle—and is bellying up to the bar. "Did I get shafted yet?" Mack murmurs in his ear.

Without taking his eyes off the board, Simon gives a slight shake of the head. Then he whispers, "Oops. There you are."

"Number 340. Well, isn't that ironic?"

Before Simon can ask what he means by that, Bobby the bartender shouts, "Whoever has the lowest number, the good news is, you get a six-pack of Black Label, on the house!"

It's poor Casey Klein, his classmate from Books and Printing. Wearing a sickly smile, Casey is ushered to the bar, where half a dozen luckier students take turns buying him drinks; he downs them desperately, one after another, as if hoping to disqualify himself by virtue of alcohol poisoning.

When the boisterous crowd thins out enough so they can hear themselves talk, Mack says, "So, what's your magic number, Froggy?"

"113."

"Ouch. Anything with a 13 in it can't be good."

"Well, I probably don't have to worry until next year sometime; maybe by then it'll all be over, over there. No singing, please."

"I wasn't going to. Let's go sit down, man." As they head for a table, Mack intercepts the waitress and orders a Chief Justice Burger. "I haven't had a decent meal since they locked me up—except for the one you guys brought."

"So, if they released you, does that mean they found you not guilty?"

Mack does his Stan Laurel head rub. "Not exactly."

"Oh? What exactly *does* it mean?"

"It means the judge gave me a choice: I could do two years in prison--"

"*What?*"

"—*or* I could join the Army."

"Jesus! What did you tell him?"

The big guy shrugs. "Well, I don't want a felony on my record, so I figure the Army is the lesser of two evils. At least when I've done my time, I can go back to school on the GI Bill. *And--*" He leans across the table and adds, confidentially, "—if I work it right, I'll get an early out."

"How?"

"My old reliable knee, don't you see? One bad jump out of a chopper or whatever, and I'll go straight from 1-A to 4-F."

"What makes you think they'll take you in the first place?"

"They already have. After the hearing, the cops kindly escorted me to the recruiting station. I guess they figured that, once I enlisted, I was the Army's problem, not theirs. After all that sitting around, my knee was doing okay; the recruiting officer never suspected a thing."

"Aw, Mack. What if they ship you to Nam?"

"Not to worry. For every grunt on the front lines, there's four or five support personnel; those are pretty good odds. "

"Who told you that? No, let me guess. The recruiting officer, right?"

"Well, yeah." Suddenly he brightens and his voice gains several decibels. "Hey! Crazy Maisie! Pull up a chair!"

When he's repeated his sad story for her benefit, the flower child takes one of his big hands in both of her little ones and says softly, "You know, we've got a network that helps draft resisters get to Canada and find work and so on."

"I know, but I wouldn't be a draft dodger. I'd be a deserter."

"Even so, you'd be safe."

"Maybe. But I'd never be able to come back. Hey, I'll be fine; trust me. I just wish I could've--" He breaks off as the waitress sets food in front of him. When she's gone, he continues. "I just wish I could've dug up more stuff about what the lab rats are up to."

Maisie shrugs. "You did what you could, Mack. You never saw anything about Agent Orange, huh?"

"Nope; sorry."

"We're going to try and open up that whole can of worms. So far it's just rumors, though. They're doing a good job of covering it up."

Simon eases his way into the conversation. "Um, I know somebody who has first-hand knowledge." He nods toward where Frank is engaged in a duel with the Devil.

"Your *amigo*?" says Mack.

"Sort of. Is it okay if he joins us?"

"Can we trust him?" asks Maisie.

Simon considers a moment, then says, "Yeah, you can."

Frank is not exactly a social person, but the offer of a free drink wins him over. Once the introductions are out of the way, Mack says, "So, you got to fool around with Agent Orange?"

Simon winces. "Um, sorry, Frank. Mack is not known for his subtlety and tact. I know you said you were tired of talking about it, but, uh, Maisie was just saying—"

"You know what the SDS is, right?" interrupts Maisie. When Frank nods, she goes on. "Well, if we can get more info on Agent Orange and its effects, we're going to make a big stink about it, one that the administration and the press can't ignore. We don't think the labs here are into it, but Mack thinks they are developing some kind of defoliant. He worked as a janitor in the Med Sci building until . . . well, until now."

Frank gives the big guy a surprised look. "You were a spy for the SDS?"

"I guess you could say that."

"Far out." Frank gazes into his drink thoughtfully. "Okay," he says, finally. "Just tell me one thing."

"What's that?" asks Maisie.

Frank's gaunt, ruined face forms a crooked smile. "Is the job still open?"

CHAPTER THIRTY-FOUR

The university is only too happy to hire a veteran; it makes them look good. Once Frank starts work, Simon doesn't see much of him. Mack is lying low, too, staying out of trouble while he waits to be called up for his physical. His old teammates are providing lodging for him, passing him around from person to person like a medicine ball.

Simon himself is even more of a hermit than usual, studying for upcoming exams and grinding out a term paper that was due weeks ago. To cope with the stress, he puts in an hour or two of *kata* whenever the wrestling room is free. He also holds the weekly self-defense class as usual. But he stays away from Karate Club, not caring to put his sails in the path of Alec's wind, which is no doubt blowing cold and bitter.

He can't avoid the scumbag's influence altogether, though. On the first day of exam week, Gabriela shows up for their study date with a message from Dr. E, asking them to stop by his office. "It is about your—*our* paper, Simon, and I do not think it is good news."

In fact, the news could hardly be worse. Apparently, when Alec made that remark about not being so sure the codex would be published, he wasn't just blowing smoke. "I received a telephone call from Mitch Reid at *JRL*," says Espinoza. "He was extremely upset—angry and embarrassed."

"Why?" asks Simon. "He doesn't like our paper?"

"No, no, that is not it at all. He is very enthusiastic about your work. He called it 'astonishing,' I believe."

"Oh. Good. But what's the problem, then?"

"Before he could submit it for peer review, he was summoned by the president of the university and told that under no circumstances was he to publish the paper."

"*Vixe Maria!*" breathes Gabriela. "*Porque razão?*"

"It seems that one of school's largest benefactors contacted the president and warned him that, if it is published, they will withdraw all their grant money."

Simon is too stunned to speak. Gabriela is too indignant not to. "Who is getting all this grant money? Not the literature department, I will bet."

Espinoza shrugs. "The president would not say."

"I think we can guess," says Simon, bleakly. "Their research lab. And it's not hard to figure out who that big benefactor is."

"So, what do we do now?" asks Gabriela.

"I can offer the piece to other journals," says the professor.

Simon glances at Gabriela. No doubt she's thinking the same thing he is: That's exactly what Weiss will expect them to do, and he'll pull the same diabolical trick. "Um, let us give it some thought, okay?"

"If you insist. But I would not wait too long. In the meantime, I will tell Dr. Reid to destroy his copy. At least that will keep it out of the mystery man's hands."

• • •

Simon and Gabriela head across campus arm in arm in glum silence. Finally Simon says, "What are you thinking?"

"I am thinking that we should submit the paper ourselves. Somewhere that Dr. Vice and his minions will not expect."

"Something besides a literature journal, you mean?"

"*Exatamente.*"

"Okay. Any suggestions?"

"Well, what about a *history* journal?"

"I don't know anything about them."

"Neither do I, really. But I know someone who does."

They've been trying all along to keep Mrs. Pitman out of the equation, both for her sake—they don't want her drugged and interrogated—and for their own; they also don't want her letting the cat out of the bag. But she's a smart lady, and she's aware that something serious and maybe sinister is going on. When she offers them tea and sympathy, they can no longer bear to keep her in the dark.

"Just do not ask us where the codex is, please, Evie. It is better if you do not know."

Though Mrs. Pitman seems a bit hurt, she agrees. Briefly, they recount their efforts to decipher the journal, and Dr. Vice's efforts to get hold of it or at least prevent its publication. Much of this isn't exactly news to her; she's been putting two and two together for a long time, but she didn't want to poke her nose in where it wasn't welcome.

"So," Simon concludes, "we thought if we sent the paper someplace that's not so obvious . . . "

"But still widely read and influential," finishes Evie.

"Right."

"May I suggest *World History Quarterly*? To paraphrase a popular song, My opinion is, it's the cream of the crop." If Mack were here, thinks Simon, he'd launch into a travesty of "My Guy." "Of course," Evie goes on, "I may be biased."

"You have published with them, yes?"

Evie nods modestly. "And, until fairly recently, they called upon me for peer reviews."

"Do you think they'd be interested?" asks Simon.

"I'm certain of it. You'd need to establish that the codex is genuine, of course, but that should be no problem. I can sign an affidavit to that effect. So can Dr. Beebe. "

"Dr. B—Beebe?" Simon very nearly slips and says "Booby."

"He examined and dated it, many years ago." She smiles slyly. "And though he may not be a stimulating lecturer, he does know his books." Mrs. Pitman jots down a name and address on a memo pad and hands it to Gabriela. "Get your manuscript in the mail right away. I'll give the editor a call to let him know it's coming."

•

The current week is even hairier than the previous one, what with taking exams and awaiting a reply from *WHQ* and Mack being ordered to Fort Hayes for his physical. One of those ordeals has a blessedly positive outcome: Simon scores a

B plus on his Spanish Lit final and an A minus in Books and Printing. The latter is sheer luck. A major portion of the test involves dating an antique book based solely on a list of its physical details. The hypothetical volume bears a close resemblance to the Vicente codex.

The second source of stress—the fate of the deciphered cipher—remains unresolved.

The outcome of the third is ambiguous. As unlikely as it seems, Mack is classified 1-A--thanks to the cortisone Doc Savage injected into his knee several days earlier. The upside, of course, is that Mack won't be going back to jail, at least not right away. The downside is, he could be bound for somewhere even worse. For the next two months, though, he's going no farther than boot camp at Fort Knox.

Simon spends as much of Christmas week with the big guy as possible. He needs a break from his studies, anyway. The new year is soon enough to Buckle Down and do some heavy-duty research on Renaissance codes and ciphers.

Not only does Gabriela make good on her promise of a Brazilian dinner, she extends the invitation to Mack and Frank. To Simon's surprise, Frank actually accepts. "I hope they won't be offended if I don't eat much. Or talk much, either."

"Don't worry," says Simon. "Mack will eat enough—and talk enough--to make up for the rest of us."

The food is amazing, from the appetizer of cheese fried in garlic, to the entrée of fish stew made with coconut milk (sent to Gabriela by her *padrinho*), to the dessert of tapioca crepes with banana filling. The conversation is good, too, lubricated by a couple of bottles of *vinho fino*, courtesy of Mrs. Pitman. Cases full of artifacts weren't the only thing her husband brought back from his expeditions.

For most of the meal, they manage to skate over the sobering topics that lurk just beneath the surface. It's not until Mack is on his third glass of wine that he cracks the ice by asking Frank how he's feeling. Frank glances about uncomfortably. "I would really rather not discuss it."

Simon does his best to defuse the situation. "Like I said, Mack isn't big on subtlety and tact."

Mack gives a sheepish shrug. "Sorry, man. I just wondered if you were able to handle the job okay."

"You are working?" asks Gabriela.

"Yeah," murmurs Frank. "I got Mack's old job as a janitor."

"Have you found any good stuff in the wastebaskets?" Mack wants to know.

Simon gives him a perturbed glance. "Uh, Mack. I'm not sure we should be discussing this?"

"Okay, okay. I thought we were all on the same side."

"We are, but . . ."

Gabriela springs up from her chair. "Who wants to help me wash up?"

"I will," says Frank, with evident relief.

As they carry the dishes to the sink, Mrs. Pitman leans in to Simon and Mack and says, "Don't worry, gentlemen; you're not giving anything away. Maisie keeps me informed about what the SDS is up to. You see, I was part of the movement back when it was called the Intercollegiate Socialist Society." By way of changing the subject, she gestures at the kitchen walls, which are hung with holly and evergreen boughs adorned with lights and tinsel. "Doesn't the place look Christmassy? Speaking of which, Simon, don't let me forget; I have a present for you."

"A present? You didn't need to--"

"Oh, shush. It didn't cost me anything."

Simon wishes he'd thought to buy something for her. He has a gift for Gabriela, but he's been holding off, uncertain how she'll feel about it. This seems like a good time to give Mack his gift, though, before he's too drunk to appreciate it.

The big guy rips off the wrapping to reveal a bound notebook and a package of Bic pens. "Ohhhkay," he says, momentarily baffled. Then he laughs. "Oh, I get it. This is a subtle hint that I'm supposed to write you."

"Right on."

"Hey, I'll try. You know me."

"Yes, yes I do."

Once the other guys are gone, Simon works up the nerve to give Gabriela her gift, but before he can, Mrs. Pitman claps her hands and announces, "It's present time! Hmm. That sounds a bit odd, doesn't it? Obviously it's the present time, as opposed to Christmas Past, or Christmas Yet to Come." An uncharacteristic giggle escapes her. "You know what they say; there's no time like the present."

Gabriela whispers in Simon's ear, "I don't think she is accustomed to have so much wine." She turns to Mrs. Pitman. "Where is it, Evie?"

Smiling mischievously, the old woman taps the side of her head. "Up here. But. First you must sit down, and pour us each a glass of wine." She burps delicately and giggles again. "Perhaps not a full glass for me. Good. Now. If I were Father Christmas—sorry, I picked that up in England—if I were Santa— or *Papai Noel*--what is the one thing you would ask me for?"

Simon hesitates; Gabriela doesn't. "To have our paper published."

Evie claps her hands together. "Oh, good! Because the editor of *WHQ* phoned me yesterday. It will appear in the Spring number. They don't require a peer review, since I vouched for you. So!" She raises her glass. "To your success!"

"To defeating Dr. Vice and his minions!" gloats Gabriela.

"To the two lovey--lovely ladies--" Simon is not accustomed to so much wine, either. "--without whom it would not have been possible!"

They clink their glasses and drain them. "I think," says Mrs. Pitman, muzzily, "that I'm ready for a lie down, now." With Gabriela's help, she makes her way unsteadily to her room.

When Gabriela returns, she's carrying a flat gift-wrapped package. "This is for you, Simon. I hope you like it."

"Um, thanks. I didn't-- I wasn't--"

"Oh, stop mumbling and open it."

It's an Astrud Gilberto album titled, oddly, "September 17, 1969." "Oh, wow! This is great! I, um, the only thing is—uh--"

"*Que?*"

"Well, I don't have a record player."

She shrugs and smiles. "Then I suppose you will just have to listen to it on mine."

Simon is feeling distinctly warm, and it's not just from the wine. "Oh. Okay. Sure. Hang on." He stumbles to the coat rack and pulls from the pocket of his jacket a tiny square package.

She examines it cautiously. "This looks almost like a . . . . "

"*Que?*"

"Well, like a ring box."

"That's because it is."

She gives him a startled look. "Simon! Why would you--?"

"Just open it, okay?"

"Okay," she says doubtfully. Unlike Mack, she peels the package slowly and carefully, making Simon even more anxious. She pries open the little box carefully, too, as though afraid of what she'll find. "Oh! It's not a . . . What *is* it?"

"It's a P F Magic Ring. I got it when I was twelve, with the purchase of P F Flyers--those are tennis shoes. I didn't really want the shoes, just the ring. You can use it to send secret messages." The ring is a miniature version of the fifteenth-century Alberti disk. The clear plastic dial in the center has a regular alphabet around the rim; circling it, on the outer part of the ring, is a jumbled-up alphabet—part of which reads "WEAR PFS."

"I love it!" cries Gabriela. "Send me a message, so I can decipher it, please!"

Simon is blushing again. "Um, I already did. It's in the secret compartment. Just pull off the dial, and look under that piece of green foil. Yeah. Now, stick the dial back on and turn it so the A is pointing to the P on the outer ring. Good."

It takes Gabriela only a minute to jot down the plaintext. "O MOK MON?" Frowning, she scratches her head. "*Cocô*. I must have done something wrong."

"No," says Simon nervously. "That's right."

"But what does--? Oh. I remember. They are the last words that Aleala said to Vicente."

Simon swallows hard. "Yep."

"Oh, Simon." Sniffling a little, she slips off one of her bulky silver rings and replaces it with the magic decoder. Then, standing on tiptoe, she wraps her arms around his neck and kisses him quickly, right on the lips. "This is the best Christmas present I ever got."

• • •

Though Simon writes to Mack regularly, he doesn't really expect to hear much from the big guy, and his expectations are met. Over the next eight weeks, he receives a total of two letters. Neither one contains anything very startling or informative. The first is mainly just a droll account of all the "sadistic shit" that the drill sergeants put them through. "If that last line is blacked out, that means they're censoring our mail. They said they wouldn't, but ya never know."

The second letter contains a comment so bizarre that Simon can't help wondering whether the sadistic shit has driven Mack over the edge or around the bend. He rereads it half a dozen times, trying to make some sense of it: "Tell

Rhonda that she has my permission to wear my Phi Beta Kappa pin, whole-heartedly."

When he meets Gabriela at the Gedunk, in between bouts of researching, he shows her the letter. She's as baffled as he is. "Phi Beta Kappa? Is that not some kind of big, important honor?"

"Uh-huh. And they give you a key, not a pin. Obviously Mack doesn't have one, and even if he did, he wouldn't give it to Rhonda." Sipping at his *café*, he studies the sentence as if it's a line of ciphertext. Hmm. There's a thought. For once, his habit of overthinking and analyzing pays off. "Oh, wait a second. Pin. . . Whole. . . Pinhole!" He plasters the page to the nearest window. "Well, look at that, would you? He actually remembered what I told him about the pinhole code!"

"Oh, good! I miss our deciphering! Read me the letters, Simon. I will copy them down."

"*S-u-p-l-y-s-g-t-s-i-c*-period. Got it?"

"*Claro.* Go on."

"*S-p-r-a-d-w-a-o-i-n-n-a-m*-the number one-*m-o-a-g-o*-period. *T-h-e-r-s-t-i-l-u-s-i-n-i-t.* That's it."

"*É verdade?* It makes no sense. Is it enciphered?"

"I don't think so. I think he's just using abbreviations. *Suply.* That's got to be Supply. And *sgt* is short for Sergeant. So. *Supply Sergeant sick. Sprayed with AO—* Agent Orange—*in Nam one month ago. They're still using it.*" Simon claps a hand to his forehead. "Holy shit. When Nixon said no more chemical or biological weapons, he was lying."

CHAPTER THIRTY-FIVE

Simon needs to show Mack's message to Frank; unfortunately, he doesn't know where Frank is living these days. He's not about to visit him at the Ratitorium, where he might run into Alec--not that he's afraid of the jerk; he just doesn't want to have to deal with him. Apparently Alec is still confident that he and Dr. Vice have foiled Simon's plans. On the rare occasion when they spot each other crossing campus, Alec gives him a cocky wave and calls, "*Osu, senpai!*" As far as Simon can tell, the scumbag's nose is as straight and finely chiseled as ever. He doesn't tell this to Gabriela; she'd be so disappointed.

Frank did mention once that he hangs out a lot at the art studio, and that's where Simon finds him, sculpting a foot-long lump of clay. Simon gives a low whistle. "*Oye, que bien!*" He's seeing a side of Frank that he didn't know existed.

"Thanks, man. This is just a model. I want to do it about ten times this size."

Though the piece is pretty stylized, you can still tell what it represents: A hunched figure being attacked by some kind of huge bird with talons—sort of a cross between an eagle and an airplane. "Are you going to do it in metal?"

Frank shrugs. "Nah, probably plaster. The prof wants me to try different mediums."

"Cool. Hey, listen; I got a message from Mack. He says—um—he says they're still using Agent Orange over there."

Frank goes rigid. Then he draws back his knife-like modeling tool and plunges it into the spot where the raptor's heart would be. "God *damn* them! If I was still over there, I'd plant a bomb in every one of their fucking aircraft!" He's so worked up that he breaks into a coughing fit.

Simon has never seen this side of him, either; he's always been so laid back. "Uh, sorry, man. I—I didn't mean to upset you."

Frank takes a ragged breath and gets the coughing under control. "No, no, you were right to tell me. I'll let the SDS know. See if Mack can find out any more details, okay?"

"I'll try. He doesn't write very often."

"Where is he now?"

"Still at Fort Knox. He's starting communications school."

Frank winces. "That's a sure ticket to Nam."

"Shit."

"He probably won't see any combat, though. Just tell him to stay away from barrels with orange stripes." Frank sets his sculpting tool aside and wipes his hands on a gray-streaked towel. "What did his message say, exactly?" Simon hands him the plaintext. "This is good, but it's not enough. SDS needs solid evidence, and I've been trying to dig up some. I'm pretty sure Mack is right about them working on a new defoliant. Who knows what the hell *that'll* do to people? I'll keep looking."

"Just be careful, okay?"

Frank gives a sarcastic laugh that he can't keep from becoming a cough. "It's way too late for that, *amigo*."

●　　　●　　　●

The next two months are mostly uneventful. Mack doesn't have much to say about AIT, and he doesn't send any more pinhole messages. Simon spends most of his time on research and the rest on studying—often with Gabriela's help--for his sole course, a seminar on Latin American Literature. He also starts up an adult karate class; true to her promise, Felicia the Lawson's Lady shows up for every session, along with several fellow townies.

Then, around the middle of April--to use Mack's phrase--the excrement starts to hit the air circulating device. A week after Vicente's journal appears in *WHQ*, Simon receives the first of a long string of letters from scholars representing a whole slew of disciplines: Renaissance Studies, Portuguese Lit, European History, Anthropology, Organic Chemistry. They hail from places all over the map. Most are just requests for more information about the codex. But several mention the possibility of doctoral studies or a teaching position or some combination of the two.

Though the attention is gratifying, it's also overwhelming. Simon still has a ton of work to do on his master's. Despite his habit of trying to please everyone, he's forced to put the information requests aside for the time being; he replies only to the most intriguing job offers, asking for time to give the matter some thought. Then he attacks his research with even more intensity—the kind he used in his showdown with Alec.

Speak of the Devil, they say, and he'll appear. When Alec turns up, Simon is at a study carrel in the Briggs with his nose in a biography of Mary, Queen of Scots—during her imprisonment, she wrote messages on the pages of novels as a way of communicating with friends. Simon is so focused that he barely notices when a voice says, "Well, well. Long time, no see." It's not until Alec reaches out and flips the cover of the book that Simon turns to glare at him. "Don't hit me, *senpai!*" Alec pleads in mock terror, guarding his nose with one hand.

"Ha, ha. Very funny. What are you doing here, Alec?"

"Hey, I just wanted to congratulate you. It's been brought to my attention that you got your little paper published after all."

Simon doesn't care to discuss the matter; he merely shrugs.

"You must be pretty proud of yourselves." Alec leans in closer and says coolly, "But you remember how I said this isn't over yet? Well, guess what, Hannay Bananay? It *still* ain't over. You don't seem to understand, my friend, how much power a corporation like AllChemi actually has. But you'll find out, I guarantee you. In the meantime--" He gives Simon's shoulder a consoling pat. "--enjoy your moment of triumph."

When Simon and Gabriela connect over dinner at Mrs. Pitman's, he replays the one-sided conversation for her. "It may be true," she says, "that AllChemi is very powerful. But what can they do at this point? Everyone knows now where to find the *o-dai.*"

"Uh-huh," says Simon thoughtfully. "That's what worries me. The term *everyone* includes Dr. Vice and his minions."

•   •   •

Without his noticing, April gives way to May, and still the SDS hasn't accumulated enough damning evidence to stage an effective demonstration. As it turns out, maybe it's just as well.

On Monday, May 4, students at Kent State, protesting the bombing of Cambodia, are fired on by National Guard troops. Four students are killed; nine others are wounded. Ten days later, there's a second massacre in Mississippi, at Jackson State. Hundreds of colleges across the country, fearing a similar situation, cancel classes or end the school year early. Not Van Dyne. It's a pretty conservative campus, and the administration holds off a while, gambling that its students won't be eager to blow off a whole semester this close to the end.

For a while, it looks as if the gamble will pay off. The place stays relatively quiet. But then, halfway through finals week, Simon gets another missive from Mack—from overseas this time. He's been assigned to the 37th Signal Battalion, headquartered at Da Nang Air Force Base, near Saigon. He seems confident that he's well out of harm's way—and in any case, he says, he may not be there long. Though he got another cortisone shot while he was on leave, his knee is starting to go all wonky again. "Guess I won't be so good at wrestling now. Holy cow; hard to imagine you being able to pin me."

"More pinholes?" says Gabriela.

"Yep." Apparently Mack isn't taking any chances; these holes are so tiny that Simon has to hold the letter right up to the bulb of the desk lamp in order to see them. "Ready?"

"*Sim*. Sock it to me."

"Okay, here we go. *M-a-y-f-o-r-t-e-e-n-f-r-e-n-d-h-o-o-s-h-u-e-y-p-i-l-o-t-d-u-m-p-t-w-e-n-y-b-b-l-a-o-d-o-n-g-l-i-n-g-r-t-f-r-o-m-b-b-l*-period. *B-r-o-k-e-o-p-e-n-w-a-x*."

"Got it!" says Gabriela. "Let me see. *May . . . fourteen*, I guess. *Friend who's . . . huey?*"

"That's a kind of helicopter."

"Oh. *Friend who's Huey pilot dumped twenty . . . bbl?*"

"Barrels, maybe?"

"*Twenty barrels Agent Orange dong ling*--I suppose that is a province or something?--*right from barrel. Broke open wax.* Wax?"

"That *w* may be short for *with*."

"So, they broke open the barrels with an *ax*?"

"I guess so."

"That does not sound normal."

"No. It sounds like some kind of rogue operation."

"*Rogue?*"

"*Ilícito.*" Simon scans her plaintext. "You're getting really good at this."

"*Obrigada.*"

"*De nada.* Um, Gabriela?"

279

"*Sim?*"

"Why does *Dong Ling* sound so familiar?"

"I don't know. I thought so, too. Oh! You know what? I think it was in the codex!"

Simon stares at her. "Shit. You're right. It's where the *ma-bri* lived."

"The Monkey Forest?"

"Yeah. The Monkey Forest. Where the *o-dai* grew." Simon feels suddenly weak. His body sinks down on the sofa; his heart sinks even farther. "Good god," he murmurs. "They wiped it all out. Alec said it wasn't over yet. I guess he was right."

As devastated as he is, Simon sees one small silver lining: This is just the sort of solid info the SDS has been waiting for. He'd better not use Frank as his liaison again; he's liable to go off the deep end and blow something up.

"Are you all right, Simon?"

"Um, yeah. More or less. I just need to--" He breaks off, unsure how much Gabriela knows about the SDS and their plans. There's no point in getting her involved in this, maybe getting her in trouble. "I just need a drink. Is there any of that wine left?"

"*Sim*. I will get it."

"No, no, you go ahead and study. I'll be back in little bit."

The wine was just an excuse, of course. He passes through the kitchen and down the hallway to Mrs. Pitman's room, where he raps softly on the door. "Evie? Are you awake? Can I talk to you for a second?"

She answers the door in a bulky bathrobe and slippers. "Of course. Won't you come in?"

"No, no. I just wanted to show you this." He hands her the plaintext of Mack's message.

Reading it, she gives a small gasp of dismay. "Oh, no. I was hoping they had stopped all that. Where is Dong Ling?"

"In Laos. It's, um, it's where Vicente discovered the *o-dai* vine."

"Oh, dear lord. And the Agent Orange will destroy it?"

Simon nods grimly. "Even if some survives, it'll be contaminated."

"What an awful waste. So sad; so senseless. May I give this information to the SDS?"

"Please do."

"Thank you. You know," she whispers, as though someone might overhear, "Frank just gave us an even juicier bit of information. While he was cleaning one of the offices, he found part of a sheet of carbon paper that someone failed to dispose of. It was from a letter—to AllChemi, no doubt—saying that the lab was testing the new defoliant on rabbits, and it showed none of the adverse effects of 2,4,5-T."

"2,4,5-T?"

"We think it's one of the chemicals in Agent Orange. So. We have enough evidence now to make our case." Evie grips one of Simon's hands with unexpected firmness. "You mustn't breathe a word of this. No one is to know about the protest until it happens. We don't want the police there--or, god forbid, the National Guard."

"I understand." He starts to leave, then turns back. "Um, listen, Evie. Could you—could you let me know about the protest? I mean, when you're going to have it?"

"It'll have to be soon; the semester's almost over." She gives him a look that holds an unmistakable challenge. "Are you planning to join us?"

"I, uh, I don't know. I'm—I'm thinking about it."

"Good," she says. "Think very hard."

Simon turns the matter over in his mind a hundred times, looking at it from every angle. It would undoubtedly turn into a thousand times except that, on Friday afternoon, Evie waylays him at the Briggs and says softly, "Tomorrow, nine a.m., Student Center."

In the morning, he finds one reason after another to delay: He needs a shave. He needs to round up a bandanna and a water bottle, in case of tear gas. There aren't any clean cereal bowls; he needs to wash them—all of them. What he *really* needs to do, though, is to figure out why he's stalling. Is he hoping the protest will start without him, and it'll be too late to join in? Maybe. Maybe, like last time, he can just sort of hang around on the fringes, so he's almost a part of it, but not quite—with the protesters in spirit, if not in body.

But of course, like every event involving more than three people, this one doesn't start as scheduled. When Simon arrives, students are milling around outside the Student Center, chatting and laughing, happy to be done with exams, discussing their plans for the summer, as blithe and buoyant as though Kent State never happened, as though lives are not being lost this very moment in a cause that was lost long ago. They're here in body, but not in spirit.

Most of them, anyway. Maisie and the other SDS mainstays are holding a war council—make that a *peace* council. Several dedicated members are handing out leaflets to the few passers-by who are out and about this early. Four young women with flowers painted on their faces are stapling squares of cardboard to strips of lath and printing slogans on them with felt-tip markers.

As for Simon, he just stands there looking around, wondering why he came, wondering whether any of this will make a difference, or enough difference, anyway, to be worth risking his academic career for. His life could even be at risk if he gets booted out of school and into the Army's waiting arms. One of the flower children glances up at him. "Hey," she says. "You want a sign?"

That's exactly what he wants—a sign. Some kind of unmistakable indication of what he's supposed to do. Not that it's likely to happen. No, he's on his own, here. There's no *sensei* showing him what moves to make. There's no professor feeding him the facts he needs to know to pass the course. His father's not around, either, to offer his parental wisdom.

But some of the advice his dad gave when he *was* around has stuck with Simon. One of the things he said was, "Sometimes defending yourself isn't enough. Sometimes you have to strike back—not to try and defeat or destroy your opponent, just to stop him." Simon put that advice to use in his showdown with Alec. Well, maybe it's time he used it again.

He's been on the defensive long enough. He's spent most of the past year trying to stay out of the clutches of Uncle Sam and Dr. Vice and his minions. But it's become increasingly clear that just avoiding the Devil's henchmen isn't enough. Somehow they've got to be stopped, regardless of the risk.

"Hey, Clyde!" calls the girl. "You want a sign or don't you?"

Simon surveys the message she's printing in glaring red letters: NO MORE LIES! "Um, yeah," says Simon. "Sure." As he picks up the sign and shoulders it, he catches sight of Evie, who's standing next to Maisie, holding on to her friend's arm. The old woman smiles and nods her approval, as if he's passed some sort of test--one that has no effect on your GPA or your class standing but that determines where you stand on the things that really matter.

Though the guy with the massive Afro is carrying the megaphone again, he's not using it; they don't want to let the administration know the game is afoot until it's too late. The ringleaders circulate through the crowd, spreading the word: They're going to move out now, quickly and quietly, and congregate in front of the Medical Sciences Center.

"Go!" calls Maisie, barely loud enough to be heard, and the others pass on the command. The protesters surge forward like a horde of Visigoths—and in fact, a couple of his Visigoths are here—a silent, nonviolent horde armed only with signs reading A DAY WITH AGENT ORANGE IS LIKE A DAY WITHOUT SUNSHINE, and NIXXXON IS TOXXXIC and STOP POISONING PEOPLE. And this time Simon doesn't hang back; he's right in the thick of things.

When the protestors are still the length of a football field from the Med Sci building, the front rank suddenly comes to a halt; the rest of the students bunch up behind them, like cars in a traffic jam. Maisie and Mrs. Pitman, who are bringing up the rear, move up next to Simon. "What's going on?" demands Maisie.

Simon is tall enough to actually see what lies ahead of them. It's not a pretty sight. The broad front steps of the building are lined with uniformed soldiers carrying M-1s and riot guns. "Um, I think it's the National Guard."

"The National Guard?" echoes Mrs. Pitman in dismay. "How on earth did they know--?"

Maisie is looking grim and angry, but not exactly surprised. "My guess is, we have a plant."

"A *plant*?"

"Police or FBI or CIA, pretending to be one of us." She climbs onto the stone wall that surrounds a bed of ornamental plants. Cupping her hands around her mouth, she shouts, "Don't let them stop us! Keep moving!" The young man with the megaphone repeats her message, the words bouncing off the building's ugly concrete façade.

The protesters advance slowly, reluctantly; no doubt many of them are thinking about the outcome of that other clash between university students and Weekend Warriors, the one at Kent State. As Simon is carried along by the crowd, from the corner of his eye he notices a movement in one of the third-floor windows. He glances up, half expecting to see a sniper getting into position. But no, it's Frank Ávila, clad in his white custodial coverall, leaning out the open window. Frank spots him and gives a mock salute. Simon raises his NO MORE LIES! sign and Frank nods in acknowledgement.

The megaphone man starts chanting, "Stop Poisoning People! Stop Poisoning People!" The front line of demonstrators, who are now only a few yards from the Guardsmen, take up the chant and it spreads through the crowd, growing ever louder and more confident. Simon follows suit, shouting the slogan at the top of his voice, trying to make up for all those times he failed to join in.

To his amazement, the line of soldiers slowly parts in the center, as if clearing a path for the protestors to enter the building. But of course that's not the reason at all. They're only making way for a trio of men in business suits, striped shirts and silk ties—the accepted uniform of non-military leaders. The three are not mere men, however; they're what the counterculture calls The Man—the president of the university, flanked by the Dean of Arts and Science and the chair of the Med Sci Department.

The president holds up a hand to silence the protestors; he looks rather taken aback when they go right on chanting. Leaning over, he says something to the Guard's commanding officer, a lieutenant who could pass for a student himself. The officer approaches the megaphone carrier; without a word, he wrests the device from the black guy's grasp and hands it over to the president.

"Thank you!" Amplified, the head honcho's ordinarily cultivated, persuasive voice sounds distorted, almost demonic. "Ladies and gentlemen! I respect your right to protest but--" He's interrupted by a raucous chorus of laughter and catcalls. "--but I'm afraid you're a bit misguided!" He waves one of the SDS leaflets. "You accuse the university of helping to develop chemical and biological weapons! I promise you that we are doing nothing of the sort!"

Simon glances up at the third floor window, to see whether Frank is taking all this in. He is. With a look of disgust and despair, he spreads his hands helplessly as if to say, "What's the use?"

The president's claim is greeted with a cacophony of comments and questions, drowning out all his attempts to deliver more phony assurances. The Guard lieutenant commandeers the megaphone and cranks up the volume. "People! This protest is over! I order you to disperse! If you do not comply, we will take whatever action is necessary!"

The crowd responds with more laughter and jeers. But when the Guardsmen start unpacking their gas masks, the voices take on an edge of alarm, and some of the students begin glancing about, looking for escape routes. "Oh, shit!" says Simon. He turns to Maisie, who's too short to see what's going on. "They're going to gas us! Get Evie out of here!"

Maisie nods; pushing other protesters aside, she guides the old woman toward the fringes of the crowd. Simon turns his attention back to the steps, where the Weekend Warriors are clumsily strapping on their masks. The men who carry riot guns begin loading them with tear-gas canisters. The demonstration is quickly descending into chaos. Some of the students are standing fast, still shouting and brandishing their signs, but far more of them are dispersing, heading for some safer spot. Simon digs out his bandanna and drenches it with water from his bottle.

Though the lieutenant hasn't quite got his own mask under control, he has one arm held aloft, poised to give the signal that will launch the gas grenades. "Ready!" he shouts, his voice muffled by the rubber mask.

If he says anything more, no one hears it because, in the next instant, there's a fearful explosion close at hand and a wave of sound engulfs the crowd. It's infinitely louder and more jarring than the crack of an M-1 or the whump of a riot gun. It's more like a sonic boom, as if a jet has passed over, a few yards above their heads. Shards of glass descend upon them like jagged hail; Simon, who is hunched over with his arms protecting his head, faintly hears the stuff shattering on the stones. He can hear people screaming, too, but to his stunned ears they sound dim and distant.

He glances upward and sees smoke billowing from the third-floor window where, a few minutes before, Frank Ávila was leaning out, watching the little drama unfold below him. "Jesus Christ!" Simon gasps; he can barely hear his own voice. "Frank!" Without thinking, he scrambles for the entrance.

Half of the Guardsmen are rushing into the building, while the other half seize the few remaining protestors. The president is still standing in the same spot on the steps, gazing about dumbly, incredulously. But when Simon tries to push past him, the man grabs hold of his sleeve and shouts, "You can't go in there, son!"

Simon reacts the same way he would in freestyle sparring; he flings his arm upward, breaking the president's grip and shoving him off balance. The man slips on the scattered glass and, with a hoarse cry, falls to his knees. Simon hesitates for a moment, debating whether or not to help him. But Frank surely needs his help a lot more; he bolts toward the revolving door.

He doesn't quite make it. When he's a few feet from the entrance, something strikes him in the back of the head and he collapses onto the concrete.

One of the cherished myths of those Saturday matinee serials Simon grew up with is that it's a simple matter to put a person—a palace guard, say, or some other minion—out of commission for a good long time just by socking him in the jaw or whacking him over the head. Well, it is theoretically possible; it's just not very likely. It might work on Mrs. Pitman, for instance. But anyone who's reasonably strong and fit probably isn't going to black out for more than a few seconds, even if he's been hit with the butt of an M1 rifle.

Though Simon isn't unconscious, neither is he in any condition to fight back or to escape. He's so disoriented and in so much pain, all he can do is let himself be dragged to the police van, transported to the county jail, and tossed into a holding cell—the same one Mack occupied—along with a dozen other "rioters."

Over the next twenty-four hours or so—it's hard to be sure, for when he fell he totaled his father's watch—the students are questioned one by one, to determine whether anyone besides Frank Ávila was involved in the bombing of the chemistry lab. Though Simon's head is killing him and his hands and knees are covered with cuts, he realizes that he could be a lot worse off. If he'd made it to the third floor, he would have looked, at best, like a friend of the bomber and at worst like an accomplice. As it is, he's routinely grilled like all the others. When it's clear that Frank acted alone, they're released. Though no one specifically says so and Simon is afraid to ask, it's also clear that Frank died in the blast.

Gabriela is waiting for him outside the jail, standing next to Mrs. Pitman's vintage Chevy. Simon doesn't feel much like talking, and she doesn't push him. She just drives him to the house, makes an ice pack and a *café com leite* for him, and lets him sack out on the sofa in the library. When she wakes him for dinner, he finally feels clear-headed enough to say what's on his mind. "I, uh, I guess Frank was killed."

"*Sim*. It was on the news. They say the bomb completely destroyed the lab."

"Aw, the poor idiot." He sinks his head into his hands. "I wonder if he even tried to get out."

"I don't suppose we will ever know. He was so sick; maybe he saw no point in it."

"Maybe not. I just—I just wish he'd *said* something, you know? Maybe I could have talked him out of it."

"I think he did not want his friends to be involved."

"I . . . I never exactly thought of us as friends. But I guess we were."

Gabriela strokes his head lightly with her fingertips. "You should not feel guilty, Simon. It was his choice. Just as it was your choice to join the protest."

"Yeah. Yeah, I guess so."

"Are you sorry that you did?"

"Not really." He sighs heavily and takes a swig of wine. "You know, they're probably going to kick me out."

"The university?"

"Uh-huh. I mean, I knocked down the president. He's not going to let me get off scot-free."

"But what if Dr. Espinoza and Evie spoke to him? Surely that would help."

"Maybe. But I'm not counting on it. I'm going to assume the worst."

"What is the worst?"

"That I'll get drafted, I guess."

"Oh, Simon, I hope not!"

"Me, too."

"If they do draft you, will you go?"

He shakes his head, then regrets it when the pain strikes again.

"But what else can you do?" asks Gabriela. "Will you go to Canada?"

"No. I'd just be avoiding things again."

"What, then?"

Simon takes his time in answering. He's certain of what he wants to say; he's just not sure how Gabriela is going to take it. He drains the glass of wine. "I, um, I thought about this a lot while we were locked up. I even discussed it with some of the other protesters. And I decided that, no matter what happens--whether I stay in school or not--I'm going to . . . I'm going to register as a CO."

"A CO?"

"A conscientious objector."

"Oh."

Simon waits for her to say something more, but she doesn't and, as practiced as he is at reading people's intentions, he can't manage to decipher hers. "Um, I hope that won't— I mean, maybe you won't want to--"

Gabriela holds up a hand, the one with the Magic Decoder Ring, to silence him. "Simon. It does not matter what *I* want. It is your choice."

"Okay, but-- I mean, I wouldn't anything to . . . you know . . ."

"To come between us?"

"Yeah."

Simon sees that old wary look come into her dark eyes again. "I cannot promise anything," she says. And then, unexpectedly--as when the meaning of a mysterious passage of ciphertext suddenly becomes clear—her lovely mouth forms a faint smile. "But I do not think that will happen."

•   •   •

One of the obligatory scenes in those Saturday morning movie serials was the final battle between the hero and the bad guys. There'll be no such showdown in this story, because the fact is, the bad guys have disappeared. Alec hasn't been seen on campus since Frank destroyed the lab. Maybe he's on some sort of sabbatical until the place is up and running again—if it ever is. Or maybe, despite Alec's failure to get the codex, Dr. Vice's offer of a job with AllChemi still stands, and he's gone off to Delaware.

As for the mystery man himself . . . well, what reason would he have to return to the scene of the crime? He's accomplished his mission. He's rid the world of the pesky plant that threatened to make all his company's relatively useless but very profitable medicines obsolete.

Perhaps the destruction of the lab will be a minor setback for AllChemi, but it's certainly not going to keep them from developing new and more efficient and more insidious chemical weapons. After all, there are plenty of other universities and research centers all over the country—all over the world--that are more than willing to do the Devil's work for him.

ABOUT THE AUTHOR

Gary Blackwood has published over thirty novels and nonfiction books for young readers and adults. *The Shakespeare Stealer* and *Shakespeare's Scribe* were on American Library Association's list of Best Books for Young Adults and *Smithsonian Magazine's* Notable Books. *The Year of the Hangman* was on the Best Books for Young Adults list and *School Library Journal's* Best Books. *Around the World in 100 Days* was a Smithsonian Notable and one of *Kirkus Reviews'* Best Books for Teens. His adult novels include two Victorian mysteries, *Bucket's List* and *Bucket's Brigade*. He's also a widely produced playwright.

NOTE FROM THE AUTHOR

Word-of-mouth is crucial for any author to succeed. If you enjoyed *The Devil to Pay*, please leave a review online—anywhere you are able. Even if it's just a sentence or two. It would make all the difference and would be very much appreciated.

Thanks!
Gary Blackwood

We hope you enjoyed reading this title from:

BLACK ROSE writing™

www.blackrosewriting.com

Subscribe to our mailing list – *The Rosevine* – and receive **FREE** books,
daily deals, and stay current with news about upcoming
releases and our hottest authors.
Scan the QR code below to sign up.

Already a subscriber? Please accept a sincere thank you for being a fan of
Black Rose Writing authors.

View other Black Rose Writing titles at
www.blackrosewriting.com/books and use promo code
PRINT to receive a **20% discount** when purchasing.

CPSIA information can be obtained
at www.ICGtesting.com
Printed in the USA
LVHW091504010622
720238LV00012B/131